When Dark Warriors invade her country, it is up to Princess Kamarie to seek out the legendary king's warrior and request his aid. The feisty princess has spent her life dreaming of adventure and is thrilled to be tasked with such a quest. There's only one thing that can dampen the princess's excitement: Oraeyn. The squire views his task of protecting the princess on her journey as an inglorious assignment and makes no attempt to hide his disappointment.

Despite a rocky start to their journey – in which Oraeyn throws the obnoxious princess in a river just to get her to call him by name – the travelers soon learn that they must depend upon one another if they are to locate the man they have been sent to find. The adventure merely begins when they meet Brant: a warrior with a mysterious past. He joins their cause readily, his heart smoldering with a vendetta Kamarie cannot completely understand. But whether she trusts him or not, the hope of their world rests on the steel he wears at his side….

The Minstrel's Song

King's Warrior

Second Son

Yorien's Hand

Minstrel's Call

KING'S WARRIOR

BOOK ONE OF
"THE MINSTREL'S SONG"

JENELLE LEANNE SCHMIDT

This is a work of fiction. All of the characters, organizations, and events portrayed in this novel are either products of the author's imagination or are used fictitiously.

KING'S WARRIOR

ISBN: 1463605935
ISBN-13: 978-1463605933

www.stormcavestudios.com

DEDICATION

To my family: you are my biggest fans, and the source of my greatest inspiration. Without you, Brant would never have been more than a farmer, restricted to the first chapter; Kiernan Kane would have just been a wandering bard; and the world of Aomigh might never have existed... there certainly would have never been a sequel.

ACKNOWLEDGMENTS

I want to thank my dad, for giving me the idea in the first place, for being my biggest fan and my toughest critic, and for always believing in me. Thanks for being my content editor.

My husband, for letting me spend countless hours editing and re-writing, and for never once failing to believe that I would succeed.

Shannon, for the hours you spent correcting my punctuation errors, my capitalization inconsistencies, and various other mechanical errors. Thanks for making the work fun, too!

Angelina, for the beautiful cover you designed, and the hours of work that went into getting it just right.

Grant and Evan, for all the time and effort you've put into the "business side" of publishing and marketing a book.

My mom and sister for being my "cheering section" and leaving me notes of encouragement as this process has unfolded.

I love you guys all so much! Thanks for being my "team." This book would not exist without all of you.

PROLOGUE

Graldon, King of the dragons, mighty lord of the skies over Aom-igh, handed the golden sword to the mere man who stood before him. "This one thing will I give thee."

His voice thundered eerily in the huge cavern, resounding off the walls and shaking the floor. The words sounded strange coming off his tongue, for dragons are not accustomed to speaking with men. The Dragon Tongue, or Old Kraïc, is an old language; it is the language of the sea and the land that existed at the beginning of time and remained unchanged throughout the years, unlike the language of men, which changed and developed countless times and continues to do so. Dragons understand and can speak the language of men, but they scoff at it for it is a young and uneducated language. Its sounds are not nearly so grand as those of Old Kraïc, which has a melody like the waves rolling on the shore and the thunder rumbling in the sky and the earth shaking as it splits.

The man knelt down before the great dragon and held the gift in his hands reverently. "I thank you for this, at least."

The huge, green-scaled dragon gazed at the human before him coolly, but his golden eyes shimmered with something like laughter. "Thinkst thou, little one, that I care so deeply about the affairs of men? Thinkst thou that I would come to thy aid and breathe fire upon thy enemies for thee, vanquishing them? No, in the way of my ancestors before me I, too, shall let thee fight thine own battles."

The man before him remained silent, as is proper and courteous before the dragon king. Although a king in his own right, Llian knew better than to anger a dragon. He sighed, his shoulders hunched and his form bent. His head sank lower, and his face crumpled. His people now faced the greatest threat that their land had ever seen. The dark sails of Llycaelon had been spotted a few weeks ago, but they had not come in force. Instead the enemy had crept in quietly and secretly in small groups, attacking outposts and then fading into the shadows. Fear reigned throughout the countryside and King Llian had come to the dragons in desperation. And here King Graldon was refusing to come to his aid.

"But Aom-igh is your home too. Will you let it be overrun by these Dark Warriors?"

"Thinkst thou that we myth-folk care which human rules other humans? Should I come running to thee whenever a young dragonling challenges my authority?"

Llian blinked, "Is that what you think this is?"

"If thou canst not defeat thine enemies, then thou shouldst not be king."

Llian stared at the floor of the cave, an angry flush rising across his face. He felt like a young boy who has just been reprimanded in front of all his friends for something he did not do.

"We have our own problems, human," Graldon said, his voice quieter. Llian looked up in surprise, meeting the great dragon's eyes and seeing there a kinship he had not expected. After a moment, he nodded. This, he could understand. He too, had needed to deal with rebellions and would-be usurpers, and this he read in Graldon's eyes. The dragon king was not telling him that he would not help but rather that he could not help.

"However," Graldon continued, "I tell thee this: the Fang Blade is no ordinary sword. Its deadly blade was formed from one of my own great teeth and the handle was created from one of my own silver scales, and in its forging it was imbued with dragon magic. It will serve thee and thy descendants and it shall neither break nor rust as other swords do. But know this as well: the sword has a will of its own, and it does not grant its holder *magic, but only brings out what is deep within him already. An evil man can do only evil with the Fang Blade, but a man of noble character and a good heart shalt be able to do mighty works with that sword in his hand. Be careful of whose hands thou dost allow the blade to fall into once thou art done with it."*

The man before him rose and seemed a little more satisfied. Graldon laughed, a mighty and terrifying sound coming from between those powerful jaws.

"Thou would have more from me?" he asked. "Thou thinkst to command the King of the dragons? Thou thinkst to ask for yet more on top of this great gift that I have granted thee?" He eyed the brave man before him who neither cowered nor shrank at his words, and a deep respect for this man filled Graldon's dragonish heart as he spoke again. "Well then, King Llian, one more thing shall I grant thee - perhaps you will scoff at this as well, but I warn you, the word of a dragon is not to be taken lightly. I promise you this: if Aom-igh is ever in such need again, the dragons will not hesitate to come to thy aid."

The great wizard, perhaps the last of the great wizards, stood looking out towards the sea. His stormy gray eyes were bright with unshed tears as he watched the waves rolling in and out. His king was dying at last. King Llian had earned his rest, but he would be sorely missed.

"Scelwhyn," the king's voice was growing weaker but his strength of will was strong as steel.

Scelwhyn turned away from the window and attended his king. "Yes, your majesty?"

"One last thing, I would ask of you," King Llian said. "I would ask you to look into the mists of the future and tell me if there is any chance that the darkness will ever return to our land. If our enemies in Llycaelon will never return, I want the sword destroyed so that it will never fall into the wrong hands. But if it will be needed again by our people, then I bid you hide it somewhere where it will be kept safe until it is once more needed to protect and defend."

Scelwhyn nodded, and then he fell silent for a long time, searching. At last he spoke. His voice was shaky and it seemed to echo, but the words were clear. He said:

> *When day is swallowed by night*
> *And the wanderer takes the road*
> *And the flame once more*
> *Burns bright:*
> *The youth will arise,*
> *The sword will awake,*
> *The dragons will fly*
> *And the enemy break.*

King Llian listened hard and then he fell back upon his bed, "Then hide the sword well, my old friend," he whispered, then he breathed his last and flew from this life, the life he had lived so well and fought for so bravely.

So died King Llian, ruler of Aom-igh, slayer of the Dark Warriors, holder of the Sword of Light, and the one who spoke with Dragons as an equal. In life, he was a noble man who loved his people and fought on their behalf. In death, he was surely welcomed home by Cruithaor Elchiyl.

-From the diaries of Master Scelwhyn
Penned in the year seven thousand one hundred eighty-four

CHAPTER
ONE

She felt the horse beneath her tense, muscles coiling, and leaned forward as together they leapt the fallen tree. They flew through the air and landed cleanly on the other side. The sound of pounding hooves filled her ears as they continued cantering down the road. Kamarie filed the fallen tree in her mind, tucking its location away. She would have to remember to tell her father about it; King Arnaud liked to keep the roads around the palace clear, especially the roads leading to Ayollan.

Kamarie urged Tor to go faster, wrapping strands of his silvery-gray mane around her hands. She was late, and Darby would be worried. She had not meant to wander so far from home on her daily ride, but her tutors had been particularly demanding that morning and Kamarie was frustrated. Why was all this so hard for her? The niceties of court etiquette gave her fits, politics was slightly easier, and history was one of her best subjects, but today she had been unable to grasp even the simplest of her lessons. And so, at her first opportunity, she had slipped out to saddle up Tor and go for a ride to clear her head. They had wandered through fields and over streams, chatting with the occasional farmer or merchant who happened to be passing by, and Kamarie had lost all track of time. Now the Dragon's Eye was beginning to set and the chill of evening hung in the air. Her sable hair streamed behind her as Tor carried her at a gallop back to the palace. A fork in the road appeared before her; without hesitation, Kamarie chose the left-hand path, despite the fact that it would take her through the forest. The roads were safe, and although the forest was dark and sometimes sheltered rogues, she was not concerned. The forest road was the shorter route. And the sword at her side was not merely for show, after all.

When Kamarie reached the stables, she threw Tor's reins to a stable-boy - something she never did - because if she took the time to care for the horse herself she would miss dinner all together.

"Princess, where have you been?" Darby sighed, as Kamarie entered her rooms. The elderly woman wrinkled her nose. "You smell like the stables again. I have been looking for you everywhere."

"Relax, Darby," Kamarie smiled. "There's plenty of time before dinner."

"Not if you don't hurry!" The gray-haired woman ushered the princess across her grand bedroom to the smaller room where her bath had been drawn up and waited, the water quickly growing cool. "You need to wash that smell off you and then I'll work on your hair. You really don't have much time."

When Kamarie emerged from her bath, clean and smelling of roses, she was dressed in a sapphire gown that matched her eyes and had been made from the finest satin in the realm. Darby sat her down in front of her mirror and fussed over the princess' long, dark hair, combing, pinning, and arranging, all the while clicking her tongue disapprovingly. Kamarie smiled at her reflection, her blue eyes twinkling mischievously.

"Who is our guest of honor tonight, Darby?"

"Prince Elroy of Roalthae, Princess, as you would know very well if you paid better attention to your schedule."

"Ah yes, Elroy," Kamarie sighed. "What do you know about him, Darby? I've only met him formally, and we've never talked. At least he's a bit older than me, unlike the Duke of Lan-Point."

Darby grinned at the memory. "That was definitely a surprise."

Kamarie rolled her eyes. As she neared marrying age, her father had begun receiving letters requesting permission to court his daughter. As the only child of the King of Aom-igh, Princess Kamarie was an ideal match for any nobleman with the slightest ambition. King Arnaud tried to filter out the most horrifying requests, but some surprises still occurred. They had exchanged correspondence with the Duke of Lan-Point, a small holding on the southern end of Iolanver and one of the four barrier islands directly to the east of Aom-igh. The duke wrote eloquently and respectfully, so Arnaud and Kamarie had agreed to invite him to the palace for a visit. When he arrived, they had discovered that he was extremely young, no more than five, and that his letters had been written by a well-meaning steward who simply wanted his young duke to be accorded the honor that an invitation to King Arnaud's palace would engender. King Arnaud had politely but firmly informed the steward that in the future he should be honest with his king, as it would save everyone subsequent embarrassment.

"He was sweet, exactly what I would like to have in a little brother," Kamarie said.

"But not in a suitor."

Kamarie smiled. "No... well, yes, but fifteen or twenty years older."

"Well let's see, what do I know of Prince Elroy," Darby mused, holding barrettes up to Kamarie's hair and considering. "Mmmm, he is the ruler of Roalthae."

"Obviously."

Roalthae was the largest and northernmost of the four barrier islands that stood directly between Aom-igh and open oceans. The barrier islands had always been friendly with Aom-igh, but they each had their own rulers. Of those rulers, three were married, leaving Prince Elroy as one of the best matches for Kamarie. In Roalthae, the ruler was given the title of "Prince" until he married and produced an heir, at which time his title would be changed to "King." It was a strange system but one that worked well. As such, Prince Elroy was a worthy match for the Princess of Aom-igh, and it would be an attractive match for Elroy as well, since he would gain a larger throne than the one he currently occupied and could choose to either appoint one of his future heirs as Prince and future King of Roalthae or raise a deserving cousin to that position if he only had one heir. Add to all this Kamarie's beauty and status as a wife and it was certainly an opportunity that the Prince of Roalthae would covet.

"Well, you know what he looks like: tall, handsome, blue eyes, dark hair, square jaw. He is said to be a fair ruler, although I have heard rumors that he is quite a bit sterner than your father. He keeps his country in line by threat of the sword, if you catch my meaning. However, that could simply be because he has no wife to temper him, and no heir to give him a feeling of security about his position."

"What about his temperament?"

"I've heard he is an amiable man. If he has ambitions he keeps them closely guarded, he didn't even write to your father until a few weeks ago, and you've already entertained dozens of would-be suitors. When I've seen him on formal occasions he seems friendly enough, but a bit aloof."

Kamarie twisted her mouth in thought. "Well, I just hope he isn't a complete bore. It doesn't sound like he's an ideal match for me, but I suppose I should give him a fair chance. Maybe he'll surprise me and be an interesting conversationalist." After a moment she grinned ruefully, thinking about some of the wild stories that were still told about her younger days. "Maybe we'll surprise each other."

Darby smiled and patted the top of Kamarie's head gently. "You will be fine. Remember, your father has given you complete authority over your choice. Even if Prince Elroy is the best match for you politically, if you can't stand the man you only have to suffer through one dinner in his company. At least, until you are queen, and then it will be your duty to host these sorts of occasions and mingle with your nobles."

"Thanks for the comfort, Darby." Kamarie grimaced. Then she stood up. "How do I look?"

"Lovely." Darby smiled fondly at her young charge. "Don't worry, I'll be at your side, as always."

While Princess Kamarie descended the stairs of the palace towards the formal dining hall, far away to the south a young boy sat and watched as the Dragon's Eye sank down in the sky and kissed the horizon. It had been a long, difficult climb to the top of Mount Theran, but Yole was convinced that it had been worth it. It had taken him nearly a week, but now he rested on the top of the world. It was the most free he had ever felt. He tilted his head back and let waves of cool wind wash over his face. By holding his arms out and closing his eyes, he could almost imagine he was flying. He relaxed and let his imagination take him soaring. In his mind's eye he could see the village below him; the white fluffy sheep and the sleek brown cattle dotting the fields; he could also see the tiny houses of the peasants who tended the pastures and the animals. With his eyes closed and his mind wandering above the plains, he could almost hear the haunting melody of the pipes played by the shepherds in the valleys.

Yole loved the music that came from the shepherd's pipes; that music was the only thing he could remember from his past. He could not remember much, but he could remember the music. His childhood seemed a blur to him. Fragments of memories danced around inside his head of places, people, and occurrences that could not possibly have happened to him. And there was a face: it stared down at him with bright eyes that somehow seemed to be the wrong color blue. The rosy lips parted gently as though saying something in a soft voice, and a tear glistened on the soft, pink cheek before falling to his hand where he could remember playing with it like a bauble. Of course, Yole knew that part of the memory couldn't be real. The face looked at him in a fond mixture of joy and sorrow. He believed that the face belonged to his mother, but if the truth were to be told, Yole was not sure that he had ever *had* a mother.

Yole could not remember a time when he had not been on his own. Never had there been a time when he truly belonged to anyone and this nomadic life was all he knew. There were moments when he began to feel as though he had found a place and family to call home, only to find himself alone, bewildered, and searching once again. His most recent out-casting burned in his memory, and his cheek still stung from the rebuke he had received.

Yole had hired-on to tend the herds of a generous family this Warm-Term, but he would not be shepherding in Peak's Shadow again. Something had happened, and he had been told in no uncertain terms that he must leave and never return. There was fear, yet understanding, in Brant's eyes as he told Yole to head for the Mountains of Dusk. Yole was bewildered as to what he had done to make himself an outcast by this family and this village that he had begun to claim as his own. Yole was a bit of a loner but not one to make enemies. He took orders and did what he was told, no questions asked. He knew better than to touch what belonged to others, and he followed all the unwritten rules that came with having no heritage to speak of.

The day was warm and slow. The type of day that makes one want to lie down in the long, cool grass and just pass the hours being idle. Yole was in the pasture watching Brant's flock, listening to the pipe music that neighboring shepherds were playing in their fields. The music intertwined and danced over the ground to where Yole was sitting. Pipe music was like that: it was light and floating, and the wind could carry it farther than most other types of music. Yole had always wanted to learn to play the pipes, but he had no one to teach him. As he listened, Yole felt perfectly content watching the sheep and letting the music wash over him. The longing was still there, of course, the longing that never quite left him, but Yole managed to ignore it.

The *music enchanted and mesmerized Yole. He remembered falling asleep, but had no idea how long, or deeply he slept. He did know that he had a flying dream and was now awake in a cold sweat of fear. Yole loved these dreams of flying, loved that feeling of being up so high that no one in all the world could reach him. He loved waking with vivid recall of soaring through the skies, yet he also knew with every such dream, that anger, fear, and confusion soon followed.*

Yole did not have to wait long. Within moments he heard shouting from all directions. He lay still; knowing, with that deep, insightful knowledge that possessed him at the most inopportune times, that the shouts meant trouble, and they were meant for him.

"Father, I found him!" Brant's son called out loudly.

Schea was Brant's oldest child, only a few years younger than Yole himself, but for some reason he was frightened and would come no closer until his father arrived. Brant himself had no such hesitancy. He walked over to where Yole was lying and grabbed him by his tunic, lifting him to his feet. Yole opened his mouth to ask what was wrong, but he did not get the chance. An unexpected slap across his face rendered him speechless for a moment; the blow did not hurt, much, but it did take him by surprise.

"Wh-what was that for?" he asked.

"That was for putting my family in danger!" Brant's voice was quiet, but deadly. "How dare you come into my home and endanger my family in this way? How did you dare to presume that you were under my protection?"

Yole stared into Brant's dark, angry eyes in bewilderment. "I-I-I…"

"No excuses! Go back to where you came from, this town will not tolerate your presence here any longer!" Brant said with force. "You must leave, I cannot protect you."

Brant paused and seemed for the first time to notice Yole's confused and frightened expression; his tone softened and he laid a gentle hand on the boy's shoulder. "Now listen to me. I will not harm you and I will not let them hunt you. I will not have you caged or beaten or killed while I can prevent it. The longer you remain here, the greater your danger. I have known these villagers for many years and they have seen hard and desperate times. The King's protection does not always reach this far. They are not cruel or vengeful, but they are very, very serious about protecting their families and their livelihoods; they will do whatever that requires, so you must leave and leave quickly. I lost five sheep today and I can ill afford to lose any more. I will provide you with provisions for a fortnight and then you will fend for yourself. Head along the north end of Peak's Shadow and it will take you deep into the Mountains of Dusk. I will keep the villagers from following you, but if you are not well into the mountains within a fortnight, you will be at their mercy. Do you understand me, son?" Brant's voice was almost compassionate now. Then, almost as an afterthought, he added something Yole could not grasp, something that kept him awake at night as he puzzled over it for a long time afterwards: *"And one more thing, if you must live near people, you really ought to be more careful."*

At the time, Yole merely nodded meekly. He had discovered that it was best not to argue or complain about what he did not understand. He was expected to understand. And he was expected to obey.

Far below Mount Theran and Yole, in the village of Peak's Shadow, Brant stared at the setting Dragon's Eye with a hard look on his face. There was trouble in Aom-igh, and it was spreading, there was no doubt about that. What trouble, he did not know, but trouble nonetheless. He could feel it coming, there had been signs everywhere: first there had been Yole, and now there were whispers of a coming war and an increase in the number of strangers passing through villages. It could not mean anything good. Even though he was tucked away in Peak's Shadow, Brant maintained his contacts in order to stay abreast of the happenings in Aom-igh. Just because all had been quiet for over twenty years did not mean that he could relax his guard. He wondered for a moment about Yole, the boy had been gone for almost a week now, and Brant hoped that he had made his way through the Mountains of Dusk and found some place where he could be accepted, although these days that was unlikely...

Brant remembered when he had first come to Peak's Shadow, the people were a friendly lot, though they did not welcome strangers readily. It had taken time to win their trust. He and his wife had made this village their home, where they became part of the quiet lifestyle that surrounded them. This was precisely as Brant wanted. He had come to Peak's Shadow for peace and quiet and rest, and here he had found it. Life in Peak's Shadow was good, with a loving wife, two wonderful children, a strong herd of cattle, and more than enough silly sheep. They owned a quaint, smallish cottage that he had built himself on a property with a spacious pasture, watered by a charming creek that gurgled and sang to itself. There was so much that life had to offer if a man worked hard and made a point of noticing and enjoying the little things.

He had tried to live a simple life; had tried to bury his past, although he never forgot. He had hoped to be able to work hard enough now, and for a good long time, so that he could live a peaceful, restful life when he got to that age that was considered "old." But now, with an ominous premonition weighing in his mind, this desire for peace and solitude brought with it a vulnerability to the dangers of life he had never sensed before... had never feared before.

"Father!" His son came running up to him. Brant looked down at the little boy and felt a pang in his heart. He longed so to protect these little ones.

"What is it Schea?" he asked softly.

"Ryder and I found a lizard! Down by the creek! Come and see." The little boy pulled on his father's cloak and pointed.

Brant laughed, and the dark clouds that had seemed to hang about him all morning dissipated in his merriment. He allowed his son to pull him along towards the pasture creek. His wife, Imojean, laid her hand on his shoulder. He turned his head to look at her; she was smiling. He smiled back, as her presence chased away the last of his fears. He loved her dearly.

"Dinner will be ready soon," she said. "Could you whistle for Kali on your way back from the creek? She's out playing with the baby sheep."

"They're called lambs dear," he teased her with a grin on his face.

"I couldn't tell Kali that!" Imojean exclaimed. "Her favorite meal is lamb."

Perhaps it was the look on her face, half playful, pretending to be shocked and hurt, and half loving. But it gave Brant an odd feeling. He leaned closer and kissed her. He wasn't sure why he did it, he would see her again in a few minutes, but he kissed her as though he would never see her again.

"I'll bring Kali," he said. As he walked away, he was surprised to find that tears had sprung to his eyes.

The lizard was pretty neat, Brant had to admit, all slimy looking with dark green spots. Its tongue flicked in and out, causing Schea and his friend Ryder to shriek with laughter. Brant smiled at the boys' antics.

"Look, look!" Schea yelled. The lizard had apparently grown tired of its audience for it was now slithering off the rock towards the water with as much dignity as could possibly be expected from a lizard.

"That's our cue boys," Brant said. "Time for dinner."

"Can Ryder come over for dinner?" Schea pleaded.

"No, not tonight Schea. How 'bout tomorrow?" Brant promised quickly as his son's face fell.

At the promise of tomorrow the little boys brightened. "I hear my ma calling anyway," Ryder said. "See you tomorrow Schea!" he called over his shoulder as he skipped off towards home.

Schea turned to his father. "We have to go get Kali," he said earnestly. "She won't hear if we whistle."

"Why not?" Brant asked, slightly perplexed by his son's suddenly serious gaze.

"Because, she's in make-believe world. She can't hear the sounds in this world," Schea said importantly as he repeated what his sister had told him.

Brant laughed. "Oh, she is, eh? Well, we'll just have to go rescue her back into our world. Let's go!"

Schea hurried along, running to keep up with his father's long strides. Brant suddenly stopped short, overwhelmed by the scene before him. Kali was sitting in the field, the long grass matted down where she had been playing. Two baby sheep were frolicking around her and one was lying next to her with its head on her lap. She was framed with a halo of brightness. Her blond hair gently blowing in the breeze and catching the light of the setting Dragon's Eye, her green eyes sparkled and shone as she looked up at her father and brother standing before her, entranced by the scene.

"Papa, the baby sheep were trying to eat my dress!" she giggled, and her young voice wafted through the air like tiny wind chimes.

Sharing this small bit of information she stood up. She was a year younger than her brother, but she was older (or perhaps wiser) than anyone Brant had ever known. She had a faraway look in her eyes more often than not. Her dreams of fairy worlds and her odd little speeches about magic endeared her to him as much as did her matter-of-fact way of saying things. Hers was a life lived without fear. Once, she had been very sick and he had been worried that she might not pull through, and it had been Kali who had comforted him. She was only three at the time, but already she was speaking in full, strangely grown-up sentences. Brant sighed as the memory came back to him in a rush; it was one he would never forget.

He had been sitting by her bedside. It was night and she was burning up with a fever, coughing badly. The physician had treated her, but said it was too soon to tell if she would recover. The medicine was helping her sleep, but her breathing was labored and painful. Brant had put his head in his hands and whispered a prayer to Cruithaor Elchiyl when she had suddenly stirred. Her green eyes flickered open, looking glassy in the candlelight. She touched his arm and said, "Papa, you don't have to worry about me. If I die, don't be sad. I'll be in the world of the cearaphiym where everything is full of light, looking down at you and saying, 'Don't cry for me, it doesn't hurt anymore, it doesn't hurt anymore Papa.' So I want you to promise that you won't be sad." He had promised in a choked voice, and had rejoiced when she had gotten well again.

"Come on," Brant smiled, "your mother has dinner waiting for us."

When Kamarie finally entered the Long Hall, she noticed that it was crowded for a private dinner. She frowned slightly and then wiped the expression from her face and smiled pleasantly, mentally counting how many people were assembled. As she wound through the courtiers and greeted them with smiles and a few soft words, she realized that almost all the nobles in Aom-igh had been gathered for this dinner. She saw that Sir Garen was also in attendance, as well as the other senior knights, and she knew that something was wrong. This was obviously not going to be a private dinner with a would-be suitor. For a moment, Kamarie felt a sense of panic. Surely her father wouldn't have pledged her to Prince Elroy without her permission. She glanced around frantically, expertly concealing the wild emotion she felt, looking for her father. She found him already near the head of the table. He was speaking in low tones to one of his senior knights and his expression was grave; he looked more serious than Kamarie could ever remember seeing him. Concern tugged at her thoughts as she noticed that in the midst of all the people assembled in the Hall, Prince Elroy was nowhere to be seen. She tuned into the mood around her and felt at once both relief and apprehension. There was tension and expectation, but mostly there was uncertainty. This audience had not been gathered to hear of an engagement, but something much more serious. Something more ominous.

King Arnaud straightened and raised his chin, signalling for all to be seated. A servant blew a short blast on a tiny trumpet and the courtiers quickly and gracefully flowed to their tables, waiting to be seated. Across the room, King Arnaud caught his daughter's eye and, with a slight motion of his head, invited her to sit next to him and her mother, Queen Zara.

Kamarie moved across the floor in something like a daze. Questions tumbled together in her head. Normally, she would have felt extremely awkward to be walking across a huge room with so many eyes suddenly turned on her. The only thing that kept her mind alert were the whispers as she passed through the gaze and scrutiny of supposed friends.

"She's certainly grown in the past year, do you remember at the Cold-Term banquet last year when she tripped over the fountain and fell into the punch bowl?" one "lady" whispered to the next.

"Oh yes, but my favorite story is when she dressed like a peasant, parading into this Hall carrying a wooden sword!"

Then came the snicker. No, courtiers were too mannerly to snicker, so it must have been a cough. Kamarie kept her temper under control and smiled directly at the ladies who were whispering behind their handkerchiefs, causing both of them to jump conspicuously and curtsy respectfully. Oh yes, there were advantages to knowing how to play this game, Kamarie thought pleasantly. Besides, the event with the wooden sword happened eleven years ago.

As she took her place between the King and Queen, the princess congratulated herself on how far she really had come. Most of her lessons could be dreadfully dull and boring, but she could recite every one of them flawlessly. To her parents' and tutors' delight, she had seen her mistakes as challenges to be overcome and had taken great pains to learn how to dance without landing in the punch bowl, sit down without knocking over the table, and walk through a room of snickering guests without tripping over her own dress. Though Kamarie still could not see the use of these arts, except as a tool to avoid whisperings and ridicule, she had set out to master them, and master them she did.

Her mother whispered, "Beautifully done, my daughter."

Kamarie squeezed her mother's hand. "What is going on?"

"Prince Elroy sent a message to tell us that he has been unavoidably detained and will not be joining us tonight, or perhaps ever."

Kamarie had never seen her mother frightened, yet Queen Zara's tone struck a chord that sent a chill through her. She glanced at her mother questioningly.

"Is something wrong?"

Zara smiled for the benefit of those nearby, and whispered, "You must be brave now, darling." Then she turned away, leaving Kamarie confused and questioning.

King Arnaud stood and raised his hand. A hush filled the room. Kamarie noticed the underlying tension that filled the Long Hall. This uncertain feel was present when she arrived, but she had been so focused on not embarrassing herself that she had not fully appreciated it. Now, in this eerie silence, it was the only thing she was aware of.

Her father held up a small piece of parchment and said, "Prince Elroy has declared war on Aom-igh." Arnaud's words fell like stone in the tomb-like silence of the hall, and then cautious whispers rose to the rafters as questions of alarm tumbled together.

King Arnaud raised his hand and spoke again, his calm silencing the whispers. "I have sent trusted men to Roalthae to learn the meaning of this threat. We do not know but we can guess that Elroy has allied himself with the Dark Country."

Kamarie felt an icy hand creep down her spine at these words. The Dark Country was only spoken of in whispers. Six hundred forty-nine years had passed since King Llian had defended against their invasion, but fear of this Warrior Kingdom lived on in legend and the people of Aom-igh could not talk about the Dark Country without recalling those dark and evil times.

Kamarie stopped contemplating the Dark Country and turned her attention back to her father.

"Since Prince Elroy had hoped to court our daughter, we can only assume that he means to take by force what he could have gained through marriage. As I do not know his plans, it is reasonable to assume that Kamarie is in danger. For this reason, I am sending her south, to stay until the danger has past."

She was to be sent away? Kamarie looked up, her bright blue eyes widening. In her outrage, she promptly forgot every single etiquette lesson she had ever learned and raised her voice for all to hear. "No!" she cried, rising out of her chair. "I will not be sent away. I will remain right here where I belong. I will not cower in safety with our people in danger!"

King Arnaud smiled kindly at his daughter, she reminded him so much of himself in his younger days. "Kamarie," he said firmly in a quiet tone meant only for her hearing, "we will speak of this later."

At the warning in his brown eyes, Kamarie fell silent and sat back down. As her father continued with further instructions, Kamarie let the words wash over her. She kept a pleasant look on her face, picking at her food, while her mind was spinning with fury at the prospect of being sent away without even being consulted.

When at long last the dinner was over and their guests had departed, with grim faces and pledges to return in the morning for a full council of war, Kamarie turned to her parents, her eyes flashing. Arnaud glanced at her and placed a weary arm around her shoulders. Kamarie stiffened but accepted the hug impatiently.

"Let's not do this here," Zara said.

"Right," Arnaud turned and led the way to their private family quarters in the castle. In the midst of their public lives, these quarters were a tiny, but beloved, haven that all three members of the royal family were grateful to have.

When they had settled into the older, thread-bare and comfortable couches in the family den, Kamarie opened her mouth to complain, but Arnaud raised a hand, forestalling her tirade.

"Kamarie, it is not what you think."

"Not what I think? What am I supposed to think? I walked into that room tonight fearing that I had been pledged to Prince Elroy without my approval, which would have been bad enough, but to be *sent away* without even discussing it with me first? How can you do this to me? Where am I supposed to go?"

"Kamarie, let your father speak." Zara sat down next to her daughter and patted her hand gently.

"I have an assignment for you, but it must be kept secret. I needed an excuse, something to keep anyone from guessing the real reason that I am sending you away from the palace. Fortunately, it is common knowledge that Prince Elroy was intending to court you."

Kamarie felt her anger receding. She sat back quietly and let her father continue.

"There is a man that I need to send a message to. I cannot entrust any normal courier with this message, and I cannot let word get out that I am trying to reach him. I need someone I can trust, and at this moment, the number of people that I can both trust *and* spare is very small."

Kamarie nodded, at once both placated and intrigued. "So that is why you are sending me."

"Exactly. His name is Brant, and he was once the King's Warrior. I need you to find him, the last I knew, he was living near Peak's Shadow, and ask him to come to our aid. I will give you a note so he will know I sent you, since he is not likely to recognize you."

"Who is he? Why do you need him?"

Arnaud sighed. "He helped keep me on the throne when King Jairem first proclaimed me as his heir. He was my right hand man for the first years of my reign, and he was a brother to me before that. He knew me when I was just Arnaud. Besides that, he is an excellent warrior and a brilliant strategist, and I will need both in order to win this war."

"I see," Kamarie said. "Forgive me for losing my temper, I just want to help so much, and the idea of being sent away without any opportunity to do something, anything, was more than I could stand. I would be honored to undertake this mission."

"Thank you," Arnaud replied wryly. "I thought you would understand, if you gave me a chance to explain."

Kamarie nodded, barely hearing his words; her quick mind was racing to plan out her journey. For a moment, she slipped into a pleasant daydream. She would be the traveling princess in disguise that none would recognize but all would love. If she was lucky, bandits might attack their party, steal their money and kidnap her escorts. She, of course, would slip noiselessly into the forest and then, when her attackers least expected, she would rescue her friends and they would travel on; maybe the bandits would even be of the breed that was loyal to their king, stealing from the rich and giving to the poor and all that. Then they would offer to be their guides through the forest and sharpen their survival skills as their band grew. This trip was definitely starting to have possibilities.

Kamarie grinned and Zara squeezed her shoulder, bringing her out of her daydream. "You must leave as soon as possible. Darby will travel with you, of course, and your father has arranged for one of the squires to escort you on your journey."

The castle was turned upside down within a few days. Soldiers and diplomats were everywhere, taking stock of their weapons and options. Dining halls and ballrooms were exchanged for mapping and strategy rooms as Arnaud readied his people for war. The countryside was now a training ground where the sound of metal on metal never ceased.

Kamarie's own preparations were underway as well. While it felt strange to be leaving the palace not knowing when she would return, there was a deep contentment growing inside of her. Trading long gowns, pointless sheer shawls and diamond-studded, uncomfortable shoes for sturdy boots, leather cloaks and woolen tunics was far more to her liking. These clothes were more practical for the adventure ahead and far more comfortable for the activities she preferred.

Understanding his daughter's heart more than she guessed, King Arnaud asked Sir Garen to present Kamarie with her own sword. She received it gracefully, doing her best to hide her delight, but she fooled no one as she easily sheathed the familiar weapon and looked up with a glow in her eyes. Queen Zara may have been surprised, but King Arnaud quietly shared the glow with his princess.

Kamarie was to depart within forty-eight hours. Darby had shown little reaction to the news that they were traveling south. All she had said was, "Humph, I suppose it couldn't be helped."

Oraeyn, a young squire about the same age as Kamarie, would be the only other companion on this journey. He had the misfortune to be training under a knight who had two squires. The other squire was older and would be going to battle with his knight-mentor. Oraeyn was not pleased with this new assignment, but nobody had asked him so he gritted his teeth and bore his disappointment alone. This was to have been his first big battle and the ache of being sent away grated on his nerves. Oraeyn glared at Kamarie and Darby every time he saw them over the next two days. Neither one of them seemed to notice his silent attack, which only added to his frustration.

Kamarie spent much of her time finding out all she could about this King's Warrior. Since her mission was supposed to be secret, she asked her questions as innocently as she could, expressing her interest as pure curiosity due to rumors and gossip she had heard. She tried to speak with her father, but he was preoccupied with other tasks and did not seem eager to answer her questions.

"I'm sorry, darling," Zara replied when Kamarie came to her, "I do not know Brant well, but your father trusts him and my heart tells me he is worthy of that trust. My only comfort in sending you away is that your purpose is to find him. More than that, I cannot say."

In frustration, Kamarie turned to Darby. "If he and my father were so close, why have I never heard him mentioned before?" she asked, as the elderly maid folded up some clothes to be packed for their journey.

"Well, dearie, he's been gone from your father's service a long while now, before you were born, I believe. I never got to know him, although I saw him around the palace quite a bit at the beginning of your father's reign, but he and your father were quite close, at least according to your mother. Closer than brothers is how she described them once, if I'm remembering correctly." And that was all that Darby would say on the subject, so Kamarie hunted elsewhere for information.

She found Sir Garen in the armory polishing his sword. He was the oldest and wisest knight in Aom-igh. It was common knowledge that he was undefeated with a sword and his history in battle required an age he did not show. He directed all combat training with a demanding eye and his knights both loved and feared him. Garen would be one upon whom Arnaud would rely in this coming battle. Garen insisted that knights take care of their own armor and weapons, and he led by example.

"Sir Garen?" Kamarie asked.

"Yes, Princess? I suppose you've come to learn about Brant."

"What?" Kamarie was puzzled.

"The King's Warrior, his name is Brant."

"Yes, I know... I was just wondering..."

Garen grinned. "I know all about your mission, Princess. It was my idea."

"Oh. Well, yes, I was wondering what you knew about him?"

Garen sighed. "Precious little. He arrived with your father when King Arnaud was summoned to court to be named as King Jairem's heir." Garen's eyes took on a far-away look as he sat back, lost in memory. "They were just boys at the time, but there was something about the way that one carried himself. It spoke of nobility and pride and self-assurance, the kind that a man gets when he's been in battle more than once and faced enemies that meant business. Oh, he tried to hide it, tried to stay in the background and let Arnaud take all the scrutiny, but he couldn't escape the notice of everyone. Some noticed and some thought a mistake had been made, that Brant was the real heir. King Jairem insisted though, and so did Brant. He could have taken the throne, there were quite a few who would have given it to him," here Garen chuckled, "Arnaud himself was one of them, but that Brant... he never seemed to want it."

"He wasn't ambitious?"

"Not in that way. He was content to become Arnaud's Warrior, to wander the realm and bring justice where it was needed and report problems back to his King. Then, in the year you were born, he came to the palace one time, just briefly, submitting his resignation, asking the king to let him out of his oath, his sworn bond. Seems he had met a woman and he wanted to settle down and pursue a life with her. The land was settled and at peace, and Brant had done so much... well, your father granted his request, didn't even think about it."

Kamarie frowned. "Thank you, Sir Garen."

"You be careful on your journey now, do you understand me?"

"What do you mean?"

"I just mean that you shouldn't go looking for trouble," Garen replied.

Kamarie grinned and left the armory without saying a word. She had much to think about and she felt that, even with all the information Garen had shared, this King's Warrior was an even bigger mystery than before.

The morning of the departure was cloudy, and by the time Kamarie, Darby, and Oraeyn were ready to set out the sky let loose with a cold downpour of rain. Queen Zara's pale blue eyes searched the horizon anxiously. She turned to her husband. "Do you think they really ought to...?" she did not finish the question, but Kamarie knew what her mother had been going to say. She was actually wondering the same thing herself. She did not relish starting out in the rain, nor was she going to get too excited about setting up camp or sleeping outside if it continued like this. It was a miserable day for traveling.

King Arnaud replied to the half-asked question, "Your tracks will be washed away by the rain; your cloaks are of good, solid cloth; and your horses are well trained and will not mind the weather. The longer you stay here in the palace, the harder it will be to leave in secret. Also, you may as well get used to this weather, you will certainly run into more on your way to Peak's Shadow."

Kamarie believed him and steeled herself inwardly. Her father had come to the throne in unlikely fashion. He had been raised by his aunt and uncle on a farm in southern Aom-igh with no knowledge that his real parents were distant relatives to the king. The king before Arnaud had never had any children. The distantly related Arnaud, living in the country and completely unaware of his royal blood, had been King Jairem's choice to succeed him to the throne. King Jairem had searched the country far and wide for someone with the right family history as well as the right sort of character and had found Arnaud. Kamarie's father had been set on the throne somewhat against his will. His life growing up had not been the sort that most royalty considered their right and privilege. Kamarie knew her father had spent many cold nights tending sheep before his appointment to the throne of Aom-igh.

Outwardly the king smiled cheerfully when he spoke of the weather they would run into, but inwardly he was worried. He did not know what was in store for his kingdom; all he had was a guess. He had allowed a few rumors to escape the walls of the palace encouraging the belief that Kamarie would be traveling the country in royal style, surrounded by an entourage, with the purpose of expressing encouragement and hope among their people. He calculated that sending her on this urgent mission, off the beaten path, in peasant attire, with only two companions would keep her unnoticed. He needed her to reach Peak's Shadow unharmed and undetected. Not only for her sake, but for her companions and for Brant as well. He knew what Brant's presence would add to their chances and he feared this may be known to their enemies as well.

He turned to Oraeyn. "Do you remember the directions?"

The boy nodded. "Yes, sir, like I know my own sword."

Arnaud was satisfied. He knew this capable squire was disappointed at being given these orders and taken away from the impending battle, but someday perhaps he would understand just how important this mission was. *When he meets Brant, I don't think he will remain disappointed,* Arnaud smiled to himself. Someday, the king was sure, this youth would make a fine knight.

Zara held Kamarie close as the rain poured down on them. "Be careful Kamarie," she whispered almost pleadingly. Then she turned to Oraeyn. "You watch over them." It was not a request.

Arnaud hugged Kamarie and handed her a small piece of paper with his seal on it before she expertly mounted her horse. Kamarie met his eyes and smiled as she slipped the note into a secret pocket on the inside of her cloak.

"Don't worry, Father, we will find Brant."

Arnaud put an arm around Zara as the three travelers rode off into the rain. "They will find Brant, and we will see them again."

Zara stared after her daughter. "I hope so," she whispered, "I hope so."

Together they turned and walked back inside. The private farewell took place behind the stable and away from prying eyes. No one knew when the Princess was leaving, and King Arnaud intended to keep it that way. Meanwhile, he now had to prepare his country for war, and a weariness settled over Arnaud that would not pass for many long days.

CHAPTER
TWO

"No, we're supposed to go *that* way!" Oraeyn yelled in exasperation, pointing south.

The three travelers had been wandering through the woods for a good part of the morning now, and Oraeyn was fed up with the Princess Kamarie *and* her royal maid. He knew which way they were supposed to go, but Kamarie seemed to think that her input had something to do with where they would end up. Oraeyn was frustrated, cold, wet, tired, and hungry, and he would have sworn that the fool girl *wanted* them to end up in some kind of danger.

"Oh look! The river," Kamarie pointed out coolly.

Imagine the nerve of that silly stable boy thinking he knew this forest better than she did! She was convinced that he would not be of any help when bandits attacked them. She had not counted on a spoilsport squire coming along on her adventure.

"And which way do you think we should follow the river, your highness?" Oraeyn asked through gritted teeth.

"That way, of course," Kamarie said, pointing upstream, which she knew full well was the wrong direction, back towards the palace, just to annoy him; it worked.

"Fine!" Oraeyn exploded. "Have it your way! But when we show up back at the palace, I'm *not* going to take the blame for getting us lost, I know which way we are supposed to go, and you, apparently, have no experience in following directions at all! You want to go up-river… then… you… *go* up-river!" He knew he was sputtering, but he no longer cared, "I, on the other hand, am going to go down-river, through the Mountains of Dusk, and into the village called Peak's Shadow, to find your father's friend and explain why you are not with me. But I won't have to explain that will I? Because you *know* where you're going. You *know* your way around, don't you?"

"Of course I knew we had to head down-river, stable boy," Kamarie said in a chilly tone. As he began his tirade, Kamarie was simply amused, but by the time he finished, she was no longer amused and in no mood to explain that she had been teasing.

At that, Oraeyn completely lost any and all grip he had on his loosely controlled frustration. What right did she have to treat him like this? She was only a princess, after all. And he was a squire, in training to become a defender of her nation. Without people like him, she might have been born a peasant's daughter. The nerve of her referring to him as a stable boy!

He dismounted from his chestnut horse and marched over to her. Glaring up at her through the rain that had been pouring down on them all day, he grabbed her arm and yanked her out of the saddle. She let out a startled yelp and started beating on him with her fists. He had to admit, the girl could throw a punch. He swung her into his arms and turned as she started yelling and protesting.

"Now, young man…" Darby started, but stopped when he threw her a withering glare.

"I am not going to hurt her. I am just going to teach her that she can't treat people the way she does and get away with it," he said.

He slowly and deliberately carried Kamarie to the riverbank and dumped her into the four feet of chilly, slow-moving water. He watched until she came up, making sure that she was not hurt. Then he turned and walked back to his horse.

Kamarie was outraged. She came up sputtering and coughing. *How dare he? How* dare *he!* The water was not overly cold, and the rain had already soaked her through, but it was the principle of the thing. Who did he think he was to be throwing the Princess of the Realm into a muddy river?

Oraeyn had returned to the side of the river and was now stretching a hand out to her. She grabbed it and spitefully put all her weight into trying to tug him into the river as well, but Oraeyn had prepared himself for such an antic and he held firm until he had pulled her out of the river and set her on the firm floor of the forest again. Immediately she turned and slapped him across the face. Or at least, she tried to. He had been expecting the blow and he blocked it, but he was not prepared for her second blow. Her fist connected painfully with his jaw causing him to blink in surprise. Then he wordlessly handed her the thick, dry blanket he had gone to get out of his saddlebags. Kamarie snatched it out of his hands and wrapped it around herself haughtily.

"My name is Oraeyn, Princess," the squire said firmly. "Not 'stable boy' or 'squire,' it is Oraeyn. And from now on, we are going to follow the directions that your father gave to me. Is that understood?"

Kamarie glowered at him beneath wet lashes and shivered in the cold rain. "I am the Princess Kamarie, Oraeyn, and you have no authority to order me about. However, I am quite willing to trust you with the directions from now on." Mustering any and all dignity she had left, she turned on her heel and marched over to her horse, her head held high.

She did not look as though she had been taught a lesson. Oraeyn noted ruefully, she almost managed to look as though it had been her idea to take a swim in the river all along. The look she gave him made him wonder just exactly who had really won that round. *Oh well, at least she used my name,* he thought to himself resignedly.

Yole was lost. He had been wandering through the Mountains of Dusk for nearly a week and had no idea which direction he was heading. He did not know if he was getting any nearer to the end of the mountains or if he was going back in the direction that he had come. It was not an uncomfortable feeling, being lost, Yole had been lost before. In fact, he had been lost for most of his short life. He had never been lost in the middle of the Mountains of Dusk though, and it was quickly becoming a frightening experience for the young boy. He sheltered in small caves that he stumbled across, and each night he heard the noises of hungry animals all around him.

Yole had oftentimes fended for himself, but that was when he was in a village. In villages there were people, and many people were compassionate and kind-hearted. In villages he could find scraps if kind-hearted people were scarce. There was a little bit of warmth that a smart boy could find by curling up in a doorway or next to a wall. With people nearby it was easy to be brave and grown-up. Now Yole was faced with wilderness, hunger, and loneliness, and people were nowhere to be found. For the first time, Yole was truly alone.

He was quickly running out of food and the weather looked to turn ugly. The sky had been dark all morning, and now thunderheads were rolling in. For the first time in his short life, Yole found that he was faced with fear. A panicked terror was clawing its way up his throat and he tried in vain to choke it down, he tried to talk to himself sternly, but it was of no use. He walked along, dragging his feet and scuffing the toes of his well-worn boots on the rocky ground. Then, with a flash of lightning and a crash of thunder, the downpour that the sky had been promising all day came in full measure. The rain was cold and relentless. Within moments, Yole was drenched and soaked to the skin. He looked around for shelter as the water dripped into his eyes and rolled down to the end of his nose. He soon spotted another cave; the one good thing about these mountains was the abundant supply of good, dry caves, if one knew where to look.

Scrambling up over rocks and tripping over the uneven ground, Yole made it to the cave and sat down, breathing hard. A sharp pain in his arm made him look down in weary bemusement. His elbow was dripping blood from where he had dragged it across a sharp rock in his hurry to get inside the cave. He wrung out his tunic as best as he could and washed out the cut with the excess water, pressing his hand against the wound to stop the bleeding. A blast of cold wind came howling through the cave causing him to shudder and his teeth to chatter. Suddenly, the urge to cry came over him. He was cold and lonely and wet, his elbow was bleeding, and he was tired of spending his nights in caves. He wanted to get out of these mountains, and he was, after all, only a young boy. Tossing his useless and soggy cloak to one side, Yole curled up on the hard cave floor. He laid his head on his arms and cried himself to sleep.

Yole awoke to the sounds of birds singing. His head hurt and he was starving. For a moment, he did not know where he was. Shaking his head, he stood up and slowly surveyed his surroundings. The cave he had stumbled upon in the night was much larger than he had first thought. He could not even see the back of it.

The first thing on his mind was food. He sat down and opened his pack. There was still a little food left. If he was careful and if he could find his way out of the mountains soon, his supply would last long enough. He did not have to worry about starving yet. It was a beautiful morning, bright and golden, with no trace of the black and gloomy fears of the night before.

His stomach no longer growling, Yole was now curious to

see how far back the cave went. Getting up, he walked into the dark cavern. As he walked, the cave narrowed slightly and became more tunnel-like. He noted with amazement that the tunnel did not seem to be getting any darker. He could not see very well, but the darkness was not pitch-black either. He could see the walls of the tunnel, and he had no real difficulty seeing what was in front of him. He had never been afraid of the dark; in fact, he could not remember it ever being so dark that he couldn't see. He had no fear of tunnels or caves either, although he could not recall ever being in one before coming to the Mountains of Dusk.

The tunnel seemed to go on forever, and Yole started to think that it might be a good idea to give up and turn back. At first he had nurtured the vain belief that the tunnel would lead to the other side of the Mountains of Dusk, but now that seemed unlikely. This tunnel might not lead anywhere at all. What if he had walked all this way just to end up right back in the cave he had spent the night in? With these doubts tumbling about in his mind, Yole's pace lessened considerably. As he slowed down and got ready to turn back, he saw something shining up ahead. Cautiously, he crept deeper into the tunnel. Then suddenly he realized that what he was seeing was daylight.

With a shout of joy, Yole ran towards the light. It grew brighter and brighter until it almost seemed as if there could be no possible way to fit any more light into one area. He stopped when the tunnel turned into a cave once more. It was not the cave that he had come from nor was it like any cave he had ever seen before. It was a huge, open space filled with richly colored and transparent rock formations of so many different varieties they made his head spin. The Dragon's Eye was shining through a small opening set at window height on the opposite wall reflecting off and refracting through the various surfaces with a visual design that almost mirrored the enchantment Yole experienced when he heard the shepherd's pipes. However, the music of the pipes was never enough, while the light display in this chamber was so powerful that Yole had to close his eyes.

As Yole's eyes adjusted to the light, he saw something that made all the light in the room seem dim. It was a beautiful yet strange arrangement of stalagmites and stalactites. Yole could not have said with any conviction that they had just grown that way; it looked as though the placement was too purposeful for them to have formed naturally, but surely it was not possible to *grow* such things. In the center of the cave was a ring of alternating stalagmites and stalactites, they were closely placed, but not so close that there were no spaces between. Yole approached the ring and peered through one of the spaces, curious to know what secret this rock formation held.

"There they are," Kamarie whispered, "the Mountains of Dusk."

Indeed, the mountains were visible. They were by no means close, peeking up over the horizon in the faraway, hazy distance, at the very edge of vision. They had risen into view overnight. Despite their arguments and the wet weather over the past few days, the three travelers had been making pretty good time. Kamarie had been as good as her word about not questioning Oraeyn's directions, though she had questioned just about everything else.

"What are we waiting for?" Kamarie asked. "Let's go!" She kicked her horse sharply and started to speed towards the mountains, but Oraeyn pulled his horse in front of hers, causing Tor to come to a very quick stop.

"Hold on there Princess," he said, "there…" he started, but of course, Kamarie would not let him finish.

"What is your problem?" she asked in exasperation. "You want to get there faster, and you don't want to continue at all, you want me to follow your directions, yet you have hardly been taking the role of leader, I don't understand you at all! Why shouldn't we keep going, there's plenty of daylight left."

"If you would take a look at the sky," Oraeyn said, in a quiet tone that made Kamarie's shouts seem so much louder than they had actually been.

Kamarie sighed in frustration, *this trip has not been much of an adventure yet*, she thought. Then she looked up towards the sky. It had been dark all day, but now off on the horizon was a large black cloud. She did not know what it meant, but it frightened her.

"What does it mean, Oraeyn?" she asked in a small voice.

"It means there is a storm coming, and we need to find shelter, fast," Oraeyn replied steadily.

A gust of cold wind blew around them, and Kamarie shuddered. Then Darby's voice came floating over to them, "Master Oraeyn, I do believe I have found us a suitable shelter to pass the storm. If you would come and take a look?"

Kamarie and Oraeyn rode over to Darby and looked at the shelter she had found. It was a clump of underbrush growing together so tightly that it made a nearly airtight ceiling of sorts. Underneath this thatched roof was enough room for the three of them to lie down comfortably.

"It's perfect," Oraeyn said. "Now, let's get a fire started and cook our meal before that gets here," he added, pointing briefly at the large, ominous cloud.

He scraped a shallow hole in the ground, grabbed some dead leaves and dry twigs, and struck his flint and steel.

"Would one of you go and get some wood so we can keep this fire going long enough to cook our food?"

"I'll get the wood," Kamarie volunteered. At Oraeyn's surprised look she added defensively, "I'm not completely helpless."

"No offense, Princess," Oraeyn said hastily, "but do you know how…"

"Yes," Kamarie said, cutting him off, "you want sticks about the same size that aren't green inside. And you want them about this long," she held her hands about a foot and a half apart, "and by the way, you can stop calling me 'Princess', I have a name too, you know."

"Where did you learn about firewood, Prin…Kamarie?" Oraeyn asked in open astonishment.

"I can read," Kamarie replied, "all the adventure books tell you how to make a fire and keep it going."

Oraeyn shook his head; this princess would probably never cease to bewilder him. One moment she seemed to know absolutely nothing about the wilderness or survival. The very basics of survival and direction were mysteries to her, she could not distinguish between upstream and downstream, she could not tell when a storm was coming; and yet, she knew how to start a fire and what kind of wood to use, and the food she had cooked along the journey had been edible, no, it had been better than edible. And he had to admit; she wore the sword at her side as if she had been born to it. He rubbed his jaw where she had hit him when he had thrown her in the river; it had bruised. *Where had the princess learned how to punch like that?* he wondered.

"You could say something like, 'thank you, Kamarie, that would be helpful,' rather than just sitting there staring at me in disbelief," Kamarie said.

Her words shook Oraeyn out of his thoughts. "That *would* be helpful, Kamarie, thank you," he said. She nodded and as she turned, he asked, "And would you mind telling me where you learned to carry a sword and punch like a knight, and where you learned how to ride?"

She looked at him in surprise for a moment. Then she laughed and said, "Yes, I would mind," and she darted off deeper into the forest before he could say anything else.

As Oraeyn started the fire and kept it going, Darby spread out their bed-rolls inside their makeshift cave of underbrush. She untacked the horses, fed them, and blanketed them so they would not feel the cold, especially if it rained later that evening. Oraeyn liked Darby. She reminded him of his mother, someone who worked hard and never complained. She was a woman of few words. The only thing he could not fathom at first was her loyalty to Kamarie, but now he was starting to understand it a little bit better. He had set off on this trip believing that Kamarie was a spoiled, bratty princess. Now he was starting to see that she had a great sense of fun, she was not completely helpless in the wilderness, and though she was exasperating, she had an irrepressible personality that drew him. He was finding that he actually enjoyed their fights, if only because it kept the journey from becoming tedious. He also liked the game of wills that had sprung up between them, though he would never have admitted to it.

Suddenly Darby was at his shoulder. He glanced up at her and noticed the worry on her face. "What is it, Darby?"

"The storm is near, and Princess Kamarie has not returned," she said anxiously. "Her Highness has been gone for a long time."

Oraeyn frowned. How long had he been lost in thought? Had Kamarie really been gone so long? One glance at his fire told him that she ought to have been back by now.

He gave Darby a reassuring look, "I will find her, maybe she got lost, I'm sure she isn't in any real danger, and I bet if she is she could probably talk her way out of it." His humor did not bring a smile to Darby's face, so he continued, "Can you watch the fire and make sure it doesn't go out?"

Grabbing his sword belt, Oraeyn set out after Kamarie. He was an excellent hunter; his mentoring knight had often praised him on his skill at tracking. He was impressed by the lack of trail that Kamarie had left, but he was also puzzled by it. He would have to find out where she had learned these survival skills. He could read her trail, but it would have been a struggle for many less skilled in the art of tracking.

Suddenly, her trail disappeared. Oraeyn was mystified. He thought at first he had somehow missed something, but disregarded that thought. In the twilight, he took note of his surroundings, and then, with his sword, poked at the ground before him. The ground ahead would not support his weight, and there was a depression that he could see in the developing darkness. He looked around and found what he sought. Sheathing his sword, he grabbed a sturdy stick and cautiously lay down on his stomach and inched towards the edge of the depression. He held his stick with both hands under his chin, perpendicular to his body. As he inched forward, the ground under him suddenly gave way. With a yell, he fell, but not far. The hole was too narrow for his makeshift staff, and it was now the only thing that kept him from falling.

Holding onto the stick for dear life, Oraeyn called out, "Kamarie? Are you there?"

"Oraeyn?" the reply was a mixture of incredulity and relief.

"Kamarie! Are you all right?" he asked.

"Yes, I'm a little shaken up, and I think there are some scrapes on my knees. But other than that I'm okay," she said.

"How did you find me?"

"I tracked you," Oraeyn said as he pulled himself up on his staff, as he did so, thanking Cruithaor Elchiyl that the stick didn't break beneath his weight. With a little effort, he was able to pull himself out of the narrow hole. Then he peered down. "Can you see me, Kamarie?"

"Yes, I can."

"How far down would you say you are?" he asked, holding his breath, hoping it was not too far.

"Ten or twelve feet. I'm not really sure. If I could stand on my own shoulders, I would almost be able to climb out," she said.

Oraeyn let his breath out in a sigh of relief, and said, "I'm going to lower a stick down to you, tell me if you can reach it. If you can, then grab a hold of it and let me pull you out."

"Do you think that will work?" Kamarie asked. "What if I can't hold on?"

"Then we will try again. I will get you out of there." When he got no reply, he lowered the staff down.

"I've got it," Kamarie called, as he felt her grab the end of it. "All right," she yelled, "pull me up."

It was more difficult to pull her up than he had first thought that it would be. The stick did not work as well as a rope would have, or even a proper staff, and the process was a slow one. But after what seemed like eons of pulling, Kamarie's head appeared and she grabbed the edge of the hole. Oraeyn grabbed her wrists and pulled her out of the hole. He set Kamarie on her feet, but as he released her she started to collapse.

"Whoa," Oraeyn said, reaching out to support her again, "are you okay?"

She nodded shakily as he helped her to sit down. It was a few moments before she could do anything but stare at the spot where the forest floor gave way, her would-be prison, and shiver. Eventually, she looked up from her trance and stared at him as if she was not quite sure she believed he was actually there, "I was so afra…" she stopped, lifted her chin slightly, and started again, "I didn't think you would come."

Now it was Oraeyn's turn to stare. "Why wouldn't I come?" he asked in bewilderment.

"B-because I…" Kamarie's voice started to tremble; she took a deep breath and regained control of herself, "Because I have been so rotten to you. And also because I knew my trail would be very difficult to follow."

Uncertain as to how he was supposed to respond, and afraid that she would give way to hysteria at any moment, Oraeyn said, "I'm a pretty good tracker." He hesitated, then continued, "And you haven't really been that bad. I mean… I shouldn't have risen to the occasion so often. You are the princess after all, and I've been treating you as if I was expecting you to be something you're not."

A flush of anger rose in Kamarie's cheeks. "What is that supposed to mean?"

"I didn't mean that in a bad way," Oraeyn quickly explained. "I mean you can't help the fact that you've been waited on your entire life and you expect everyone to do so. You've been entitled to it, so I could hardly expect you to quit treating everyone like servants."

"For your information…" Kamarie stopped.

Who am I? She thought to herself, *I am not the person that he thinks I am… am I? And if I am, then what can I do to change?*

She hesitated and then continued in a different vein instead of defending herself, "I had started to gather the firewood when I fell down that hole, so I suppose I will have to start over again. Only this time I'll watch out for holes in the ground," she smiled at him winningly.

"Uh, yeah." Oraeyn stared at the creature before him in confusion. *Who is this girl?* He asked himself, as he said, "How about we gather that firewood on our way back towards the camp? Darby probably thinks we've run out on her by now."

Kamarie laughed, "Probably."

As they walked back to their campsite, Oraeyn gathered up the courage to say, "Can I ask you a question?"

"Sure," Kamarie said.

"Just where did you learn how to use a sword?"

Startled, Kamarie almost dropped her firewood. Then she turned away and picked up another stick, "How did you know I can use a sword?" she asked, keeping her gaze down, studying the ground intently for firewood.

"One swordsman knows another," Oraeyn said simply. "The way you wear your sword gives you away to anyone who knows anything about weapons."

Kamarie's face darkened, and she seemed to be struggling with herself. There was silence for a moment, and then she sighed heavily. She looked up from the ground and held his gaze solemnly.

"I'm afraid I haven't been quite honest with you. I'm not exactly what I seem. I mean, of course I'm the princess, and my name is Kamarie, but I'm not an ordinary princess. You see… well, I begged Sir Garen into training me as his squire."

Oraeyn looked startled. "Sir…Garen? He agreed? And your parents?"

"No, my parents did not know, and perhaps they still don't, although I am pretty sure that my father suspects. It took a lot of convincing to get Sir Garen to teach me since it had to be in secret. Every night when I was supposed to be in bed, I would climb out the window, and Sir Garen and I would ride out into the forest where he taught me swordsmanship, the code of chivalry, archery, tracking, riding, how to make a fire, everything you've been learning."

"You've been actually training as a squire, a real squire, under Garen's tutelage." Oraeyn was stunned. Garen had stopped training squires several years ago. He was a hero of Aom-igh, and now he taught the younger squires history and was the head commander of all the regular knights. He was revered by squires and knights alike. Though past his prime, he was still strong and could out-track, out-ride, and out-fight many of the best knights in the kingdom. King Arnaud trusted the defense of his country to Garen, and that was all the honor that this great warrior needed.

"Well, yes," Kamarie said.

Then Oraeyn looked sharply at her. "So what has all of this been?"

"All of what?"

"Why did you point up-river? Why have you been acting like you know nothing about being out here in the wilderness? Why have you been acting like a spoiled princess if you aren't one?"

Kamarie glanced at him shamefacedly then looked away, unable to meet his gaze. "Well, partially because I wanted to keep my training a secret, and partially because I don't have a whole lot of real experience... I know the concepts of direction and finding my way, but I haven't had a lot of time to put those concepts into practice." She turned away and picked up another stick to hide her furious blushing.

Oraeyn looked skeptical. "You wanted to keep it secret," he said slowly. There was a long pause, and then, "Did you think you couldn't trust me? Is that why you thought I wouldn't come rescue you from that pit?"

Kamarie blushed again and cast her gaze downwards again. Then she straightened, still standing with her back towards him.

Without turning around, she stiffly nodded, once. Oraeyn saw the nod and the look on his face turned sad.

"I'm sorry you felt that way."

Kamarie turned to face him now. "Oraeyn, my kingdom is in danger, and I don't know where the danger is coming from. It is quite possible that there are traitors inside Aom-igh already, even inside the castle. I had to be careful, for everyone's sake."

He nodded slowly, his eyes sympathetic. "I understand. I think you did right. I am sorry I gave you such a hard time."

"No!" Kamarie exclaimed. "It's a good thing you did, that's how I knew I could trust you."

He stared at her in total bewilderment for a moment, and then they both started laughing. As they walked back together, Oraeyn asked her about her training and Kamarie answered.

"What do you plan to do with your training?" Oraeyn finally asked, when they were almost back at the camp.

Kamarie's face sobered as she paused and faced Oraeyn. "Did you know that in King Artair's day, the women were trained as warriors too? They didn't fight on the front lines, but they were the last line of defense against invasion. They were often trained as archers, although they learned the sword and spear as well."

Oraeyn's eyes widened. "Then you plan to become a knight?"

Kamarie sighed. "No, not really."

"Why not?"

"There isn't time. I'm the princess, and in two years I come of age, I don't have time to go through the intensive training that you will undergo next year in order to reach knighthood. I have too many other responsibilities that will demand my attention."

"So all this has been, what, a game? A distraction? Why go through it?"

"To be useful," Kamarie smiled faintly. "I've read the histories, and I admired the system that King Artair set up. Even if an invading force made it through his army, they still hadn't conquered Aom-igh, because they had to get through that final line of defense, the women protecting their homes, and they were trained and capable of defending their homes. I may be queen someday, I would like to be able to defend my people, should the need arise."

"You've put a lot of thought into this, I'm impressed. Have you spoken to your father about it?"

"Not yet, but I wish now that I had."

"Father," Schea said while he helped Brant round up a few straggling sheep. "I just remembered. Ryder and I found a hole in the fence down by the South Pasture. We put some sticks over the hole, but we couldn't lift the big boards that had fallen."

Brant looked up, surprised. "Did you find the hole today?"

Schea looked uncomfortable. "Um... no, I'm sorry, Father, it was um... a couple of weeks ago. Right before the... um... right before you had to send Yole away. It's the part of the fence that's closest to the forest, and we haven't been all the way out to the forest in a while."

"Well, you must have done a good job with those sticks, none of our livestock has gone missing."

"Yeah, but I shouldn't have forgot."

"It's all right, son. No harm done."

Schea perked up a bit as he realized his father wasn't disappointed in him. A few moments later they heard Imojean ringing the dinner bell and Kali joined them, a bunch of violets held gently in her left hand.

"Thank you for telling me Schea, safeguarding our livestock is our life's blood," Brant said. It was good that the boy had remembered; sheep and cattle could be lost if a patched fence went too long unnoticed. "You and Kali go up to the house for dinner. Tell your mother I'll be late, and that I said to go ahead and start dinner without me. I want to go look at the fence."

"Yes, sir," Schea and Kali turned towards the house.

"I'll beat you to the house!" Brant heard Schea challenge Kali.

"Not if I beat you first!" Kali retorted.

Brant smiled. She might seem to belong in fairyland sometimes, but she was very much a rancher's daughter as well, and a tough one at that. Her thoughtful, gentle, and airy nature was a good balance to Schea, who was always very much a little boy. The two fought and argued more than their fair share, Brant sometimes thought, but they always made up and were best friends again soon afterwards. He turned towards the south and sighed. The Dragon's Eye had begun to set, and it would be dark by the time he reached the fence, but it was not something he wanted to leave unchecked till tomorrow.

The fence was not too bad, but it was a good thing that Schea and Ryder had found it. Severe winds had damaged a portion of the fence, which could have eventually caused some major problems. The sticks that the boys had used to patch the hole were still in place, which was probably why none of the sheep or cattle had escaped yet. Brant removed the patch, smiling to himself as he did so, proud of his son's ingenuity, and started putting the fence timbers back into place. He re-tied the wire and pushed mud into the holes where the heavy timbers fit into the posts, confident this repair would safeguard his herd until he could get his tools down here to fix it properly. As he was finishing his final repairs, Brant heard a scream from somewhere behind him. Startled, he turned his head and looked over his shoulder towards his house. Black smoke billowing up into the sky sent alarm slicing through his heart. The fence concern vanished and he took off across the pasture at a sprint. When he reached the path that led up out of the pasture to his home, he realized that the smoke was pouring out of all the windows in his house.

His first panicked thought was that Imojean had accidentally left the flue shut or that some hot coals had fallen out of the stove and onto the floor; but as he drew closer, a more urgent dread filled his senses. There was no sign of life around the house. No shouts to the children to get buckets of water, no movement of any sort inside that would have told him that anyone was trying to beat out the flames. There was no noise at all except for the roaring of the fire, no movement except for the raging flames that lapped hungrily at everything they touched. He dashed up the path to the house and stopped suddenly, dropping to his knees on the dusty ground with an anguished cry.

In front of him, face down on the path only a few feet from the front door of his house, lay Schea and Kali. He knew before he touched them that they were dead. A lump formed in his throat making it impossible to swallow. Pain seared across his chest and he could not breathe. He stared blankly at the dark stain on the ground around his precious children.

Standing up now, he looked towards the house. Blazing ashes were flying up into the sky and falling back to the ground like little comets. Flames were shooting up through the roof and pouring out through the windows. The fire was slurping greedily at the little shutters he had taken such pains to put in for Imojean, the pretty green paint was bubbling as it melted.

Something broke loose inside of Brant; half screaming, half sobbing he stumbled towards his house, crying, "Imojean! Imojean!"

He burst in through the front door and was immediately thrown back by the intense heat and smoke. He pulled his shirt up over his nose and mouth and stepped back through the door; frantically he scanned the room searching, searching. He found her. She was lying on the floor with destruction all around her. The whole scene unfolded in his mind's eye. Imojean had been humming to herself, maybe even singing, setting the table for dinner as she waited for her family to arrive from the fields. She could hear the patter of her children's feet as they raced up the path, and then there was silence. She looked out the window to see what was taking so long... that must have been the scream he had heard, the one that had been cut off so abruptly by the dagger sticking out of her back.

He's found me, the thought froze the blood in his veins. *After all these years, he has finally tracked me down.*

A section of the roof crackled and fell a few feet in front of him, pulling him out of his thoughts and reminding him that he stood inside a house that was ablaze. He made his way to Imojean and picked her up. Kissing her forehead gently, he carried her to the bed and laid her there as carefully as he could. Then he ran back outside and picked up Schea. A warrior's burial in fire he could give his family, at the very least he could give them that, he who had brought this upon them. Cradling his son in his arms and kissing his face, he carried the limp body of his son back to the house and laid him next to his mother. Then he went back for Kali. When he picked her up, she moaned. He knelt down on the path quickly, his eyes brimming with hope.

"Kali?" he spoke her name in a quivering, astonished voice, amazed that she was still alive, "Kali?"

"Papa?" she whispered, her eyelids fluttering open. She pressed her small hand to the knife wound in her side. "It hurts papa."

His eyes filled with tears. "I know, honey."

"They set the house on fire," she choked on the words and spit blood.

"It's okay, it's going to be okay."

"They killed Schea. I screamed, I knew you would come..." her eyes started to glaze over.

"No! Kali! Don't go, stay with me darling, please. We'll make it, we'll be okay." Brant was not sure what he was saying, but he knew that he had to keep her talking, had to keep her from going to sleep or his entire world would fall apart. He had seen her wound, so he knew there was no hope, but his mind clung to hope with stubborn ferocity. Tears streamed down his face as he begged his daughter to live.

Her eyes focused on his face and her little hand touched his cheek, brushing away the tears. "I knew you'd come," she whispered again. Then her eyes closed and her hand fell back down. She was gone. The bonds of flesh no longer held her spirit. Brant, convulsed in sobs, could almost see her face, shining with a gentle, golden smile as she reached her little hand down to him from the realm above and said, "Don't. Don't cry for me, Papa. It doesn't hurt anymore."

CHAPTER

THREE

Brant, desolate and exhausted, watched through a haze of tears as his house burned to the ground and the wind scattered the ashes across the hills and the fields. The black specks fluttered across the green grass, oddly out of place against the bright sky and the glow of the setting Dragon's Eye. He was void of feeling. This tragedy was happening to someone else, somewhere far away. Brant half-believed that he would soon wake up and be surrounded by his happy family once again. This nightmare would become a thing that had never, *could* never have, happened. Imojean would come running out of the doorway that was not on fire and dance, laughing, into his arms again. Schea, grinning, little, dark-haired Schea, would tug on his cloak and tell him to come see his newest find down by the creek. Presently, his sweet, faraway dreamer, the golden haired Kali would appear to explain the fairy ring she had found. His world would fill up with magic and laughter again, and they would all sit together eating the dinner that had never even been set on the table. Tears rolled down his face, unheeded. He stood frozen in place, watching all his dreams, hopes, and work die inside hungry flames that devoured everything he held dear.

He knew he had been standing in the same spot for a long time. He could feel it in the dull ache creeping up his legs and lower back, but he could not move. He could not tear his eyes away from the destruction. As the last flames died out, and his life lay before him in a pile of blackened charcoal and ashes, a fury welled up within Brant, an intensity of emotion he had never known. The rage shoved sorrow aside, tucking it into an aching, throbbing little ball in the corner of his heart, and then his fury consumed him, burning through him with a force like the fire that had just destroyed his life. He had tried so hard, so hard to leave his past behind him, to lead a normal, quiet life, raising his family in a remote place, taking up a peaceful existence, and doing everything he could to blend into the normal crowd. But his past had caught up to him; his world had been taken from him, brutally ripped out of his grasp. And now he had nowhere to turn but back the way he had come. How had this happened? How had they found him? And most importantly, why now?

Tears streamed from his eyes. "They were just children, innocents... how could you?"

Finally, the storm that had been threatening all day broke loose and swirled around him. Flashes of blazing light flared across the sky in streaks followed closely by the deafening roar of thunder. The rain poured down in sheets, drenching Brant within seconds.

As if echoing the weather, the storm in Brant's heart burst out of his grasp in all its fury. Raising his voice in defiance, Brant shouted out into the storm. "I will find you!" he yelled, his deep voice rising above the raging squall, "I know who you are, and I will find you!"

Queen Zara stood staring out of the window with a sorrowful and pensive look on her lovely face. She turned to

Arnaud. "Do you think that they are all right?" she asked in a hushed voice filled with the quietness that comes from living for days on end under great strain.

Arnaud smiled reassuringly. "I'm sure they are."

"I know that the boy, Oraeyn, is capable enough, and I know that training to be a knight is not easy work. I know that he is prepared, but it is Kamarie that I am worried about," Zara said. "I know I shouldn't, Oraeyn will look after her, and of course Darby will too, but she has never been out in the forest without a proper escort. I can't help but think that at this very moment she is probably cold and frightened. The forest is not exactly the safest place in Aom-igh for her to be traveling. Maybe she should have stayed here." Zara bit her lip and wrinkled her brow.

King Arnaud laid a gentle hand on his wife's shoulder. "I believe Kamarie is better suited to the journey than you might think," he said with a twinkle in his eye. "She is going to be fine. The trip to the village on the other side of the Mountains of Dusk is a long one, but I am sure that Oraeyn will get them to Peak's Shadow safely. And when they get there, I have every confidence that Brant will be able to protect her. I sent him a message through Oraeyn, asking him to look after Kamarie and find her a safe place to stay until this threat is past."

Zara smiled wanly. "I know, I just worry. She is so headstrong, I suppose I worry mostly that she will refuse to be left somewhere safe, even by Brant... you know I have every confidence in his abilities, but it has been a long time, a very long time..."

"I'm sure he has not forgotten how to take care of himself," Arnaud smiled.

Zara nodded and said nothing more. Despite his soothing words, Arnaud was filled with anxiety. He had not seen or had any contact with Brant for many years, and he was not even sure if the man was still living in the village of Peak's Shadow. Brant had always been a wanderer, but that had been back in their much younger years, even before Arnaud had found himself the unsuspecting heir to the throne of Aom-igh and long before

Brant had met Imojean and settled down into the simpler, peaceful life of a rancher and farmer.

However, King Arnaud's greater fear was that this lull in the storm would continue, that nothing would happen, and that they would all start to let down their guard. Then, when even he no longer expected an attack, the flood would come. He was not afraid of facing that flood, but he did fear that they could be swept away by it when they least expected it. The one certainty he had was that when the time came to take up arms, he would be there, fighting alongside his warriors.

As the warm rays of light from the Dragon's Eye peered over the horizon heralding the dawn of a new day, Brant awoke. As he pushed himself up, the tangles of half-remembered dreams and hours of deep sleep still clung to him as he stared at his surroundings in dazed confusion. Then the flood hit him as he remembered the events of the night before.

He had stood in the rain and watched his house burn down until he could no longer hold sleep at bay. The events of the day had overwhelmed him, causing him to sleep more deeply than ever before. He had ended up falling asleep on the ground outside his house, and now he was covered in a layer of caked mud and soot.

In a state of determined shock, Brant took a step towards the smoldering remains of his once happy home and then stopped as he realized that there was nothing left, nothing to salvage. Although his heart felt numb, the blazing fury from the night before when he had screamed into the storm was still smoldering in the depths of his heart. The difference this morning was that now he was thinking clearly. The rage and need for revenge was boiling beneath a cold layer of logic. He had once again taken on the mantel that had made him so dangerous so many years before.

Turning away from the pile of blackened timber, Brant walked deliberately down towards the South Pasture. There was a pond bordering the edge of the South Pasture that served as a boundary between his own land and his neighbor's. He could wash the mud, soot, and filth off his skin and from his clothes in the pond, and then he would ask Jonsten for the loan of a horse. He had his own horses, but he was certain his barn had been burned by his enemies. After that, he would go into the village for supplies and then he would hunt down these murderers. But right now his first step was to get to the pond without collapsing beneath the weight of despair.

When he reached the water, he dove in. Staying under for as long as he could, Brant felt a welcome release from the horrors of the night before. It was peaceful and quiet under the surface of the water; he could not even hear the roaring in his ears that had started when he heard that first scream. He relaxed in the soothing grasp of the cool water, cradled in its embrace. He hung suspended in the darkness and the silence. Finally, Brant was forced to surface. He swam over to the far shore, letting the swimming motion through the water wash most of the mud from his clothes. He reached the shore on the other side of the pond and worked on cleaning the soot and dirt from his hair and clothes. When he was done, he was not prepared for what met his eyes as he looked up.

A few hundred feet from the shore where Jonsten's home had once stood was another pile of burned timbers, beams, and ashes. There was no sign of life anywhere around the remains of the house. In renewed horror, Brant quickly scanned the area, looking in the direction that his other neighbors' houses were supposed to be standing. Instead of the pretty little homes, he only saw faint clouds of smoke where houses should have been. The rain had put out the fires, but some of the embers still smoldered, and thin wisps of smoke rose into the air. The realization that he was the only living person left in Peak's Shadow dawned upon him, leaving him gasping for air. His village and his life had been turned into a pile of rubble overnight. There was nothing left now. Questions raced through his mind like stampeding horses. Was all of Aom-igh in danger, or had he been the sole target of this attack? One other idea was surfacing in the back of his mind; he tried to push it away, thinking it was ludicrous. But, could it be? Was it possible that the murderer was so determined to kill him that his very presence in this country was putting all of Aom-igh in danger? But that could not be, that would make the killer a madman, and Brant knew that the man who hunted him was anything but mad. He stared at the ruins of the village he loved in numb disbelief as water dripped down from his dark hair and rolled down his face.

He had been so certain that he was the target of the attack, so certain that he knew his enemy, but this... could so much have changed over the years? Could his enemy's jealousy have so consumed him that honor no longer had any meaning? Brant's mind reeled and he changed his line of thinking, unwilling to contemplate what that might mean.

Suddenly Brant let out a harsh and bitter laugh. If he *had* been the target, then his enemy, whoever he was, was a terrible marksman.

Setting his jaw, Brant made a decision and headed back with long, determined strides past what had been his home without even glancing at it. He found the small mound that he was looking for and started digging. Two feet down, he hit something hard. Working more quickly now, he dug wider and finally was able to see the entire top of a long wooden box. With a little effort, Brant was able to pull the box out of the hole and set it on the ground next to him.

Heaving a sigh filled with the weight of many memories, Brant knelt next to the box and ran his hand across the top of it. He hesitated when he touched the latch.

"I buried this thinking I would never see it again, hoping I would never see it again. But something inside me could not believe that I would never need it again," he muttered to himself. He breathed deep, and then shrugged the residue of the memories away.

With no hesitation now, he turned the latch and lifted the lid. Inside the box were remnants of days that Brant had tried to forget, had tried to put behind him. A shirt of chain mail, a brightly shining sword that was deceptively plain-looking, a wickedly sharp throwing dagger, a shield with the design of a flame leaping out of a cluster of stars etched on the front in bright colors that seemed to mute the Dragon's Eye itself, and a leather vest decorated with a miniature version of the same symbol.

Brant rifled through the items; then he lifted the sword out of the box and stood up straight. The hilt fit into his hand as though he had never laid the blade to rest. He went through a practice pattern with grace and perfection, almost as though sixteen years of forgetting had never occurred. With much less hesitation now, Brant pulled out the sword belt and strapped it around himself, sheathing the beautiful, but deadly, blade. He glanced at the shield longingly, but knew it was an impractical desire that he had, to bring it along with him; it would only hinder his progress. He also passed by the chain mail shirt in favor of the lighter, leather vest with his emblem of stars and flame imprinted on the left side. With not a little regret, Brant put the shield and shirt back in the box. Then he placed the box back in the hole and covered it up again.

Finally, he headed towards his barn. He was relieved to find it still standing. It seemed it was the only building for miles that had escaped the devastation the rest of the village had been subjected to. The stables were a good distance from the house, down by the paddocks the sheep were herded into every night. A small hillock and a healthy line of pine trees stood between the house and the barn, which was most likely the only thing that had kept it from being burned to the ground like his home. Whatever the reason, chance or the guiding hand of Cruithaor Elchiyl, Brant muttered a quiet "thank you" as he slipped into the barn.

"Easy, Legend," he muttered softly to the big brown gelding inside the barn. As he spoke the horse's name, he felt a pang.

Schea and Kali had named the horse when he brought it home. He patted the horse's shaggy neck and memories of his family flooded through his mind.

Legend snorted and shook his head. Brant sighed and got the horse tacked up. Loading the horse's saddle-bags with grain and weapons, Brant swung himself up onto Legend's back and headed towards the mountains.

As Yole cautiously approached the ring of rock that was shooting light in all directions, he was frightened. It was a different emotion for him; he rarely ever felt frightened by anything. But this strange rock formation sent shivers of fear all through his body and made the skin on the back of his neck tingle in warning. And yet, the formation also fascinated him. He was entranced by curiosity. He moved towards it against his own will. He could not control his own legs; whatever the ring was guarding was singing, calling to him, a call he could not resist.

He crept closer, closer, always closer to the opening in the ring of rock, until finally he was standing right in front of it. He stopped, uncertain, feeling as though he were trespassing on forbidden territory; but he had come this far, and he could not turn back now. He took another step and then he was standing in the opening, gazing towards the interior of the naturally formed room. Now the light was so bright it was blinding him. Another step and he was inside the ring with the treasure it guarded. As his eyes adjusted to the brightness, he saw that it came from a table-like pillar in the middle of the small room. A ring of golden flames, which accounted for the eerie, life-like quality of the light, surrounded the table. Lying in the middle of the table was an object that Yole could not see clearly. He was filled with an insatiable desire to move forward to get a better look at it, but the sensation of fear returned and stopped him in his tracks. Frozen, he stood there for a moment, and then he reached deep down inside himself and found a tiny remnant of courage.

He approached the table, as close as he could get without being burned. In the middle of the table lay a sword. The blade was pure gold. The firelight made it shine and shimmer. The hilt was plain, almost nondescript, but then Yole rubbed his eyes and stared again. Because of the gleaming brightness flashing from the golden blade, the hilt was overwhelmed at first glance but closer inspection proved that it was made out of translucent silver. A brown strap of leather was wrapped around the hilt, making it easier to grasp. The sword was grace and beauty incarnate, and Yole wondered how many people had fallen to this lethal blade's bite. The edge gleamed as though just sharpened, and the deadly point made Yole shudder as his gaze fell upon it.

In a trance, Yole reached for the beautiful sword. As he stretched his hand out to grasp the hilt, a dancing flame reached up and singed his arm, jerking him out of his dazed state. With a yell, Yole leaped back from the table, rubbing his arm. The sword was beyond his reach.

"The fire..." Yole narrowed his eyes. Was it possible that the fire had reacted with a will of its own? Keeping his eyes on the flames, Yole again reached towards the sword. A flame blazed brighter and Yole snatched his arm back just in time, but the fire followed his movement and only subsided after his arm was safely back at his side. Yole whistled, his eyes big. The message was clear: he could look, but he was not allowed to touch this strange sword.

He wondered to whom the sword belonged. "What master craftsman formed this blade?" he asked aloud. "And from what did he form it?"

"A dragon's tooth." The reply echoed around the cavern and caused Yole to jump in sudden fear. He fled the ringed formation and hid behind a boulder, his heart racing. He had been trespassing, and now the guard of the ring would make him pay for trying to take the treasure.

A very old man emerged from behind the ring of light and looked directly at Yole's hiding place. "Do you wish to know the secret of the sword or not?"

Yole crept out from behind his rock. "Y-yes."

"The blade was created from a dragon's tooth. And the hilt was made from a dragon's scale."

"That's it? That's all you're going to say about it? You're not going to tell me why the sword is here or who made it?"

"I only answer questions that I am asked, I don't read minds."

"Please, please tell me."

"It's a story you want, I see. Well, children normally do enjoy these types of things. Very well," the robed figure said. "I shall answer your questions."

Yole did not like being called a child, even by this very old man. However, he did not say anything to contradict him for fear that he would not continue.

"The sword that you gaze upon in wonder was made many years ago when dragons were plentiful and humans did not fear them so much."

"When was that? Haven't the dragons been gone for a long time? It's so rare to see one," Yole could not help interrupting.

The old figure paused, "I said it happened a long time ago... six centuries ago, that's not the point. There came a time when King Llian of Aom-igh faced invasion from his enemies. The Dark Country had arrived on his shores, bent on conquering Aom-igh and making it their own, and they were winning. In desperation, King Llian journeyed into the Mountains of Dusk where he beseeched the King of the dragons to come to his aid. The dragons consulted among themselves and decided they could not fight in this war. They did not fear the Dark Country, although perhaps they should have. Instead, they agreed that they would make a sword for this human king that might help him defeat his enemies. They told him to return three days hence.

"After Llian left, the King of the dragons sacrificed one of his sharp teeth and one of his silver scales. Deep in the heart of these very mountains the dragons forged the golden blade you saw within the ring, and from the scale they created the hilt. With tooth and scale they forged a unique weapon of power and presented this gift to the grateful, yet still uncertain, King Llian.

"The wizard Scelwhyn created a special sheath for the blade and binding for the hilt, and King Llian carried this treasure into battle. The blade is infused with dragon magic, and since King Llian had considerable power running through his own veins, the sword became a weapon of great might in his hands; with it, he defeated his enemies and chased them out of his country.

"However, even good kings do not live forever. Years later, when King Llian lay on his death bed, he made one last request of his great friend, Scelwhyn. Thus, the wizard created this cave as a protection for the great blade so that no one would be able to mis-use this weapon. He built the strange rock formation you entered and infused it with magic that would protect the sword. As you have seen for yourself, the sword cannot be removed from that table."

"But surely there must be some way for the sword to be removed!" Yole cried in dismay.

"Yes, there certainly is one way. The only one who can take the sword from that table is King Llian himself."

"But... but you just said that King Llian died."

"Would you stop interrupting and let me finish? The only one who can take the sword from that table is King Llian himself, or one of his direct descendants. However, since the line of the kingship has become so tangled and twisted, who knows if any, or even one, of his direct descendants still exists. Perhaps the sword and its aid have truly been lost to us forever."

"Isn't King Arnaud descended from Llian?"

"No," the old man replied. "I believe he is descended from Llian's brother, Veli."

Yole pondered that a moment. "So if the sword can only be held by one of the direct descendants of King Llian..."

"Ignorant child! The sword can be held by anyone who wishes to hold it. Why do you think King Llian ordered this spell to be cast? He desired to keep it out of the wrong hands! The sword will obey any master. King Llian and his chief wizard knew this, and they foresaw what evil use the blade could be put to."

Yole blinked. Then a new question occurred to him. "How do you know all of this?"

The figure laughed. "Because I am a dragon!"

Then, before Yole could recover from his shock and disbelief, there was a flash of light and when Yole had recovered enough to look around, he saw that the robed figure had vanished. Yole searched the cave and looked behind the rocks and the stalagmites, but the figure, the... dragon...? had completely disappeared.

Darby *had* been worried, and she was ready to turn around and march all three of them home when Oraeyn and Kamarie explained what had happened with the hunter's trap. But they eventually got her calmed down enough to realize that nobody had been hurt.

"This trip is going to be the death of me, I declare," she said, sitting down. "I don't know what will become of us. I don't know if I can take it much longer."

"I'm really quite all right," Kamarie reassured her maid. "Oraeyn rescued me and I didn't get hurt at all. And I'll know to take a walking stick with me next time I go gathering wood alone."

"And that is supposed to make me feel better?" Darby asked in an exasperated tone. "If it was up to me, there wouldn't be any chance of a next time. If it was up to me, I'd march you straight back home this instant. But it isn't up to me, I suppose."

"No, Darby, it isn't up to you," Kamarie said. "We can't give up and go home just because I had a fall. We couldn't give up and go home even if something worse had happened because home isn't any safer than these forests."

"I know," Darby replied with a sigh. *I just wanted to make sure you knew that,* she thought to herself.

At that moment Oraeyn turned from the fire and said, "Dinner's ready."

They ate their meal and then bedded down for the evening, with Oraeyn taking the first watch. The night was cold and dark, and the fire had long since gone out because of the steady, pouring rain. He liked taking the first watch; it gave him time to think about the day's events, and tonight he had a lot to mull over. The princess was also a squire-in-training. He could hardly believe it, even though he knew that it had to be true. Kamarie did make more sense now that he knew about the lessons that Garen had been giving her. She had a lot of courage, this princess; he thought, training to be a knight was not an easy feat, he knew from experience. There had been times when he had wanted to give up himself, but at least he had the other squires to rely on, and he didn't really have any other options, while the princess certainly did. But Kamarie had to keep her training completely secret. She could not talk to anyone; she had to bear all the difficulties of the training and pretend that she was not in training whenever anyone was around. She also had to deal with knowing that certain aspects of her training would remain incomplete, such as learning directions and finding her way without the Dragon's Eye to guide her. And at the end of it all, she would have to leave it behind: she would never be a knight, and she would never be acknowledged for her hard work. Oraeyn did not know if he could do that. The promise of knighthood, of honor and respect, was often all that kept him going. To train with no hope of that reward... He felt a touch on his shoulder and jerked out of his thoughts, all senses alert, his muscles tight and ready for a fight.

"It's my watch," Kamarie's voice was filled with silent laughter, she knew that she had startled him. "You didn't wake me up."

He relaxed. "It's not nice to sneak up on people."

She did laugh now, but quietly, so as not to disturb Darby. "Go get some sleep, I'll keep the bandits at bay."

Glaring at her, but knowing that she could not see his glare in the darkness of the starless night, Oraeyn went to his bedroll. Suddenly his exhaustion caught up with him and he fell asleep almost before he had time to lie down.

The next morning dawned bright and fresh, with no trace of the dark storm that had ruled the night. Oraeyn struggled to open his sleep-filled eyes and stretched his arms above his head with a noise that sounded like something between a yawn and a groan. The morning air was chilly, yet un-warmed by the Dragon's Eye.

"Good morning," a too cheery voice sounded in his ears. "Get up! We have an absolutely perfect day before us, we shouldn't waste any of it."

Oraeyn groaned again, nobody should be allowed to sound that chipper this early in the morning. In order to better show his disgust, he pointedly rolled over, away from the voice, and pulled his blanket up over his head. Someone started pulling at his blanket, but he held it down around him until they gave up.

"I'll get up when I'm good and ready," he growled.

The blanket pulling stopped, and he was left alone. With a regretful sigh that he had to get up and leave his warm blankets, Oraeyn sat up and looked around him to get his bearings. He had to admit it did show all the promising signs of being a beautiful day for traveling. Just then Kamarie came back, carrying a plate of fried ham and biscuits with pieces of fruit adorning the side. She handed him the plate and a glass of water, which he accepted gratefully.

"You sure are a grouch in the morning," she said cheerfully. "Especially for a squire. Aren't knights supposed to spring out of bed, ready for their next battle?"

"I'm not a knight yet," Oraeyn growled.

Oraeyn did not trust himself to say anything more. It would have been very easy for him to snap back and tell her that she was annoyingly cheerful in the morning, but he could not see the result being very beneficial, so he held his tongue and bit into a hard biscuit. At this, Kamarie breezed away, leaving the shelter of the bushes to go get the horses ready for another days' journey, much to Oraeyn's relief. He would grudgingly admit that he admired the girl, but she could also be the most frustrating person he had ever met.

Within moments, he had eaten breakfast, washed his face in a basin of cold water that someone had left for him, and gotten his boots on. With that done, Oraeyn felt much more ready to face the day. He walked out of the cover of the bushes, carrying his folded bedroll, and went over to where Kamarie was saddling up the horses. After he had attached his bedroll to his chestnut horse, Oraeyn set about destroying the evidence of their camp. It was not likely that they were being followed, but in the unlikely event of that happening, their pursuers would get no help from him. He stepped back to study his handiwork, and then made a few adjustments until he was satisfied. A good tracker would give this place one glance and find no clues; a great tracker would see that there had been a camp here at one time, but would not be able to figure out when. Sir Garen would be able to decipher the clues, but Oraeyn seriously doubted that there was anyone else, anywhere else, with Sir Garen's abilities.

Finally, the three travelers set out once more towards the Mountains of Dusk. Their course had been fairly easy the past few days; the forest was mostly on flat ground, and there had been the occasional open fields that they had raced through. But now they were heading into the foothills of the mountains, and the journey became more difficult. As they rode along, over rolling hills, the mountains came more sharply into view. Kamarie grew excited: here, finally, the journey would really start. She had never been as far as the Mountains of Dusk before; the feeling of wandering into unfamiliar territory exhilarated her.

Oraeyn noticed a change coming over Kamarie and studied her, puzzled. She leaned forward a little more in her saddle, her cheeks flushed and her blue eyes sparkled with excitement. There had been a lot of silence during the journey today, and Oraeyn was growing tired of it.

"Are you all right, Kamarie?" he questioned.

She looked at him with a bright smile. "Of course! We're getting closer and closer to the Mountains of Dusk, and the journey is really beginning now."

Her tone was light, and yet there seemed to be a dark undercurrent to her words, almost as if... Oraeyn pushed the thought out of his mind, but still it lingered there in the back of his thoughts: almost as if she was afraid. He knew the thought was ludicrous; so far Kamarie had been the bravest of all of them, certainly the bravest girl he had ever met. She had no reason to fear the Mountains, but that tone was there: he had heard it, had seen a shadow pass through her eyes. He knew she had never been as far as the mountains before; but then, neither had he. He had never gotten that far, even when journeying with his mentor-knight.

"Yes, the journey is really beginning now," Oraeyn said. "We have come through the forest, we have refrained from killing one another, and now we are in the foothills of the Mountains of Dusk, we can no longer speak of turning back," he finished and watched Kamarie's reaction to his words.

She nodded, as if to herself, and then her eyes got big as he finished. She turned to stare at him, her face a mix of emotions. Her eyes flashed with what looked like anger, but her mouth twitched in something resembling concealed laughter. He was not quite sure what he had said to merit this reaction, but he braced himself for an argument.

"'Refrained from killing one another'?" Kamarie burst out in mock outrage. "Perhaps I refrained from killing you, but I'm sure that throwing me in the river was a direct attempt on your part to do away with me!"

Oraeyn sputtered in surprise and confusion. "I was not!" he said. "I knew how deep the river was and I knew that it wasn't moving fast, otherwise I never would have..." He broke off as he caught a glimpse of Kamarie's face. She was laughing now, again, at him. He tensed, then forced himself to relax, knowing that the comment had been a joke but still not liking it. He decided that he would never understand this girl. Or maybe he would just never understand her sense of humor.

Oraeyn glanced over towards where Darby was riding. Her face was implacable, a mask that could not be read. But there was a look in her eye that told him she had heard the exchange and found it humorous as well. Hunching his shoulders, Oraeyn pulled up the hood of his cloak and glowered ahead of him. He was quickly getting tired of Kamarie's jokes, and he was also tired of being surrounded and outnumbered by women… all two of them.

As they rode along, Oraeyn came up with an idea that just might keep him from being laughed at. He decided that from now on, he was going to keep his mouth shut. Just as he decided upon this new course of action, he heard a sound. It was a musical sound but light, like the music from the pan pipes that he had heard upon occasion when traveling the countryside. This music was somehow lighter, though, and impossibly stronger for such an airy sound. It pulled at him, tugging at the very core of his being.

"Do you hear that?" he asked, forgetting his resolution of the moment before.

"Hear what?" Kamarie asked.

"That… that!" Oraeyn could not believe she did not understand what he was talking about.

Kamarie stared at him. "That what?"

"That sound, that music, that beautiful, beautiful sound! How can you not hear it?" He gazed at her in disbelief.

Shaking her head, Kamarie stopped her horse and cocked her head. A look of intense concentration washed over her face as she threw all her energy into listening. After a moment or two, she straightened and laughed. "You got me," she said, grinning, "you really had me going there."

"I'm not joking!" Oraeyn cried in distress. "Are you telling me that you really cannot hear that music?"

"That's what I'm saying, I don't hear a thing that sounds like music," Kamarie said apologetically.

"But…" Oraeyn turned to Darby. "Can you hear it?" he demanded.

Darby shook her head, "I'm sorry Master Oraeyn, but I don't hear anything that sounds like what you have described."

Oraeyn ground his teeth in frustration. Neither of them could hear it, and yet, there it was, whatever it was, growing louder and more full, more vibrant with every passing moment. It filled his ears, filled him with a longing to follow it until he felt that he would surely die if he did not answer the call. But he did not know how he could explain that to Kamarie and Darby. How could he explain a summons they could not hear?

"I don't know what it is," he started, "but it is calling me. I feel like I am being ripped apart inside just because I am not moving towards the sound. Please…" he stopped, not knowing what he could possibly be saying 'please' for. Then it hit him. He wanted to answer the call; he had to go find what was making that music. He dropped his head in defeat, not knowing what to do.

Kamarie watched Oraeyn closely as he uttered his last words; she could tell that he was not trying to fool her. His face was open, honest, with a faraway look of longing deep in his dark green eyes. She strained her ears, listening for something, anything that resembled the sound he had described. After a few long moments of silence, she relaxed and dropped her shoulders.

Shaking her head, Kamarie stared at Oraeyn. "I don't hear anything out of the ordinary. I hear birds, and the grass blowing in the wind, but I don't hear anything that sounds like music. I think we should probably keep going Oraeyn… Oraeyn!"

Kamarie said his name sharply, trying to get his attention, but it was no use. Oraeyn was staring straight ahead with an expectant, far-off look on his face. Kamarie could tell that he was no longer hearing the sounds of this world; he was solely aware of the enchanted music only he could hear. She rode up and tapped him on the shoulder but got no response. She waved her hands in front of his face but only received a blank stare. Finally, in desperation, she pulled him from his saddle and placed her hands over his ears. Oraeyn jumped, as if he had been burned, and his eyes became clear again.

"What? Where?" He gazed at Kamarie in confusion and then asked, "How long?"

"We have been trying to get your attention for three or four minutes," Kamarie yelled, loud enough for him to be able to hear her while her hands were still covering his ears.

He trembled. "It seemed like hours. But it was so beautiful." He pushed her hands from his ears. "The music…" he stopped.

"Is it still there?" Kamarie asked, hoping she would not have to cover his ears again. That would make the journey rather difficult.

"Yes," Oraeyn sighed, "but it is fainter now, softer, not so insistent."

"Well, that's a relief," Darby interjected.

Darby felt a twinge of sadness that she could not hear the melody that was so apparent to the young man. She had seen enough of Oraeyn in the past few days together to know there was a depth and seriousness to him that indicated unusual paths may be in store for him. She said none of this, however, preferring to keep her own council.

Aloud, she continued, "If you are willing, I believe we really need to keep going. Our mission to find Brant has to be the priority. I don't think we have time to seek this haunted music, young man, especially when Kamarie and I are unable to help you in the search."

"Haunted," Oraeyn muttered, "that is a good way to describe it. A haunting melody… an eerie, ghostlike tune that belongs in a deep, dark forest, or on a foggy moor. A music that…"

"Darby is right," Kamarie said quickly before Oraeyn could continue about the music that she could not hear. "It is getting late and we have not been making very good time lately."

Darby nodded in agreement, though with a heavy heart.

Oraeyn glanced up at the Dragon's Eye, at its highest point signaling the middle of the day, and then he nodded with a sigh. "The music seems to be coming from inside the mountains anyway, perhaps our path will cross some place where we can all hear the music."

Kamarie shot a suspicious glance at Oraeyn. She was not entirely certain that he had truly snapped out of his trance. She decided to keep very alert, to make sure he was not allowing this music, that only he could hear, to pull them off their path and away from their goal. She intended to reach her father's friend in Peak's Shadow, and nothing was going to distract her from that goal, unless it was something that would help her country. With a renewed determination and refreshed thoughts of their goals and purpose, the three travelers set off once more traveling ever deeper into the Mountains of Dusk.

CHAPTER

FOUR

Although they had made fantastic time in getting to the foothills and the journey had only taken approximately two weeks, so far the Mountains of Dusk were much larger and the journey across them was taking much longer than Kamarie had anticipated. Once in the heart of the mountain chain, they faced the difficult task of keeping to the seldom-traveled path. The road became nearly invisible at times and far more difficult to navigate. Often they had to dismount and lead their horses around or over obstacles. The ground was rough and rocky, filled with dangerous stretches where slipping and falling was a constant threat.

Oraeyn was leading the little group, picking his steps carefully, trying to follow the ill-marked road. Kamarie watched him closely and was quickly growing concerned. He claimed that the music had grown fainter, that it no longer tugged at him, but with every step they took the look in his eyes became more distant and the expression on his face became more eager, almost expectant. The further they went, the lighter Oraeyn's step became: almost as if he were racing to answer a very insistent summons. They still seemed to be traveling in the correct direction so Kamarie had said nothing yet, but she was still concerned that they could easily be drawn from their goal. If their path was taking them closer to the source of Oraeyn's haunted music, she feared that she would not be able to keep him from answering the call that only he could hear. Deep down, Kamarie also feared for Oraeyn; she did not know what the music meant, could not understand how it tugged at his heart, but she feared that it could mean danger for him.

As they journeyed on through the seemingly endless mountains, the path that they were on turned very steep, much steeper than anything that they had come across in the mountains so far. The peaks and heights were all around them now, and this difficult path had been their only clue to finding their way through the mountains to Peak's Shadow. So far the ill-marked road had kept them at a relatively low altitude and it had been easy to start taking it for granted, focusing on other things. But now, as the path sloped upwards at an alarming angle, Kamarie was forced to turn her full attention to what she was doing so as to keep Tor from panicking or slipping. As they continued upwards, the path eventually started to even out and seemed to be leading them towards a large, cavernous opening that looked like it could be the beginning of a tunnel through the mountain.

"Do we have to go in there?" Kamarie's voice was strong, but there was a tremble in her hands where she was holding Tor's reins.

Oraeyn looked back at her. "I can go in first and come back to tell you if it's all right, if you want," he said sympathetically. He could not fault her for not wanting to go into a dark cave without knowing where it led.

"That sounds like a goo…" Darby started, but the princess cut her off before she could finish.

Kamarie sat up, straightened her shoulders, and took a breath. "N-no," she said a little shakily, "we will all go in together." She heeled Tor into a slow walk, and the three of them cautiously approached the cave opening. Suddenly, Oraeyn stopped.

"Who are you?" he demanded suspiciously.

Taken aback, Kamarie and Darby stopped, shared a questioning glance, and then scanned the path before them. At first, Kamarie could not see who or what Oraeyn was talking to, and for a moment, she thought that the young man had gone completely insane. Then she rubbed her eyes and saw the figure standing at the mouth of the cave.

It was a boy, eleven or twelve years old, certainly no older. He was small and slight for his age and looked as though he had never had a truly decent meal in his life; his size made him appear very young, but his face bore intelligence and wisdom that belied his height. He was dirty and disheveled, and his clothes were in tatters. His feet were bare, and there was dried blood on both of his knees. He was gazing at them with a look of bewildered amazement on his face. He had fiery golden-red hair that looked as wild as the rest of him; it sprang from his head in untamed curls. His eyes were a deep amber color, too light to be brown but too dark to be anything else; they reminded Kamarie of molten gold or lava, and they flashed with a mixture of defiance, sorrow, and surprise. Before she could think about what she was doing, Kamarie dismounted and approached the boy.

"What is your name?" she asked gently as she walked towards him with an outstretched hand.

The boy shrank from her hand as if it were deadly poison. He glanced up at her and their eyes locked. A shock went through Kamarie as she felt a recognition of something long forgotten shoot into her. The youth seemed to experience the same thing, for he went rigid, and looked at her sharply. His face suddenly looked too old, too wise for his apparent youthful age.

"My name is Yole," the boy said hesitantly. "Who are you? I didn't know there was anyone else in these mountains."

"I am Kamarie, and my two companions are Oraeyn and Darby," Kamarie said, still puzzling over what she had seen in the youth's eyes. It had seemed as though she was looking through a window and seeing a very different world than the one she had expected. There was something strangely familiar about this youth, like a part of a dream that has faded with time but was never completely forgotten.

Oraeyn stepped forward. "What are you doing out here alone?"

Yole glanced at his feet. "I was working for a man in the village of Peak's Shadow."

Kamarie's eyes met Oraeyn's in startled recognition; he nodded and touched the hilt of his sword as if expecting an attack. Yole continued without noticing their reaction to the name that he had uttered, "I fell asleep while I was watching the herd. I know I shouldn't have, but I was listening to the other shepherds' playing their pipes and the music just made me feel drowsy and tired and I couldn't help but fall asleep.

"The next thing I knew, Brant was waking me up and telling me that I had to leave, that I should be more careful around people. I think he was accusing me of stealing sheep or something, but I *didn't*. I don't have any use for sheep of my own. I wouldn't know what to do with them. I certainly don't have any place to put them," Yole's tone was open and slightly confused. "I've been wandering through these mountains trying to find my way out for a long time now. I don't have any food left, and I think I'm lost." He sniffed, and wiped his nose with his grimy hand.

Kamarie winced and said, "We have some food."

At the same time, Oraeyn asked, "Did you say *Brant?*"

The boy looked at Kamarie gratefully, then turned to Oraeyn. "Yes sir. The man I worked for was named Brant."

"Well, now, that's just the man that we need to find, isn't it?" Darby said, causing them all to jump. It was sometimes fairly easy to forget that Darby was even there she spoke so little.

"Yes, Darby, it is," Kamarie said, surprised that she had not been as quick as either Darby or Oraeyn to make that connection. Perhaps it was the strange tug of familiarity that she felt towards the boy, or perhaps it was the worry about Oraeyn, but either way Kamarie was glad to be reminded of their mission.

"He's a good man," Yole said quickly, darting a look at them as if he thought they would start accusing him of being ungrateful, "looks out for his people. He's not really the leader of the village or anything, but everyone looks up to him. Whenever there's trouble, it's brought to Brant, and he deals with it, never saw anyone more fair in his treatment of others. And his family is nice too: kind, generous people. I don't hold a thing against them. I don't know what I did, but I know I probably deserved to be kicked out, because Brant wouldn't ever issue a punishment if it weren't deserved."

"Does he still bend knee to his King?" Kamarie asked thoughtfully.

Yole stared at her. "Of course he does!" he exclaimed. "I told you, he's a good man, follows the rules. Fair. Of course he bends knee to King Arnaud, he thinks very highly of him, he always speaks of the king with respect and admiration. He's a man of character, Brant is, loyal to the end."

"All right, all right!" Kamarie held up her hands. "I was not questioning his character. We just have to be careful in these difficult days."

The defensiveness went out of Yole's eyes. "I'm sorry too, but Brant, he was good to me. Paid me more than I deserved, sent me out with plenty of food, well, it *would* have been enough food if I hadn't gotten lost. Most of the other people I worked for used whips when they sent me away. I was chased out of one town by the villagers, they threw rocks and threatened to kill me if I ever came back."

Oraeyn stared at him. "*What* did you do?"

"I don't know, really," he said, "but it must have been something awful."

"Did you ever consider, young man," Darby suddenly spoke up, "that perhaps *they* were in the wrong?"

Yole's eyes got big, and he looked scared. "No! Never! I wouldn't even let the thought enter my head. I just broke some rule and had to be punished for it, that's all."

Kamarie looked at him sympathetically. "We are not trying to get a confession out of you, we are just trying to better understand, we do not wish you any harm. You do not have to be afraid of us."

Yole looked trustingly at her. "I believe you," he said, "I don't know why, but I do believe you." He glanced distrustfully at Oraeyn and Darby, and Kamarie understood what he was saying.

"These are my friends, they do not wish you any harm either. We are all on the same side," she said, "would you like to travel with us? We promise we won't chase you away. If you decide to travel with us, you have the King's protection on you. I give my word that we will not harm you and neither will anyone else so long as I can prevent it."

The boy looked thoughtful for a moment, then he said, "But you are going to Peak's Shadow. I can't go back there, Miss."

"You can if you are with me," Kamarie said proudly, her head high and her blue eyes flashing. At that moment, Oraeyn thought that she looked every inch the Princess of the Realm, and she was suddenly, startlingly, beautiful.

"Well, I suppose…" Yole said quietly, "I would like to … to…" he stopped, a shy and timid look on his face that made him suddenly appear young.

"Like to what?" Kamarie asked kindly.

Looking up, Yole gave his first smile, and tentatively said, "To *belong*."

Kamarie was a little taken aback, not knowing what to say to the young boy. But it was Oraeyn who spoke, "Consider yourself one of us then, you can even ride with me."

Yole looked up at the older boy with an expression of pure joy on his face. From that moment on, Oraeyn was his hero, and the youth did everything he could to emulate Oraeyn's every move.

"Well, now that we've spent all this time out here, we might as well just get back to our journey," Darby's voice reminded them all of what they were supposed to be doing. "Yole, have you been inside that cave up there?"

The boy hesitated. "Y-yes."

"Does it go anywhere? Or is it just a big cave?" Oraeyn asked.

"It's a tunnel that will take you to the other side of the mountain," Yole replied.

"Good, then we are on the right path," Kamarie breathed a sigh of relief, "let's go!"

They spurred their horses on towards the cave, Yole riding behind Oraeyn on the big chestnut gelding. As they got closer to the cave, the music became more and more insistent; it seemed to pierce right through Oraeyn and into the deepest areas in his heart. It called, beckoned, and pulled at him until he thought he might be ripped from the saddle of his horse if he did nothing to answer it. He could not believe that the others could not hear the beautiful melody, but he dared say nothing, after the way that his first mention of the music had been received.

Finally, they reached the opening of the cave. According to Yole, there was only one tunnel, so they did not have to worry about getting lost. Inside the cave, the music echoed and bounced off the walls, sweet and lilting, dark and haunting until Oraeyn could not bear it anymore. He let out a yell and dropped off of his horse, kneeling on the ground with his hands over his ears. Kamarie stopped short when she heard Oraeyn's cry of distress; reining Tor around sharply she dismounted and ran to Oraeyn.

"Are you all right? What's wrong?" she questioned him, concerned and confused.

Oraeyn moaned, "It's here. It's all around me; I can't get away from it! I tried, Kamarie, I tried, but I can't… can't push it away any more. If I don't answer the call it will kill me, I cannot pass through this cave without finding the source. It's tearing me apart!" His last words ended in a cry of anguish as tears sprang into his eyes.

Kamarie knelt next to him and took his head in her hands, raising it until she was looking into his eyes. He was in obvious torment, and it hurt her to see it. "Are you sure it is somewhere in this cave?" she asked quietly.

"I am more sure of it than I have ever been of anything in my entire life," was the shaky reply.

"Then you must find it," Kamarie said, "and I will help you."

"How can you help?" Oraeyn's distress was clear. "You can't hear the music; you can't find the source."

Suddenly, Yole was next to them. "I can take you to it."

Kamarie looked at him sharply. "You can hear the music?"

"No," Yole said, "but I know where it is coming from." Then an excited look came into his eyes as he regarded Oraeyn, "Y-you're *him*!"

"Him who?" Kamarie asked.

"The... but it couldn't be, the dragon thought none existed... but it has to be... and you're him!"

"Dragon?" Kamarie asked, she knew there had been dragons in Aom-igh at one time long ago, but they had gone into hiding many years prior and no one had seen or heard from one since. Some believed that they were actually just a legend or a myth, although Kamarie had been taught that they were real. In any case, everyone believed that they were extinct.

"Never mind, I'll take you to it!" Yole took off down the tunnel.

Leading the horses, Kamarie, Oraeyn, and Darby followed the boy a few more steps, then the tunnel abruptly changed directions. Suddenly, they were standing in the room full of light. Kamarie and Darby stood, transfixed by the sight of the ring of stalagmites and stalactites. Oraeyn started to walk, slowly, as if in a trance, towards the ring of rock. He stopped when he reached it and put a hand up to shield his eyes. There was a moment of hesitation, and then he stepped forward and entered the ring.

"Oraeyn!" Kamarie leaped after him, but was too late. The stalagmites seemed to get larger and larger, and the spaces between them slowly vanished, leaving Kamarie, Darby, and Yole in darkness once more.

"It!" Yole yelped and then gulped in fear. "It didn't do *that* before."

"Before?" Kamarie asked.

"When I went in, it didn't close up behind me," Yole answered.

A few seconds, that seemed to last for years, passed, and then a burst of light shot out from one side of the ring. The spaces opened up again, and suddenly the room was flooded with light once more.

"Oraeyn!" Kamarie shouted, desperately hoping he was all right.

For a breathless moment of terror, no answer came. Then, there he was, striding out of the ring of light. Kamarie held up a hand to shield her eyes, the squire seemed taller somehow, older, and in his hand was a glowing blade that shimmered and threw off golden sparks of light. His stride was sure, and his steps were light. When he got closer, he lifted the sword high; it was beautiful, pure gold, and yet somehow it seemed to carry a light within it that glowed and filled the cavern with sparkling rainbows. The handle looked as though it might have been made of silver, and it seemed to fit in Oraeyn's hand as though it had been made for him.

Then he sheathed the sword and became Oraeyn again. Kamarie vaguely wondered what had happened to his old sword and sheath, but she pushed the question aside. When the sword was no longer in sight, it seemed as though the room was suddenly empty, and Kamarie was filled with an unexplainable ache.

"It *is* you." Yole breathed in awe.

Oraeyn looked at them. "I found it."

Brant did not know where to begin looking for the murderer, but he felt a pull towards the Mountains of Dusk. He had always trusted his hunches in the past. He had avoided danger and even death many times before by following his instincts, so, he headed off in the direction that he had sent Yole just a few weeks before. Had it been such a short time ago? It seemed as though ages had rushed by over the past few days. He had lost everything dear to him, had dug up and reclaimed his past, and now felt ready for anything. His senses were keen and his reflexes were as sharp as they had ever been. He was not certain what danger he was following, but he knew that it was heading north, towards the castle of Aom-igh, towards King Arnaud and the capital city of Ayollan. He also knew that it was terrible and merciless, guided by some dark madness that put them all in danger.

Brant thought of Arnaud as he rode. They had been friends years ago, when Arnaud was just a youth, a farm boy really. Arnaud had saved his life, although at the time he had not been aware that he was saving Brant's life. *And*, Brant thought, *if he had known then whom he was saving, he probably would have just as soon let me die.* But Brant knew, and Brant remembered.

It was Arnaud who had given him the chance to start a new life, who had befriended him when everyone dear to him had turned him away. Arnaud found him on the border of the Harshlands and brought this stranger home. Brant remembered that day as if it had just happened.

He had been running all day, through this blistering desert of burning sand and sharp stones in this strange land. He knew he could not stop, or they would catch him. His little boat had been completely ruined when it crashed up against this shore the night before, and he had been running ever since. They were there, only a step behind him. They could travel so swiftly, so silently; how had he ever hoped to escape? And now he was here, in this horrible wasteland, this rocky, harsh place with the Dragon's Eye beating down on him mercilessly. He squinted ahead of him, barely able to see his own hand in front of his face anymore; it was too bright, too hot. He would die from thirst and exhaustion if he stayed here. How could anything survive in this horrible wilderness? Was there any end to this place?

He had finally given way to exhaustion and fallen down, accepting his fate. Death would be kinder than they would be. Then he heard a noise. Had they caught up to him so fast?

"Hey? Are you all right? Do you need some help?" a voice from the sky asked.

Brant rolled over onto his back and saw the face of a young boy, maybe in his early teens, anxiously peering at him. He sat up and stretched. "I must have fallen asleep," he lied.

"You fell asleep? While in the Harshlands? Do you know how dangerous that could have been?" The boy's voice was full of incredulity, but there was also a note of awe in it at the bravery of this youth who appeared to be the same age as he. Arnaud had paused for a moment, and then asked, "Do you have any place to go? My name is Arnaud."

Brant looked at him blankly. "No, I don't have any place to go. And my name is Brant."

"You don't?" Arnaud looked surprised. "Well, you can come home with me then, Brant." He rolled the name around on his tongue as if it tasted strange. "If you're willing to work, we can give you a place to stay."

Brant had accepted Arnaud's offer, and that was how the friendship had begun. Arnaud had even been the one to introduce him to Imojean. A pang sliced through Brant's heart, Imojean... he shook his head. If he started thinking about what he could not change he would never get anywhere, and he might go mad in the process. He had grieved, and now he must move on. He must be stronger than his enemies, he must be... *Oh Imojean,* he thought in despair, *I tried so hard to leave it all behind, for you... for you.*

He did not know why he felt so certain that this attack had been directed at him, but he did. He was absolutely sure that after all these years his past was rising up to haunt him. And he decided that even if he were wrong, those who had done this would pay, would pay dearly. Pictures of his family and his lost, happy life danced in his head as he rode towards the Mountains of Dusk. Faces that he had loved dearly rose up before him. Voices of those whom he had embraced with his whole heart as he had never embraced anyone before whispered in his ears. A terrible gnawing ache welled up within his heart. With a shout of rage and pain he kicked Legend into a gallop. He was running again, but this time he was not running away. He would never run away again.

CHAPTER
FIVE

The young knight was out of breath but composed as he came before King Arnaud. Eight days earlier, Arnaud had decided to make a move, and while he knew that it was risky, it was better than sitting around waiting for the worst to happen. He sent a team of seven spies over to Roalthae to discover what was happening in the barrier islands under the rule of Prince Elroy. The man standing before him was one of those seven, but he was the only one who had returned.

Struggling to regain his composure, the spy began, "As you know, Sire, my team and I arrived in Roalthae six days ago. After hiding our craft, we headed towards the capital city. Along the way, we noticed several peculiar things. The fields had been harvested early, ringing of hammers at the forges filled the air. The countryside was quiet, yet the cities were ablaze with people, unusual for this time of year. This made us cautious. We traveled the city and saw that the forges were filled with newly-formed weaponry. Roalthae is preparing for war."

Arnaud nodded. "We assumed as much. Go on."

"We made our way to the center of the Capital and gained entry into the palace grounds. Disguising myself as a servant, I reached the corridors near the Throne Room where I caught glimpses of Prince Elroy and his thoughts. He has pledged his allegiance to the King of the Dark Country."

"How do you know this?"

"There was a foreigner in the throne room with the Prince."

"How do you know he was a foreigner?"

"His height, for one thing. The people of Roalthae tend to be small in stature, but this man was taller than Your Majesty and his shoulders were as broad as that of an ox. Also, his hair and eyes were very dark, and most of the Roalthaens have lighter hair and eyes."

"It wasn't the King of the Dark Country himself?"

The spy shook his head. "I do not believe so. Prince Elroy deferred to him, but not as an equal, more like an advisor he has to put up with. I overheard some of their conversation and they were speaking of a 'King Seamas,' which led me to believe that the Dark Country's King and most of their forces are still either in the Dark Country or only just beginning their voyage of conquest."

"So their intent is to conquer?"

The spy hesitated. "I am not sure. From what little I overheard, I think the throne of Aom-igh has been promised to Elroy for his help."

"For his treachery, you mean," Arnaud growled.

"Yes, Sire," the spy continued, "but from what I heard, I do not think it is this King Seamas' intent to rule over Aom-igh. It sounds more as though he is searching for something, something important enough to him that he cares not if our country is destroyed in the hunt. He believes we are hiding something from him, or harboring some criminal."

"Is that all you learned?"

"No, I also learned that Roalthae will not be contributing men to the invasion."

"What?"

"You heard me correctly, Sire. Roalthae is providing weapons, ships, and their shores as a staging ground for their attack. We have not yet seen any sign of an invasion because the Dark Country lacks a navy. Prince Elroy is providing transport. Llycaelon will invade when their manpower matches the armada of Roalthae."

"Interesting," King Arnaud turned thoughtful. "We can use that information to our advantage. You couldn't discover the Dark King's motivation for attacking us?"

The young man shook his head. "Forgive me, Sire, but I do not think that King Seamas has told his own men very much about what, or who, they are looking for. I listened to as much as I could and stayed beyond the point of safety to glean as much information as I was able. I know how important this mission was, but nobody seems to know much more than what I've told you."

"And the rest of my men?"

"They remain hidden throughout the city, waiting to learn more."

"Good," Arnaud said. "You have done well, Justan."

"Thank you, Sire."

"I don't understand," Kamarie said slowly, looking around once more, as though she might find some new information or clue she had overlooked that would provide her with the missing piece of the puzzle.

They had reached Peak's Shadow at last, but there was no one to greet them. The last few miles of the journey had been filled with heightened spirits and laughter, for Yole assured them that they were nearing their destination. What they found at the edge of the mountains quickly reduced their merriment to a bewildered, and somewhat fearful, silence.

Yole was leading the way when they came out of the mountains, but at the sight of Brant's home he suddenly stopped with a stricken look on his face. What was Brant's home was now no more than a pile of ashes. There was no sign of life anywhere. The entire valley was eerily quiet, as if even the animals were afraid to break the sacred silence.

They found themselves at a loss in deciding what steps should be taken next. Following directions from Yole, Oraeyn continued townward to learn if anyone knew what had happened to Brant and his family. The others stayed at the remains of Brant's house to see if they could discover anything.

As she was puzzling over what could have happened, Kamarie heard hoof-beats coming; she looked up to see Oraeyn returning from his search. He slid off of his horse and came over, a little out of breath and looking as though he was carrying a heavy weight. When he faced them, there was a deeply puzzled and worried look in his eyes.

"There is no one left," he said between gulps of air.

Darby glanced at him in disbelief. "Just what do you mean when you say, 'no one left' young man?"

Oraeyn stared up at them, a pained expression on his face. "I mean, *no one*. Every house in the area looks just like this one: a pile of ash and burned logs. No one is left, either they all departed the village suddenly and it's some weird custom around here to burn your home before moving, or they were all killed."

"All killed? What makes you think they were killed?" Kamarie asked.

"What else could this mean? Why else would we find a village that had been burned to the ground with no villagers? If this were an accident, there would be a whole village full of people around here somewhere, building new houses or looking for somewhere to go. If they were leaving the area and heading through the mountains to the north, we would have heard or seen something of them, don't you think? And there might even be a few left here who did not wish to move. But there is not a living soul to be found, not a single one. So you tell me, does this look like an accident, or does it look like it was a massacre?"

Kamarie had to admit; he had a point.

"But who would do such a thing?" Yole asked.

"You forget, we are being threatened by either Roalthae, the Dark Country, or both. These are dangerous times," Darby reminded them all.

"So, do you think…?" Kamarie stopped, not wanting Yole to hear her question.

Yole looked at her with wide and frightened amber eyes as he realized what she had been going to ask. "Brant… do you think he's dead too?"

Kamarie dropped her eyes, unable to meet the boy's gaze, unable to deny her fears yet not wanting to confirm them either. As her gaze dropped, she saw footprints on the dusty ground. Dropping from her horse she landed in a crouch, studying the marks closely. She touched them lightly, and then followed with her eyes the direction in which they were heading. She straightened and met the eager looks of her companions.

"Someone survived. We can't know if that someone is Brant or the killer or someone else; but a person standing here, left this spot just a few hours ago. That someone has the answers to at least some of our questions."

Oraeyn nodded. "Then we must follow those tracks, where do they lead?"

Kamarie grimaced, "That's the hard part, they go back the way we came, into the mountains."

Darby sighed. "I'm getting too old for gallivanting around the countryside, especially when I travel for days to get to one place, only to find out that I actually need to go back the way I came from. Can't we at least eat first?"

Kamarie smiled sympathetically. "All right Darby, we will eat first, but then we must hurry before darkness hides our trail, I have questions, and I mean to find the answers."

They ate quickly. No one was eager to turn around and head back to the mountains they had just escaped, but there was nothing else to do. They followed the trail with surprising ease; their prey had not bothered to cover his tracks.

"Well, there are two possibilities," Oraeyn said when they stopped to make camp for the night. "Either, the person we are following is the attacker and figures that there was no one left to follow him, or the person we are following is a sole survivor from the attack and is bent on revenge, figuring that his enemy thinks he is dead so leaving a clear trail doesn't matter."

"I would like to believe that it is a survivor," Kamarie said as she rolled out her blankets, "because then it will be easier to question him."

"True," Oraeyn granted, "but then how many answers do you think he will be able or willing to provide?"

Kamarie saw the wisdom in that, but did not feel like admitting it. "I'm going to get a few more sticks to throw on the fire," was all she said.

"I'll come with you," Oraeyn offered. "We ought to be more careful than we have been, especially now."

Kamarie looked sober, and they walked together to a lone stand of timber. While they were picking up sticks that would work as firewood, Kamarie finally gathered the courage to ask the question that had been burning in her mind for a while.

"Oraeyn," she started.

"Yes?"

"What... what happened in the cave?"

"What do you mean?"

"I mean, with the ring of rock, and the sword, and the music that came when you were carrying the sword and then stopped when you sheathed it? What did it all mean? Yole said, 'you are him,' but... him who? I haven't even seen the sword since you first came out of that strange place." There was a tiny bit of a wistful reproach in her voice.

Oraeyn looked down for a moment, then he said, "I don't know what it all means. The music called me, but since the sword was making the music, I guess you could say that the sword called me. I know it sounds crazy, but I asked Yole to tell me what he knew about the sword. He tried, but his answer didn't really make any sense. He says he talked to a dragon that looked like a man, and he says the dragon told him a story about the sword being a gift from the dragons to King Llian a long time ago. Apparently when King Llian died he arranged to hide the sword in that cave and leave a spell on it so that no one could remove it from the cave unless it was a direct descendant of King Llian…" Oraeyn trailed off, looking slightly uncomfortable. "But… um… none of it really sounds plausible to me. Yole said that he couldn't take the sword, but he's a lot shorter than me, maybe he just couldn't reach it. I don't know if I believe the story about the dragon."

Kamarie looked at him. His face was unreadable in the dark, but his voice held a tone of embarrassment. She asked, "Who were your parents?"

"I-I don't know. I never knew them," Oraeyn replied. "I was found as a child by Tenrod, my mentor-knight. He found me when I was really little, before I can even remember. He raised me and trained me as a squire. If he hadn't told me the story of how he found me, I would have believed that he was my father."

"So, it's possible. You could be a descendant of King Llian," Kamarie said. "He was something like a great-great-great-great uncle or second cousin four times removed of my father's, and he was one of the greatest kings of Aom-igh. But his only son left the throne in the hands of a cousin and vanished. That's why the line of rulers of Aom-igh has been so odd; the reign is almost never passed from father to son. So… I mean; it's possible… you could be…"

"I don't know," Oraeyn's tone was harsh. "I'm sorry, I didn't mean to snap at you, I just… it's too much," he laughed. "I mean, can you imagine me the direct descendent of the greatest king Aom-igh has ever seen? Look, I don't know why the sword called me, it just did. Maybe I am a great great something of this Llian, but I don't want to be. I'm an orphan, I'm an orphan who got lucky enough to be raised by a knight and trained as a squire, that's all I want. That's all I've ever wanted. I don't want…" he trailed off, as though uncertain how to continue.

Kamarie suddenly felt self-conscious, not knowing what she could say or do that might help. On an impulse, she reached out tentatively and touched his shoulder. "It's okay, Oraeyn," she said quietly, "nobody expects you to be anything but what you are. You are Oraeyn, and a sword cannot change that; an ancestor cannot change that."

Oraeyn relaxed at her words, and there was a comfortable silence for a moment while they gathered some more wood; when they had enough wood they headed back to the camp. As they entered the circle of light and dancing shadows that the flickering campfire sent off, Oraeyn said quickly, "Thanks, Kamarie."

Brant had stopped for the night. The trail he was on was not a difficult one to follow, and the darkness was not a problem, but he was tired and he knew that Legend could use a rest as well. If he did not stop now, he would have to stop later, and by that time he would only be even more tired and would need to rest longer. He found a small cave without difficulty, more a small opening or shallow depression in the side of a wall of rock, really, but it would serve as a relatively safe place to sleep for a few hours. He turned Legend out to graze on the sparse grass in the nearby area. The horse was well-trained and would not wander far. He surveyed the land in front of him before allowing himself to relax; there was nothing in sight that told him anything of whoever he was tailing, but something, some extra warrior sense perhaps, told him danger was still there in front of him and that he should proceed with care. As he crawled into the small cave, he glanced behind him, back towards the way that he had come, and tensed. There was a glow from a campfire, only several miles behind him. Thoughts raced through his mind, each one more worrisome than the last, but no matter who was following him it was obvious that he could not sleep yet. Putting rest out of his mind, Brant cautiously crept back the way that he had come.

Oraeyn was half asleep when he heard the faint noise. It was nothing loud or even obvious, just a slight difference in the silence, really, but it was enough to alert his trained senses to the possible threat. In an instant he was up with his sword half drawn. He looked around in confusion. He saw nothing; there was no visible threat, but the strange prickle on the back of his neck told him something was near. That was when he realized he had been falling asleep when he was supposed to be on guard. Shaking his head to clear it, he started pacing back and forth; he dared not sit down now that he knew how tired he was.

Brant silently kicked himself as he realized that he had somehow given himself away and had woken the man sitting by the campfire. Quietly now, and with more care, Brant moved towards the campfire; when he was about twenty feet away, he stopped and surveyed the area. The man standing guard was now pacing back and forth, probably trying to keep himself awake. Behind him under an outcropping of rock there were the forms of three other people who appeared to be sleeping. He wondered if he should try to talk with them or if he should just get rid of them. Weighing his options, he decided that it was less risky to try talking first. His attackers were ahead of him, had to be ahead of him. Even if these people were bandits or enemies, it was very likely that they did not know what he looked like. Besides, if he attacked first and they were not the ones he was looking for, innocent blood might be shed, and that was not what Brant wanted.

His decision made, Brant stood up and strode into the circle of light offered by the campfire. "Hello there, friend," he said, loudly enough to startle the guard but quietly enough that his greeting could not be mistaken for a threat.

Oraeyn jumped and grasped the hilt of his sword as he turned towards the person who had spoken. The voice was deep, and there was something strong and good about it. As the man strode into the light, Oraeyn studied the visitor warily. The stranger was tall. He was lean and muscular, and he wore his sword easily. He moved with deadly grace, like a falcon that could whirl and dive upon its prey with lightning speed. The man strode noisily into their camp, but Oraeyn knew he could have gotten much closer without ever being noticed; he instinctively recognized that this man was dangerous.

Brant knew he was being studied, but he didn't mind, it gave him a moment to study the man before him as well. The guard was much younger than he had first thought. The boy was a good-looking youth with green eyes and light brown hair that was trimmed short like a squire's, he was tall, but a good three inches shorter than Brant. At his side he carried a sword that Brant would have liked to look at more closely. It was obvious that the boy was experienced with the weapon, but Brant doubted he had ever used it in real combat. The youth had an unseasoned look about his face. There was something in the eyes that told Brant this young man had never had to stare death in the face. He was probably a squire, Brant decided; he was not young enough for a page.

"Who goes there?" Oraeyn asked firmly.

"A lone traveler looking for some company," came Brant's casual reply.

"Oraeyn? Who are you talking to?" Kamarie sat up, blinking. Then she noticed the stranger and in one motion she went from lying on the ground half asleep, to wide-awake and standing up with her sword drawn.

Although Brant felt a wave of admiration at the girl's swift response to the situation, he knew he must quickly put both of them at ease before they got themselves hurt. "I see before me two knights, or at least squires. I did not realize I was in such esteemed company," he said, hoping that these two were, in fact, in the employ of the king.

They both relaxed a bit, but the girl still gripped her sword as she asked, "And who are you?"

"I am merely a lone traveler journeying through Aom-igh, I saw your campfire and came over hoping to join you. The road can get very lonely at times, and it has been a long time since I have conversed with other people," Brant lied.

Just then the smaller of the two remaining sleeping figures groaned, stretched, and sat up. When he saw the face of the child, Brant jerked in recognition. The boy rubbed his eyes and looked up at the young guard.

"Is it morning already?" he asked sleepily.

"No, it's not morning, we were just joined by this lone traveler whose name is… What is your name? You have not yet told us," Oraeyn said.

"Brant!" Yole yelped as he recognized the stranger. "You're alive!"

Brant stiffened, all senses alert and ready to flee or fight to the death, whichever course of action was demanded. But, as if he had not already been surprised enough for one night, the girl smiled warmly and relaxed with a relieved sigh; then she approached him with a friendly smile and an outstretched hand.

"Brant, we have been looking for you. I am so glad we found you. When we saw the village we feared the worst."

Brant retreated from the outstretched hand in distrust. "Who are you and why were you looking for me?"

The girl looked a bit taken aback, then she smiled easily. "I'm sorry, I forgot that you weren't really expecting us. I am Princess Kamarie, daughter of King Arnaud and Queen Zara. These are my traveling companions: Oraeyn, who, as you already guessed, is a squire. And this is Yole, but you already know him. And that," she pointed over towards the last remaining sleeping figure, "is my maid Darby, but you will have to meet her in the morning, because she is not very sociable tonight."

Brant stared at her warily, studying her features. She did not look much like Arnaud, but there was something about her smile that reminded him of his old friend, and that look in her eyes was the same one Arnaud had always gotten when he had to corral some stubborn farm animal. She definitely favored her mother.

Brant bowed. "Princess Kamarie, forgive the impertinence of my questions, but why were you seeking me?"

Now the princess's face turned grave. "Because Aom-igh is in danger. There is an army gathering in Roalthae; we have been told that our ally Prince Elroy may have committed treason by joining forces with the Dark Country across the Stained Sea. That is not yet certain, but we have been preparing for the worst. My father sent my companions and myself to you in the hopes that we would find safety under your protection. When we traveled to your home and found the village destroyed we feared that you had been killed. I am very glad to find that you survived."

"I wish I could say the same for my family and my neighbors." Brant's voice was quiet.

Kamarie looked at him and saw, for a moment, how deep his hurt was. Her heart went out to him as she considered his loss. Although she had just met him, she felt as though she had known him all her life, and she was overcome by a desperate longing to ease or share some of his grief. She tried to think of the right thing to say or do to help comfort him. She had seen people hurting before because of the loss of a loved one and had noticed how awkward and tentative their friends always seemed to be at comforting them. She hated the way that so many people could not seem to effectively reach out to those who were in pain. She hesitated for a brief instant, and then did the most un-princess-like thing she could think of, trying as she did so not to convey through her actions just how awkward she felt. She threw her arms around Brant and said softly, "I'm sorry."

Brant was taken by complete surprise. He stood quite still and rigid for a moment, and then he tentatively hugged the girl back. When she stepped away, he shook his head and smiled. "Thank you," he said, not sure whether he ought to laugh or cry.

The next morning dawned bright and clear, but there was a hint of storm clouds gathering on the distant eastern horizon. Brant had already retrieved his horse and provisions. Darby was a little confused, having missed the goings on of the night before, but after eyeing him shrewdly she announced, "Sure, he looks about the same as I remember him," and accepted the fact that Brant was who he said he was with no complaints. She just muttered to herself about how she ought to have been woken up and that it was "indecent" of them to have let her sleep through "all that excitement." But she did not seem to mind the fact that she had gotten more sleep than the rest of them.

"So what are we supposed to do now?" Oraeyn asked as they quickly finished breakfast.

"What do you mean? We found Brant and now we continue as planned," Kamarie said around a mouthful of berries.

"As planned?" Oraeyn asked. "As planned what? The plan was to find Brant, tell him of the need for his help, and then he was supposed to find a safe place for us to stay until all of this is over. That's the only plan there ever was."

"But I thought... I thought we were supposed to bring Brant back to my father... what do you mean?" Kamarie asked.

"Unfortunately it's not as simple as either of those plans anymore," Brant said. "I believe the danger to Aom-igh is related to the attack on Peak's Shadow. I must either continue to follow those who killed my family, or I must return immediately to your father and offer my assistance. Of course, his need is greater than my own. Although I intended to hunt my attacker, I did not know of the danger to the rest of the country. I will abandon my own quest for now and respond to King Arnaud's request first. I cannot give you a safe place to stay anymore; Peak's Shadow *was* the safe place, and it is no more."

"I still don't see why our enemies chose to attack such a random village in the middle of the country. Nor how they got their agents so far inland without anyone seeing their ships," Oraeyn said, "but I agree with you that we cannot continue as planned."

"We ought to do as my father commanded," Kamarie said reluctantly. "I would much rather be a part of the fight, and I know that being my escort has taken you away from your first real battle as well, Oraeyn, but I should not go against my fathers' orders."

"Your father didn't know that Brant's village would be the first place to be attacked, he didn't know that by the time we reached Peak's Shadow, Brant would already be aware of the danger. We cannot put our safety above that of Aom-igh's," Oraeyn said.

"The situation has indeed changed, Arnaud must be told of what is coming," Brant said. "I can give you directions to another possible safe haven, but I cannot take you there myself. Would that be acceptable?"

"No," Kamarie said, a light crossing her face. "We are coming with you. Traveling under your protection is the best safe place you can give us, and it does not defy my father's orders."

"I doubt your father would agree with that," Brant said wryly. "It will be dangerous in my company should my enemies discover that they were not completely successful in their mission to wipe out my village."

"But that is the whole point. If your attackers discover that someone escaped their attack, they will be watching for a lone survivor. They will not expect a group of five travelers who seem, at first glance, to be harmless and defenseless. We will give you an edge: the element of surprise." Kamarie's words were convincing, but Brant still had his doubts.

"If you get hurt, Arnaud will never forgive me," he said, starting to waver.

"We are not defenseless," Kamarie shot back, her eyes flashing in a mixture of anger and pride. "Oraeyn and I are both squires in training and are both capable warriors. Yole and Darby are also more than they appear. Together, we are a force to be reckoned with."

As she held her head high, Brant believed her. He knew that she was not lying about the training; if her quick motion from sleep to wakefulness the night before had not convinced him, the casual way she wore her sword would have. He could tell that she would be able to hold her own in a fight, if only because anyone facing her would be slow in realizing that she was more than she seemed. At length he relented, "All right. I just want you to know that it might be safer to stay behind."

He threw that in as his last bid, hoping that perhaps it would cause them to change their minds; but he was granted no such luck. Kamarie smiled. "I know. I do not expect you to protect us, we can do very well without your protection."

Brant smiled wryly, he had no doubts that they could do just that. He was sure that if they got into any sort of trouble, Kamarie would be able to talk them out of it, if nothing else. Then he sobered, but he did know what they were up against and Kamarie did not. Silently he vowed to his King and his friend that he would protect this princess; then he nodded. Without another word, Brant strode north towards Ayollan. His four new traveling companions scrambled to keep up with their new guide.

As they started out, he said casually, "From now on, we will forgo the campfire. Speed is the best service we can now offer to Arnaud."

Darby spoke up, "No campfire? And how do you expect us to set up camp, or eat well without creating some sort of evidence that will need to be hidden?"

Brant grinned to himself at the naiveté of his little group. "We will camp and even the wild animals won't know that we've been there."

It was *good* to be traveling again, to be on the move again. It was good to sleep on the hard ground under the stars, good to be on the trail of the enemy. His mind was sharp; his instincts alert. *I have stayed in one place for too long. I had almost forgotten what it was like to wander. I had almost forgotten what it felt like to carry a sword… I had almost forgotten how much I liked it,* he thought, and he smiled his first real smile since Imojean's death.

The words of the returning spy sent a ripple through the army of Aom-igh: the attack was coming, and the enemy was strong. The knights hefted their weapons and stood ready to fight. Their love of King and country rose up within their hearts almost to bursting, and each one of them knew that he would risk his life protecting either.

King Arnaud's heart swelled with pride as he walked among his men. A dangerous enemy was approaching and his men would be fighting the unknown tactics of the Dark Country, a land that was only spoken of in whispers. All that was really known about the Dark Country was that it was the realm of the fiercest warriors ever trained, but fantastical tales had grown up around the truth so that many believed that the people of the Dark Country were monsters, only barely resembling humans. Nonetheless, the knights of the realm were steadfast and brave. And yet, the lull continued. No dark sails appeared on the horizon; no army marched in from any direction. All was still, and the looming threat of danger seemed as if it had been imagined. The knights started to relax; laughter and teasing were heard on the walls again. King Arnaud remained tense and grew more and more uneasy as the days passed and the flood did not come. Even his beloved wife was starting to question the reality of a threat.

"Arnaud," she started quietly; he was in the library, studying everything that could be found about the Dark Country, but there was precious little, and the search was beginning to seem futile.

He looked up wearily. "Yes, dear?"

"Don't you think… well, nothing has happened… so don't you think that maybe we could send someone to bring Kamarie back?" Zara asked tentatively.

Arnaud stood up, worry and weariness lined his face. "Zara, we cannot do that yet. Remember the report from Roalthae. We must act with courage and wisdom until we know for certain that no threat exists. I cannot bring Kamarie back if there is still a chance there might be an invasion."

"Isn't the fact that no enemy has come evidence enough that there is no danger?" Zara asked. "Maybe Elroy is simply preparing to export weapons for a price. Maybe he is preparing some sort of presentation in hopes of winning Kamarie's affection."

"Zara," Arnaud's voice was firm.

Zara looked down. "I miss her," she said softly.

Arnaud embraced his wife. "As do I."

Then Zara looked up at him. "I know you are right, I just hoped perhaps..." She trailed off. "I had an idea. I think you should study the journals of King Llian."

"Why?"

"Six hundred fifty years ago, King Llian faced an invasion from the Dark Country and defeated them. He was also a renowned historian. His journals are the most accurate history we posess. He wrote about his battles and victories. Surely he wrote about the invasion he faced from the Dark Country."

Arnaud's eyes sparked with interest. "Darling, you are a genius. That is the weapon I have been seeking these many days." He kissed Zara and hurried to locate these precious journals eager to see what help might be had from this new source.

The journals were dusty from disuse and falling apart. The bindings were cracked and the leather covers worn. The pages were yellowed and the edges crumbled at the touch. The words on the pages, however, were what Arnaud was interested in, and they were whole and oddly unchanged by the time that had touched the rest of the books. Later that night, Arnaud commented on this to Zara but she simply smiled.

"Scelwhyn most likely laid a spell of keeping on the journals."

"Ah, yes. Well, you would know," Arnaud smiled back.

The first few volumes of the ancient, crumbling pages were written in a quick youth's hand and told of how Llian had come to the throne. The story was interesting; apparently the boy had been just a child when he was chosen by the people as the first ruler of Aom-igh. The journal was not very clear on why the boy had been chosen as king, the man was humble and did not laud his own talents and victories much. Perhaps that was why his journals were said to be so historically accurate, Arnaud thought;

they did not seem to be overly biased in any direction. They were written with clear, simple, and objective descriptions of events. Although he was curious to read the earlier writings in more detail, it was the later journals that held Arnaud's attention. Here, the pages spoke of the invasion of the Dark Country. As he read, fascinated by the skill and cunning of the Dark Warriors, Arnaud felt his heart sinking within him. How could they possibly hope to stand against such ferocity, such strategy, such well-trained fighting styles? Battle was what the Dark Warriors were born and bred for. Arnaud was proud of his people, and he had great faith in their devotion and in their fighting spirit, but he questioned if that would be enough. Was he sending his men against an enemy that could outnumber and overpower them?

He continued reading, searching for any piece of information that would help him prevail against this great threat. Aom-igh had turned away the Dark Country once before under the rule of King Llian, and Arnaud was determined that they could and would do so again.

Our enemies are finally upon us. We have known they were coming for some time now, but there has been no visible threat for so long that even I was starting to think that the danger had passed. The warriors from the Dark Country came in a wave of onslaught and then retreated. They have been making random, quick strikes at us that never last long enough for us to do any damage. They are here in great numbers and their warriors are capable and ruthless.

Arnaud skimmed a little further; he knew about the wait, knew about the fact that the warriors of the Dark Country were trained in combat from a very young age. Also, King Llian's notes seemed to be telling him that people in the Dark Country aged differently, more slowly, than people in the rest of the world. Their life spans were much longer than most, and they spent much of their lives training to be warriors. He had a sudden, fleeting, nagging thought tug at the corner of his mind, distracting him from his reading for a moment. Something about that information seemed suddenly terribly important. Arnaud looked up from the book and tried to catch the thought. It was something he should know, something he should remember, he could feel it on the tip of his brain... but no, now it was gone, fled as if it had never been. If it was important, he hoped he would remember before it was too late, but now he had to keep reading.

His eyes caught an interesting fragment of a sentence as he was skimming through the pages and stopped, reading more closely. *I went to enlist the help of the dragons today. King Graldon is reluctant to join in the actual fight, but he understands his people are in danger too if the Dark Country prevails. He instructed me to return in a few days, and I replied I did not know if we had a few days left.*

The next journal entry told of how the people of Aom-igh had continued to hold the Dark Warriors at bay and King Arnaud skimmed most of that until the writing came back to Llian's mission to find the dragons. *I returned to the dragons hoping to be granted some form, any form of help. When I arrived in the Mountains of Dusk...* Arnaud stopped reading, perplexed, how could King Llian have traveled from the castle to the mountains in one day?

Leaving the page marked, Arnaud went and found his wife to ask her how this was possible. At his question, Zara smiled and answered, "Scelwhyn, was very powerful, one of the very last truly powerful wizards, as you well know. He was the last known wizard alive to master the art of trekking. The art has since been lost to us. His magic is what enabled King Llian to travel many miles in a few short minutes."

"I see," King Arnaud was impressed and suddenly wished that he had Scelwhyn's aid once more. He could have used it.

"Are you finding anything of use?"

"Nothing so far, but I haven't finished reading all of Llian's journals yet," Arnaud sighed. "So far everything seems to be saying that the Dark Warriors are a match that we will not be able to win against on our own. It's too bad that the dragons have disappeared from Aom-igh; we could use their help now. I'm wishing for a couple of wizards too," he added jokingly, but his eyes were serious.

Zara's expression sobered. "If it comes to that, you know we will do everything in our power, but we do have limits."

"I know... I wish I knew why the wizards' line died out, for that matter, I wish I knew where the dragons went."

"You will find something that will help."

Arnaud smiled wanly. "I hope so, for all of us, I hope so."

When Zara left, he returned to his reading. He was getting frustrated and was starting to feel as though he ought to look elsewhere for answers to his questions. But then, as he kept reading, he began to see a ray of hope.

When I arrived in the Mountains of Dusk, I approached the King of the dragons once more. He told me he had decided against joining our cause. He did not consider the threat great enough to risk personal injury for the sake of human lives. The dragons have never been very cause-oriented, and I was not surprised at their decision; however, I was disappointed and discouraged and started to turn to leave, completely disheartened. Then King Graldon stopped me and said something that lifted my spirits.

He spoke in Old Kraïc, but Scelwhyn was there with me to interpret. "We will not fight in your war, but we will contribute this one thing."

I turned back towards him to find that he was holding a sword out to me as a gift. The dragons had fashioned the golden blade from one of the teeth of King Graldon himself, and the hilt was crafted from one of his silver scales.

"This blade," he said, "will not break or wear with time, and it will never fail you or your line when facing an enemy. We hope this sword will help you defeat the threat you speak of." I thanked him and turned to go. Before I left, he added one more thing, "If Aom-igh is ever in this great a danger again, you have my word that the dragons will not hesitate to join you in combat."

I left the dragons feeling both cheered and defeated. I was glad of their gift and their promise, but I truly hope that Aom-igh is never in this much danger again. I hope this gift never needs to be used again, and I hope we never have reason to hold the dragons to their promise.

Arnaud quickly scanned the next few pages; the sword in the hands of King Llian had truly been the weapon that had turned the tide. The enemy had been repulsed and forced to return home. The last few pages were written in a shaky, scrawling script by Llian as he lay on his deathbed. He described the cave that he had ordered Scelwhyn to create and the stipulations that bound the sword. There, the book ended. Arnaud flipped to the next page and found it blank. But then, as Arnaud watched in amazed wonder, words slowly appeared:

You who now read this, be it in days nearby or in the far distance of years to come, are once again in danger from the Dark Country across the sea. They were driven back by the sword of light, but not defeated. Great King Llian, Defender of his people, lies cold in the tomb, and his mighty Fang Blade is hidden and protected by spells you cannot unravel. But do not despair; there is yet hope:

> *When day is swallowed by night*
> *And the wanderer takes the road*
> *And the flame once more*
> *Burns bright:*
> *The youth will arise,*
> *The sword will awake,*
> *The dragons will fly*
> *And the enemy break.*

As quickly as they had appeared, the words vanished once more, leaving Arnaud to puzzle out the meaning of the cryptic message.

CHAPTER
SIX

Oraeyn was troubled by the way Brant was traveling. Although the man seemed certain of where he was going, they were not following any visible trail, and Oraeyn was furious to discover that he himself was completely lost. It wasn't that he didn't trust Brant - his King certainly seemed to think highly of the man - but Oraeyn was not used to being kept in the dark, and it was frustrating him. They were making it through the mountains in record time, once Brant showed them how to push their horses without exhausting them completely. Since they were supposedly headed towards the castle Oraeyn felt that they should have reached something familiar by now, but everywhere he turned all he saw was unfamiliar wilderness. At least they were headed in the right direction, but other than that Oraeyn had no idea where they were.

"Brant," Oraeyn said quietly as he rode up beside the man, "I need to talk to you about something."

"Speak," Brant said without looking at him.

"How do you know that we are on the right track?" Oraeyn asked, "I haven't seen any sign of a trail, how do you know that we are going in the right direction?"

"We are going in the right direction," Brant said simply.

Oraeyn stared at him, speechless. He waited for a more specific answer, but Brant did not seem inclined to say anything more. At length, Oraeyn made a small, exasperated noise.

Brant looked up at him. "Perhaps this will help: I'm sure you all have at least a few questions about me that I can answer, although many of them I cannot. Tonight when we make camp, I will explain the few things that I can, is that acceptable?"

Oraeyn nodded and then allowed his horse to drift back towards Kamarie. She looked at him questioningly.

"I still don't know if I trust this man," he whispered. "Maybe we were better off before we found him."

Kamarie frowned. "Brant said he would return with us to the palace, so far he has given us no indication that he is deceiving us or that he has gone back on his word. We would have no real idea of what to do next if we weren't following Brant. I think we should trust him; my father does."

"You can trust him," Yole's quiet voice suddenly intruded on their private conversation, startling Oraeyn; he had not known that the boy was listening to their conversation.

"How do you know?" Oraeyn asked suspiciously. "We have to be very careful who we trust. I'm not saying that I *don't* trust Brant, I'm just saying that I don't *know* if I trust him; there's a difference."

Yole nodded, but did not seem satisfied, though he said no more. A thoughtful silence fell over the group as they traveled, a silence that lasted for quite some time. When they finally stopped for the night, they were each amazed yet again at how easy it was to set up camp without leaving any traces of their passing. Brant's skills as a woodsman and a tracker seemed to know no bounds. Even Oraeyn was impressed enough to feel slightly remorseful that he had doubted the man.

"Once we get completely out of the mountains, this procedure becomes more difficult," Brant told them after they had gotten settled for the night, "because you have to deal with upsetting more plant life and trampling down the grass and the underbrush, but for now this will do. One good thing about the forest though, it is much easier to forage for food when you get into wooded areas."

After a quick supper, the weary travelers gathered as the Dragon's Eye set in the glowing sky. All eyes were on Brant, and there was a feeling of expectancy in the air. Brant glanced around and then sighed quietly.

"I promised young Oraeyn that I would answer at least some of your questions tonight. Listen closely, for I do not have time to repeat myself, and if there are any interruptions, I will be silenced. In time, you may grow to understand the need for this care."

The four of them leaned in closely so that they would be able to catch everything that the man they called Brant was going to say. A hush fell over the group as he began his story.

"You already know my village was attacked and destroyed several days ago. The attacker did not leave any visible trail to your eyes and you may well be wondering how I knew which way to follow. I sense Oraeyn is not the only one of you who has questions about me. I hope I answered some of your questions, or at least assuaged some of your doubts when we set up camp tonight. Now I am going to answer a few more of your questions.

"First of all, the ones who attacked my village were warriors from the Dark Country. I know much about the Dark Country and its people, I cannot tell you why or how I learned this information. Suffice to say that I am familiar with the Dark Warriors and I know how to identify their handiwork and how to track them. They do not leave a trail that is easy to find, which is why you have not been able to see the tracks I originally followed into the mountains. I also have reason to believe that the attack on my village was directed solely at me, but once again I cannot tell you why." Brant stopped speaking and sat back.

No one dared to say anything; for fear that he was not done. Nobody wanted to interrupt him after his warning. After a few moments, Brant continued.

"Secondly, am I heading towards the palace, or am I still tracking my enemies? The answer is that I gave you my word I would return to the palace with you, and that is what I intend to do. I am still keeping an eye out for our enemies, but I am not intending to actively pursue them unless I am forced to. If you are unfamiliar with the trail I am following, that is because you do not know this area as well as you should. I spent years wandering this countryside before either of you young ones were born, when I was the King's Warrior, so I assure you that I do know where I am and where I am going."

Oraeyn shifted uncomfortably. His mind was overflowing with even more questions than he had had before Brant's answers. The questions that Brant had not answered were the questions that Oraeyn most wanted the answers to. He wanted to know and understand the "how" and the "why" behind Brant, not just this superficial information that told him nothing.

Nobody seemed satisfied with Brant's answers, except for Darby. She nodded slowly to herself and smiled, but no one seemed to notice Darby; they were all intent on Brant, waiting to see if he was going to say anything more. Oraeyn thought that he was about to burst from keeping all his comments and questions inside, but it was Kamarie who spoke first.

"But you haven't told us anything!" she burst out in dismay. "All you have done is told us that you plan to keep your promise to return with us to the castle."

Brant eyed her coolly. "I have said all that I can, Princess Kamarie."

Kamarie glowered at him, her normally bright blue eyes looked dark and stormy, and Oraeyn tried to think of something to say that would be acceptable as a truce. Coming up with nothing, he turned and asked Brant, "Why will you not tell us how you know so much about the Dark Warriors and the Dark Country?"

Brant opened his mouth to answer, and then he looked at Oraeyn thoughtfully for a moment. When he finally spoke, it sounded as though he was choosing each word very carefully.

"I will tell you this: I am on your side in this battle. I want Aom-igh to survive, and I will do everything in my power to further that goal. Arnaud," Brant paused and looked at Kamarie, "your father, is my good friend, and I am in his service for a debt I owe. He, himself, is unaware that I owe him anything, which only makes my allegiance stronger."

All of them puzzled over Brant's words. Kamarie was awed by his fervor but annoyed by his lack of clarity. To her, it seemed as though he was speaking in unsolvable riddles for no other reason than to irk them and glean amusement from their confusion.

However, the truth of the matter was that Brant was not amused; he was watching Darby carefully as he spoke, and his demeanor became very cautious as he noted her reaction. She smiled at him, knowing that he was watching her, and then she nodded slowly as if to say, "I know who you are, and I know the meaning behind your words."

Brant shook himself and looked away. He found the older woman altogether too disconcerting. She seemed to know far too much. He knew that she did not look like anyone's idea of a threat; she was short and round and looked very much like someone who did not really know what was going on much of the time. But this appearance seemed to work to her advantage almost too well. Her brown eyes were sparkling with intelligence, and she did not let much slip by her. Brant decided he would have to be careful of this woman, she had secrets about her.

The night passed too quickly for all of them except, of course, for Brant. As they ate a quick, cold breakfast, Brant told them that they were coming close to the end of the mountains.

"If we can move quickly, we should be able to reach the castle in three days."

Darby sighed. "I thought we were traveling quickly," she muttered.

"Three days? It took us a week to get to the mountains," Kamarie's voice rose in dismay.

"I know I've been pushing you, but we all know how important it is to reach the castle before our enemies. I know shortcuts once we're out of the mountains."

There were a few sighs as he spoke, but nobody voiced their complaint as they readied their horses and concealed their meager camp. Brant watched them each appraisingly. He was surprised at how quickly he had grown accustomed to their presence, how comfortable he felt with them. He tried to steel himself against such feelings; it was better not to get attached, better to be stone. However, he could not help but admire his companions. Although at first glance they did not seem to be anything special, they took his orders well, they did their best to keep up with the grueling pace he was setting, and they had not done much complaining. Brant could not keep the small smile from tugging at the corners of his lips. King Arnaud could be proud of his daughter, he thought. She had discipline, courage, compassion, and a smattering of diplomacy in her irrepressible personality. Kamarie would make a fine queen someday. Brant determined to tell Arnaud that when they reached the palace, if his old friend didn't already know it.

Arnaud was puzzling over the rhyme. The second half of the poem made sense. He did not know who the "youth" was, but the sword it talked about was almost certainly the sword of the great King Llian. It was the first half of the rhyme, however, that was the mystery. He had written down the poem and showed it to Zara, but she had not been able to make any sense of it either.

"Are you still puzzling over that riddle?" Zara asked as she shivered into the room.

It was early, and morning was peeking up over the western horizon. Pink streaks of light were causing the darkness of the night to appear pale and watery. The stars were winking out and the Dragon's Eye was starting to rise up in all its blazing glory to replace the smaller, paler light of the Toreth.

"I can't figure this out," Arnaud said wearily. "I know the answer is here, but I don't have enough of the pieces to make sense of it. Who is the wanderer? What does it mean that the dragons will fly? The only part I understand is the part about the sword, and that only because it's right there in the journal on the page before the prophecy."

Zara came and looked over his shoulder, reading aloud, "'When day is swallowed by night,' could we be the day and the Dark Country the night?" she asked. "Perhaps that line is talking about the danger we face now."

Arnaud nodded. "Yes, but I don't like the word 'swallowed' then."

Zara managed a half smile that looked more like a grimace than a grin. "Ever seeing doom and destruction, aren't you?"

"No, not ever, just right now. As long as I expect the worst I cannot be taken by surprise, but I don't know how much longer I can continue expecting the worst," Arnaud sighed. "I don't know what more I can do, and yet I fear that I am letting our people down."

Zara hugged him. "You take too much on yourself."

"This is our greatest time of need, and I have nothing. I have a riddle I don't know the answer to. I have a vision of what is coming, and I cannot fight it. I have a country that is looking to me to protect them, and I have no idea how I am going to do so. Perhaps I am taking too much on myself, but there is no one else."

"Sir!" The door of the library opened and a young squire came rushing in, breathless and excited.

"What is it?" Arnaud stood up, expecting to hear that the enemy had at last arrived and the waiting would finally end.

"There are some people here to see you, your majesty, I told them… but they say their news is very important."

Arnaud was suddenly on guard. "Who is it?"

"I don't know, I couldn't see their faces because of their long cloaks, but there's five of them. They all look as though they have been traveling for a while. They say that they must speak with you. Will you receive them?"

King Arnaud furrowed his brow. "I will. Bring them to the Hall. I will meet them in ten minutes. If that is not acceptable, send them on their way."

The squire bowed. "I will tell them, your majesty."

Queen Zara's blue eyes searched Arnaud's face questioningly. "Who do you think it is?"

"I have no idea. I wasn't expecting anyone."

Ten minutes later, King Arnaud and Queen Zara were in the Hall, waiting to see who these strangers were who sought an audience with them. The five cloaked figures entered and Arnaud was rendered speechless for a moment. Zara, however, sprang from her throne instantly and crossed the room in several quick strides, gathering her daughter in her arms and hugging her tightly.

"Kamarie, you're safe, and you're home."

Kamarie smiled, hugging her mother back. "Yes," she spoke quickly, "we must talk to you and father. I do not know how much you have learned about our enemy, but we have some information that is very important."

Arnaud approached, a little less quickly and also hugged his daughter tightly. Then he faced her with a questioning and worried look on his face.

"I am glad to see you safely home, but I must admit I am a bit puzzled. I gave Oraeyn strict instructions. Could you not find Brant?"

"Father," Kamarie replied, "the situation is graver than we thought. Peak's Shadow has been attacked and there is nothing left."

Arnaud felt his breath leave his chest and for a moment he found it hard to speak. "What? Nothing? What do you mean?"

Kamarie lowered her eyes. "I think Brant should explain."

Arnaud looked up at the tallest member of the group and his eyes widened in relief and concern at the sight of his old friend. He reached out and clasped his friend's arm.

"Brant! It is good to see you, my old friend." Arnaud peered into Brant's face. "The years have certainly been kind to you," he exclaimed. Then he paused, processing what Kamarie had just said, "Imojean...?"

Brant shook his head, and Arnaud read the raw grief in the man's eyes.

"I am so sorry," Arnaud's voice grew thick. "Schea and Kali?"

Zara's eyes grew misty as Brant nodded wordlessly. She reached out and laid a hand on his arm.

"I never got to meet your wife, not really," she said. "Arnaud read me the letters you sent when your children were born. I wish I had gotten the chance to know your family. If there is anything we can do..."

"Thank you, both of you," Brant replied, his voice carefully steady, "but what I need right now is to focus on our enemies and create a plan for stopping them."

"Arnaud has been practically living in the library trying to find any information that will help us to turn back this threat. If you have anything to add, it is most welcome," Zara said.

There was a tumbling of words as the five travelers all tried to pour out their story at once. Eventually the chatter subsided, and they deferred to Brant to explain most of the latest events. After Brant described what had been happening in the south over the past few weeks, there was a long pause. Finally, Arnaud spoke.

"So you are telling me that there is a Dark Warrior, perhaps more than one, in Aom-igh already? And he... they are on the loose?"

"Yes, your majesty," Brant replied.

"How did they get so far inland?"

"I mean to find that out."

"Is there anything else?" Arnaud asked, recognizing something in his friend's eyes that told him Brant was holding something back.

"I believe I was the target of the attack on my village."

"What? Why?"

Brant pursed his lips. "I would prefer not to speculate on that just now."

"But you do believe that you are the reason for this entire threat?" Arnaud asked.

Brant dropped his eyes. "Yes, I believe so."

"I think you flatter yourself. Why would anyone from the Dark Country be after you?" Arnaud paused, giving Brant another chance to explain but the other man remained silent. Arnaud continued, "My intelligence tells me that other islands have allied themselves with the Dark Country already; apparently Roalthae joined willingly. Prince Elroy is the sovereign over the barrier islands, which means that the Dark Country did not have to struggle for their foothold there. And then there is the prophecy I found."

Brant started at the word "prophecy" and then he lowered his gaze self-consciously as he felt the gazes of the others fall upon him. His face turned dark and he muttered something under his breath about "superstition," and then fell silent.

"What prophecy?" Kamarie asked. She had remained silent throughout the entire conversation, but this bit of news was enough to spark her curiosity.

Arnaud pulled out the piece of paper that he had copied the poem onto and showed it to them. "I have not been very successful in figuring out its meaning, perhaps you can provide some insights. I only know the sword that the riddle mentions is the Lost Sword of King Llian."

At his words, Oraeyn jumped a bit. He quickly scanned the short poem, and his hand strayed unconsciously to the hilt of his sword. Nobody noticed the movement, but Oraeyn felt as though he was suddenly the object of far too much unwanted attention. He did not believe what he was reading, that the sword he carried was the sword of King Llian; it couldn't be. He started to speak, but Brant was already talking.

"I know what one of the lines means."

"Which one?" Arnaud asked.

"The one about the dragons. It means that you must send someone to find the dragons and wake them after all these years of hiding. And I know who you should send."

"What? But the dragons disappeared generations ago; the mission would be doomed before it even began. And who could I send?"

"The dragons retreated, they did not vanish; you know that, Sire. And I think you should send Oraeyn, Darby, Yole, Kamarie, and me to find their refuge and remind them of their promise."

"No!" Zara exclaimed.

"Zara..." Brant began, but Zara interrupted.

"I just got my daughter back after weeks of worrying about her. I am not about to let her wander the country looking for some of the most dangerous creatures that have ever lived."

"They are generally peaceful," Brant replied mildly.

"Once, perhaps, but that was before they felt threatened and exiled themselves into hiding."

"Mother, please, I want to go," Kamarie spoke up. Brant gave her a sharp look, but Kamarie held her chin high.

"Arnaud, may I speak with you and the queen alone for a moment?" Brant asked.

Arnaud looked at the faces of those around him and nodded. "Perhaps that would be best. Kamarie, take your friends to the kitchens and see if the kitchen staff can rustle up some food for your companions. Dinner is not for a few hours and you all look as though you could use a good meal or two. Have some food and drink sent up for Brant as well."

Kamarie wanted to argue, but she recognized the look in her father's eyes and knew that no amount of arguing was going to change his mind. She nodded and led the others down towards the kitchens.

Once they were alone, Zara turned to Brant. Her eyes were flashing angrily, her lips set in a thin line, her cheeks flushed. "Do you even know where to start looking for the hiding place of the myth-folk?" she demanded.

"I don't, but I know someone who does." Brant replied. "As do you... if I am correct in my guess." He stared at Zara unblinkingly until she lowered her gaze and blushed.

"I forget that you know more about the secrets of Aom-igh than most," she muttered. "That doesn't mean I am convinced though."

"Zara," Arnaud laid a placating hand on his wife's shoulder, "let us hear the man out. I am sure Brant has his reasons for suggesting something that sounds so preposterous."

Brant nodded. "Thank you, I do. There is a legend, a story, if you will, that Aom-igh was attacked by the Dark Country during King Llian's reign."

"I have been reading his journals," Arnaud replied.

"Have you come across the part where he asked the dragons for help?"

"I had skimmed over that a bit, actually," Arnaud admitted. Then I found the prophecy and I have been focusing on that."

"Well, he did ask the dragons for help. King Graldon, I believe it was." Brant glanced questioningly at Zara, who nodded, her eyes filling with grudging respect. "The dragons chose not to fight directly; instead, they gave King Llian a magical sword and with it he defeated the Dark Country."

"Yes, but we don't know where that sword is," Arnaud replied.

Brant smiled, a small, half smile. "It is closer than you think, but I'll get to that later. King Graldon also promised that the dragons would come to our aid if Aom-igh ever faced such a grave threat again. The dragons may be many things, but liars they are not. They hold their honor and their word as highly as any knight of the realm."

"You are making a good case for sending an emissary," Zara said, "but you haven't explained why it should be our daughter."

"Who else from the royal family is there?" Brant asked. "Zara, you of all people should know that it would be improper to send the King of the dragons anything less than a royal emissary, that is why King Llian himself went to Graldon all those years ago. He understood the proper etiquette that should be used when addressing the myth-folk. Arnaud is needed here, overseeing the defense of Aom-igh. Zara, you are the heart of your people. They will remain strong as long as they see your strength. Kamarie is the only choice for this mission."

"Darby will go as well, if only for my sake," Zara replied.

"And Oraeyn too, I suppose."

"Oraeyn has to go for another reason," Brant said, "for he is carrying King Llian's sword at his side."

Arnaud looked up, startled. "What? How do you know?"

Brant's mouth quirked in a crooked smile. "I just do."

"But that means..." Zara's eyes widened and she shared a long look with her husband. "Brant, do you realize what that means?"

"I believe I do," Brant replied. Arnaud merely looked thoughtful.

"But what about Yole?" Arnaud asked. "Surely the boy is too young to be included on such a dangerous quest?"

"It will be beneficial to him for reasons I wish to keep to myself for now," Brant replied. Arnaud frowned, but let it slide; he knew Brant well enough to know that the man would not divulge one word more than he should.

Zara grimaced. "I don't have to like it, but I can't argue against your logic. Kamarie can go, along with Darby and Oraeyn. But Brant, we are entrusting her to your care, is that understood?"

Brant nodded solemnly.

"I don't like your odds, but I can't deny that having the dragons reminded of their promised alliance would be beneficial to all of Aom-igh," Arnaud paused. "All right, Brant, time is of the essence. Make ready your band, succeed in your mission, and return to us as quickly as possible. We no longer wonder *if* there is to be an attack. Now the question is simply when. We are all at risk here, and our dear friend has already lost too much. I would avoid war at any price, but if it is thrust upon me, and more importantly on our people, then our enemy will suffer the calamity."

"I have one request," Zara spoke quickly. "I have been unable to contact my sister, Leila. She lives in the Harshlands, and we could use her help. When you have completed your quest, would you journey to her home and ask her for her aid in our fight? She will be needed."

Brant bowed his head. "Of course, my Lady."

CHAPTER
SEVEN

"Where, exactly, are we going?" Kamarie asked Brant as they set out once more. She was trying not to be too nosy. She knew that Brant must have said something profound to her parents to get them to agree to include her on this quest, and she did not have any desire to do or say anything that might make Brant regret speaking on her behalf.

"We are going to the Pearl Cove to look up an old friend of mine," Brant replied. "She will be able to help us in our search for the dragons."

"The Pearl Cove!" Kamarie yelped. "Do we have to go *there?*"

"What's the Pearl Cove?" Yole asked.

"It is merely a beach that is covered in pure white sand. The beach is long and wide with dunes of white sand everywhere. The beach slopes down to the ocean and is surrounded by great cliffs that form a sort of natural roof of protection over the entire area," Brant replied.

"Yes, that is how you would describe what it looks like," Kamarie agreed, "or at least, that's the way most of the stories

I've heard make it sound. But the Pearl Cove is much more than just that. The place is full of legends and myths that are told by travelers; I've heard many of the stories the knights tell, and from what they say, the Pearl Cove is a place you want toavoid. 'It is a place many have visited but few have returned. It is dangerous, surrounded by a thunderstorm and a wall of old magic,'" she quoted. "The place is also inhabited by unspeakable monsters and other dangerous creatures."

Brant smiled a little. "What you say is true and yet incorrect. The magic is old, but it is also new. Many unusual creatures do seek haven on the Pearl Cove, and yes, the place can be dangerous for the wrong people. It is also true that very few of the people who have journeyed to its crystalline shores ever returned, but the reasons for that are not what you think they are. Besides, you of all people should want to visit the Cove."

Kamarie wrinkled her brow in confusion. "Why should I want to visit Pearl Cove?"

Brant seemed about to answer when suddenly Darby seemed to suffer from a fit of coughing. The elderly woman doubled over and began choking and gasping, and they had to stop their horses in order to help her. Brant hurried to get her a cup of water from a nearby stream, and she drank it thankfully, apologizing profusely for delaying their journey. Once she could breathe normally, they continued on their way, but the conversation lapsed and Brant never answered Kamarie's question.

Oraeyn was once again pondering the mystery that seemed to surround their guide and companion. He wondered how Brant managed to answer so many questions without telling them anything and what exactly he meant by saying that the magic was old as well as new. Everything that came out of Brant's mouth seemed to be yet another mystery to solve. The man spoke with such confidence and cool assurance that it was very difficult not to believe that he knew what he was talking about. But even so, Brant's words gave away so little that he always left Oraeyn puzzling over what hidden meaning could be behind what he had said.

Yole was concerned by Kamarie's words. The Pearl Cove did not seem to be a very safe place to be traveling to. He was not sure that he was very comforted by Brant's description either. He was beginning to like these people very much, and he really enjoyed having his own horse, but he did not at all like the idea of riding into a place that was dangerous and full of fierce creatures.

King Arnaud had offered to lend Yole a horse of his own from the royal stables. Yole had chosen a small, gentle roan mare that had an interesting white marking on her forehead; Yole could not figure out what he thought the mark looked like. He had chosen the horse because it was the most even-tempered and non-threatening mount in the stables. He was unused to horses and for some reason they made him nervous.

The group rode in silence for a long time, each of them wrapped in their own thoughts. Yole was not sure he wanted to find any dragons. If they did happen to find some, who was to say that the dragons would not eat them first and then ask questions later? He did not like that idea at all and tried to shake it from his mind, but the further they rode, the more real the vision of being eaten by a large, ferocious, fire-breathing lizard with wings became to him.

Kamarie was not afraid of the idea of facing dragons, but she was worried that the mighty creatures would not remember their promise. All they had was the scrawling handwritten journal of a king who had been dead for over six hundred years. Perhaps all the dragons who could remember the promise had died out or been killed, or maybe they had never actually said they would help and it was just King Llian's wishful thinking that had made him write that. She worried about it for a while but realized it was a useless exercise until she knew for sure, so she focused her concentration on learning how to direct Tor without using her reins, the way Brant commanded his horse.

Oraeyn was not thinking about dragons. He was not even thinking about their mission at hand. All he could think about was the sword he now carried at his side and the poem King Arnaud had read to them. It seemed like every time he turned around, someone was talking about King Llian's sword. Yole claimed that Oraeyn's sword and the Lost Sword were one and the same, but the boy had also said a dragon that looked like an old man had told him this. That was just too hard to believe. Yet, Oraeyn could not deny that the sword had called him and only him. He could not deny that finding the sword in the mountains was a very odd occurrence, especially since the sword had been protected in such an unusual way. But he could not believe, or perhaps did not want to believe, that the sword was truly King Llian's.

As evening approached, the travelers came upon a small farmhouse. There was a garden on either side of the path that led up to the door. The few windows were lit with candles that looked cheery and inviting. There was a tattered barn behind the house and a gurgling brook running between them.

"Let's see if we can spend the night here," Brant said, swinging down from his horse.

He walked up the path and knocked on the door. There were a few moments of silence, and then the heavy wooden door swung open and a man greeted them. His family was crowding around behind him trying to get a glimpse of the strangers.

"Hello, travelers," the man's voice was a bit wary. "What is your business here?"

"We are just passing through. Can we trouble you for a place to sleep?" Brant replied easily.

The man relaxed a bit and opened the door a bit wider. "Any King's Man is welcome in my home. My name is Jhens, and this is my wife Chara, and my sons, Kent and Shaun. And this little one," he pointed at the tiny little girl who had brown curls and bright, curious brown eyes, "this is Wren."

Brant nodded a greeting at each of them and smiled at Wren. He said, "My name is Schea, this is Karen, Olin, Dara, and Yvan. We thank you for your hospitality."

Kamarie shot Brant a questioning look when he introduced her as Karen, but he shook his head slightly so she kept quiet. Jhens showed the five of them to the barn.

"I am sorry that we do not have anything more comfortable for you, but my house is small and this hayloft is the best I have to offer. Chara made the blankets though, and they are very comfortable and quite warm. You can come inside and have dinner with us if you'd like."

"It is better than sleeping on the road," Brant replied, "and we will appreciate a roof over our heads tonight as well. You do not have to feed us."

"Please, I insist," Jhens said.

Brant frowned. "Well, if you insist, then we thank you. A warm meal is much better than cold rations from our saddlebags. We will be in as soon as we've taken care of our horses."

When Jhens had left, Kamarie asked, "Why did you introduce us like that? Why didn't you tell him our real names? Don't you trust him? He seems harmless to me."

Brant met her questioning gaze. "I had thought that such a small detail would be obvious," he said in a low voice. "Dark Warriors already annihilated an entire village because they were either looking for me, or because they somehow found out that you were coming, which I highly doubt; however, we cannot rule it out. We are now on a critically important journey, and it is certain we will be hunted. We cannot endanger this family with our real identities. What a person does not know he cannot be forced to tell."

Kamarie nodded, hearing the wisdom in Brant's words. "I see."

When they had finished caring for their horses, the five travelers entered Jhens' home and ate a delicious meal of chicken stew with his family. The three children asked questions endlessly and seemed impressed with what they heard. The others let

Brant field the questions, only speaking when they felt that they could do so without revealing their true identities or purpose. After dinner, Jhens invited them to sit with the family around the fire and they accepted, feeling unable to excuse themselves without being rude.

As they made themselves comfortable in the cozy living room, little Wren climbed up into Brant's lap. Kamarie watched in amusement as the tiny child curled up and laid her head on Brant's chest. But then she felt a pain go through her when she glanced up at Brant's face. There were tears glistening in this warrior's dark eyes. Kamarie blinked and looked away, trying not to stare. When she returned her gaze once more, the tears were gone, and Kamarie wondered if they had really been there or if it had just been a trick of the light and shadows being cast about the room by the flames in the fireplace.

By the time they headed out to the barn, Wren had drifted off to sleep on Brant's lap and both of the young boys were yawning. Jhens invited them to breakfast with his family in the morning.

"We cannot linger," Brant said. "Thank you for your hospitality. Ma'am," he turned to Chara, "the food was worthy of the King's table!"

Chara blushed. "It is kind of you to say so."

The night was still and quiet as the weary travelers laid out their blankets in the hayloft and drifted off to sleep. Kamarie fell asleep almost immediately and slipped into a dream about home. She was riding Tor through the long grass of the forest in the early morning light. The wind was blowing across her face and whipping through her hair. She reveled in the feeling of traveling so fast above the ground, almost as if she were flying, and then suddenly she was flying, soaring on the back of a winged horse, high above the ground.

In an instant, Kamarie was jerked into wakefulness by something. She lay still for a moment, trying to determine what had woken her. It had not been a sound, or any movement she could detect; it was more as though the night had shifted a little, become colder perhaps, or the air had moved slightly. From where she was lying, she darted her eyes back and forth, trying to peer through the darkness. In the pale light of the Toreth coming through a large hole in the roof, she saw something peek up over the top of the ladder that led to the hayloft they were sleeping in. A dark figure climbed up over the top of the ladder and crept towards them. Kamarie remained still, not sure what she should do. Slowly, she slid her right hand across the floor to her sword. She gripped the hilt firmly and waited, every muscle tensed to spring up and challenge the intruder as it approached silently through the hay towards her. Even as her heart was racing and her muscles tightened to jump, Kamarie could not help but admire the silence with which the figure moved. As she tensed to rise, however, Brant silently exploded from his bedroll and ran his sword cleanly through the invader's chest. The death stroke was so quick that the figure crumpled and fell without a sound. Kamarie clenched her teeth to keep from crying out. She was amazed at how quickly and gracefully Brant had reacted; yet it terrified her as well. The motion had been so fluid, so natural, and so final that it frightened her.

Brant pulled his sword away, then knelt and wiped it clean. Kamarie silently stood up and joined him. The dead man was lying on the ground, a pool of blood next to him glinted in the light of the Toreth. Kamarie cringed but felt as though she could not look away. The man's face was angular, and as she looked at him, she could see a hardness in his jaw. His dark hair fell back from his face, but it probably fell into his eyes when he was upright. Kamarie closed her eyes and then opened them again as Brant reached over and touched the invader's neck. Kamarie shuddered, the matter of fact way Brant was acting about this man he had just killed terrified her more than her would-be attacker had. And seeing him now so very normal, handsome even, had brought her visions of their enemies as dark, faceless figures or monsters creeping towards them with evil intent crashing down around her ears. Their enemies were simply men.

"He is dead," Brant said in a low, emotionless voice, without looking at Kamarie.

"Who is it?" she asked in a hushed whisper.

"A Dark Warrior."

"The same one you were following into the mountains?" Kamarie asked, trying to dispel the darkness of death with normal conversation.

"I hope so, but there is no way to tell."

Oraeyn was suddenly standing next to them. "That was the most amazing thing I ever saw. I barely had enough time to sit up before you jumped up and ran him through like it was nothing. I can't believe how quickly you moved."

Brant put a finger to his lips but it was too late; Yole was suddenly sitting up and rubbing his eyes. "What's going on?"

Kamarie looked at him, then glanced at the dead man lying at Brant's feet and quickly moved so she was sitting between Yole and the figure. She heard Brant and Oraeyn moving the man behind her as she reached over and patted Yole's head. She felt a need to protect the boy from what had just happened.

"I woke up because I thought I heard something; Oraeyn and Brant are going to check it out, but it was probably just one of our horses kicking at his stall," Kamarie said the first thing that came into her head.

The boy moved away from her and she could just barely see that he was glaring at her in the dimly lit hayloft. Kamarie suddenly realized that he probably took her gesture of patting him on the head as an insult. She pulled her hand away; she had not meant to treat him like a child. She had really been trying to calm herself down more than anything, but she knew Yole would not understand that, especially since she had just lied to him about the Dark Warrior. Yole was not really that young, but he was small for his age and often seemed younger than he was.

She tried to think of something to say that would be sufficient as an apology for the insult. "I'm sorry, the noise I heard scared me," she said quietly, trying to explain that it was *she* who needed comforting.

Yole was not one to hold a grudge, and he recognized that no offense had been intended; so he grinned quickly and said, "Good-night," and then lay back down. Within moments his breathing had slowed and deepened and Kamarie knew he was asleep. She went back to her own bedroll, and as she lay down, she suddenly began shaking.

Kamarie had never seen anyone killed for real. And it had been so fast, so easy. The man had died without even a chance to defend himself. There had been no glory, no honor in what Brant had done. A small thought tugged at the corner of her mind. *And what about what the Dark Warrior did? Where was the honor or nobility in what he did? To slaughter an entire village, to kill innocent women and children, to kill Brant's family, what about that?* Kamarie shook her head lost in thought. The Dark Warrior would most certainly have killed them if Brant had not acted as quickly as he had. The man was probably one of those who had showed no mercy to the women and children of Peak's Shadow, but something still did not seem right deep within Kamarie's heart. After Brant and Oraeyn returned, with assurances that Jhens and his family were unharmed, she waited for Oraeyn to lie down and then she went over to where Brant was keeping vigil.

"How could you do that?" she asked quietly.

Brant patted the hay beside him, inviting her to sit down and join him. Kamarie sat, drawing her knees up under her chin and wrapping her arms around her legs. She shivered, and Brant wrapped his cloak around her shoulders. They sat together quietly for a moment.

At length, Kamarie began to speak, "I mean, how could you kill someone without allowing them the chance to defend themselves? Where is the honor in that? Where is the glory in catching someone unawares and killing them without giving him a fair chance? He was so young... I thought... I didn't realize..." She stopped and looked up at Brant, the tears in her eyes expressing all the fear, doubt, and questions she could not verbalize.

Brant looked at her sadly and shook his head. "There is no honor in that," he said softly, and his dark eyes were haunted. "There was no honor in the way that my family and friends were slaughtered either, they too were not given a chance to defend themselves. That is how war is, though. There is very little fair play in a war, there is only doing what you must do to keep the ones you love safe. It is true; there was no honor, no glory, and no nobility in what I did. But I did what I had to do to keep all of us safe, I killed a man so he would not kill us. Perhaps you are right and there is no honor in that, but it is what had to be done."

"I see." Kamarie sighed. "It's not the way they make it sound, is it? I mean in the stories and songs."

Brant shook his head. "Not really, no."

They sat in silence together for a while longer. As they stared out at the night, Kamarie felt their relationship change. Over the past few hours, Brant had become a little more like family and a little less of a stranger. He was still mysterious and she still had dozens of questions that she would have liked to ask him, but she began to think that perhaps her questions didn't matter as much as she had thought. It was enough that Brant was himself and that she was learning to trust him. As she returned to her bedroll to try to get a little more sleep before dawn, Kamarie felt safer than she had in weeks.

The next morning, Darby woke them all with a smile and a pleasant "good-morning" that none of them really appreciated except for Yole. The body of the Dark Warrior had disappeared while Kamarie slept, but she refrained from asking what had happened to it.

"Sure *she's* bright and chipper this morning, she wasn't awake for last night's goings on," Oraeyn grumbled quietly to Kamarie.

Kamarie smiled a little and said in a light tone, "Somehow I'm beginning to think that it would not have made a difference."

Oraeyn threw a glance in Darby's direction and noted the bright smile and the twinkle in the old maid's eyes and gave a grudging nod. "You're probably right."

Darby was, in fact, aware of what had happened the night before. She had woken up at about the same time as Kamarie and Oraeyn and watched the entire exchange through narrowed eyes. She had known instinctively that her help was not needed, she was confident that Brant had been completely alert since the intruder had first entered the barn. The man was as tense as a coiled spring, and he practically slept with one eye and both ears open. She had listened to Kamarie talking with Yole and had watched when the princess had gone over to talk with Brant. When she had heard the exchange between Brant and Kamarie, she had relaxed, smiled, and returned to her own quiet vigil, sensing her own growing approval of this mysterious and dangerous man. Of course, none of them, not even Brant who noticed everything, were aware of this, and Darby was sure that she liked it that way.

The five travelers departed early the next morning, eager to put the previous evening's events behind them. Kamarie left a pile of silver staters and a note on the front stoop, thanking Jhens and Chara for their hospitality and kindness, freely given.

As the five travelers got back on the road, they soon found that their spirits were light and their hearts were less heavy. The new dawn and the welcome light of the Dragon's Eye brought new hope with it, and for a while at least, their mission seemed less daunting.

Calyssia knew that travelers were headed towards the Pearl Cove. She always knew when people were coming, and she knew their purpose. It had always been that way. It was how she had set up the Cove over two hundred years ago. The shield warned her in advance.

The Pearl Cove was her home, her domain, and she liked it that way. It also had to remain that way. She had only set foot outside the Cove once in nearly seventy years. The shield of illusion and perpetual storm depended on her presence. The occasional traveler made it through, seeking glory, fame, or safety but no one could find or enter her domain without her permission. However, now events were unfolding, leaving her uncertain about the future.

These travelers were different. They were not coming for glory or for safety; they were coming for some other purpose. They were seeking her, and specifically they were seeking information only she could provide. She did not know who they were, she never knew that, but she did know that these who sought her were unique.

She also understood that a darkness was coming to Aom-igh and that it was threatening to sweep over the whole land with death and destruction. When it came, it would likely destroy her as well. She was tired, too tired, already. She would not be able to hold it at bay. Granted, she would be able to defend against it for a while but, in the end, she too would be defeated.

Understanding this, she also knew that the coming strangers could possibly alter this course. They heralded a chance for the land, but they also signaled an end to her domain. She waited for them expectantly, but she also feared their arrival. There were five of them, and they were near. She dreaded their arrival as it portended the destruction of her beloved Pearl Cove, but she would welcome them as their arrival could save all of Aom-igh.

The five traveled for some time across the plains, and then the Mountains of Dusk once again surrounded them. Brant explained that they were crossing the mountains at their narrowest point and that this was the only easy pass they would find through the mountains.

"The only other path through the mountains that is this short," he continued to say, "is where the river winds through them in the east. But that path is neither easy nor is it safe. And it is on the wrong side of the country as well, since it leads into the Harshlands."

Traveling along the path Brant showed them was more like walking on the floor of a ravine with two great rock walls rising up on either side of them. The height of the walls and the steepness of them made Kamarie dizzy when she looked up, and it was hard not to look up. The walls on either side of them were breathtaking and awe-inspiring, and she could not pull her eyes from them.

"Who is this friend of yours that lives in the Pearl Cove?" Kamarie asked for lack of anything else to say and to keep her eyes away from the towering cliffs.

Brant smiled a bit and said in a mysterious tone of voice, "You might say that she is the Keeper."

"The keeper of what?" Oraeyn asked curiously.

"The Keeper of the Cove."

"And that, once again, tells us exactly nothing," Kamarie whispered to Oraeyn, throwing a look of annoyance at Brant.

Oraeyn could not help it, he laughed. His laugh was contagious and Kamarie started laughing, and then Yole began to laugh as well, even though he did not have any idea what the joke was. Brant glanced back at them with a puzzled look on his face, which only made them laugh harder. The tensions of the past days drifted away on the lazy breeze as the travelers began to talk and joke and laugh together. The day of traveling passed so quickly that when Brant stopped they were all surprised. They had made it through the mountain pass, and there was a forest before them. The travelers exchanged excited smiles; it was so refreshing to see green grass and growth around them after the long journey through the rough-hewn mountain pass.

"We will make camp here tonight," Brant said. "And tomorrow, you will meet the Keeper of the Cove."

Kamarie was curious to find out who this Keeper of the Cove was. Brant obviously knew her, but he was not telling them any more than usual. Kamarie had grown up hearing awful tales about Pearl Cove. Most people avoided even talking about this place, and here she was, actually seeking it out. She drifted off to sleep, after sharing thoughts of the Cove with her guardian. Kamarie felt anticipation and dread, but Darby spoke of the Cove in an oddly unbridled excitement.

On their way the next morning, before the Dragon's Eye had completely risen over the horizon, Kamarie was reminded of all the times she had snuck out at first light to ride Tor and work with Garen for her secret squire lessons. Though she had only left home a few weeks ago to travel to Peak's Shadow, Kamarie felt as though remembering those times were as shadows of a half-forgotten dream.

They rode into the forest, and everyone but Brant stopped short in surprise. What had appeared as a large and ominous wood the night before was only a shallow line of trees. Immediately before them now was a tempest. It was a very odd experience, standing next to a grove of trees with the Dragon's Eye beating down on their heads and warming them while there was a furious storm raging just ahead. No more than thirty paces away the sky was black and full of dark angry thunderheads. There was a roaring, howling wind bending trees to the ground. Relentless, blinding rain crashed down from the sky as waves from the ocean crashed against a mountain wall. Lightning blasts streaked continuously across the dark sky, followed faithfully by thunderclaps that shook the ground. To call the storm simply "beautiful" or "terrifying" would not have done it justice.

Yole shivered and a moan escaped his lips, but it was lost in the spectacle. The power of the storm held them. Finally, Brant spoke, breaking the spell.

"That is where we are headed."

Oraeyn shook himself and found that he had been gripping the hilt of his sword so tightly that it was making his hand ache. He glanced back at Kamarie, but it was Darby who caught his attention. The look on her face was almost transforming. For a moment she was sitting straighter and looked taller. There was a smile on her face that made her appear far younger than usual. Her graying hair, which was normally pulled tightly back in a bun, was blowing around her in waves of golden brown.

Oraeyn took his hand off of the hilt of his sword and rubbed his eyes. When he looked up again, Darby was the same as she had always been. She was sitting on her pony with her shoulders hunched a little, her gray hair pulled back tightly. She looked at him sharply, but there was a twinkle in the depths of her brown eyes that Oraeyn found very unsettling.

The storm in front of them was a daunting sight, even Brant seemed a little awed by the display, but he had seen it before. He urged them on, leading them into the beauty and terror that surrounded Pearl Cove. As they entered, the storm appeared more terrible, only now they were surrounded by its rage. They were drenched as they fought their way through the waves of rain while lightning struck the ground all around. The deafening crack of thunder was a giant whip cracking just above their heads, and it was all they could do to keep their mounts under control. The wind tore at their faces and fingers, making it impossible to move and freezing them to the bone.

Brant looked back and saw that Yole was in grave danger, and he knew he had to get them through this storm and fast. Sliding off his horse, Brant grasped the reins of Yole's horse and started walking straight through the storm. Fighting against the wind and the rain and trudging along with his head bent and rain streaming down his face in rivers, he led Yole's horse behind him. Oraeyn and Kamarie dismounted and grabbed their horses' reins, desperately keeping their eyes on Brant and following his lead. Darby rode behind them, looking for all the world as though she was out for an afternoon stroll through the courtyard but no one had time to notice the lack of effect that the storm had upon her.

They seemed to be in the grip of the storm for an eternity. They wrapped their rain sodden cloaks tightly around themselves and continued slowly through the tempest, following Brant. Then, as suddenly as they had entered the storm, they left it behind. It was as though they had walked through a door and into a totally different house. They were standing on a strip of grassy plain with the welcome warmth of the Dragon's Eye once more beating down on them, drying them out and warming them. As they wrung out their cloaks, they looked around to get their bearings. The storm behind them had vanished completely, and the land in front of them was nothing but rolling, emerald hills as far as the eye could see.

"Where is Pearl Cove?" Yole asked, swinging his head around in confusion.

"Right there," Brant pointed straight ahead of them.

Yole stared at him as though he had gone crazy. "That's nothing but a green pasture."

"It is an illusion, lad," Brant said, smiling at the boy, "a green pasture is what she wants you to see."

"The Keeper?" Kamarie asked. "What is she like? Is she a sorceress?"

Brant looked at her and his mouth twitched in a mysterious smile as he replied, "I think that I will let her introduce herself."

When they had dried out a bit and gotten their breath back, Brant led them a little further away from the storm. Almost instantly there appeared a steep drop-off directly in front of them. Kamarie gasped and stopped before she stepped off of the cliff. She looked down to where white, foaming waves were crashing up against the sharp, jagged rocks so far below.

"I can't step off of that, I'll be smashed on the rocks," she whispered.

As if in the far distance, she heard someone say something about a ferocious beast that was coming to attack him. Just then, Darby looked over at Kamarie and saw her face going white. She stood in front of the girl and took her by the shoulders.

"Kamarie, it is just an illusion. An *illusion*, it is not real. Do you understand me?"

Kamarie gulped a little and nodded slowly, staring down at the jutting rocks. She took a deep breath and color started to return to her cheeks. Before she could stop to think about it any longer, she bravely stepped forward off the cliff. For a split second she envisioned her foot coming down on thin air and imagined falling to her death on the sharp rocks and crashing waves, and her heart beat a little faster. Then she was on the other side. Kamarie looked up, blinking, and saw the others.

They were all standing on a beach of pure white sand under a sky of the deepest blue. Oraeyn was standing next to her. He leaned over to whisper something in her ear.

"I couldn't see the illusion," he said.

"What?" Kamarie was taken by surprise. "You mean you could see through it?"

"No, not through it exactly, but all I could see was a gray wall. No cliff like you said you saw, and no wild animals like Yole saw. Just a gray wall that looked about as sturdy as billowing smoke."

Kamarie stared at him. "I don't understand."

"Me neither, but don't tell anyone about it, okay? At least, not yet."

"Why?"

"Because I think it has something to do with the sword," Oraeyn admitted quietly.

"All right," Kamarie agreed slowly, then she glanced over to where Brant and Yole were standing, a few paces away. "Where is Darby?"

"Right here," a musical voice said behind her.

Kamarie and Oraeyn turned around and gaped in astonishment. Emerging from the barrier of illusion was a tall, trim young lady with long, flowing, golden brown hair and brightly dancing brown eyes. She was dressed in traveling clothes, but somehow she managed to give off the impression that she was wearing a gown of the finest fabric, embossed with jewels and embroidered with thread spun from gold and silver. She was smiling, and there was a hint of laughter in her eyes.

"Excuse me, ma'am," Oraeyn said, ducking his head, "we did not see you."

"Is that the Keeper?" Kamarie whispered to Brant.

Brant merely shook his head, his eyes wide.

"Of course not, I just came through," the lady said lightly. She looked down at her ill-fitting clothes and grimaced. "Well, that was unexpected. I know my appearance is a bit of a shock, it surprised me a little too. I did not realize that my sister's wall of illusion would dissemble my own."

"Who are you?" Brant's voice made them all jump slightly as he strode up behind them. He had a questioning look on his face.

"Don't tell me you don't remember me, Brant. We have met before, you know." Her smile hinted her delight at returning the mystery to this mysterious man.

Brant started, and then he shook his head and his shoulders dropped, "In truth, Lady, I do *not* remember you. Forgive my memory lapse."

Yole looked up at the tall lady and said quietly and unabashedly, "You're beautiful."

The lady laughed, a pleasant sound, and said, "But don't you recognize me either young Yole?"

Yole shook his head wordlessly. Brant looked hard at the apparition; then suddenly he straightened and stepped back. He looked surprised. "Darby?"

Kamarie stared. "Not possible," she breathed in disbelief. But, yes, the eyes were the same, though there were no other visible similarities.

"Yes," the lady laughed again, "I have been Darby for the past seventeen years. But my real name is Dylanna."

Brant's eyes widened in shocked recognition. "Of course, there were four of you."

Kamarie was brimming with questions, they all were, but before anyone had a chance to ask any of them, another figure approached. The figure was a tall, willowy woman with white-blond hair and mint green eyes. She bore a striking resemblance to Darby-who-was-now-Dylanna. She walked as though she were gliding over the sand. She was dressed in a loose, flowing white gown that shimmered in the light of the Dragon's Eye. Her face was young, but her eyes held the wisdom of ages.

She fixed each of them with a cool, green-eyed gaze.

"You could have warned me that you were the one coming to visit, sister," she said in a wry tone. "I would have made an easier path for you to come through."

"Sister!" Kamarie yelped, but no one paid any attention to her outburst.

"Forgive me, Calyssia," Dylanna said, stepping forward to embrace the woman. "I was in disguise and couldn't spare the energy. The storm was not as bad as the rumors say."

Calyssia sighed. "No, I suppose it wouldn't be."

Dylanna shot her a sharp, questioning look, but Calyssia only smiled the barest hint of a smile and turned to the rest of the group, greeting them individually, "Welcome, Princess Kamarie, our meeting is long overdue, although I did come to your christening, not that you would remember that." She reached out a slender hand and held Kamarie's chin for an instant, and Kamarie saw an ocean of regret and something like love reflected in the Keeper's eyes. Then Calyssia turned to the others. "Welcome, sword-holder. Welcome, fiery youngling. Welcome, wanderer, I see that you no longer travel alone. Welcome, travelers to the Pearl Cove; I am the Keeper of the Cove, my name is Calyssia."

"Greetings, Calyssia," Brant said, bowing slightly, "we have come to ask for your help."

Calyssia nodded faintly, and there was pain in her gaze. "I know," she turned and beckoned for them to follow her. "Come."

They followed her through the shimmering white dunes of sand to a place where a single, silver tree stood by itself. The tree was very tall and the trunk was huge, yet the whole plant looked frail and delicate. At the base of the tree there was a door.

"Welcome to my home," Calyssia said.

Oraeyn thought that her voice sounded sad, and he wanted to know why. But he did not speak as they went through the doorway. Once inside, the companions found themselves in a large, comfortable room. Calyssia motioned for them to sit down.

"Now tell me, what brings you to Pearl Cove?" Calyssia asked as she sat across from them.

Brant quickly recounted the events of the past few weeks, starting by describing the destruction of his home; the others added things to his story when they thought he was leaving out important details. When he had finished, Calyssia sat back and sighed. Her face was weary, and she looked down at her hands.

"And so now you want me to help you find the dragons."

It was not a question, and there was a note of resignation in her voice and that same hint of sadness as well. Brant nodded, and Calyssia looked hard at each of them.

"And why should I help you? Aom-igh is not my responsibility," she said.

"Aom-igh is your home!" Kamarie sputtered in an outraged and hurt tone.

Brant put a hand on Kamarie's shoulder and said calmly, "Because you know what is coming, and even you cannot hold it back forever."

Oraeyn, Kamarie, and Yole held their breath. There was a pause, and then Calyssia laughed but there was no true merriment in it.

"You are almost too clever for your own good sometimes, dear wanderer," she said, her voice light, and then she became more solemn. "You are right, wandering firebrand, even I cannot hold the Dark Country back forever; of course, I must help you. You were also right in believing that I know where the dragons are. I do indeed know where their retreat is, but finding the dragons themselves may not be an easy task, or a quick one. I can only show you the way; I cannot travel with you. But it is now late, and I need rest. We will continue in the morning."

"Thank you, Calyssia," Kamarie said gratefully.

"Do not thank me yet, dear child," Calyssia said fondly. "Your search for the dragons will be long and hard, and even though you find them, it may still be too late to save Aom-igh."

Kamarie's face fell slightly, but Calyssia continued, "Do not despair yet, for it is always in the face of the greatest danger when the courageous find a way to rise up and conquer."

Kamarie's eyes sparked with hope, but she did not say anything more. Yole walked up and yawned.

"Good-night, Kamarie. Good-night, Pearl Lady."

Calyssia laughed slightly as Kamarie ruffled Yole's hair and said, "Good-night, Yole. You were very brave today."

He smiled sleepily, not really noticing that she was once again treating him like a child. Or perhaps, if he did notice, he did not truly mind anymore. There was a safety and a peace in this place that made him feel small and young, but he did not mind that very much either. There was nothing here to prove, nothing to fight, and no real reason to mind being young; it was better to be a child in this place. Yole was not exactly sure why this was, and he was not at all sure if he was even thinking straight anymore, but he was too tired to dwell on it, so he yawned again and put the odd thoughts out of his mind.

Calyssia smiled compassionately at him. "She is right, not many people can face my wall of illusion with half as much courage as you did." Then she whispered, "Continue being brave, young one, for you may need all of your courage yet. I cannot see very far into your future."

Not hearing the last part, Yole yawned again. "Good night," he said and padded off to bed.

The rest of them followed Yole's good example and went to sleep. The night was quiet and peaceful, and the weary travelers all enjoyed the most restful and refreshing night of sleep that any of them could ever remember having in a long time.

CHAPTER
EIGHT

Calyssia woke them early to a breakfast of refreshment they had never experienced before. They then made ready for an immediate start when Calyssia stated, "You will need to leave your horses behind for this part of your journey."

Kamarie frowned and patted Tor's neck anxiously. "You'll take good care of him?"

"I promise," Calyssia assured her. "They will be waiting for your return. They may feel a bit abandoned for a while, but I assure you it would be far crueler to take them on this next leg of your quest."

Kamarie nodded and turned to her horse. "You need to stay here for a while," she whispered to the big silver stallion. "I'll be back soon. I promise."

Tor shook his head up and down as if to say, "Don't worry." And then Kamarie hoisted her pack over one shoulder and followed after the others. Calyssia led the way through the white sand. In the early morning light, the land shone as though it were made of crystal.

As they walked through the Cove, Oraeyn noticed that they were not alone. There were people all around them, peering out from behind sand dunes, giving them curious looks. There were also some very strange creatures that were watching them. Oraeyn abruptly realized how the rumors had started about Pearl Cove. If the storm and the wall of illusion had not been enough to start stories about this place, the strange animals would have. And then he realized something else, the people that were watching them must be people who had traveled here and disappeared. But Brant had been right; they had not disappeared for the same reasons that most would think. These people had come and decided not to leave because they wanted to stay, not because they had been killed or forced to stay. He could feel the peace and the safety of this place. It was like being wrapped up in a warm blanket by a fire while a storm raged outside. The peace of Pearl Cove seemed to affect them all. Silence permeated their conversation as they followed Calyssia. It seemed wrong to introduce voices to this strange, beautiful land.

Calyssia led them to a large bluff on the edge of her domain. Beyond was the ocean itself. The adjoining beach sloped gracefully down to meet the water and they could see the Dragon's Eye sparkling off the crests of the waves.

Seemingly unaware of their questioning looks, Calyssia approached a pearl-white dune immediately before the rising bluff. As she got closer, she said something unintelligible. The sand started to shake and quiver, causing the ground beneath them to shift in something like a minor earthquake, making it hard to keep their balance. Slowly, a round hole emerged on the front of the dune and grew in size. Finally, the shaking stopped and what had once been a sand dune was now the mouth of an enormous dark cave.

"This is where your journey starts," Calyssia said, gesturing towards the opening. "This cave is the last gateway that exists on this side."

"What does that mean?" Yole asked.

Calyssia spoke quietly, "When the dragons retreated from the land of men, two hundred years ago, this is where they went. There is a world of tunnels and caves beneath the surface of Aom-igh that most people never know about. I am the last gate keeper on the outside."

Yole frowned and asked, "So if someone wants to find the dragons they always have to come and find you first?"

Calyssia nodded to Yole. Then, as if she could hear the worry in Kamarie's mind, she added, "If you manage to find them, you will soon discover that the dragons have very long memories."

Oraeyn's mind suddenly made a connection, and he spoke without thinking, "The dragons vanished two hundred years ago, yet you know where they are and you are the gate keeper to their domain. Just how old are you?"

Calyssia met his gaze. "I have seen the turn of three centuries."

It was just the tiniest bit unnerving to hear the Lady tell them that she was three hundred years old when she did not look a day over thirty.

"Don't look so shocked Oraeyn," Dylanna said. "I'm two hundred and seven myself."

Kamarie's eyes widened, and she shook her head in surprise and wonder. "After this, I'd believe anything," she said, "but I still have so many questions."

"Not now child," Calyssia said gently. "Though I might wish to sit with you and speak with you at length, I have not the time now. Know that your questions will all be answered eventually. I know that they are burning on your mind and that you are confused and want answers, but we do not have time for answers now. Dylanna will probably explain some things and provide you with some of the answers you so desire as you travel through the land of the dragons, but I suspect that she will not explain things as thoroughly as you might want her to."

"Now there's a big surprise," Kamarie muttered.

"You will find that the tunnels are lit by Ember Stones, so you should not have any difficulty seeing or finding your way through the realm of the dragons. I wish you all speed and success in your search. I truly wish I could do more for you than that," Calyssia said in a tone of farewell.

"You have done quite enough," Brant said, uttering the formal words of thanks and bowing his head slightly with the respect that was due the Keeper.

"You remembered," Calyssia smiled.

"How could I forget?" Brant replied.

Calyssia nodded her head in acknowledgement, then she motioned towards the opening in the side of the sand dune once more. She stepped back in order to allow the travelers to enter the doorway. When all five of them had stepped through the entryway, Calyssia called out one final farewell, and the ground shook again. A moment later, the door had closed behind them a final time.

For lack of any other options, they began walking forward, blinking in the dim light that seemed dark after the brilliance of the Dragon's Eye. As they started forward, they found that the path wound around in a spiral and the ground sloped downwards.

"You notice something?" Kamarie said after a little while.

"What?" Oraeyn asked.

"This tunnel is human sized. How big are dragons? If they're anything like the beasts described in the storybooks, then they could not ever use this tunnel, could they? They wouldn't fit," Kamarie was puzzled.

"Dragons *are* the large, winged creatures that you see in the pictures of storybooks," Brant answered, having overheard Kamarie's question. "You are right in understanding they cannot use this tunnel. They never expected to use this particular entrance because they created it for the use of humans like us who are in need. When and if the dragons ever leave their underground tunnels and caves to go out into the world above ground, they leave through their own doors that only open from the inside."

"How would you know that?" Dylanna demanded.

"I spoke with Calyssia late into the early morning hours. I wanted to know any information she could provide that may help us.

"How do they get back in here if the only gate that opens from the outside is in Pearl Cove?" Oraeyn asked.

"The gate we just came through is the only gate that humans can use from the outside," Brant explained. "The dragons can go in and out through any of their gates."

"These Ember Stones are pretty neat," Yole said abruptly, trailing his hand along the wall.

The caves had been carved out of a hard stone that looked something like marble or perhaps granite, and the Ember Stones lined the walls and the ceiling of the tunnels. The stones were cool to the touch and seemed to generate their own light. Some of the stones were a pale turquoise or light rose color, but the clear or white ones seemed to be the most common colors. The glow of the Ember Stones lit the tunnels fairly well, making visibility possible, although nothing could really replace the light of the Dragon's Eye. As Yole's hand brushed them, they seemed to glow more brightly for an instant, but nobody noticed this except Brant.

"It must have taken a long time to build these tunnels and caves," Oraeyn said.

"The dragons built these tunnels thousands of years ago, even before King Llian's reign. Nobody truly recalls the original intent for these tunnels. Even the *dragons* forgot them during their centuries above ground. They lived mostly in the Mountains of Dusk until about two hundred years ago, when they rediscovered the tunnels and sought refuge here. More and more myth-folk retreated into the tunnels until they no longer journeyed the world of daylight," Dylanna said.

"Why did they come back down here? Why don't they return to the Mountains of Dusk and live above ground?" Kamarie asked.

"There were many reasons for the dragons' retreat to the underworld," Dylanna said quietly. "The main reason was because dragons have longer memories than humans do. Dragons were once the great defenders of Aom-igh, and then they became simply inhabitants of Aom-igh as the people united under a king and were able to defend themselves. As the years went by and the dragons were no longer actively involved, people started to forget them. When people start forgetting things, they stop understanding the things that they have forgotten, and people fear what they cannot understand.

"Dragons live longer than humans do, and they remember more. You see, they remembered their guardianship of old. They were once revered and held in high esteem and their friendship was treasured. But we no longer recalled those times, and instead we feared and mistrusted them. So, they departed.

"What began as a safe haven for the dragons has become a haven for others as well. Many other forgotten creatures have sought refuge here when their friendship and trust was no longer valued." Dylanna stopped speaking as they finally came to the end of the winding path.

Here, the ground evened out and continued straight in front of them, no longer sloping downwards. The tunnel widened, and the ceiling was much higher. Large creatures could easily stampede through this great hall, and Yole suddenly felt very small as he stood at the threshold. It suddenly became very easy to imagine great scaled, winged dragons moving through the tunnel, their claws clicking against the hard, smooth, marble floor and smoke curling from their powerful jaws full of blade-sharp teeth. Yet somehow, although he felt very small and out of place, Yole had a strange feeling of truly being *home* for the first time in his short life.

"Here is where the journey really begins," Kamarie said softly to herself. "After this, there is no turning back."

"How in the world do they tell time down here?" Oraeyn wondered out loud.

Nobody had a good response to that question. In awed silence, the five travelers walked forward. They were somewhat overwhelmed by the immense underground grandeur they were entering.

Although the tunnels were amazingly crafted and beautiful to look upon, trekking through them soon proved to be monotonous. There was no change in color or scenery, no difference in the lighting from one part of the tunnel to the next. They had not seen, or sensed, any sign of another living creature. All of them soon grew tired of walking through the endless rock tunnels. There was anxious tension in the air at the thought of how easily they could become lost forever.

"Tell us a story, Dylanna," Yole finally begged out of sheer boredom.

"What would you like to hear about, Yole?" Dylanna asked kindly.

"About you. Are you really two hundred and seven?" Yole asked, his tone saying clearly that he did not believe it.

Dylanna laughed. "Yes, I really am." At his suspicious glance she asked, "Is it truly so hard for you to believe?"

Yole nodded vigorously, "You don't *look* old, I mean, you did before when you were Darby, but you don't now."

"I haven't really changed, Yole, just my name and appearance have," Dylanna said gently.

"And the way you talk," Yole added.

"Well, I would like to hear some kind of explanation," Kamarie said. "Perhaps it is true that you have not really changed, but you have not exactly been really you either, so much of who I think you are was just a façade."

"Dear Princess Kamarie, you have grown very wise since we started traveling. The story will make our journey seem to pass more quickly," Dylanna paused, allowing the silence to begin the story.

"I remember when the dragons retreated," she started, "I was just a child…"

Oraeyn snorted. "A child of *forty*."

Dylanna nodded with a smile and continued, "Yes, I age differently than you do, and for a wizard forty and even fifty is still in the realm of childhood. It was gradual at first. The dragons of Aom-igh wanted to remain in the Mountains of Dusk that had been their home for so long, but they were also tired of being feared. King Llian had been dead for several hundred years and just as his great sword had apparently been lost, many memories were truly lost as well. Graldon, the King of the dragons was growing old and tired, and so he allowed his people to slip quietly out of the mountains and down to the tunnels.

"Not everyone forgot, some people still remembered the bright days of the rule of the dragons, some people still believed that the dragons should live in peace alongside humans in the daylight of Aom-igh. But the dragons had lost faith in us. Not a single dragon-ward had been discovered in hundreds of years; therefore, the dragons did not see any reason to remain."

"Hold on, you lost me again. What is a dragon-ward?" Oraeyn asked.

Brant answered, "They were also known as dragon riders. They are very rare human children born with special abilities. Taught in the old ways, they study dragon lore, magic, and Old Kraïc, the dragon tongue. They have an uncanny sixth sense with animals, which allows them to communicate completely, without speaking. A dragon knows when his ward has been born and will spend the rest of his life searching for his ward. When joined, their bond is immediate and permanent until they die. At one time, most dragons had a ward, and they were an invincible army in the sky, guardians of those on the ground. But as trust and friendship deteriorated, fewer of these special children were born."

"They were not always such a rarity. In fact, there used to be just as many wards as there were dragons," Dylanna interjected.

"But as the dragons became more and more reclusive, fewer and fewer wards were born. The wards were always the link between dragons and humans, and their absence made it even harder for the two races to find common ground. Some of us believe that it is not so much that these special children are no longer born, but that those who are born are not taught what they need to learn, so they live and die with an empty spot within them, like an ache or a hole that could never be completely healed or filled."

"I don't really understand," Kamarie said, "what happens when the two find each other?"

"It is like meeting someone and knowing instantly that the two of you will be best friends," Dylanna said.

"Or like having a talking horse that flies," Brant threw in sarcastically.

Dylanna gave Brant a look of irritation. But Oraeyn and Kamarie laughed. Brant was continually surprising them. As soon as they started thinking that they knew him, he did something unexpected.

Dylanna then said, "Back to the story, as the dragons disappeared, my sister Calyssia pleaded with the dragons, asking that they not leave Aom-igh completely. Out of respect for my father, love for Calyssia, and honor for his promise to King Llian, Graldon finally relented and allowed there to be one entrance to the tunnels on the conditions that Calyssia, his ward, be the Keeper of the entryway and that she only allow people to pass through in times of greatest need. I think that it was mostly an arrangement for his own benefit, for Graldon had a very difficult time accepting the fact that Calyssia refused to move down into the tunnels, and Calyssia never forgave herself for abandoning him. I think she blames herself for his death, even though Graldon was very old, even by dragons' standards."

"Who was your father that the dragons would respect him so?" Oraeyn asked.

"Calyssia was a dragon ward? The ward of the *King* of the dragons?" Kamarie gasped.

"My father was Scelwhyn, great mage and advisor to King Llian," Dylanna said proudly. "My sisters and I are his only descendants. Many things disappeared when the dragons did, including wizards and mages. My sisters and I are the only wizardesses left in all of Aom-igh now."

"Scelwhyn!" Oraeyn exclaimed, then he gave a low whistle. "Wow."

"How many sisters do you have?" Kamarie asked.

"I have three sisters, Calyssia is the eldest, I am the second," Dylanna paused for a moment and then continued, "and Zara is the youngest."

Kamarie started and spoke in a loud, surprised voice, "Zara!" She stopped and then, in a quieter tone, she asked, "My mother?"

Dylanna nodded.

"So you are my aunt?"

Dylanna nodded again.

"And Aunt Leila is also a wizardess?"

Dylanna nodded.

"And Scelwhyn was my grandfather?"

Once more, Dylanna nodded.

"I'm only half-human?"

"Yes, that is true. Your grandfather was a full-blooded wizard."

Kamarie felt as though her world were spinning out of control. Her vision blurred and then cleared and then blurred again as she tried to process this information.

"Why have I never been told?"

"You would have been told on your twenty-first birthday," Dylanna replied. "Your parents wanted you to have as normal a childhood as possible. Your mother chose to abandon her training and live as human a life as possible. She wanted you to have that opportunity as well."

"Will I age differently too?"

Dylanna bit her lip. "We don't really know. Our history and lore do not tell us much in this regard. It is possible, although you have given every indication that you are aging in the normal, human way."

Kamarie thought about that for a moment, then in a small voice she asked, "So what does that make me? Am I only half human? I *can't* be the granddaughter of a wizard who lived to be over seven hundred years old!"

Oddly enough, it was not Dylanna who answered these desperate questions. "It makes you the Princess of Aom-igh, daughter of King Arnaud and Queen Zara," Oraeyn said quietly, "it makes you Kamarie, the same person that you have always been; who your grandparents were cannot change that."

Kamarie calmed down and smiled wryly as she heard her own words being repeated back to her. "Sounds like you heard that from someone very wise."

Oraeyn did not smile. "I did," he said earnestly.

They continued on for a long time, until Yole started complaining about his sore feet and his hungry tummy. Kamarie was glad he had spoken up, for she was also tired of walking, as well as quite hungry, but she had not wanted to be the one to ask for a rest. She didn't want to slow the group down, so she had stubbornly decided that she could keep walking for as long as Brant could – a more ambitious decision than she realized.

They sat down to eat and rest, all of them ready for a break. After eating and stretching their aching muscles a bit, Brant insisted that they go further before they stopped for the night. Although all of them were sure that he could not possibly know what time of day it was, they were not about to argue over something so trivial. They stood up and folded their packs once more, getting ready to press on for a little while longer at least.

"Ssstrangersss," an alien, hissing, whispery voice suddenly filled the air around them, causing them to huddle together a bit.

Yole jumped. "What was that?"

"I don't know," Kamarie said in a breath that could barely be called a whisper.

They were standing in a large cave with tunnels extending in all directions. In the dim light, Kamarie could not see very well, but she had the uncomfortable feeling they were being watched by creatures who could see just fine.

"Ssstrangersss and intrudersss," now more voices echoed around them.

"Hhhhumansss," a voice hissed menacingly.

"Friends," Dylanna called out.

There was silence, and then a voice spoke again, "Whhho sssayss… friendsss?"

"I say friends. I, Dylanna, second-daughter of Scelwhyn."

The voices hissed, and now they sounded a little less menacing and a bit more thoughtful, "Sssscelwhhhyn, dragon-friend."

"Will you take us to the King of the dragons?" Dylanna asked.

"Will you take us to Graldon?" Kamarie cried out without thinking. In the days to come, Kamarie often wondered why she had not remembered the end of Dylanna's story. But at the moment she felt more afraid of the voices in the darkness than she had ever been of anything and fear made her speak without thinking.

"Graldon isss dead," came the mournful reply, "hisss sssuccessor is Rhendak. Long live the Kiiiiing."

"Will you take us to Rhendak then?" Oraeyn questioned hopefully.

"We asssk questionsss," the reply was harsh, "whhoo are you? What do you want in Krayghentalisss?"

Dylanna's voice rang out, "We are here to speak to Rhendak, the King of the dragons, our message is for him alone."

There was a muted hissing that sounded like a consultation, then the reply came, "We will take you to Rhendak."

A creature emerged from the shadows, but it was not what they had been expecting. The creature was not a dragon at all; instead, they were faced with a small gryphon. It did not look anything like the fierce pictures that Kamarie had seen. For one thing, it was much smaller than she had expected, maybe twice the size of a mountain lion. It had the head, beak, and wings of an eagle, and his eyes were fierce and proud; he held his head at an erect angle and there was a haughty, yet curious way about the manner with which he gazed at each of them. The gryphon's body and legs were that of a lion's, gracefully muscular and powerful. The tail also looked like a lion's, flicking back and forth, but there were sharp, deadly stingers at the end of the tail.

"My name is Iarrdek," the gryphon said slowly, clicking harshly on the last consonant of his name.

Yole noticed that the creature did not hiss when he took the time to form his words carefully. He spoke in deep, intelligent tones; his beak clicked between some of his words, giving his speech a harsh quality.

"How far is it to the dragons?" Yole asked nervously.

"Not far," Iarrdek clicked in an ominous tone.

The five of them followed the gryphon cautiously. They walked several paces behind him, none of them wanting to get very close to the sharp stingers on that tail. The gryphon stalked in front of them, leading the way down the path on their left.

Oraeyn marveled at the grace with which the animal moved. The muscles in his shoulders and legs stretched easily as he walked along in front of them. Watching the gryphon move was like watching a lazy river, his every motion full of fluidity and confidence.

They continued down the long tunnel for a while in silence. The presence of Iarrdek made them loath to speak of their mission, and no one could think of anything else appropriate to say. They were also very aware that they were being constantly watched. The tunnels suddenly seemed full of unseen eyes. It made the younger travelers a little jumpy, knowing that there were many invisible, intelligent creatures watching them as they walked through the long tunnels. Kamarie felt as though she were trespassing on forbidden ground. Oraeyn was growing restless and defensive, almost wishing that one of the creatures would try something; he was ready for a good fight. He was tired of this endless journey through the caves and tunnels and yearned to see the light of day once more. Yole was growing more nervous by the second; he could feel the tensions in the air and was worried that something would happen. Brant and Dylanna, however, seemed unperturbed by their surroundings and walked easily and comfortably behind their guide.

The gryphon turned into a cave to the right, leaving the straight path that they had been following. The new tunnel was probably considered a curving, twisting, winding path, but to the five humans it was too large for them to be able to tell the difference from the last tunnel that they had been in. Now the gryphon began to take more turns into new tunnels and he took them past and through some very large caves.

This maze must really be as large as all of Aom-igh itself, Kamarie thought to herself, *supposedly many creatures live down here, but they sure are good at keeping themselves hidden. I cannot believe that all of this is down here and nobody knows about it up in Aom-igh. I bet even father does not know about this maze.*

Most of the others were thinking much the same thing, and it would have been easy to believe that they were really the only living beings in the tunnels had it not been for the feel of the unseen forbidding eyes that watched them from the shadows. The sense of hostility was so thick Oraeyn felt like he was making his way through spider webs, it was there and tangible, but he could not see or fight it.

"Sure is a long way for being not far," Oraeyn grumbled only loud enough for Kamarie to hear.

"Apparently 'not far' is a lot farther than you might think," Kamarie shot back with a quiet laugh.

Brant overheard and smiled to himself, sure that *his* idea of "not far" would not suit Oraeyn or Kamarie either. He kept his amusement to himself, not adding anything to their conversation. Silence weighed heavily upon them once more, the gryphon's paws and their soft-soled leather boots made very little sound at all on the smooth rock floor.

"Wait-t here," Iarrdek said, stopping abruptly in front of a huge, dark portal. "I must-t announce you."

The gryphon disappeared while the travelers waited, shifting a little nervously. That is to say, Oraeyn, Kamarie, and Yole shifted about in nervous anticipation; Brant and Dylanna stood still and quiet. Brant was standing within a shadow and had his arms folded, so motionless that it would have been very easy to miss him unless one looked closely. His face was hard and unreadable. His muscles were tense and although he looked relaxed, he also gave the impression that he would be able to spring into action at a split-second's notice. Oraeyn wondered if the man was truly as comfortable as he seemed or if he was just very good at hiding his own restlessness.

Dylanna, on the other hand, would not have been easy to overlook. She stood very tall in the brightest part of the tunnel, her head erect and proud. She was surrounded by a dim glow of white light from the Ember Stones. Outlined in the eerie light, she looked every bit the daughter of Scelwhyn, favored friend of the dragons.

At the same time that the travelers were following Iarrdek through the tunnels of Krayghentaliss, a squire was racing into the royal library in a breathless state of excitement and fear. He skidded to a halt, remembering his manners almost a fraction of a second too late, and bowed.

"Your Majesty."

"What is it?" King Arnaud asked wearily; he had been up all night studying as many of the manuscripts and history books that he could find on the historical war between Aom-igh and the Dark Country.

"There are ships coming from the south-east, bearing the markings of Iolanver," the squire said, "we cannot tell if they are friend or foe, they are several hours away yet, but Garen sent me to inform you, your Majesty."

Arnaud straightened. Iolanver was one of the barrier islands, and therefore subject to the rule of Prince Elroy. "Show me."

They hurried to the tower where they could observe the approaching ships. When Arnaud reached the top, a guard on duty turned at his approach and bowed.

"Your Majesty," he began.

That had been hard to get used to, and still was difficult to accept, the whole "Your Majesty" business. Growing up as a commoner, people had names not titles. He had wanted to issue a decree eliminating these ridiculous formalities, but the idea had not been well received, especially by those who preferred to keep their own titles. He resigned himself to this lost hope. He pulled his train of thought back to the present, focusing on what the guard was telling him.

"We just spotted them through the lens a few minutes ago. The sails bear the seal of Iolanver, Your Majesty."

There it was again, the title that granted him the respect due a king, and yet it placed an insurmountable barrier between him and his people. Arnaud shook his head; now was not the time to be thinking about trivial details like that, especially ones he could not change.

Arnaud took the lens and saw the standard on the sails. He straightened. "Keep an eye on them. They may be here on Elroy's business, or they may be refugees trying to defect from Elroy's rule. Either way, we cannot be too careful. Send a ship and learn their business. Treat them as dangerous until we know otherwise."

"I hear and obey, Majesty," the guard clapped his fist to his heart.

Arnaud winced at the salute as much as at the title. He knew they were intended as symbols of respect, but he still found himself wishing that the barrier between ruler and subject were not quite so large. He descended from the tower back into the main part of the palace. As he walked past Zara, she read his face easily and reached out to put her hand on his shoulder.

"The throne of the king is sometimes a lonely spot to be," she said in a quiet, soothing tone, her eyes full of compassion and understanding.

"It's silly of me to be dwelling on such little matters when the whole of Aom-igh is at risk," Arnaud sighed. "I know. Especially now, I thought I had gotten used to it years ago. But still it weighs on me, now more than ever. The courtiers are always putting on a show to impress me, trying to gain influence and power. The knights are real enough, but I can never quite get past the bowing and 'your majesty-ing' to really talk to them or get to know them, and I think that the honest, hardworking farmers almost fear me. I am tired, Zara, tired of the weight of this crown, tired of the loneliness of the throne. I want to have a real conversation about weather and crops and the land without being looked at in cautious trust. I want to shake a man's hand and not have him wondering what I am going to punish him for. I have tried to be a good ruler, and I am going to see this war through; I will stay on the throne for as long as Aom-igh needs me, but I cannot help hoping that somehow Aom-igh will not need me for much longer."

Zara looked at him with a look of pure understanding on her face. "No country needs a great ruler. It needs a good ruler. One who inspires his people to greatness, and that is what you have done for the people of Aom-igh. You have paved the road and made the path much easier for your successor."

Arnaud smiled at her. "You always know what to say," he said fondly.

She laughed a little at that, and then turned serious. "Have you found anything more in the library?"

"Yes, I have," Arnaud turned his attention to business, blocking out all the other minor irritations, "and there are ships from Iolanver heading this way. I have sent a restriction ship to learn their business and instructed the men to regard them as a threat."

Zara nodded, her face grave. Then she sighed. "Everything is upside down from how it should be. Those ships should be our allies, and here we are preparing to receive them as spies or a trap. The man who sought to court our daughter has declared war upon us and our daughter..." she stopped, biting her lip.

"They will find the dragons," Arnaud said, picking up on her mood change, although he did not feel certain of this himself, "and they *will* come back to us."

Zara smiled wearily. "I know, deep in my heart I know that, but it is hard to keep my fears from rising. Can one be full of hope and full of dread at the same time?"

Arnaud nodded quietly. "Yes, I believe that is more common than being entirely full of one or the other."

Zara smiled again, but she could not find any words, her heart was too full. There was a mixture of sorrow and hope shining in her deep blue eyes.

Prince Elroy stood on his shoreline looking towards Aom-igh. He thought about the invasion plans made known to him earlier that morning. Llycaelon, the Dark Country, did indeed have only a small number of ships. They were not a trading or sea-faring people, though apparently that policy was changing. For reasons unknown, Llycaelon was bringing war to Aom-igh and they had recruited the services of Prince Elroy and his island nation, Roalthae, as a staging point from which to attack. There were many reasons this alliance was beneficial to Llcyaelon, and Elroy thought it a marvelous plan.

It was an even better plan, in Prince Elroy's opinion, since he did not have to put his own men in danger. The warriors of Llycaelon had made no attempt to hide their disdain when he had offered his knights to the cause. They simply and firmly informed him that they had no need of his assistance, other than the use of his island and ships from which to launch their attack. Elroy did not understand why King Seamas was so intent on conquering Aom-igh. The Dark Warrior, or rather "aethalon," which is the correct term for warriors from Llycaelon, who stood at his side and passed him information from King Seamas had told him very little. As far as Prince Elroy had been able to surmise, the King of Llycaelon believed that Aom-igh had either stolen something or was harboring a criminal or traitor and King

Seamas wanted it, him, or both returned. Elroy did not care about the motivations, all he knew was that King Seamas had no interest in ruling Aom-igh once he had retrieved the item or person he had lost. Prince Elroy had been promised the throne and wealth of Aom-igh in return for his allegiance. True, he could gain the throne through marriage to Princess Kamarie, but Llycaelon offered him the chance to seize power now, power that would not be shared. That thought appealed greatly to Prince Elroy.

Tobias, the aethalon assigned to watch over Prince Elroy, knew the ambitions swirling in the thoughts of this foolish young lord. He also knew that King Seamas had no intention of ruling Aom-igh once he achieved his own purpose. Promising the Kingship to the young prince cost him nothing. Tobias hunched his shoulders and an expression of misery haunted his face. He was among the few who really knew what King Seamas was seeking. Why was Seamas convinced that his treasure or prey was in Aom-igh? Who else could have known? Not for the first time, Tobias wondered how much the king truly knew and how much he guessed. At great peril to himself, Tobias had kept the truth from Seamas for nearly thirty years, and the king could not have failed to notice that his most trusted advisor and friend had somehow either been tricked or had been lying throughout time. Perhaps that was why he had been assigned to watch over Prince Elroy, far away from Llycaelon and his own people where he might have offered opposing counsel to this unprovoked invasion. Would his advice have made any difference with the King? Seamas had slowly surrounded himself with men who sought their own purposes, not the interests of Llycaelon, men of political ambition and false flattery who would not hesitate to twist the King's thoughts to their own advantage. Undoubtedly it was they who had convinced Seamas that Tobias was needed at Prince Elroy's side in far-distant Roalthae. Tobias shuddered. He had been trying to ignore it for years now, but he now knew, too late, that his king's sorrow, grief, and doubt had crossed over into madness. And now, when his king needed his advice and direction the most, Tobias had been sentenced to Roalthae, leaving Seamas at the mercy of these unscrupulous advisors. A sudden fear clutched Tobias by the heart. Perhaps... perhaps the king had not discovered his treachery on his own. In his unstable state, how could he? But the three men closest to him these days, they had resources, they had ambition, and they had no qualms in using the king's grief and jealousy to further their own ends. What if they had somehow discovered the secret Tobias kept from his King? What if they had told the king, playing on his madness, playing on the rage that would come in response to this new information? Not only had he been removed as chief advisor to the king, was he now to be portrayed as a traitor in order to justify this pointless and dishonorable war? Tobias hoped against this thought, but a voice in his heart whispered that it was so.

Iarrdek reappeared after a few minutes and stood before them. His tail was flicking back and forth like a cat's but he was otherwise rigidly still.

"Rhendak will ssee you now," the gryphon hissed.

Slowly, cautiously, the five of them walked through the entrance of the cave in front of them. Upon entering the cave, they were suddenly bombarded with light. They stood, blinking and raising their hands to shield their eyes. Even with their eyes covered, for a few moments it was very difficult to open their eyes for more than a second or two at a time. As their eyes adjusted and the five travelers were able to see again, they began to gaze about them in openmouthed wonder at their surroundings. Even Brant seemed to be a little taken by surprise, although he concealed it very well. The scene that met their eyes was spectacular.

This Great Hall was linear in shape, rather than curved, and its immenseness dwarfed any other space they had ever seen, above or below ground. The walls were covered in countless golden Ember Stones, the most rare and precious of all jewels.

In each corner was a huge, blazing fire that only multiplied the blinding light contained in the Great Hall. Perhaps not as bright as the Dragon's Eye, Kamarie thought, but certainly taking second place to nothing else.

Yole tugged on Kamarie's sleeve, and when she looked down at him to see what it was that he wanted, he could do nothing more than stare wordlessly at the sight in front of them. His eyes were large and round and glowed with fear. Kamarie followed his gaze with her eyes, and suddenly she felt as overawed as Yole looked.

Standing like sentries in two rows in front of them were giant creatures that could only be dragons. Though Brant had given them a brief description of what dragons looked like, his description fell far short of reality. These beasts were huge, far bigger than even Yole had expected, and he had expected them to be pretty big. They had powerful jaws and rows of golden, gleaming, sharp teeth. Their scaled shoulders and legs were well muscled and strong. Their scales were all different colors, but most of the dragons were red or gold. Some of the dragons, however, were different shades of green or silver and a very few even had a blueish tinge to their scales. They had large feet that arched up a little bit because of their long, strong claws which ended in slightly curved talons that were masterfully designed for slashing and tearing apart enemy or prey. Folded along their backs were large, powerfully built, leathery, wings of shining silver or bronze, varying with the color of each dragon.

Unsure as to what was expected, the travelers followed Dylanna's lead and walked past the rows of dragons. Awaiting them at the end of this gauntlet was Rhendak, King of the dragons. This dragon had to be the king. He was huge, larger than any other creature they had ever seen, with silvery green scales and silver wings. Hot steam surrounded him as he stared at them with unblinking, golden glowing eyes.

"Iarrdek told me of you," the booming voice erupting from Rhendak shook them as the sound echoed around the hall, reverberating off the walls and emblazoning the corner fires. "I want to hear your story from your mouths."

"King of the dragons, we salute you," Dylanna said smoothly, standing in front of the others.

She bowed, and her companions obediently followed suit.

"I am Dylanna, second-daughter of Scelwhyn," she said, and then motioned for the rest of them to introduce themselves.

"I am Princess Kamarie, daughter of King Arnaud and Queen Zara...uh, granddaughter of Scelwhyn," Kamarie stumbled through, adding the part about Scelwhyn because she really did not know what else to say.

"I am Oraeyn, knight of the realm," Oraeyn stretched the truth a bit, but he did not know what else to say either, and it seemed to be a good thing to add a title. *Perhaps dragons respect titles*, he thought.

"I am Yole, an orphan, and companion to these good people," Yole did not know where that had come from, but just saying his name seemed boring after the other introductions.

"I am Brant," Brant said simply.

The Dragon eyed each one of them carefully, and there was a sharp intake of breath when Brant introduced himself, then he spoke, "Some of your names are familiar to me. Iarrdek said that you claimed to be friends and that you had a message to deliver to none but me. I would hear that message now."

"Aom-igh is in danger," Kamarie said, speaking up before anyone else could. She was a princess after all, and it was her father's kingdom; she might as well be the one to explain. She took a deep breath and continued, "The Dark Country is once again threatening our existence. Roalthae has joined forces with the Dark Warriors and the status of our allies is uncertain. We are preparing for the worst, which is why we have come to you."

"Why come to usss? Let the humansss take care of themselves," the whisper did not come from Rhendak; it came from the sentries.

Kamarie whirled around, an angry flush rising in her cheeks. "I was told that dragons have long memories," she said loudly and clearly, "but perhaps now you only remember what you want to remember. I did not think that I would have to remind you of your promise but I see you now for what you are."

Kamarie felt a sudden, passionate fury rising up within her, and the sting of tears pushed at her eyes, but she forced it back. She wanted to beat her fists against the unfeeling creature, but she refused to allow herself to make a scene. She would not permit her emotions to show in front of these lizards; she was Princess of the realm, and as such she would act with dignity.

Rhendak's head came back and his golden eyes widened in disbelief as she spoke. When she had finished, he opened his mouth a bit, showing his teeth. Yole wanted to jump behind Kamarie in panic. Though he put up a brave front, these dragons filled him with an icy terror. The fear of these huge, dazzling creatures welled up within him as if to choke him, but then a sound came from deep within the King of the dragons; it was a rumble that grew into a full-fledged roar. Rhendak was laughing!

"I like your spirit," he said when he had stopped laughing, "not many people in your position, standing in our Hall, miles underground, outnumbered and surrounded by creatures that you have probably only seen in unflattering pictures and who could easily rip you into shreds without thinking about it, would have the audacity to yell at us. And yet, you are right as well. The dragons did make a promise, years ago, to King Llian. We promised that we would not hesitate to help if the Dark Country ever threatened again.

"However, that promise was made in Graldon's time, not ours. And it was made over six hundred years ago. Things have changed drastically since then, things that my predecessor could not have foreseen. Therefore, I cannot say at this moment whether or not we will or can help. This is a matter for the Council of Elders."

Kamarie slumped a little, dejected and disappointed.

"You will be given a room to stay in while we hold council," Rhendak said in his booming voice as he nodded to Iarrdek.

The tone of his voice clearly said that he was done, and that they should leave. Iarrdek approached and motioned for them to follow. Leaving the Great Hall was a little anticlimactic, Kamarie thought to herself. She had gone before Rhendak full of hopes and dreams of the dragons rallying behind her and the others, all ready to go charging up into the light of day to turn away the evils of the Dark Country; but now she was leaving without even a glimmer of hope. She had seen the looks of distrust, she had heard the whispers of the sentries, and she knew that all the creatures down here hated her and all that she stood for. She felt even more deeply than ever that she and her friends did not belong down here. This maze was for non-humans only, it was off limits, a place they had trespassed upon from sheer desperation; and now they were being turned away.

"This whole trip was a waste of time," Oraeyn muttered under his breath, and Kamarie heard her own thoughts echoed in his words.

Iarrdek led them to a decent-sized room. There were some large couches and chairs that looked like they would have been the right size for a gryphon in the room. There were also large bowls of water and some enormous plates of fruit and vegetables.

"Iarrdek," Dylanna said before the gryphon could leave, "what did Rhendak mean when he said that things have changed?"

Iarrdek hesitated for a moment, and then he replied, choosing his words carefully, "At first, when the dragons and the other creatures such as myself retreated down here to the tunnels, it seemed like a good idea. We were no longer hunted, and we lived in harmony. It seemed as though we had found the perfect solution. But as the years passed, something has been happening that we have no control over."

He paused as if debating with himself, then continued, "Our numbers grow smaller each year. Not just the dragons, but all of us. Our elders are sickly and dying, and not many younglings are born to any species. Even the younger dragons have been dying.

We do not know why this is or how to stop it. But there are very few of us now." Iarrdek stopped suddenly. "I do not know if I ought to be telling you this…." He bobbed his head in uncertainty, and then quickly exited the room.

Oraeyn looked to Brant and Dylanna. "They are dying? Why?"

Brant had a dark look on his face, and Dylanna shrugged.

"Brant?" Kamarie asked quietly, "What's wrong?"

He looked at Kamarie; she was so young, too young to be bearing all the weight that she took upon herself. Oraeyn too, and yet they had each borne their share of the load willingly, uncomplaining. They had come all this way to save their country, they had come knowing that the quest was all but hopeless, and yet they had come anyway. Brant shivered inside, *I was that young once, and I was also too young for the load that I bore, too young for the burden that I have carried for so long.* Some memories surfaced and he tried to push them down, realizing that the others were waiting for an answer.

"Nothing is wrong," he said in the same gentle, reassuring voice that he had always used when his daughter Kali had picked up on one of his darker moods, "I was just trying to figure out what has been responsible for all the deaths that Iarrdek spoke of."

They pondered this question in silence for a while, but none of them was able to think very clearly. Without realizing it, they had been traveling for two days straight without rest. Now, as their weariness caught up to them, one by one they drifted into a deep and dreamless sleep.

As the restriction ship sent by Arnaud drew closer, the foreign ship threw up the white flag almost immediately. With a certain wary caution, the Knights of Aom-igh boarded the ship from Iolanver. What they found was definitely not what they had been expecting.

The ship had very obviously seen its better days. The mast was crooked, the sails were tattered, and the hold was leaking. The deck was covered in trash and there was an air of death about the ship.

The crew of the vessel was unexpected. Instead of grim, fearsome warriors, the crew was a motley bunch. They were not all from Iolanver. They were men, women, and children from all islands in the chain, with the exception of Roalthae. They were ragged and had not eaten in over a week. Their clothes hung from them in tatters, and not one of them looked clean. They stared at the soldiers in fear, but there was a glimmer of hope in their wide, staring, hungry eyes as the soldiers began to attend to their needs.

The vessel was guided in to shore and arrangements were made to care for these newly arrived refugees. Fear permeated all movement, but there was that constant light of hope within each of their eyes.

CHAPTER
NINE

King Arnaud paced back and forth across the room. Pacing was something that he had never used to do. He found now that it helped him think more clearly, and so he continued pacing. He was thinking about the message he had received regarding the vessel from Iolanver. The meaning was unclear, and that disturbed him.

The ship boasted no crew, but only a full passenger list of exhausted, starving families. Arnaud did not know what he was going to do. He could not trust anyone, could not allow foreigners, potential enemies, to roam freely in his kingdom. He decided that he could do nothing more than wait for these people to be brought before him, no decisions could be made before he at least listened to their story.

The group before him was a larger one than he had expected, perhaps two hundred in total. They looked as described, which could be remedied with food and rest. They were worn, but not beaten.

A young man stepped forward and tried to spread his arms in a gesture that said they did not mean any harm. Unfortunately, he was not able to do so because his arms were still tied behind his back. He grinned ruefully and dropped to his knees before Arnaud. He looked up meekly and Arnaud was struck by the hope that was in the man's eyes.

"What is your story?" King Arnaud asked.

"Your Majesty, as you can tell, we are not all from Iolanver. However, we all believe the same thing. The families with me are loyal to Aom-igh. We have seen what is happening in Roalthae and we are against it. Prince Elroy has broken his alliance with Aom-igh and is prepared to commit great treachery against those who would call him friend. He will not stop with Aom-igh, but will continue until all the Barrier Islands are under his rule. We would see him stopped, and we pledge our service to you, Sire, in order to safeguard freedom for our own lands."

"How can I trust you?" King Arnaud asked.

The man kneeling before him shook his head. "We have nothing to gain, and everything to lose by bringing our families to your shores, were treachery our purpose."

Arnaud pondered. He took in the looks of hope on the faces of the women and the older children. He took in the words of the man kneeling on the hard stone floor. He took in the desperation in the eyes of the other men. At length, he nodded.

"No, I can see that. Garen, see to their needs and receive their bond of allegiance. Their valor now and loyalty beyond is a most welcome gift, one we can ill-affored to refuse. Safeguard these families and equip the men for the battle to come."

One of the women gasped in relief and burst into tears, obviously frightening the small child she held in her arms. The baby began to wail and the mother choked back her tears, a tiny smile on her face as she comforted the child. The man kneeling on the floor bowed his head and tears of gratitude fell from his eyes, splashing a little on the stones beneath him.

"Thank you, Your Majesty. It will be our honor to fight alongside such a man of compassion as yourself."

Arnaud reached down and helped the soldier to his feet. "The honor and responsibility is mine, young man, to command the devotion and loyalty you have laid before me. My fear of the battle ahead has been diminished by your gift this day. Garen, proceed quickly." Arnaud left the room and for the first time in many weeks, he was reminded that, occasionally, it was good to be the king.

The travelers slept for a long time, much longer than they intended. There was something about the air in the underground realm of Krayghentaliss, maybe it was the smell of old magic, or perhaps it was because they had not really slept in over two days, but for whatever reason, they slept long and soundly. Later, they all agreed that they had never had a better night's sleep than the night they spent in the realm of the myth-folk.

Brant was the first to wake; he rubbed his eyes and wondered what had woken him. Then he froze. He suddenly realized how deeply he had slept, that his guard had been completely down. Anyone could have come in and killed them all, and he would not have woken to stop it. He quickly glanced around, taking in his surroundings and making sure that Kamarie, Oraeyn, Yole, and Dylanna were all still there. They were, and he relaxed, or, at least, he relaxed as much as he could. Brant was a coiled spring at all times. He was very disconcerted at having slept so well and so long. He wondered about the food that they had been given right before they fell asleep, perhaps something had been added to it to make them sleep longer so as to give the Dragon Council more time to discuss what was to be done about the above-worlders' request.

Slowly, the others woke, stretching and yawning. As most people did not keep an internal clock as accurately as Brant did, no one else realized just how long they had slept. Brant did not care to alert them to it either; he realized it would do no good since they could not change what had happened now, and he also realized it would only serve to upset Kamarie.

A few minutes after they were all awake, a creature stuck its head in through the door. Seeing that they were alert, it entered the room.

"Good, you are awake," the creature said. "I am here to serve you breakfast."

Brant studied it warily. "Is there anything magical in our food?"

The creature looked hurt. "Of course not."

Kamarie had been staring, quite unabashedly at the figure before them. It was the most beautiful thing she had ever seen. It was a horse, but such a horse! The creature was silvery black, almost blue-black, and it had wide, intelligent eyes. The creature appeared powerful and delicate all at the same time. But the most amazing part was that she had wings protruding from her back: great, large, glossy black wings like an eagle's with very fine and intricate feathers. They were folded along her back, but Kamarie could envision that when those wings were spread it would make the horse look very fierce indeed.

"What are you?" Yole breathed in wonder.

"I am a pegasus," the creature laughed a little at the boy's wide-eyed gaze of astonishment.

"What is your name?" Oraeyn asked.

"Rhynellewhyn," the pegasus answered, "but now is not the time for talking, now is the time for eating, and as soon as you are finished with your breakfast, I have been instructed to bring you before King Rhendak and the Elders." As the travelers started to rush through their meal, Rhynellewhyn said, "There is no need to rush. Dragons are a patient race. They made their decision two days ago."

"Two days ago!" Kamarie raised her voice in disbelief. "How long did we sleep?"

"You slept through three nights and two days, it is the third day since you first appeared before King Rhendak."

"But, anything could be happening up in Aom-igh!" Kamarie exclaimed. "We've been down here for far too long!"

"You needed the rest," Rhynellewhyn replied, "and Rhendak sent a scout up to see what was happening above-realm."

"What is happening? Has the Dark Country come?" Dylanna asked in concern.

"Well, perhaps not in the way that you mean. But there are many, smaller groups of, as you say, Dark Warriors, throughout Aom-igh. From all sides, they are approaching the capital city, except from the side they are expected. It will be many days before a concerted attack could occur, but the war is indeed underway."

"We have to leave as soon as possible," Kamarie said.

"Eat first," Rhynellewhyn ordered.

When they had finished their breakfast, which would have been delicious had they not been so distressed, Rhynellewhyn led them back to the Great Hall where Rhendak and the Elders awaited. The Hall was different from the way any of them remembered. There was no intimidating line of sentries this time, just a few dragons before them. Oraeyn guessed that they were the Elders. The fires were still burning, but not quite as brightly as they had been before. As they approached, Rhendak beckoned with a huge claw and the travelers edged forward.

"We have decided," Rhendak's voice was again startling, it was so loud.

Just then, the Dragon King shook his head in surprise and he looked directly at Yole; his eyes darkened. "Come here, youngling Yole."

Yole stared back and forth from Kamarie to Oraeyn, his amber eyes wide with fear and confusion. Then his face took on a resigned look, he took a deep breath, and he stepped forward to confront the King of the dragons.

"Yes, Y-your Majesty?" Yole said, his voice only trembling once.

Rhendak looked at the boy who was trying so hard not to tremble in fear. He leaned forward until his snout was only inches from Yole's. Yole flinched slightly and closed his eyes tightly, screwing his face up, but other than that he did not move or back away. Kamarie and Oraeyn both watched in admiration of Yole's courage.

Rhendak lifted his head up and let out a short laugh. "I am not going to *eat* you, boy."

Yole opened his eyes one at a time and allowed his face to relax from its scrunched up position. "You're not?" His voice said that he did not believe the dragon's words.

The King of the dragons shook his head. "No, I merely noticed something about you that somehow escaped my attention the first time you and your friends came before me, although I do not know how." The dragon's voice lowered and he sounded puzzled.

"You noticed something about *me?*" Yole asked timidly, then, choosing his next words cautiously, he asked suspiciously, "What did you notice?"

"You, young Yole, are one of our Lost."

Dylanna's head shot up in surprise at these words. Kamarie and Oraeyn exchanged questioning looks, completely confused by Rhendak's words. Only Brant remained unfazed by what Rhendak had revealed. He stood as silent and as still as the cavern walls. Anyone looking closely would have seen the ghost of a smile flit through his stormy dark eyes; no one, however, was watching Brant.

"Lost what?" Yole's voice was quiet and more than a little afraid.

Rhendak's head came up, and the other dragons began muttering in surprise.

"Hhhee doessn't know!" The whispered voices hissed, echoing around the room.

"You don't know?" Rhendak asked in what appeared to be utter shock.

"Should I?" Yole asked, shaking his head in bewildered confusion, his eyes were worried and upset.

"You are one of us, a lost dragon," Rhendak said kindly.

Yole stared in uncomprehending silence; he suddenly found that he could not speak. His mouth was dry and he had a burning sensation at the back of his throat. He made a gasping sound and managed to choke out a mangled, "What?" before he started to sway. As the meaning in Rhendak's words began to sink in, Yole's face turned paler than the sand in Pearl Cove and he stumbled backwards. Brant stepped forward and reached out a hand to steady the boy before he tripped or fell to the ground.

"No, he really did not know that he is a dragon," Brant confirmed it. "I did not realize he was unaware."

"You knew?" Dylanna asked.

Brant nodded, offering no further explanation.

"How…?" Kamarie began, but then she stopped as she began to connect conversations and events, she continued, thinking out loud, "Every time he got kicked out of places and did not know why… but… he *looks* human enough."

"It is called shape-shifting," Rhendak offered. Kamarie jumped, she had almost forgotten that he was there.

"Shape-shifting?" Oraeyn asked.

"Dragons are the oldest and most powerful of all the beings in the realm; therefore, we know the art of shape-shifting, or, to put it simply, the art of taking on a different form," Rhendak explained. "When we went below ground to come and live in Krayghentaliss, some of the dragons did not want to come with us, so they chose to shape-shift to human form and remain above-realm. We called them the 'lost.' Yole is one of ours who was born above-realm and was never told of his true identity. Of course, since he did not know, neither did he have any control over his power to shape-shift, and when he did shape-shift to appear in his true form, my guess is that he would only remember it as if it had been a dream."

Yole had recovered enough to comprehend what Rhendak was saying, and he spoke, "My flying dreams! They were real?"

Rhendak nodded. "Welcome home."

Yole seemed to steady himself and he stood a little straighter. His face was still pale, and Brant kept his hand on the boy's shoulder to help support him.

"Now you have a choice, Yole," Rhendak said, "you can stay here with us and learn how to shape-shift to your true form…"

Yole cut him off, "No! I want to stay with my friends."

"As I said, you can make that choice, now that you know who you are," Rhendak said.

Just then, Kamarie caught the implication in his words. "You're not going to help us!" she cried out in distress, forgetting her promise to herself not to make a scene.

Rhendak eyed her sternly. "I did not say that we were not going to help you."

"But you gave Yole a choice, to stay down here with you or to go back with us, that sounds like you're not coming to help us! What about your promise? I don't understand!"

"LET ME FINISH, CHILD!" Rhendak roared. The room resounded with his voice, shaking Kamarie's confidence. He paused, letting the echoes die, then he continued, "No, we are not going to come above-realm with you and drive the enemy away by sheer force. The Elders and myself have decided that we cannot do that, we have too many problems down here of our own. But, we will give you this," Rhendak produced a silvery-green set of shepherd's pipes.

Yole gasped in awe and gazed at the beautiful pipes with a deep longing in his amber eyes. Oraeyn suddenly felt his sword hum, he jumped and put his hand on the hilt, trying to make it stop, but it was too late. Rhendak looked straight at him and there was a curious glint in his eyes, and then he nodded but said nothing.

"What does that do?" Kamarie asked, sounding somewhat abashed and properly chastised at the rebuke.

Rhendak looked at her kindly in a way that said he did not hold her hasty words against her. "It is a call," he said, "if, during the battle, you should need their magic, then blow on the pipes. Do not worry about what melody to use, the instrument will choose its own, and the help you seek will be found, either from within or without, depending on the need."

Kamarie's face turned sober as she took the pipes Rhendak handed to her and then she gave them to Dylanna for safekeeping. She was grateful, but she was also more than a little discouraged. She had found the dragons, not an easy feat, and they were not coming to help. They were going to remain underground. They were fulfilling their promise, not by rushing to their aid and breathing fire down their enemies' throats, but rather by giving them another trinket.

"If I recall correctly, the last time the Dark Country invaded, the humans stopped it all by themselves, with the help of a special gift." Rhendak stared straight at Oraeyn as he said this, but no one else seemed to notice.

Oraeyn shifted uncomfortably under the piercing gaze. The dragon seemed to be waiting for him to offer some explanation for the sword he carried at his side. Oraeyn wished that he could give some reasonable explanation, but he realized that he had none, other than the explanation staring him in the face, which was one he could not, or would not, yet believe. Rhendak understood the silence and pressed no further. He nodded once, indicating their interview was ended.

"Thank you for your generous gift," Dylanna said, "and for your hospitality."

Rhendak bowed his head and looked straight into Dylanna's eyes, recalling an old friend. "You are welcome any time," he said graciously, then he turned directly to Brant and took the full measure of the man and added, "you are needed above-realm, Iarrdek will take you to the exit you desire."

The travelers thanked the King of the dragons again and left the Great Hall. On their way out they said good-bye to Rhynellewhyn. She seemed to be sad that they were leaving and wished them good-bye softly.

"I hope we will meet again," Kamarie said, wishing she could have gotten to know the pegasus a little better.

"I hope so too," Rhynellewhyn said; then with a shake of her head, she galloped up a tunnel and out of sight.

Iarrdek appeared from a side tunnel and stood before them, looking happy to see them again. "Where would you like to go?"

"Well, we have to get our horses at some point," Kamarie said, thinking hard, "but we should also get back to the castle, we might be needed. I hate to leave Tor, though."

"Queen Zara asked me to find her sister in the Harshlands and request her help," Brant said.

"She did?" Dylanna asked. "She said nothing to me about it."

Kamarie frowned. "I'd love to see Aunt Leila again, and if she's a wizardess I can understand why Mother wants us to ask her for help, but can't you contact her with magic or something?"

Dylanna shook her head. "Not from here, and your mother is out of practice. I'm sure she tried."

Iarrdek spoke, interrupting Kamarie's reply. "If I could offer some advice: the place where you *think* you are needed the most, is, more often than not, the place where you are needed the least."

Kamarie brightened. "Well that's simple enough," she exclaimed, "I think that my parents need me to warn them, but they probably already know about the danger. So, in all likelihood, we are not needed at the castle as much as we might be needed somewhere else."

She looked to Iarrdek to see if she had solved his riddle correctly, but he merely inclined his head and asked, "So, which exit?"

"We would like to go back to Pearl Cove, if that is possible," Dylanna said, very decisively.

"Then to Pearl Cove it is," Iarrdek said, "but the journey is two days, at the least."

Kamarie gave a resigned sigh, and they followed after Iarrdek quietly.

The darkness was coming, and she could not stop it. Calyssia sat atop the bluff on the edge of her domain and stared out to sea. The Soothing Sea was rolling peacefully and whispering to itself. It looked so beautiful that it made Calyssia's heart ache. She knew she would return there, soon. Her strength was failing her, and the weakness that crept through her body made it necessary for her to spend much of each day sitting still. Walking from one end of the Cove to the other was now a feat that caused her to become short of breath and she found herself stumbling after only a few steps.

She looked young and frail, sitting upon the dune. She had her knees tucked up under her chin, and her delicate white hands were clasped around her legs. Her pale green eyes had a far away look in them, and her long blond hair was blowing gently in the breeze.

"Milady?" a deep voice asked timidly from behind her.

Calyssia turned and looked at the man, "Yes, Wessel?" She sighed involuntarily.

"The enemy is coming here?"

She studied him, he had been one of those who had come seeking glory, and yet he had chosen to stay and remain un-honored, deciding that peace was more to be prized than fame. She wondered what would become of them all. She cared deeply for each one of the men and women who had come to her home. But those who had come were not timid, skulking creatures; they were strong, and they all knew the joy of hard work completed together. If she ceased to be, if the Pearl Cove ceased to exist, she was confident they would be able to take care of themselves.

"Yes, Wessel, they are coming, they are coming, woe to us all."

"You can't stop them." It was really more of a statement than a question, but Calyssia answered it anyway.

"No, I cannot stop them."

"So what will happen to us?"

"I do not know," Calyssia said truthfully. "I must rejoin the sea. You and your companions have a little time. If you run, you will survive and build new lives for yourselves and others.

Perhaps you will be the ones to change Aom-igh, to teach the others what I have taught you."

"Milady?"

"Or perhaps the outside world has something to teach you."

"I see."

They lapsed into a silent camaraderie. The two of them, so different, sitting amiably upon the dune-top; the tall, pale woman who looked as though a stronger breeze might carry her away, and the short, sturdy man, darkened by hard work in the heat of the Dragon's Eye. They sat together until the Eye had passed overhead and disappeared behind the horizon. The twinkling stars began to peer out of the dark expanse of sky, and the waves far below them rolled and broke on the rocks. The slight breeze carried a fine mist up to Calyssia and Wessel from the breaking waves. The tiny droplets of water bathed their faces. Calyssia breathed deeply of the salt smell of the ocean, and she smiled, content to sit in silence.

"You are dying," Wessel said, sadness in his voice. "That is why you cannot stop them."

Calyssia said nothing.

"The barrier that protects us?"

"Will fail before the morning, it is all I can give you, my strength is gone, my magic is already fading."

"Nothing will be left?"

"I do not know. My life, my strength, they are tied into the magic. I do not know how to make the barrier stand on its own."

"Is there anything we can do for you?"

Calyssia smiled. "Fight. Live. Do not mourn for me, for I am going to the sea."

Another long silence stretched between then. Finally, Wessel stood, "I will go and tell the others to make ready."

"Tell them not to fear, and tell them to stand together," Calyssia said, her voice seeming to echo the sounds of the rolling sea.

Wessel bowed slightly and turned to go. There was all the deep sorrow of farewell within her words, and he found himself blinking back tears. She was here with them still, but he knew that in her heart, their Great Lady had already left them and the Cove far behind. He did not know how the Cove People would manage without her, they had all come to love the Keeper, and now she would be leaving them.

Calyssia could hear the footsteps in the sand as he left, and she blinked back the tears that sprang to her eyes. The wanderer had come and his coming heralded the end of the Cove. But the secret that Calyssia carried with her was this: she was older than her years. Maintaining the Cove had drained her of strength and life, what life she had left when Graldon passed. She had begun to die long before, even had the wanderer not arrived, even had this enemy never threatened their shores, Calyssia could no longer hold up the barrier. She had hours, perhaps a day, and then her strength would leave her completely and she would die. Although she dreaded the alternative, it was the only one left to her. Her mother's people... the stories her father had told her of that cold, uncaring folk sent chills up her spine, but perhaps... just perhaps... she set her face towards the sea. She had no wish to die.

With heavy heart and strong resolve, Wessel brought news to the inhabitants of Pearl Cove. The Lady was leaving, the darkness was coming, and they had to ready themselves for war.

The travelers stopped to sleep for the night. Now that they had a guide, in the form of Iarrdek, they also had someone along who was able to tell them whether it was day or night, and when it was time to stop or sleep. They did not have any idea how the gryphon could keep track of the position of the Dragon's Eye from underground, but no one could argue with him about it either.

They had been traveling at a slower pace than before and had more time to notice and study their surroundings. As the novelty and frightfulness of the tunnels wore off, it was easier to see and understand how the myth-folk were able to find their way around. There were many subtle differences between the tunnels and the caves that they passed through, and at each junction of tunnels, there seemed to be directions etched into the rock floor and filled with glowing ember stones. Iarrdek explained that these maps were relatively easy to follow if one knew how to read them; he also told them that he personally had most of the tunnels memorized, and therefore did not need to even bother with the maps anymore.

As they unrolled their blankets and got ready to bed down for the night, not much was said. Each of them was wrapped up in their own thoughts, and all of them were anxious to see daylight again. Oraeyn was surprised at how easy it was to get tired in these tunnels, and he wondered briefly if it had anything to do with the lack of air circulation or the absence of light from the Dragon's Eye. As these thoughts passed through his head, something tickled at the back of his mind, something that was important, something that he ought to remember. He did not ponder it for very long, however, since he was asleep almost the instant that he laid down.

Iarrdek allowed them to sleep for a few hours, and then he woke them up again. He was very impressed by the man, Brant, though he did not comment on it. No sooner had Iarrdek lifted his head from his great paws than Brant had been on his feet, fully alert. The others woke fairly quickly as well, except for Yole. Dragon though he was, Yole was also very much a young boy, and convincing him that it was time to get up proved to take some doing. Finally, they were all awake and alert. Iarrdek provided them with food. Then they were on their way once more, traveling through the huge, continuous tunnels.

Oraeyn was more restless than ever. He kept an eye on Brant, trying to imitate the man's easy stride and appearance of infinite patience. Ever since the occurrence with the Dark Warrior in the hayloft, Brant had become Oraeyn's hero. He tried, as subtly as he could, to imitate the man's every move. It was more difficult than Brant made it look, to saunter lazily along appearing as though he had absolutely nothing better to do, especially when he was so anxious to do something, anything, other than continue wandering around underground. He longed for a challenge, a break of pace. He wanted nothing more than to escape from this never-ending pattern of sleeping, eating, and walking: endless walking.

Kamarie's thoughts lay along a similar path as Oraeyn's. In a desperate attempt to break the monotony of their journey, Kamarie suddenly began singing. The tune was light and cheerful and familiar. It was a children's song with an easy tune to follow. As soon as she began singing, Yole joined her, and within moments, they were all singing along, even Iarrdek.

Cheerily we all dance
Beneath the Dragon's Eye
Me and you together:
Children of Aom-igh.

Come circle round
And dance with us.

We work hard together
Joining to forge ahead
Toiling till Toreth-rise
And then we rest our heads.

Come circle round
And dance with me.

Come dance the dance
Of our fair land
Come join your hearts,
Come join your hands.

Come circle round
And dance with me,

Enter our dance
Come join your hands.

The music had the desired affect upon the group; it lightened their hearts. There was a spring in their step as they walked along, singing cheerfully. For a little while they were able to forget that they were miles underground, they forgot there was a war brewing in Aom-igh, forgot the dragons had declined to give them the help that they needed. Instead they dreamed of green grass and tall trees, of farmers tilling their fields and soldiers practicing their swordsmanship. They were even able to feel the wind on their faces and hear birds chirping around them.

Suddenly Brant broke the cheerful mood by stopping short and putting up a hand. "Listen!"

The others stopped singing and strained their ears to listen for the sound Brant had heard. For a moment, they heard nothing, and then their ears picked up the faint sound of a quick and steady hoofed animal following them at a very fast pace. Kamarie wondered how Brant had heard the faint sound with all of them singing.

"Someone is trying to catch up with us," Iarrdek muttered. "We will wait for them."

They waited, tension and questions growing as the hoof-beats came nearer. Soon they could make out the figure of the creature that was following them; it was a pegasus.

"Rhynellewhyn!" Kamarie exclaimed, recognizing the gentle animal first.

"Kamarie, all of you!" Rhynellewhyn gasped, slightly out of breath. "Something terrible has happened and some have pointed the finger of blame on you. I came to warn you as quickly as I could. You are in great danger!"

"Slow down, take a deep breath, what has happened?" Iarrdek asked.

Rhynellewhyn did as Iarrdek suggested and started over, "Shortly after you left, Shalintess was killed."

Iarrdek stared at her. "What?"

"Who is Shalintess?" Oraeyn asked.

"How do you know she was killed and it wasn't a natural death?" Brant asked sharply.

"Who is blaming us for what?" Yole demanded, referring to the first thing that Rhynellewhyn had said.

Rhynellewhyn swung her head back and forth between the questions. A wild look was in her normally quiet, calm eyes. Kamarie stayed silent, and then she went up and put a soothing hand on the creature's neck.

She spoke softly. "All right, Shalintess has been killed. Who is Shalintess?"

At Kamarie's voice, Rhynellewhyn calmed down visibly. "Shalintess was Rhendak's mate."

"And how do you know she was killed?" Kamarie asked.

"She was cut with a sword, although what sword could do that, no one knows."

"And there are some who are blaming us for this?" Kamarie questioned.

Rhynellewhyn nodded. "Rhendak suspects that this was done by a Dark Warrior, and many Elders believe you led him down here. Oh, not on purpose," Rhynellewhyn added hastily, seeing the looks of outrage on their faces. "But you spoke of Dark Warriors attacking Aom-igh, so naturally some concluded that they may have followed you."

"They did not follow us," Brant said firmly. "We came through the Pearl Cove, and to follow us was simply not possible. If it was a Dark Warrior, he found his own way."

"*I* don't think that you are the reason there was a Dark Warrior down here," Rhynellewhyn said quickly. "I think they would have found Krayghentaliss eventually anyway. But the others..." she trailed off, shaking her head.

"Thank you for your warning, Rhynellewhyn," Oraeyn offered. "Shouldn't we get going?"

"Wait, before you go, I wanted to see if..." Rhynellewhyn stopped, looking embarrassed.

"To see if?" Kamarie urged.

"To see if I might travel with you," Rhynellewhyn said, then added, "Please! I can be of so much help, and it has been so long since I was above-realm."

Brant looked hard at the pegasus. "No."

Rhynellewhyn looked hurt. "But I want to help."

Brant was unmoved. "No, you cannot travel with us."

"But why?" Kamarie exploded. "Why can't she come with us?"

Brant did not answer, and Dylanna looked at him sharply. "Why not, Brant?"

Brant frowned. "Have I not yet earned your trust? I have to explain every single thing before you realize that I am right," he shook his head and sighed.

Rhynellewhyn started backing away slowly, a cautious look in her blue eyes. Brant watched her with an unreadable expression on his face. Rhynellewhyn looked away, unable to meet his piercing gaze.

After a long moment, Brant spoke again, "Liars are not welcome companions."

"What?" Kamarie cried. "You think she is making up this story about Rhendak's mate being killed by a Dark Warrior?"

"I cannot say anything about Shalintess, but I know for certain this pegasus is lying to us about who...."

Before he could finish his statement, Rhynellewhyn reared up and her blue eyes flashed gold. She neighed a challenge and her voice deepened into a roar. Brant was instantly on guard. He stood in a fighter's crouch with his sword drawn and ready. Oraeyn put his hand on the hilt of his sword, but he did not draw it.

Kamarie stared at the normally gentle Pegasus in confusion, "Rhyn..." she began.

Brant cut her off, finishing his comment with quiet calm. "The reason we cannot take Rhynellewhyn along is because *that* is not Rhynellewhyn."

As Brant spoke, Rhynellewhyn's edges seemed to blur; then, suddenly before them stood a great, red dragon with gold wings.

The creature took up most of the tunnel and blocked their path. Kamarie gasped and drew her own sword, but the gesture was more of a reaction than a motion with any intent behind it.

"Iarrdek, what's going on?" Yole asked, turning towards the gryphon, then he yelped in fear.

They all spun around to find that the gryphon was gone, replaced by a smaller, gold-colored dragon. A short spurt of flame appeared from its mouth as it bared its teeth.

"You are tresspasserss here," the red dragon said fiercely, "you have brought arguments and trouble among usss."

"Tread warily, I warn you," Dylanna said. "We have the protection of your king upon us."

"Rhendak iss a fool!" the gold dragon spat.

"He is still your king!"

"Ssilence!" the red dragon roared in anger. "Rhendak made the decision to give you the pipes without our consssssent, the vote was not unanimouss. We are here to make sure that you do not leave with the pipes, our voicesss will be heard!"

"You killed Shalintess," Brant stated.

The smaller, gold dragon barked out a laugh. "Yess," he hissed.

"Sssilence!" The red dragon thundered. "Do not tell them everything!"

The gold dragon spat flame in defiance. "They will ssoon be too dead to repeat anything that they hhhear."

Kamarie felt a shudder of fear thrill through her. She looked at the huge, powerful creatures and knew that they could never escape.

The red dragon smiled, a very disconcerting sight; all his teeth showed. "True," he said, "very true."

The gold dragon shifted, looking a little uncomfortable now. "Do you really think that we ought to…?"

The red dragon cut him off, "Yess! Do not back out on me now! We have come too far to turn back." Then he fixed the travelers with a gold-eyed glare, "Thisss will be fun."

Suddenly, the red dragon lunged, making a swipe at Brant with his huge right claw. At the same instant, Brant sprang, twisting, into the air, causing the dragon's maneuver to pass harmlessly beneath him. As he jumped, he brought his sword down in an arcing counterattack. The blade hit the scales of the dragon's arm and made a loud, screeching sound, throwing off sparks, but the blade bounced off the scales without causing any damage. The great red beast let out a roar of laughter.

"Your flimsy blade of steel cannot touch *me!*" he boasted.

Dylanna grabbed Kamarie and Yole and pulled them out of the tunnel and into a side passage. She pushed them behind her and wove a pattern in the air with her hands, creating a shield across the mouth of the passage. The gold dragon remained still, uncertain about what he should do. He looked at the red dragon, the obvious leader of this endeavor. Seeing that he would get no help or direction from there, he turned and began blasting flames at Dylanna's shield. Kamarie felt that she had never been so terrified in her life as the gold flames leaped towards her only to hover a few feet in front of her face.

"Can he get through?" she asked.

Dylanna's face was tight. "Only if his strength outlasts my own."

The red dragon lashed his tail around at Brant from the right, but this time Brant was ready. He dropped backwards until he was nearly sitting down. The end of the deadly tail whipped by him, then Brant suddenly changed directions. He lunged forward and twisted the blade of his sword so that it slid in sideways between the dragon's scales. The dragon roared in pain and jerked back violently, throwing Brant off balance as he struggled to maintain his grip on the hilt of his sword.

With almost lightning fast reflexes, the dragon swiped with his left claw. Since Brant was already falling, he made a split-second decision and allowed himself to continue in that direction. He landed on his stomach and rolled out of the way as the dragon's claw passed over him inches above where his head had been. This time, however, the attack was not harmless, the dragon's swipe caught Oraeyn, who had leaped towards Brant as the older warrior fell, slicing into his right shoulder.

Oraeyn gasped in pain as blood spurted from the shallow cut. He stumbled back and pressed his left hand to the wound in order to staunch the flow. Then, gritting his teeth, he drew his sword, ignoring the pain that shot up and down his arm as he did so.

The Fang Blade, as Rhendak had called it, seemed to almost spring out of its sheath and into Oraeyn's hand. This time, as the dragon struck out, it was Oraeyn's sword that went singing through the air. The sword hit its mark as he swung it up to block the blow. But instead of bouncing harmlessly off of the armored scales as Oraeyn expected it to, the sword cleaved almost completely through the arm. The red dragon howled and lashed out again with his tail. This time Oraeyn put all the force of his arm into the swing and sliced through the end of the beast's tail.

The dragon roared again in hurt and fury, but now he backed away slowly, looking wary. Brant was up again, and the two now stood back to back, facing the two dragons. Oraeyn noticed that Kamarie, Dylanna, and Yole had slipped away to safety and that the gold dragon was clawing and throwing flames at some sort of invisible shield that kept him from reaching his prey.

"Mystak," the red dragon roared, "they have the Fang Blade, we cannot stand against them. Let us leave now while we still can!"

"NO!" Mystak screamed between flame bursts. "They know too much! We cannot allow them to escape with their lives!"

The red dragon responded, "They will never find their way out without a guide, they will wander around lost in Krayghentaliss until they run out of food and die of ssstarvation! Let usss leave!"

The gold dragon hesitated for a moment, then gave a short nod and retreated. He threw an angry look at the wizardess, and then he and the red dragon, who was holding his right claw close to his body, turned and fled down the tunnels the way they had come. As they disappeared into the darkness of the tunnels Dylanna let down her shield and she, Kamarie, and Yole cautiously stepped out into the main tunnel.

Kamarie noticed Oraeyn's cut and frowned in instant concern at the blood seeping through Oraeyn's fingers.

"Are you all right?" she asked. "Does it hurt?"

Oraeyn grimaced a bit, and rotated his arm, then he flinched and covered it with his left hand again as the blood, that had nearly been staunched, began to flow once more. He took the opportunity to show off a little.

"It's not deep, but it stings like anything," he said lightly, shrugging to show that he did not care about the pain, even though it was taking all his resolve to stand without swaying.

"Sit down and let me see to that," Kamarie ordered.

She pulled a clean strip of cloth out of the small pouch on her belt and tied it around Oraeyn's arm. He winced a little as she tightened the knot, but did not say anything.

"I'll be all right," he said. Then he stretched the truth again, "It doesn't even hurt anymore."

Kamarie smiled at him. Dylanna gave Brant a look that was somewhere between a smile of gratitude and a glare. He ignored her, and her scowl deepened.

"How did you know?" she demanded, when she found that her glare would get no response.

Brant shrugged and said nothing. Dylanna's brown eyes flashed and she clenched her fists in irritation.

"I did not know that those two were dragons, their magic is stronger than mine. I want to know how you knew!"

Brant fixed her with his dark-eyed gaze. For a moment, they matched glares. Dylanna's eyes were flashing with unchecked anger, and Brant's eyes were dark and expressionless. Suddenly, just as it seemed like the two were going to come to blows, Yole spoke up.

"What does it matter how he knew?" the boy asked. "Brant saved our lives! I'm glad he knew."

Dylanna dropped her eyes and nodded at Yole. "True," she said quietly, "very true."

Kamarie changed the subject abruptly, "So, what do we do now?" she asked. "We don't know where we are, or how to get out. We don't know where Pearl Cove is from here, and we do not know how to get there. The dragons were, in all likelihood, correct: we will have to wander around down here until we either find our way out by chance or die of starvation."

The corners of Brant's mouth twitched in a smile at Kamarie's gloomy words. "I wouldn't be so sure about that."

"What do you mean?" Oraeyn asked.

"Traitors to Rhendak they were, and the one disguised as Iarrdek was not leading us towards Pearl Cove. I had my suspicions before the other one arrived, but I did not listen to them because he was leading us on a path that goes very near to Pearl Cove. If we continue down that path," Brant pointed at a tunnel that branched to the left, "we will come to the exit we want. I'd say we are about a half hour's journey to daylight."

"You can read the maps?" Dylanna asked in disbelief.

Brant nodded, once.

"So that's how…" Dylanna began, then she stopped. "Forgive me," she said, "it is my nature to be suspicious of things that do not make sense to me. As a wizardess, I do not come across much that I do not understand. I thought you had somehow detected an illusion that I could not. I was wrong, and I am sorry for questioning you."

Brant said nothing, but Kamarie noticed his lips twitching as though he was trying not to laugh. That was impossible, of course; Brant rarely even smiled. However, she got the feeling that he was not telling them everything.

Rhendak roared out into the tunnels and fire sprayed from his mouth in huge bursts, so hot that the ember stones went dark. Shalintess, his one true love, was gone. But he was a king, so he was not allowed the luxury of grief; he was not allowed to lose his head and go on a killing rampage, as he would have liked to. As king, he must demonstrate calm and clear-headed logic, even in such a painful situation.

There had been evidence of human handiwork in the murder, and yet there was something un-human about it too. Rhendak saw the sword lying next to her, and he noted that she had numerous stab wounds. What did not add up was the fact that very few blades were any real match for a dragon's armor, except of course, for the Fang Blade. But he also knew that the holder of the Fang Blade had not been anywhere near the scene of Shalintess' death, and he also believed that the holder was unaware of what he carried at his side.

Much as he hated to do so, Rhendak called a council of the Elders. He noted that Nnyendell and Mystak were not present, but that did not raise any concern. Those two were hardly ever present at Elder meetings, a tendency that he would eventually have to address.

"Shalintess has been killed," he said in a voice heavy with sorrow.

Immediately, whispers filled the air, but he silenced them with a raised claw. "I want to…" he stopped as he heard a noise coming from one of the tunnels.

The Elders waited, thinking that he was going to say something. They were astonished when Rhendak got up and walked out. He was gone for a few minutes, and they waited in silence, a little bit perturbed at this irregularity. Then Rhendak strode back in to the Great Cavern, he had something hanging from his jaws. He walked up to the Council and set it down. They were all a little surprised to see that it was a young gryphon. What was even more disturbing was that the gryphon was tied up.

With a quick motion, Rhendak sliced through the bonds that had been holding the gryphon captive. The gryphon looked up gratefully.

"Thank you, Your Majesty," he said.

Rhendak reared back a little in surprise. "Iarrdek! What happened? I thought that I sent you with the humans, to guide them back to Pearl Cove."

"You did," Iarrdek said. "I asked them which exit they wanted to go to, and then we began. I told them to stop and rest for the night, and I must have dozed off myself, because the next thing I knew, I was being dragged somewhere. I tried to struggle or cry out for help, but found that I was tied up and had been gagged. I was not, however, blindfolded. My captor was Mystak, the gold dragon of Suden-Krayghentaliss."

The Council members started muttering to each other at this. Many of them did not seem at all surprised.

Iarrdek continued, "He was muttering to himself, not knowing that I had woken up. He seemed scared, talking about following someone else's orders or something like that. Apparently he was terrified of getting caught, because of something he had done. Something that he thought you would be upset about, Your Majesty."

Rhendak's eyes turned molten and steam began to curl out of his nose. "We have traitors among us!" he roared, and his roar was filled with anger and grief as he pieced together the events of the past day. "Nnyendell and Mystak were the two Elders who opposed helping the humans. Now they have taken their revenge on our decision by killing Shalintess and making it appear as if the humans did it. They are right now probably posing as guides for the humans, aiming to bring them to destruction."

An Elder spoke up, "Say the word, Highness, and we will be after them in a second."

Rhendak's eyes held gratitude as he looked at the black dragon who had spoken; the two had been friends for a long time. He motioned to the sentries at the entrance. "Bring them to me," he ordered. "They shall not escape my wrath or our justice."

The sentries exchanged a glance; then one of them spoke, "I am afraid we cannot do that."

CHAPTER
TEN

"We are no longer safe here," Wessel told the other inhabitants of Pearl Cove. The darkness was broken only by the soft glow of the Toreth and the flickering light from the torches.

Wessel had sounded the great horn, calling all of Pearl Cove to gather at the Crest, a large, tabular-shaped rock formation, overlooking the sea. Matters of impact were presented and discussed at the Crest, and tonight's meeting would impact them all.

"The Lady is leaving us," Wessel said quietly.

The gasps and outcries of the people and animals pierced the air. There was a mournful quality in each voice, a lament that echoed on and on across the white sand and down to the sea where it was lost in the great swells.

Wessel raised his hand. "She is leaving, and enemies are approaching even now. Calyssia has warned of a strong and deadly force at our borders. She does not know their purpose, but she does know the result. Her departure means the end of Pearl Cove."

An older woman stood up, and Wessel nodded.

"What are we to do?" she asked. "Will we flee?"

A young man jumped to his feet and shouted, "No! We must defend the Cove! This is our home! Surely we will defend our home."

An older man stood up slowly and shook his head. "When the Keeper leaves, the Cove will die, and those of us who remain will die as well."

Wessel raised his hand again for silence. "Whatever we do, we must do it together. If we all go off in different directions, we scorn what the Lady Calyssia has taught us."

Heads nodded at the wisdom of Wessel's words and the people began to calm down, though they still raised questions.

"So, do we defend our home or do we flee?"

"Does the Lady Calyssia have any final words for us in this great time of need, or has she already departed?"

"The Lady Calyssia does have a few words for you." Suddenly Calyssia was there, her voice full of sorrow and farewell, but her eyes full of excitement and wonder. "Yes, I am leaving, and I am here to wish you farewell. You have come here from many different places and for many different reasons, but you all came. You all found a place of refuge, yes, but also a place of purpose, and you all learned to live and work together.

"At some point, the student must become independent of the teacher and learn the hard way, by making his or her own decisions. This is why I am not going to tell you what to do when the enemy comes. I will only tell you this, if you stay and fight, you may be able to strike a forceful blow against the Dark Country. Know also, if you choose to stay, many of you will most certainly be killed. The Dark Warriors are skilled in warfare, and you, my friends, are not. The choice must be yours. The only request that I make..." Calyssia stopped, oddly out of breath and her face paled with the effort of standing before them. She swallowed and swayed slightly, then she continued to speak, her voice thin. "The only thing I would ask of you... is to forgive me... for not having the strength... to protect you."

With these words, Calyssia collapsed onto the sand. Wessel and his wife, Rena, were at her side in an instant. Rena sat down and lifted the Lady's head and shoulders, surprised at how light she had become. Wessel knelt beside his wife, his eyes worried. Someone brought a small cup of water and Rena held it to Calyssia's lips. The water made Calyssia's eyes flutter open and she looked into the worried eyes that peered down at her.

"The sea..." she rasped, "please... it is my only chance."

Wessel lifted the Lady into his arms. Followed by Rena and the rest of the people of the Cove, he carried Calyssia down to the water's edge. He waded out into the gentle waves and then looked down at the frail wizardess.

Rena stood beside him and her eyes narrowed in concern. "You are sure?"

Calyssia's eyes were wide and frightened. She looked very young and her eyes held a hint of panic as she looked out towards the sea. But she nodded firmly.

"I have hidden from my grief... for too long. I have hidden from my past... my mother's curse, and the pain she caused my father. It is time to face... the unknown. To see for myself..." She did not explain further and Wessel nodded.

"Good-bye," he said softly.

Rena held Calyssia's hand, as Wessel set the Gate-Keeper in the sea, then, taking his wife's hand, they both turned away and headed back to the shore and their people.

Calyssia floated on top of the water for a moment. The light of the Toreth shone down solely upon the Keeper, framing her in a shimmering, pale glow. She sank gently beneath the surface of the water. The wind blew forcefully in from the sea, carrying the fragrant smell of sea-salt and ocean-breeze to her friends, her family, waiting on the shore. Suddenly, Calyssia broke through the surface, as if her strength had suddenly returned. Her long blond hair, silver in the light of the Toreth, rippled out behind her like sweet strains of music.

The incoming waves crested around her like great, white, foaming giants, then broke and returned out to sea, trying to swallow the delicate form of the gentle creature. Yet she remained, and suddenly her laughter filled the night, borne on the wind, daring the waves to come ever closer, fearless and excited.

The waves returned her challenge and Calyssia's eyes sparkled with silvery green fire and she smiled, a genuine, delight-filled smile. She swam with powerful strokes towards the horizon, her long hair streaming behind her. She delighted in the feel of the water, rushing past her as the currents carried her far out to sea. The music of the ocean and the waves sang to her, and she sang back, swimming with reckless abandon, feeling younger than she had in years.

She turned and looked one last time upon her Pearl Cove. Oh, how she had loved it. As she looked for the final time upon this haven of peace that had been entrusted to her care, she was overcome with emotion. She remembered the magic of the sand, and the peace and security that her Cove had provided. She spotted a child watching from a dune. The child appeared as a star of pure gold, whose light burned strong, and Calyssia felt a surge of hope swell inside for the future of Aom-igh. The future was in the hearts and purposes of the children: it was no longer her concern. Calyssia waved to the child, and then to the others on the shore, and she cried out joyfully, "Fare well!" Then she dove into the depths of the sea and she was gone.

The Lady was gone. The people could all feel it. Her presence had been strong, like the warmth of the Dragon's Eye or the soft light of the Toreth. And now that guiding light, that protection, was gone, vanished into the night like a mist.

Those who had gathered shivered as the night air suddenly turned chilly and they looked to Wessel for direction. Wessel had always been respected within the Cove; he knew that the people would turn to him now that the Lady was gone. He sighed, and when he spoke, his quiet voice carried across the sands.

"The Lady told me that it might be time for us to take what we have learned to the rest of Aom-igh. She also told me that the people we have isolated ourselves from for so many years now may have something to teach us as well." He shrugged, a small motion. "I do not know what tomorrow holds, but I do know that even though I have isolated myself and my family from the rest of Aom-igh, it has never ceased to be my home. The ones who come to our shores with the intent to conquer... they threaten all of us as well. I will send my family away from here, I will ask my wife and child to carry news of this invasion to King Arnaud. But I intend to make a stand here on the shores of my home and strike a blow at this enemy. I will isolate myself from the troubles of the world no longer. I ask you to return to your homes and decide for yourselves what you will do on the morrow."

The group broke up and Wessel returned to his home with Rena and their daughter, Kaitryn. Rena made dinner and began packing their few belongings into a small sack. There were tears in her eyes as she set about these tasks.

Wessel caught his wife's hand and squeezed it gently, forcing her to stop packing for a moment. "You will take the Western Pass through the mountains. I will catch up with you when I have done all I can here."

"But what if you don't?"

"I will catch up with you."

"It has been years since you swung a sword or drew a bow," Rena glanced at the sleeping form of their young daughter on a small mattress in the corner. "She needs her father."

"I do not intend for her to lose her father," Wessel replied.

"You cannot know what will happen in the course of battle. Why must you stand and fight here? The Cove is already returning to an ordinary beach, the shield is already fading, this place is our home no longer."

"Long ago, we came to the Cove, searching for peace and Calyssia taught us strength; not in weapons or battles, but in common, everyday courage and sacrifice. We return now to Aom-igh where peace is threatened, bringing an ally to their cause. The men will make a stand here to help win the battle, and you and all of the others will travel to King Arnaud to help win the future for our shared country. This may indeed have been the purpose the Lady intended for us. I do not intend to let enemies land on our shores and invade our lands unhindered."

Rena let out a small sob and threw herself into her husband's arms. "You are right. You're right," she whispered, "but I wish it didn't have to be."

Long into the dark hours of the night they clung to each other. For despite Wessel's brave and confident words, he too worried that this was the last time he would hold his wife and look upon his daughter.

The night was a long one, for they all knew what awaited them in the days to come, and none of the Cove People could find it in themselves to get more than a few hours' rest. Following Wessel's example, the men had all decided to stand and fight.

Morning dawned with a cold, heavy fog that was unusual for Pearl Cove. Usually the weather in the Cove was bright and warm. The people arose from their beds with heavy hearts and quietly prepared themselves for the coming of the Dark Warriors. The women and children were guided towards the mountains, and their men promised to rejoin them soon. There were few tears, for their farewells had all been said the previous night.

When the women and children were safely into the mountain pass, the men readied themselves for battle. Some who had faced battle before took out swords and shields, long unused, while others made crude weapons from their tools and implements. Wessel separated the men into smaller formations and hid them in disparate locations believing that surprise and multiple attacks against their enemy would prove more effective than a single, momentary battle against a foe that was certain to win. Wessel knew that their battle was for time, not victory.

They did not have to wait long. Great ships appeared on the horizon. The size and number of the ships was enough to strike dismay into the brave hearts of the men and the few myth-folk who had long ago chosen to stay above ground in the safety of

Pearl Cove, but they held steady, their hands gripping their weapons tightly. Wessel turned to a younger man, no more than a boy, who was standing near him and gestured for him to come closer. The boy stepped forward eagerly, a long dagger held firmly in his hand.

"This is no intelligence gathering foray, as we first thought," Wessel spoke quietly. "This is the beginning of the final battle to conquer our lands. You must run, catch up with the women and children and carry a message to King Arnaud. He looks to the sea for his enemy, but he will come from the mountains. He will come from behind."

The boy's face fell slightly, but he could not hide the relief in his brown eyes. "Hurry now, lad, for this information is critical to our King!" He repeated the message. "And tell our families to run. We will not be able to hold the enemy for long, but we will do our best to give you all a fair head start on them."

The boy swallowed hard and nodded. Then he darted up and off north, towards the mountains and safety.

The armada of Dark Warriors reached the shore by nightfall. Dressed in black leather, equipped with swords and shields, the Dark Warriors wasted no time in their approach to the mountains. Their enemy was on the far side of those mountains. Suddenly, a horn blew and the unseen men of Pearl Cove attacked. The battle raged furiously, starting out well for the Cove People. They had the edge of surprise and righteous anger on their side, and their fight was desperate as well as self-sacrificing. The Dark Warriors had not been expecting to face such defiance or such passion so soon, for they had been told by Prince Elroy that this part of the coast was uninhabited by living creatures. But the training and fighting instincts drilled into the Dark Warriors soon took over, and the tide of battle turned.

Steel clashed on steel, bowstrings twanged, and the cries of dying men filled the night air as the battle raged on. The Dark Warriors fought with skill and power matching the pictures painted of them in fear-filled rumors, but the men of Pearl Cove stood fearlessly against them. Blood stained the pure white sand as good men fell to the ground and breathed their last.

Wessel was fighting for his life. He had promised his six-year-old daughter, Kaitryn that he would come and join them on their journey as soon as they had defeated the Dark Warriors. He had known it was a lie. He had known that their chance for victory was slim, but her wide, pleading blue eyes had ripped the promise from him even as the lie had torn his heart in two.

"Daddy," she had said, her curly hair framing her sweet, innocent little face, "why do we have to leave?"

"Because some very bad people are coming here, and you must leave so that you and your mommy will be safe," he had replied, kneeling in front of her.

She had thrown her tiny arms around his neck and buried her face in his shoulder. "Promise me you'll join us soon, Daddy," she had whispered, her voice thick with tears.

In a choked voice he had promised, "Just as soon as I can, Kitry, I promise."

Wessel had received several battle wounds by now; a trickle of blood was running down his face from a gash high on his forehead. His left arm burned where an arrow had struck him a glancing blow. He was breathing hard and he was exhausted. He was no warrior, though he had been fairly good with a sword, once. However, he was sorely out of practice. He was now facing two Dark Warriors, his back to a large sand dune. In desperation he went down on one knee, spinning with one leg stretched out he tripped one of the warriors even as he stabbed the other with his sword. The second warrior climbed to his feet, and the dance began. The warrior was smiling slightly, as if he knew that victory was his, relishing the fight. Wessel's face was also grim, knowing that this would be his last fight.

Coy found himself facing a man his own age. Sweat dripped down into his eyes and he blinked grimly, knowing that if he took a moment to wipe it away it might be the last thing he ever did. They had been assured that they would meet no resistance upon reaching the shore. They were part of a three-pronged invasion. What had gone wrong? Their mission was to make their way secretly through Aom-igh to the capital city of Ayollan, where they were to await their signal and then attack the enemy soldiers from the rear. They had already lost far too many men in this unexpected battle. What had been military orders now became personal as the warrior before him had just killed the man next to him, a man who had been Coy's best friend since their first years in battle training.

Coy sprang to his feet and faced the man who had just killed his friend. He had not known what to believe when setting off on this mission. He did not like the idea of a surprise attack. His training recoiled at the thought of attacking a land without warning or provocation. The reports linking Aom-igh to their enemies was unconvincing. But now that he had seen for himself how cunning the people of Aom-igh could be, how they had obviously positioned their warriors where they ought to have been least expected, and how viciously they fought, Coy was ready to believe the worst about this country he had known nothing about before less than a year ago. He faced the man before him, his face set in a dark smile. He would make the enemy pay for the death of his friend.

The warrior swung, his blade narrowly missing Wessel's face. Wessel leaned back, then stabbed forward, nicking the Dark Warrior in the arm, just at a joint in his armor, drawing first blood. The warrior's eyes narrowed and he focused his whole attention upon the man before him. Wessel lunged again, as the Dark Warrior sliced at his knees. Wessel brought his sword down in a block, and the blades screeched as they clashed. The force of the blow made Wessel's arm tingle and he barely managed to block the next slice, which this time was aimed at his left arm. He twisted his body impossibly and kicked the Dark Warrior in the stomach, pushing him away. The warrior grunted and stumbled backwards, gasping for air. Wessel used the warrior's stumble to his advantage and leaped after him, stabbing him through the heart.

The Dark Warrior crumpled, a look of astonishment on his face as he slipped into death. Wessel stood above him, breathing hard. He looked around, and saw that they were quickly losing the battle. He sighed and dropped his eyes, his heart heavy, as he saw the white coast littered with the bodies of both friends and enemies alike.

Just then, someone sounded the horn for a retreat. Wessel turned to obey the order to retreat and felt a sharp pain shoot through him. He looked down and blinked at the arrow sticking out of his side. He looked up towards the border and saw it begin to swim before his eyes. His blood dripped onto the sand and he sank to his knees, unable to cross the distance to the safety of the forest. He slowly fell to the ground and stared up at the pale blue sky. The Dragon's Eye was setting, causing the edge of the horizon to seem as though it were on fire. Pink and orange beams of light streaked across the canvas of blue above him. His breath caught at the beauty of it all, and he wondered if his wife and daughter were seeing it as well, hoping it appeared to them as beautiful and magnificent and as full of confidence as it appeared to him.

As he thought again of his family, memories swam behind his eyes. He saw his wife, Rena, as the laughing young girl who had stolen his heart. He recalled the two of them finding their way to Pearl Cove. He saw Kaitryn as a tiny baby, born inside the protective barrier of the Cove, a baby who smiled and gurgled at everyone. Then he saw her learning to walk, and he saw Rena and himself rejoicing over Kaitryn's first steps, her first words. His life had been full of happy memories that flooded over him now in comforting waves.

Weariness overtook him and Wessel closed his eyes, his only regret that he could not keep his promise. "I'm sorry Kitry," he whispered, "I'm sorry."

The tunnel they had been traveling along suddenly turned into a dead end.

"Here it is," Brant said, "the exit."

Kamarie looked at him questioningly, but said nothing. Oraeyn and Yole exchanged looks of confusion, seeing nothing in front of them but a solid rock wall.

Brant turned to Dylanna. "I do not believe I can open the door, can you?"

Dylanna raised an eyebrow as he said this, surprised that he was admitting that there was something he could not do, then she frowned at the wall. "I can try," she said in a voice of deep concentration.

She walked up to the wall and ran a hand across it, her eyes searching. She allowed her fingertips to trail lightly, exploring every tiny crack and indentation on the rough surface of the wall. Suddenly her fingers stopped at a slightly larger indentation on the wall, and a light broke over her face. She pushed at the spot and said in a commanding voice: "Arach Deiseal!"

The wall swung outwards and a bright beam of light shot down the tunnel from outside. Yole gave a cry of delight and they all rushed out into the open air once again. After so many days underground, wandering the tunnels of Krayghentaliss, the fresh air was pure joy. The Dragon's Eye beat down upon them, warming them and washing away the coldness of the caves.

Kamarie fairly danced out of the tunnel, so great was her delight at being once again above ground. She spread her arms wide and spun in circles, as if trying to gather up the warmth of the Dragon's Eye into her arms and never let go of it. She laughed in pure pleasure, and fell to her back on the soft green grass, soaking in the colors and the brightness.

Oraeyn strode out of the tunnel, envying Kamarie's reckless abandon. For a moment he wished he could show his delight with such passion. As he left the tunnel, his envy faded and he felt refreshed and renewed. His restlessness vanished, and he breathed deeply of the fresh air. Then he laughed out loud as joy swept over him.

Yole's eyes brightened, and his face flushed as he left the tunnels. He looked healthier than he had in days. Even Dylanna and Brant seemed relieved to be back above-realm. As they left Krayghentaliss, the door swung shut behind them.

"What was that you said?" Kamarie asked Dylanna, looking up from where she lay on the ground.

"Arach Deiseal?" Dylanna asked. "It's Old Kraïc for 'open.' Actually, it was just a guess, my Old Kraïc is just a touch rusty."

"What's Old Kraïc?" Yole asked. "Is it magic? This might be a little strange, but I sort of understood you. Not really the words themselves, but what you meant."

"No wonder, young Yole," Brant smiled. "Old Kraïc is not magic, rather it is the language of the dragons."

Yole fell silent, his face troubled.

"Where are we?" Oraeyn finally asked, getting past the wonder of being outside again and taking notice of their surroundings.

Brant blinked. "We are just outside the Pearl Cove, past the storm," he said, then he pointed, "right there is the bound...."

They turned to look, and Dylanna gasped. The border was gone. With an unspoken agreement they took off running to the place where the wall of illusion had been and stopped short, surveying the ruin of Pearl Cove.

Kamarie remembered the place as being dazzlingly white, sparkling with life and energy. She remembered it as though there had been a silver glow emanating from everything within the Cove. There had been something magical, some strong presence within the Cove that had made it what it was, but now that magic, that strength, had vanished. The sand was still white, but it no longer sparkled like crystals. The sky above them was still blue, but it was just a normal sky blue, not the deep sapphire that it had been in their memories. The air around them no longer shimmered with life or magic.

"What happened?" Yole asked, afraid of the answer to his question.

"The Keeper is gone." Brant's voice was sad.

A single tear slid down Dylanna's cheek and fell to the ground. The tear hit the white sand and disappeared without a trace. A few seconds later a tiny, delicate, silver shoot poked out of the ground. The others gasped in surprise at its unexpected appearance.

"It will grow into a tree, straight and tall," Dylanna murmured, "it is the last and best thing that I have to offer to Calyssia, this small memorial of all that she accomplished. It will offer shade and a place of rest for the weary, it will bear fruit for the hungry. It will neither be buffeted by the strong winds nor cut by the woodsmen, but it will be found by all who need it; just as Calyssia was."

"Where is Calyssia now, Dylanna?" Yole asked, tugging on her sleeve and looking distraught.

Dylanna looked down at the youth, an expression of kindness and deep sorrow on her face. "She has returned to the sea… she has returned to our mother."

"Your mother?" Kamarie asked.

"She was of the mer-folk."

"A *mermaid?*" Kamarie's voice rose an octave. "What else about my lineage haven't you told me?"

Dylanna shook her head. "Now you know everything," her eyes darkened and she refused to say any more on the subject.

"What about the people who lived here?" Oraeyn asked in concern.

"Many of them died here," Brant said in a low voice that sounded almost detached. They turned and looked over the Cove, their eyes falling on what Brant had already seen. Bodies lay strewn across the white beach.

"Did any survive?" Kamarie asked.

Brant nodded slowly and pointed to the ground. "It looks as though quite a few passed this way, perhaps the people had warning and were able to send the women and children to safety?"

"Calyssia would have warned them, she had strength to do that, at least," Dylanna replied.

They stood in silence for a moment, honoring the memory of the Cove and its Keeper. Then they walked around the Cove a little, but saw no sign of life anywhere.

Suddenly, Kamarie gave a start, "Tor! The horses! Where are they?" she asked, looking around frantically.

"I would guess that Calyssia sent them home," Dylanna said, her tone lifeless. Her grief was too great to care about anything else, "either that or they were killed or stolen by the Dark Warriors."

The look on Kamarie's face was very close to that of panic, so Oraeyn spoke quickly, "It's more likely that Calyssia sent them home. Horses can always find their way home you know, and Tor is very smart. Calyssia knew how much Tor meant to you, Kamarie, and I'm sure that she would have done anything in her power to keep him safe for you. She was your aunt, after all."

Kamarie brightened a bit at Oraeyn's words, hearing the truth in them. "I always said Tor was a magic horse. My Aunt Leila gave him to me... of course, that was before I had any idea my aunt was a wizardess."

Dylanna spoke quietly. "Before we leave, do you think we might go down to the shore, I want to say good-bye one last time to my sister."

They nodded and walked slowly with Dylanna down to where the waves gently rolled up onto the sand. Dylanna slipped off her shoes and strode out into the water. The others stood back at a respectful distance and looked on quietly, all of them feeling the loss of Calyssia very deeply in their hearts. Even the air grew still and cold, mourning alongside them.

Dylanna stared out at the sparkling blue-green ocean and felt the wind on her face. She had always feared the sea, heeding her father's stories about it and her mother's people more closely than her sisters had. However, as she watched the rolling waves and saw the sparkle of the light from the Dragon's Eye dancing across the water and smelled the tangy salt smell that washed up in the breeze, she began to understand why her sister had so loved the sea. She could almost feel Calyssia's touch in the water and she understood why Calyssia had built her domain so close to the water's edge, and why now, after so many years, she made the drastic choice to turn to the ocean rather than die. In deep sorrow at her sister's leaving, and yet with a quiet understanding welling up within her, Dylanna began to sing her farewell. The melody was low and haunting, and there was a hint of tears in her voice as she sang the tribute to Calyssia.

> The bright, broad seas'
> Silken back waves
> To and fro eternally.
>
> The crystal caves
> Of sparkling foam
> Echo deep beyond the grave.
>
> Calling you home
> With watery sighs
> The sea beckons you alone.
>
> Wailing winds cry
> A siren's sad song
> 'Cross the lonely expanse of sky.
>
> Away you have gone
> Beyond the deep
> To the sea you now belong.
>
> Dearest one, sleep
> I bid thee farewell
> In my heart you'll always be.

As the last notes of Dylanna's song faded, the others shook themselves, awaking from a trance. Her song had carried them out over the water and into the waves, and they were surprised to find themselves standing once more on the solid ground of the shore. She turned to them, and all traces of sadness were gone from her face as she smiled. They walked back up the beach in silence, wondering what had happened down by the water. None of them spoke as they left the Cove, feeling as though it would somehow be wrong to break the peaceful silence. It was not until they had crossed into the forest that any of them dared to utter a word.

At last, when they had left the silence of the Cove and were once again in the woods beyond the border, Kamarie dared to speak. "Well, I for one am not looking forward to walking all the way back to the castle, but I suppose there is nothing else to do."

Dylanna shook her head. "There is something else that we need to do first."

"What is that, Dylanna?" Oraeyn asked.

"We must travel to the Harshlands to see my sister Leila," Dylanna said firmly.

"Now wait a minute," Oraeyn argued, "Dark Warriors came through here less than a day ago. I know the Queen asked us to enlist the aid of your other sister, but surely the situation has changed? Surely we should warn the castle?"

"No," Brant said quietly, "I made a promise to Queen Zara. We must travel to the Harshlands."

With heavy, yet determined hearts, they made for the Harshlands. As they headed east, Kamarie felt a puzzling sense of discontentment. She wanted to be heading for home again. And yet, the Harshlands beckoned and promised adventure and challenges she could only guess at, and her heart leapt at the prospect of the unknown.

And perhaps, Kamarie thought to herself, *perhaps we will even find a way to strike a blow to the enemy whilst we journey back and forth across Aom-igh.*

Rhendak's eyes turned into two menacing slits as he glared fiercely at the two sentries who had dared to oppose his wishes. He was already angry, and now he seemed to be glowing with a fiery orange light from inside. Smoke was billowing out from his great nostrils and he bared his teeth, the shiny, sparkling rows of sharp daggers were a vision that would strike fear into even the bravest souls.

"You will do as I sssay or you will regret being born," he hissed, giving them one last chance; a chance they did not deserve.

Rhendak almost hoped that they would not take it. He needed to destroy something, and, although they did not know it, he had a very loose and slipping grasp upon his already inflamed temper. He was sick with grief at Shalintess' death, and he believed that he knew who was responsible. He suspected these two rebellious guards were now following Nnyendell and Mystak's orders, that they had probably been in on the plans for the murder. Rhendak began to see red, his temper raged hotter and his control slipped even more.

The Elders watched the scene in fascination, waiting to see what Rhendak would do. They had never seen their King like this before. Several of them were old enough to remember Graldon's reign, and many of them missed it. Graldon had been a good king, but he had also been a tough king. Graldon was the type of king who had no patience for disobedience or dissension in the ranks. He had been fair, but his word had been law, and he had ruled with an iron grip. These two traitors would never have talked back to Graldon the way they were speaking to Rhendak now. They would have been too terrified of being roasted on the spot.

The two sentries weighed their options, then decided that Rhendak was not really as fearsome as he appeared, and the older one cleared his throat nervously. "No," he said, but not as firmly as before.

Rhendak instantly lost every bit of the little control he had managed to maintain upon his temper. His green scales changed color and seemed to turn liquid silver in his fury. His eyes went glassy and a red fire burned deep within them. Several of the Elders cheered inwardly. All the Elders liked Rhendak, they had all thrown their support behind him when Graldon died, but all of them agreed he was a little too soft, a touch too forgiving. They hoped it was simply a reflection of his youth and that he would become tougher and stronger with time and experience. Each and every one of them was watching now to see whether or not Rhendak was going to follow in the great footprints of Graldon.

"Then you are traitors and spies, disloyal to your King and fellow dragons!" Rhendak roared. His head came back and sparks came out of his mouth as he asked, "You know what the penalty for treason and disobedience is?" His voice rose at the end of his speech, but it was far more a statement than a question.

They had brought their own destruction upon their heads. There was nothing they could possibly hope to do that would change Rhendak's course. He was in a blood rage and ready to lash out at the first living thing that dared to cross him. The two sentries now looked at each other in fear. Nnyendell and Mystak had assured them that King Rhendak was weak and that his grief over Shalintess' death would weaken him even more. The two traitors had assured the sentries that there was no danger at all in their job. The sentries had believed them; they had not expected this vengeful, powerful *king* of a dragon who was now standing before them.

When neither answered, an Elder spoke up, trying hard to cover his delight at Rhendak's sudden transformation, "The penalty is death, traitors cannot be allowed to live, lest they be granted the opportunity to cause even more trouble and bring harm upon others."

Rhendak stared at each of the sentries in turn until they dropped their eyes and shifted uncomfortably, then he spoke again. "Do you have any last words? Any desire to turn away from the leading of Nnyendell and Mystak and once again swear fealty to me?" He gave them one final chance, but doubted if even a plea for mercy and promises of good behavior would be sufficient enough to cause him to grant them their lives. The only reason he hesitated now was that he still hoped to get information about who the masterminds behind this plot were.

The two sentries stared at each other, then the older one snapped, "No!" Then he hissed at the younger one, "He won't do it, he's weak, he's spineless, not a real king at all."

No sooner had the sentry stopped speaking than Rhendak lashed out with his right claw. His talons hooked under the older sentry's scales and slid upwards into the soft flesh beneath, silencing him forever. Then Rhendak spat out a huge burst of searing orange flame. The fire engulfed the sentry, whose death had come so quickly he had not even had time to utter a sound. The flame was so large and so hot that when it died out, it left nothing behind; not even a pile of ashes to mark the spot where the sentry had stood only seconds before.

The younger sentry backed away, his eyes wide and round as he stared at the place where he had seen his fellow engulfed in a merciless blast of flame. Then he looked back at Rhendak. In a split second, he had made up his mind, for Rhendak was still angry and looking ready to kill again.

"Mercy, King Rhendak, mercy, Sire!" he cried, lowering his great body as close to the ground as was possible. "I know I don't deserve it, but please, grant me the chance to swear allegiance to you again, grant me the chance to prove my loyalty!"

The plea for mercy cut through Rhendak's haze, and he stopped. Rhendak cocked his head, as if weighing the words of the young sentry.

"Why should I believe anything you say?"

"I am ashamed of my actions, Sire, but what is a dragon of such a young age to do when his elders give him orders? I knew nothing of the plot against your mate, I swear it. Only let me live, or at least let me tell you what you need to know before you kill me, that I might die with a shred of honor yet."

The fire in Rhendak's eyes dimmed at the young sentry's speech. "Speak!"

"Nnyendell and Mystak plan to kill the humans that came down here and they also plan to retrieve the Charmed Pipes. They have no other followers, just myself and…" he gulped and nodded at the spot where the other sentry had been standing, "they hoped to gain a following by using the Pipes. They believe you to be too soft and merciful to lead the myth-folk and they came up with this plot to discredit and dethrone you, but I swear to you, Sire, if they were the ones behind Shalintess' murder, I knew naught of it."

Rhendak nodded, thinking quickly, "We will go now and hopefully save the humans, but I have a feeling that our help will not be necessary; they seemed rather self-sufficient. I do not believe that our two traitors are expecting their victims to be as resourceful or as strong as I know that they are. So, although we will go quickly to offer any assistance that we may, our purpose is to bring back Nnyendell and Mystak to face trial and punishment for their acts of treason."

CHAPTER ELEVEN

Dark Warriors were apparently swarming all over Aom-igh and King Arnaud had not yet seen one of them. There were reports of crops, livestock, and villages being destroyed, but as of yet, no living person could actually report seeing this enemy. Kamarie and the others had been gone for far too long. Arnaud felt deep down in his heart that their mission had ended unsuccessfully; he knew that the dragons were not coming.

Arnaud sent knights throughout the realm to respond to the reports, and yet always they were too late. He well understood he was playing into his enemy's hands, spreading his forces thinner than he could afford and thus leaving Aom-igh defenseless when the main attack should come. He knew he did not have the resources to match the Dark Country. He had hoped his studies would provide an edge that would neutralize that superiority. His ships were too few to bring the attack to Roalthae, and yet he could not simply endure these seemingly disconnected attacks on his people without response. His people were being threatened and killed and his efforts thus far to protect them had proven futile.

What was so frustrating, was that Arnaud understood he was losing a war that he could not see. He pounded his fist against the wall in frustration at his helplessness.

Suddenly Zara was there. "What is it?" she asked, looking up at him.

She knew what was wrong, but she was allowing him to talk about it, so he turned and poured out all of the turmoil that was within him to her. She listened to every word with care and understanding written across her beautiful face. She took in the look of anguish on his face, the pain in his words, the worry in his eyes, and he discovered that he felt better just talking to her.

When he had finished, she put her hand on his shoulder. "You have done all that can be done. You can only fight the battle immediately before you. You have sent protection into the countryside, which may be why the enemy does not show himself. You have promoted to service every qualified squire and able-bodied man that could be found. Our people are not as timid as you fear, and their beloved King has much more strength than he realizes. And do not forget, that your wife, and their Queen, still has a little magic left in her."

Arnaud grinned. "I'm sure glad that you're on our side." Then he took his wife's hand and turned serious, "I never wanted you to forsake your magic or your training. I understood your desire for Kamarie to have a normal childhood, but I think it's time for our daughter to learn who her mother really is."

Zara bit her lip. "When we come through this... we will talk about it then."

Traveling cross country on foot proved more difficult than Kamarie had feared. Three days had passed and the loss of their horses was greatly felt. Brant set a grueling pace, and as a result they were now into the deep wilderness, far to the south of the Mountains of Dusk. They were in the great forest that spaned the width of Aom-igh from Pearl Cove to the Harshlands. It was dark, and the trails Brant guided them through were barely wide enough for two to walk abreast. The uneven terrain, rocks, and roots twisting across their path made it difficult to keep up with Brant's long and certain strides, and made conversation impossible. At noon on the fourth day, they came upon a clearing in the middle of the forest, and as they hurried across, Yole caught up with Dylanna and asked the question that had been burning in his mind for days.

"Do these forests have names, Dylanna?"

"Yes, they do, Yole. But this forest is so old that no one knows what its true name is any more."

"Why not?"

Brant answered quietly, "Because the trees refuse to remind us."

Yole gave him a look of disbelief and Oraeyn snorted, thinking that Brant was joking. But then Dylanna spoke again, after shooting Brant a look of surprised astonishment.

"Brant gave a very good answer to your question, Yole," she responded mildly.

As they reached the other side of the clearing and continued on, deeper into the great woods on winding, narrow trails, Oraeyn found the going difficult. He seemed to be tripping over just about every root or branch that happened to cross the path. Every time he took a step it seemed as though some root or branch reached up to entangle his feet.

"Don't these trees ever end?" Oraeyn growled as he tumbled over yet another tree root.

Kamarie grinned at him as he slowly picked himself up, but she wisely chose not to make any sarcastic comments.

"If I didn't know any better, I would almost say that they are doing it on purpose," he muttered angrily, glancing up at the owner of the offending root.

Dylanna overheard him and spoke, "Don't be so sure that they aren't. These forests are full of leftover pockets of magic from the golden years during the reign of King Llian, which nobody ever bothered to clean up. Besides the magic, these woods are also inhabited by wood nymphs. They have a great sense of fun and mischief, though they are good-natured and rarely do they mean any true harm. However, I have never found them to be very helpful, nor in the least accommodating."

Oraeyn stopped and stared at Dylanna. "Well, can you tell me how to make them stop tripping me, if they are, in fact, doing it on purpose?"

Dylanna smiled. "I suppose you could always try simply asking them to stop."

Oraeyn decided right then and there that Dylanna had either gone crazy or that all of them were setting him up to be laughed at. Still, he was beyond aggravated and decided that her suggestion was worth a try. He turned to the tree whose root he had just tripped over and addressed it, feeling more than a little foolish.

"Good tree…"

Kamarie giggled, and Yole laughed out right. Even Brant and Dylanna seemed amused. Oraeyn could feel his ears turning red, and he wondered once again if this were all just a big joke somehow. Ignoring the amusement of the others, he took a deep breath and continued.

"We are on a very important journey and we need to make all haste possible. Also, falling on my face is not very comfortable and neither is it a habit I want to get used to. So would you please stop tripping me? And could you kindly send the word along to all your friends asking them not to trip me either?"

The whole tree shook slightly as though a small breeze was blowing through its branches. Oraeyn got the feeling that if trees could laugh, then this one would be. He had never seen a tree laugh before, had never believed it possible, but this one was doing a fairly good impression. He glared at the laughing tree, then spun around and marched off in the direction that they had been heading. He managed to take two steps before a root promptly, and very observably, rose up out of the ground and tripped him.

Oraeyn jumped back to his feet and rashly drew his sword. "That's it!" he cried. "This stops *now*!"

His last word rang through the forest and the sword began to glow and hum, but Oraeyn did not notice it. He was, instead, focused on the tree in front of him. He could not have said exactly what happened next. All he could remember was that one moment he was staring at the tree, willing it to stop tripping him, willing it to obey his command, and then the tree began to twist and shake violently. The leaves rustled, and for a moment Oraeyn felt that he could distinguish whispered words in the susurration. Oraeyn stepped back and stared at the tree in shock as it waved around as though caught in a ferocious windstorm.

Then, without warning, the tree stopped and was still again, as all good trees ought to be when there is no actual wind present. From behind the tree stepped a young girl, perhaps four or five years younger than himself; she was small and slight, so thin that she was almost transparent. Her skin was light brown, almost matching the trunk of the tree he had just been talking to. Her hair was long and brown, and her eyes were a deep, forest green flecked with gold that reminded him of light from the Dragon's Eye hitting the leaves of a tree. Her face was pixie-like and full of mischief, and she had long, graceful arms. The girl was dressed in a green, filmy dress that made one think the wind was blowing around her, even when there was no wind. She was altogether childlike, despite the ancient depth of her gaze.

For a moment, the whole forest seemed frozen. The girl looked at each of them in turn, a look of surprise registering in her eyes as she realized that they were all staring at her.

"Why did you pull me out?" the girl demanded in fury, storming up to stand in front of Oraeyn, who had been in the process of sheathing his sword, sensing no threat from this small girl. The top of her head barely came up to his chin and she had to throw her head back to look him in the eye, but the look on her face made Oraeyn take a step back, despite her small stature.

"Pull you out?" Oraeyn asked.

"Yes, you pulled me out, and I want to know why you did it and how you expect to put me back in again."

Oraeyn shared a puzzled look with Kamarie. Kamarie shrugged. The girl was speaking clearly, but nothing she said made sense.

"Pulled you out of where?" Oraeyn asked.

The girl fixed him with a stare that said he must be either quite stupid or very unobservant.

Then she explained in an exasperated tone, "Out of my tree, of course."

"You're a wood nymph?"

Dylanna gasped.

The wood nymph put her hands on her hips. "What did you think I was? A water nymph?" She snorted. "Water nymphs look more like her," she pointed at Kamarie, "dark hair, blue eyes and pale skin."

"Hold on," Oraeyn said, "you said that I pulled you out of your tree, how do you know it was me? Maybe it was someone else." He was certainly hoping it had been someone else.

The wood nymph fixed him with a glare. "I know it was you who pulled me out of my tree because I could see your magic from several miles away; it's glowing all around you like the light of the Dragon's Eye. You are also the only one standing here who could have possibly pulled me out of my tree. I haven't been out of my tree in a hundred years, not since I was just a sapling." She paused, her face thoughtful. "Well, I suppose I should thank you for reminding me how to leave my tree." Then her eyes sparked angrily. "But I cannot remember how to get back in! And it's *your* fault! Put me back."

Oraeyn was taken aback by the girl's fierce words, but he was more surprised by the other things she had said about him. *She can see my 'magic'?* Oraeyn thought, *what magic? I don't know anything about magic. Dylanna's a wizardess, and Calyssia was too, Yole is a dragon, he must have some magic. Brant is full of puzzles and questions, and it wouldn't surprise me one bit if he is covered in magic. Even Kamarie probably has some magic about her, considering her mother's a wizardess, never mind that she never told Kamarie about it. But me? No, not me. I don't have any kind of power, not like that.*

The girl was growing impatient and she stomped her foot. "I want to go back in my tree," she said irritably, "the Dragon's Eye hurts my eyes and my head ever so terribly, I don't like the brightness of it. When I used to come out of my tree to dance through the woods, it was always at night. I do not like being out in the daytime. I'm nocturnal! Put me back!"

"Can trees be nocturnal?" Yole asked.

The wood nymph glared at him. "I'm a wood nymph, and *I'm* nocturnal."

Yole was abashed. "Sorry," he mumbled.

"You're grumpy, for a tree," Oraeyn commented.

"Put. Me. Back. In. My. Tree." The wood nymph's voice was fierce and low. "Or you will never walk anywhere on land again without tripping every two or three steps, I swear it."

Oraeyn sighed and put his hands up. "Fine! I don't know what I did to pull you out of your tree, I certainly never meant to. But, if you think for some reason that I can put you back, I will try!" He scratched his head, trying to remember what it was that he had done shortly before the wood nymph had appeared. Then an idea hit him. He did not know if he *could* put the nymph back in the tree, because he was not at all convinced that he had been the one who had pulled her out, but he decided he might as well make a deal and get something out of the bargain.

"First, you have to promise to stop tripping me," he said fiercely, "and to pass the word on to the rest of the wood nymphs to stop tripping me on purpose, or I will pull all of you out of your trees and then I will make you forget how to get back in permanently."

The threat worked. The nymph looked at him first in derision, then in shock, then in actual fear. Her eyes darted around, and then she nodded in reluctant agreement. She threw back her head, closed her eyes, and hummed a few whispery notes that floated up on the breeze and seemed to hang over the whole forest for a moment, then the music faded away.

"Done," she said.

"Good."

He drew his sword and pointed at the wood nymph with the Fang Blade. Feeling somewhat foolish he said, "As you were!" And *willed* his words to send the wood nymph back into her tree. For a moment, nothing happened, and Oraeyn lowered his sword, disappointed and dreading a life of tripping and stumbling over tree roots. He wondered if he could get assigned to one of Aom-igh's few ships, perhaps he could help King Arnaud build up their navy when this was all over, assuming they came through the war alive. Then the nymph sprang into the air with a cry of delight. She hovered above the ground for a second and then came back down lightly. She spun in a circle, clapped her hands, and laughed excitedly, her eyes glowing.

"I remembered how to get back in!" she exclaimed, dancing around the travelers, her fragile, willowy form moving gracefully, like branches swaying in the wind. "And I can remind the others! You have freed us from our own forgetfulness!"

She danced lightly over to Oraeyn and kissed him playfully. "All my thanks! If you are ever in need, just call on the trees, we will come to your aid, the whole forest is in your debt. And I am sorry for tripping you, but oh! It was so much fun!" She laughed, kissed him again, and then vanished.

Oraeyn was too shocked to reply, and before he could think of one single thing to say, he realized that the girl had disappeared again. He glanced around, wondering if he would catch a glimpse of her again, then he heard the leaves of the tall tree that had tripped him rustle, making a noise that sounded very decidedly like joy. He looked up at the tree and smiled, knowing that the wood nymph had made it home. He caught Kamarie's eye and smiled at her, but all she offered in return was a glare.

Tobias paced around the large room that Prince Elroy had provided him. He was worried. King Seamas had arrived in Roalthae that morning, but Tobias had not yet been summoned and he feared what this might mean. The reports from Aom-igh worried him. If true, King Seamas would lose his throne forever by bringing his men and his people to dishonor. An entire village had been destroyed, and the defenseless and innocent families had been slaughtered. Tobias recalled the young Kestrel's report, reluctantly given through shame-faced eyes:

"My commanding officer was looking for someone, or ... something," the boy hesitated.

Tobias nodded patiently. The boy was a good lad, a Kestrel, in the final year of his apprenticeship and training. At the end of this campaign the lad would complete his rite of passage and enter into the ranks of the aethalons as a full-fledged warrior.

"Sir, I thought we were simply invading Aom-igh because they threatened us, but Aetoli Aoren mentioned something that they had stolen... or someone they were harboring? It wasn't very clear. He said he had orders directly from the Council and the King himself to leave behind no trace of our passing. We asked some questions in the town, and Aoren seemed to think we had found what we were sent to find. Then we burned the entire village... sir... it wasn't just fighting men we killed. Their women... they're not like ours, sir, they had no military training at all. Sir... they weren't a threat."

Tobias' eyes clouded as he remembered the report. There were plenty of men who would still stand against such acts. Any aethalon should know such an order carried a stain of dishonor with it. A good warrior followed orders but did not follow them blindly. But the order was from the Council. He frowned. The Council was manipulating the King, but how could he prove it? There was also the matter of Tobias' own dishonesty. He had lied to his King, an offense worthy of death. He had no idea if the King or anyone else knew of his treachery; only one other person had known about his lie and he believed she had taken the secret to her grave.

Tobias straightened. He would not falter now. If the King knew of his treachery and was planning to punish him accordingly, he would face it. His treason had been committed in order to protect the King himself, and he still believed it had been the right thing to do. If Seamas did not know and his

Council had found out about the fugitive some other way, well, then they could only guess at his own part in it, a part that had been so small it was possible nobody, not even the King, remembered it. It would not do to start panicking, not yet. He could still be useful to his King, and more importantly, to his country. He would serve both, with honor, and the threat of death would not alter that.

The day was sweltering and muggy with a clear, blue sky above them. The Dragon's Eye beat down on them in scorching waves. Dylanna and Kamarie had pulled their hoods up to shield their faces from the almost unbearable light. It was too hot for hoods, but Kamarie figured that it was better than having her face red and burned the next day. Oraeyn and Brant did not comment on the heat, but they looked uncomfortable. Yole, however, seemed to actually enjoy it. Kamarie envied him.

As the day wore on, Kamarie wished with all her might that it would rain. She was uncomfortably warm and sticky and tired and thirsty. When she could stand it no longer, she threw off her hood. Dylanna scolded her, but Kamarie was in no mood to listen.

"I am dying from the heat, Aunt Dylanna," Kamarie said forcefully. "I do not care if I get freckles or even burned by the Dragon's Eye, the hood retains too much warmth and I cannot wear it."

Dylanna did not say anything, but she arched an eyebrow in disapproval.

"How much farther is it to the Harshlands?" Oraeyn asked, of nobody in particular.

"Almost a six days' walk from where we now stand," Dylanna said.

Oraeyn wished that he had not asked. He was glad to see that the Dragon's Eye was riding low in the late afternoon sky and that the evening star had come out. Everyone was tired, and the tempers were running thick. It was much to everyone's relief that Brant stopped before the Eye had fully set and announced they would set up camp for the night. They put their packs down and made camp. They ate a cold meal, as Brant still would not allow them to start a fire, and as the evening grew darker they began unrolling their blankets and getting ready to sleep for a few hours.

However, no sooner had true darkness set in than Brant stiffened and held a warning finger up to his lips. The others froze, watching him, trying to read his face. Brant stood in the shadows of the evening with his head slightly cocked and his eyes drawn into narrow slits, as though he were trying to slice through the darkness of the glade to see what was hidden beyond view. He silently and swiftly drew his sword and crouched into a fighter's stance.

He looked back and met their questioning gazes for a brief second. "When I give the word, run as fast as you can, that way," he motioned in the direction that they had been going, "I will catch up with you at the border of the Harshlands."

"But..." Kamarie began.

Brant cut her off. "Hush!" he said fiercely.

She snapped her mouth shut, and Yole grabbed her hand tightly. She looked down at him. The boy was frightened, and his eyes seemed to glow in the darkness. Though Yole was a dragon and not really a child, this journey had been testing him sorely, and he was, after all, too young for such burdens. Kamarie recognized that he needed reassurance from someone older than himself that things were going to be all right. She squeezed his hand and he relaxed a little.

Suddenly Brant let out a loud yell, then shouted, "Run, now!"

Kamarie, still holding Yole's hand, turned and raced in the direction Brant had told them to go. She did not know what threatened them, but she decided she did not want to find out. They ran without any idea of direction or purpose; they just ran, the tree branches whipping at their faces and scratching up their hands and arms. The night had suddenly turned deadly, and Kamarie and Yole sought to run from its darkness.

Oraeyn heard Brant tell him to run, but he could not. He was rooted to the spot, staring towards the same spot that Brant was watching. He could not see or hear anything; there was no flicker of movement, no underbrush rustling, no twigs cracking to disturb the silence of the evening. The night was calm and still. He had no idea what was about to descend upon them, perhaps the dragons they had wounded back in Krayghentaliss or perhaps the dragons' friends, seeking revenge for their injured comrades. Perhaps it would be an army of Dark Warriors, or something even more deadly. However, whatever it was, Oraeyn knew that he could not leave Brant to face it alone, and if he ran now he could never take up his knighthood in good conscience; so he stayed at Brant's side, his whole being ready for anything. Without any warning at all, the night suddenly became much darker. Silent warriors dressed in black leather and wielding deadly blades swarmed into the clearing where Brant and Oraeyn stood. Oraeyn drew his sword, prepared to fight to the death.

Brant noticed his movement and hissed at him in a mixture of pride and frustration, "I told you to go! What are you doing?"

Oraeyn had no time to answer, for in a heartbeat, the warriors were upon them.

Kamarie heard the noise of the battle behind her, but she did not stop. She could not stop. Fear like she had never before felt urged her to run faster, farther. Yole was panting, struggling to keep up with her, his hand still tightly clasped in her own, but she could not slow down to set an easier pace for him. She had lost Dylanna as they raced into the forest, but she believed her aunt could keep up with them.

Yole was tiring quickly; he could not keep up with this pace, and yet he knew he had to. He believed, instinctively, that if they stopped they would be killed. He did not know if anyone was actually chasing them yet, but he knew they soon would be, and he was frightened. With strength born of fear and desperation, the two ran through the night until finally neither could continue further. Kamarie and Yole crept into a thick mat of underbrush and hid by concealing themselves with the deep piles of red and brown leaves that blanketed the ground each Change-Term. There were always leaves that blew into the underbrush and never got weathered down, and now Kamarie was grateful for them, as they offered a place to hide that was soft and even a little warm. Then they lay very still, hardly daring to breathe, waiting for whatever was coming. They had run late into the evening, covering many miles through unknown land. The exertion and the stress overcame them, and they slept the sleep of exhaustion.

Kamarie awoke in a panic, not knowing where she was. She sat up quickly and then the terror of the night before came back to her in a flood. She froze, almost scared again, but the light of the morning made the darkness of the night before seem so harmless. She almost laughed when she saw how far she had burrowed down into the pile of leaves; the fear had not completely gone, so she could not yet laugh about it. She pulled leaves out of her collar and sleeves and shook her hair out. The leaves, which had seemed so inviting and comfortable the night before, were surprisingly scratchy and itchy in the light of the morning.

A few feet away, Yole sat up as well, rubbing his eyes. There were leaves sticking up out of his hair, and his eyes were sleepy. He stretched his arms and then looked around, confusion written across his face. She watched as he remembered their terrified flight through the forest. His eyes widened, and he looked around frantically. He caught sight of Kamarie and relaxed.

"I thought maybe I was the only one left," he said.

"It's all right, we're safe now. Brant and Dylanna and Oraeyn will find us soon."

Yole sniffled a little, but he did not cry. "Do you know where we are? Where will we go now?"

"We will never find our campsite again, but I do know the general direction to the Harshlands. That is where we will meet the others, if our paths don't cross before we get there. We have enough food in our packs to last us for awhile. If we cannot find it, we will ask people who live along the way if they know how to get there. But we have to be careful." Kamarie paused, thinking about the family that had given them shelter on the way to Pearl Cove. "It might be best if we don't use our real names... if we meet anyone along the way. Perhaps we should try to disguise ourselves a bit as well."

Yole nodded, and Kamarie's eyes began to twinkle as she got into the spirit of the moment. Truth be told, her fear from the night before had faded quite a bit and she was feeling that their current predicament was a sort of blessing. She had never been truly alone before, and the thought of dangerous adventuring through unknown land was genuinely exhilerating.

"I will be Ian, what name will you take Kamarie?" he asked, his eyes beginning to brighten at the prospect of traveling through villages pretending to be someone else. "And how will we disguise ourselves?"

"I will be Leota," Kamarie said, grinning at the excitement of it all in spite of herself, "but we only need the false names when there are other people around."

Yole nodded, glad that he would not have to use a different name all the time. They ate a quick breakfast and then set to work disguising themselves, in case the enemy knew what they looked like. Their disguises would also safeguard any who came to their aid, Kamarie explained. Kamarie boiled skorch root and dark berries in water until they had a nice, brown liquid. Then they rubbed the stain onto their skin, making it appear as though they had been browned by the Dragon's Eye through many days of hard toil and labor in wide-open fields. Then Kamarie rubbed the liquid through Yole's hair, turning it from its normal golden-red to a dark brown.

"What about your hair Kamarie?" Yole asked, admiring his new reflection in the still pond.

Kamarie hesitated, "Dye won't stick to it because it's too dark, so I'm just going to have to bind it up tightly and hide it under my hood. I don't want to cut it," she sighed, "perhaps no one will ask me to remove my hood.

"We're about done here. Help me clean up this mess and then we have to move on... but we need to be careful we don't leave a track for anyone to follow."

"How do we do that?"

Kamarie smiled. "I'll show you, it's the first thing you learn as a squire."

"I thought that squires learned how to fight."

"We do, but only after we've learned how to avoid one. You can be my squire-in-training, if you want, I can teach you all sorts of things as we travel."

Yole looked up at her in disbelief. "Really? You'd teach me squire stuff?"

"Of course," Kamarie said, "it's not that hard. You're not too old to learn either, 'you're never too old to learn' as Garen would say. All right, we're finished here."

The two of them headed off towards the Harshlands, the squire and the young boy, the teacher and the student, the princess and the dragon.

The Dark Warriors surrounded the two fighters. There were four of them, tall and grim, wearing dark colors that blended in with the night, camouflaging them quite effectively. Oraeyn took note of the leather armor they wore and wondered if the Dark Warriors were really good enough that they didn't need metal armor or if they were simply overconfident. Oraeyn and Brant fought back to back as they had in the tunnels of Krayghentaliss, holding the Dark Warriors at bay, but Oraeyn knew that it was only a matter of time before they both became exhausted and began to make tiny mistakes that the warriors would use to their advantage. He soon discovered the answers to his questions: the warriors were indeed good enough to need very little protection, but their thin-seeming armor was deceiving, for it stopped several of his blows that made it through their defenses.

The warriors were biding their time, and Oraeyn noticed that they seemed hesitant to attack in full force. He wondered why, but had no time to puzzle it out. The enemies were jumping in and slashing at him with their swords, and it was all he could do to block their blows and defend against their attacks. He could tell that Brant was being more daring than he, the man was making as many offensive strikes as he could. Oraeyn wondered how he managed to do so and he hoped Brant would not waste his strength.

A Dark Warrior on his right thrust his sword at Oraeyn's shoulder, which he blocked and pushed away with as much force as he could. From out of the corner of his left eye he saw the other warrior's sword coming in a jab towards his head. He made a split-second decision and followed through with his defense too far, allowing himself to collapse on his right side, causing his left-side attacker's sword to pass through the air harmlessly above him. As he fell he twisted around onto his back and stabbed upwards. He felt his sword enter the Dark Warrior on his right just below his armor and then warm, sticky blood spattered down onto his face. The warrior dropped his sword and fell sideways. However, the attacker on his left recovered from his miss far more quickly than Oraeyn had anticipated. Thus, Oraeyn did not see the sword coming down at him in an arcing hiss until it was too late. His own weapon was trapped beneath the body of the dead warrior, and he was still on his back and helpless. He almost closed his eyes, anticipating the pain, but he could not quite bring himself to do so. Then he saw Brant whirl and slice his sword through the attacking warrior, killing him instantly. Oraeyn breathed again, realizing that he had not been. Brant reached down and helped him up.

"That was stupid," Oraeyn muttered.

"Yes, it was. Don't ever try that move again, unless you are in one-on-one combat, boy," Brant said angrily.

"What happened to the other two?"

Brant pointed to the ground behind him and replied, "The other escaped."

Oraeyn knelt down and pulled his sword from the dead Warrior's body, and then he carefully wiped it clean on the grass. The sword glimmered faintly, and Brant eyed it cautiously.

"Take care of that sword, boy."

Oraeyn nodded slowly. "Yes," he replied, and then he looked at Brant, "why was it like that this time?"

"What do you mean?"

"The fight, there was none of the excitement or the rush of adrenaline that there was when we fought the dragons, why?"

"Because there is no pleasure in killing," Brant seemed surprised that Oraeyn had not figured this out for himself, "we were doing a job, we were fighting for our lives. War and killing are not the glorious things that the history books record or mentor knights describe."

"But what about a country that is attacked? What about the situation we are in right now? You are surely not saying that Aom-igh should roll over and die!" Oraeyn exclaimed in horror.

"No, I am definitely not saying that!" Brant thundered. "Sometimes there is no other choice than to fight. When a country is attacked, it must defend itself, to do otherwise is cowardly and devoid of honor and no country will survive if that defines her people. Courage and honor are enough. Glory and fame mean nothing."

Oraeyn wondered at the tone of voice and the dark words, but he said nothing, pondering Brant's words. He decided that they made sense, and he also realized that he had learned something more about the man who had become his hero.

Brant then spoke again in a lighter tone. "We must get some rest, but not here; we will go deeper into the forest. Early tomorrow, we will set out to find the others."

The trail suddenly disappeared. Dylanna ground her teeth in frustration. She was not a tracker, and it had already been hard for her to follow the obvious trail that Kamarie and Yole had left as they fled through the forest the night before. She knew that they must have spent the night in the underbrush when they were too exhausted to run anymore. She also knew that in the light of the morning Kamarie had begun thinking more clearly and had started taking more care about the trail they were leaving.

So now Dylanna was stuck. There was no way that she would catch up with her niece before they reached the Harshlands, for she could no more follow a trail that she could not see than she could walk back to Ayollan on her hands. She would not use her magic, at least not now. She did not know if Dark Warriors could sense magic, and she did not want to find out while she was alone in the wilderness.

When Brant had told them to run, she had hesitated for the briefest of moments, waiting to see the enemy that had followed them. Unfortunately, Kamarie and Yole had not hesitated; they had taken off running with speed born from a terror of the unknown. When Dylanna had turned to follow, they were already out of sight. She had been able to follow the sounds they made, but she had not been able to catch up with them. Finally, she had been unable to go any farther and had stopped for the night. Early the next morning, she had picked up their trail and followed it to where Kamarie and Yole had spent the night, but from there the trail disappeared.

She weighed her options. She could see that Kamarie and Yole were still heading towards the Harshlands, and it would be pointless for her to travel back to the glade where they had been attacked. Dylanna did not doubt the outcome of the attack, but she also did not know how quickly Brant and Oraeyn would resume their search for Kamarie and Yole. Brant would know immediately that they were traveling separately from Dylanna and he would also know that Dylanna could fend for herself. Her mind made up, Dylanna started walking. Brant and Oraeyn would go for Kamarie and Yole; she would go for Leila.

"What are the Harshlands like Kamarie?" Yole asked.

They had been walking for a while in silence, and Kamarie was beginning to wonder if they would ever reach the end of the forest. She was also starting to think that perhaps the forest had no end.

"Well, I've never been there, but I've read that the Harshlands are a dry, barren place," Kamarie said, trying to remember what she had been taught. "They are very dangerous and only the bravest of men has ever dared to cross the border into them, and then only in times of greatest need. If my memory serves me correctly, the book I read indicated that very few, if any, have ever returned from the Harshlands."

Yole stood up straighter and squared his shoulders; then he looked at Kamarie with an expression of doubt and honesty written across his face and spoke quietly, "I don't think that I am one of the very bravest."

Kamarie squeezed his shoulder lightly. "Neither am I Yole, but our need is most certainly the greatest. Besides, my Aunt Leila lives in the Harshlands, so perhaps the book was wrong."

He accepted that with a slight nod of his head, and they continued on for a little while, lapsing into silence once more. Eventually, they came to a small clearing that had a stream running off to one side, filling up a little pond of clear water.

"Here is a good spot where we can stop to rest and eat," Kamarie said.

She was not tiring, but she had noticed that Yole was beginning to struggle to keep up with her long strides. He sighed in relief at her words and sank down onto the moss-covered ground. Kamarie dug down into her pack and shared out some food. They took out their canteens and filled them with the cold, clear water of the spring. Then they ate slowly, neither one of them anxious to resume their unending trek through this strange and dangerous wood. Around the clearing the trees had thinned a little, allowing them to see the sky above them. The light of the

Dragon's Eye shone down and sparkled on the surface of the rippling water of the small pool. Yole suddenly laughed and pointed over to where a whole school of fish was leaping out of the water. Their silver scales caught the rays of the Dragon's Eye and glimmered in the light.

Kamarie kicked off her shoes and walked over to the little pond. She dangled her feet in the water and gasped in shock at its coldness. The cold water was refreshing as she continued to hang her feet in the cool, clear water. Yole grinned and followed her example, sitting next to her on the bank of the pond and dangling his feet in the water. Together they sat there for a long while, enjoying the coolness that washed over their tired feet as they watched the glittering fish jump.

Kamarie's face turned solemn as she sat there. There were so many unknowns in their quest now. She did not know if their companions had made it; she did not know if they were even still alive. She did not know where the Harshlands were, nor did she know how far away they were, and she did not know for sure that they would be able to meet up with the others when they did reach their destination. The Harshlands were large and dangerous, and although Kamarie was confident that she could find them, she had no idea where inside the Harshlands her Aunt's house might be. She feared that they were traveling too slowly, that they would stray too far in the wrong direction, or that they would miss the others when they got to the Harshlands. She wondered where Brant, Oraeyn, and Dylanna were now. She hoped that they were safe and heading towards the Harshlands as she and Yole were.

Yole noticed the worried expression on her face, and he smiled at her. "Oraeyn, Brant, and Dylanna will be fine," he said, "they will be at the border of the Harshlands waiting for us and then we will all travel together again."

Kamarie gave him a quick smile, knowing that she could not speak to him of her fears. "Of course they will."

Then, reluctantly, they both stood up and set off again. As they walked, Kamarie pointed out to Yole what plants were edible and recited to him which parts of certain plants could be used for healing different ailments; she also pointed out which ones were poisonous. She named many animals that they caught glimpses of as they journeyed along and asked Yole to repeat back to her everything she taught him. Yole proved to be a surprisingly quick learner and a very good student. Before long he could recite back to her all of the plants and animals that she had pointed out to him, as well as their uses. Kamarie was impressed at the speed with which he learned, and she told the boy so. Yole beamed with pride at her praise and walked a little taller, rehearsing the things that she had taught him with more confidence.

As the Dragon's Eye began to set and the shadows grew long, Kamarie and Yole came to the edge of the forest. Before them now were long stretches of fields and farmland; far across the fields, they could see where the forest started up again. Next to where they had come out of the forest there stood a small farmhouse with a gentle cloud of smoke billowing out of a red brick chimney. Planted around the house were pretty flowers in neat little gardens. The house seemed cheerful with bright green shutters and a tidy brown door. The place looked homey and welcoming, and it was all they could do to keep from running to it and knocking on the door.

"We can sleep indoors tonight!" Yole said smiling. "I bet the owners of this house will let us sleep in their hayloft if we ask them, like we did on the way to Pearl Cove."

Kamarie shook her head, remembering the last time that they had slept in a hayloft. She could still remember the dark figure slinking towards them, his sword drawn and his menacing presence threatening them all. She remembered Brant's swift and deadly action and shuddered. She did not want to chance a Dark Warrior finding them again, especially since they did not have Brant with them this time.

"No, we will sleep in the woods tonight, and then tomorrow we can ask around in the village to see if we are still going in the right direction. We can also ask some questions to find out if any of the others have passed through this way before us. And maybe we can buy some food."

Yole did not protest her decision to stay in the forest for another night, but Kamarie could tell that he was disappointed. She could relate, for she also had allowed herself to be tempted by thoughts of a pillowy blanket and a warm bed and a fire crackling in a small fireplace. Still, she had to be cautious. There was no telling where the Dark Warriors might appear or how much they knew. This was the sort of village that they might have passed through. There was probably even an inn closer to the center of the village, an inn that would be rife with gossip that anyone could listen to in a crowded taproom, and she could not take the chance that their enemies might hear of their passing this way.

CHAPTER
TWELVE

Kamarie awoke to a sheet of cold rain falling on her face. She pulled her thin blanket up over her head and groaned in dismay. The blanket was soaked through, and the dye was running off her face in little rivers. She could hear Yole off to her left, whimpering under his breath. She looked over at him; he was huddled up in his own sopping wet blanket, gritting his teeth and shaking with cold. Kamarie marveled at his fortitude. He was cold, wet, and miserable, and yet he had not tried to wake her or get her to change her mind about spending the rest of the night in the forest. She wondered, had she been in the same predicament as he, whether or not she would have acted with the same self-control.

Probably not, she decided ruefully. It was very dark, but the Toreth was still low in the sky, meaning that the night was still very young. The prospect of staying where they were made Kamarie cringe. She sighed and looked around. The small shelter they had created was useless against the rain, and there had been no better prospects when they had hunted around earlier for a place to camp. She knew they would find no spot drier than the one they occupied now.

Kamarie stood up slowly, her own teeth chattering with cold, and she went over to where Yole was. "Let's go," she said, shaking him by the shoulder, "it is not that late yet, perhaps the owners of that house will let us dry ourselves by their fireplace until this rain lets up a bit."

As she spoke, lightning began to streak across the sky and thunder rumbled loudly. The rain beat down on them even harder. The two wet and weary travelers held their blankets over their heads to keep the water from soaking them further. They ran as fast as they could to the little house that they had seen earlier and knocked on the door.

A middle-aged woman opened the door in answer to Kamarie's knocking. She was short and plump with graying hair, sparkling eyes and a merry smile. She took one look at the two bedraggled figures standing on her doorstep and practically pulled them into the house.

"Get in here wid you, oot o' the rain," she exclaimed in a strong accent. "Come dry yerselves roond the fire and tell me what ye be doing oot of doors in weather like this."

"Thank you kindly ma'am," Yole said gratefully.

The woman led the two of them into the house, and then all three sat around the fire. The warmth of it was very welcome after the soaking rain that had chilled them to the bone. The woman bustled around and soon brought out two sets of clothes.

"My name be Marghita. These belonged to my chil'ren, when they was smaller. Now they're all grown and live doon the road a spell. Their little 'uns be too small yet fer these, so I keep 'em here till they be needed agin."

"Thank you, ma'am," Kamarie said. "My name is Leota, and this is my youngest brother, Ian. It is very nice of you to take us in on such a night. We got a little lost in the dark and I had no idea where the village inn might be."

"Oh, it be a ways from here, we're about the furthest house from it. You would ne'er had made it on a night like this 'un."

Kamarie and Yole each took turns changing in a little room where the washtub was kept, then they returned to the fire and the woman hung their wet clothes on a handy rod near the fire.

"There now, those will be dry by mornin'. This is no night to be travelin' in," the woman said. "What do you be doing oot, two youngsters like yerselves?"

"We are traveling to visit my older brother," Kamarie lied. "He lives in a small town near the border of the Harshlands, but we seem to have lost the trail."

"Ah, the Harshlands, them that lives near there be brave souls indeed," their hostess said.

"Do you know which direction from here we should go in order to get to the Harshlands?" Kamarie asked.

The woman smiled. "Jest keep going east from here and ye cannot be missing it."

Kamarie nodded. "Thank you," she said. Then after a slight pause, she went on in a more cautious tone, "You would not happen to know if any strangers have been through here in the past couple of days?"

The woman looked at her inquisitively. "I be not thinkin' so lass, but could you be describing these mysterious strangers?"

"A tall man with dark hair, and a stony face. A boy about my age with light brown hair and green eyes; he is a few inches taller than myself and carries himself like a warrior. They both carry swords. The third is a woman, she is very beautiful and slender and she has long brown hair, brown eyes and a quiet look of strength about her."

The woman shook her head. "No one like that has been through here; in fact, there has been no one new around here at all exceptin' you two."

Kamarie sighed. *At least that means no Dark Warriors either*, she thought. "Oh well, they must be traveling a bit slower than us... they're relatives of ours as well, my brother... he's getting married, that's why we're traveling so far to see him."

"Well! A wedding, that sounds grand. My congratulations to yer brother."

They sat in silence for a while, sipping some warmed tea that the woman had fixed for them. Then their hostess spoke again in a decisive tone.

"Now, I have extra blankets for ye. Ye can sleep here in this room for the rest of the night if ye be wishin' it. Me husband spent the day over in the next village at the market, 'tis but a few hours' journey and I be expecting 'im back soon, so do not be startled if ye hear the door opening. Would ye like some warm biscuits and stew? Me husband will have had a cold supper on the road, so I made fresh biscuits for him to have with hot beef stew when he gets home. I made aplenty, more than I ought, truly."

They accepted her offer eagerly. After they downed the warm food, they thanked the woman for her hospitality, promised that they would not be scared if they heard people walking around later, and then promptly fell asleep in their blankets near the hearth, surrounded by the warmth of the fire and the coziness of the cottage, their bellies full and satisfied for the first time in days. The woman studied the two forms sleeping before her fire for a while, then pursed her lips and nodded her head as if she had decided something important. Then she got up and cleaned up their dishes and went into her own room.

Kamarie woke to full alertness several hours later when she heard the door of the cottage open. She remained still, keeping her eyes shut and listening intently. After a moment she allowed her eyelids to flicker open slightly so that she could see. The fire had burned low and she could just make out a shadowy form of the tall figure standing in the doorway. She tensed, ready to spring, but then she saw their hostess run to the figure and hug him.

"Enreigh," she whispered joyfully, "how was yer trip?"

"Prosperous," he said.

The woman put a finger to her lips to shush him, and then she pointed to where Kamarie and Yole were sleeping.

"Who are they?" Enreigh asked quietly.

The woman hesitated, then said, "They say they're traveling to a brother's wedding. But I think that they might be Iosten's two runaways. He came over today and told me that two of his laborers were missin' and that he was putting out the alert for them all over town."

"I should go talk to him and find out," Enreigh said, starting to shrug back into his coat.

"Enreigh! For shame, it is late and raining. The Toreth has long been passin' the top of the sky. Ye be needing rest, ye've had a hard day's travel, and these children will be here in the morning."

He consented readily. "All right, but first thing in the morning…"

"Aye. Aye, first thing in the morning," his wife agreed.

Kamarie lay very still, thinking hard. She knew that it would be fairly easy to prove that they were not the runaway laborers. She also knew that if they left now it would look as though they were guilty and half the town would be chasing them until they were described to Iosten and he told everyone that they were not his runaways. But, staying to prove their innocence would cost them precious time, perhaps an entire day or two, and energy. In less than a moment, Kamarie had made up her mind.

She waited until she had heard no sound from the other room for a long while, and then she waited for a little longer, all the time reciting her lessons on patience silently to herself. Finally, when she was sure that their two hosts were truly asleep, she rose silently, wrapping up her bedroll and picking up her pack. She touched Yole's shoulder and shook him gently. He rolled over and groaned a little but fell silent when she touched a finger to her lips.

"Shhh."

Yole stared at her; then whispered, "What's wrong?"

Kamarie shook her head silently and mouthed the word, "Later."

They changed back into their now dry clothes and gathered up their few belongings. Then Kamarie reached into a small pouch and placed a gold ryal on the table. She knew this was overly generous, but she was grateful for the kindness of these people, her people. She also figured this gesture would allay any suspicions about them being run-away laborers, for there was no way a simple run-away would have that kind of money ... or part with it.

They carefully opened the heavy door and crept silently out of the house into the waning night. *At least,* Kamarie thought, *it finally stopped raining.*

Rhendak was seething with rage as he paced back and forth before the Council of Elders. They sat, in patient silence. The tension in the room grew unto bursting before Rhendak whirled and spoke through clenched teeth.

"I called you here to tell you of a great treachery. Nnyendell and Mystak are free and have vanished. The sentry whose worthless life I gave back to him has fled as well."

If the Elders were not expecting this piece of information, they hid it well, for they showed no great surprise. The truth was that they had almost expected as much ever since Rhendak had shown mercy to the sentry several nights before. The Council did not have the ruling power of the King, but they did hold power in their own right with their age and experience. Rhendak was young, and he relied on their experience and wisdom that age had not yet taught him. The Elders knew that Rhendak must learn the hard way discerning the difference between compassion and justice if he ever hoped to amount to anything as King of the dragons. They knew that Rhendak was strong and that he would make a good king if he could allow himself to be taught, if he could learn from his mistakes. They also knew that he was young and idealistic and that mistakes would be made before he could learn from them. Rhendak did not yet understand the deep capacity for treachery of his own people, and he was, as yet, unprepared to deal with it correctly. However, the Elders had high hopes for Rhendak. They hoped that he could do what many thought was impossible: that he could unite the people of Krayghentaliss. They could see a bright future where the dragons, pegasi, gryphons, centaurs, and unicorns came together and put aside their petty disputes to become a single mighty force, reuniting with the world above, by force if need be.

One of the Elders tapped the ground, requesting the floor. Rhendak stopped pacing and faced him, granting him permission to speak.

"What does Your Majesty propose to do?" the Elder asked.

Rhendak hesitated for a moment, holding on to his ideals of mercy for just an instant longer. Then he spoke, "They must be brought to jusssstice."

"And what is that justice, Majesty?" the Elder asked slyly.

Again, Rhendak hesitated briefly, and then he spat out the sentence that the traitors must face, "Death."

"And if the three of them will not come peaceably to face their trial and punishment?" the Elder asked cannily.

"Then kill them on sight." Rhendak did not hesitate this time, but he said the words with no relish.

The tension in the room lightened, and a few of the Elders even had to fight not to smile with pride as they saw how their young king was learning. He was beginning to understand their expectations and was beginning to see why the laws had to be so harsh. It was a pity that he had to learn of the devious minds of his people through something as great and destructive as Nnyendell and Mystak's treason, but the Elders knew that hard lessons would not be forgotten easily.

Rhendak stayed and helped outline the details surrounding the plans to capture the traitors, and then he retired to his own chamber. He was tired, and he felt as though a great burden rested upon his shoulders. He had much to think over, and he desired to be alone. Rhendak had always believed that the laws of his people were too strict and that the punishments were oftentimes too severe as well, but he began now to see why this was. The Elders had been disappointed by his idealism and merciful nature. Rhendak leaned towards mercy and they to justice. He thought they were simply old-fashioned, but now understood that their wisdom saw more clearly than his ideals. They had known the depth of treason in Nnyendell and Mystak's hearts and had tried to protect him from that evil. And yet, sadly, they had bowed to his decision, letting him learn from his own mistake.

As he pondered the events of the past few days, he began to understand things as never before. He saw the devious trickery in his fellow dragons, and as he recognized their cunning, he became aware of the guile he himself was capable of. Recognizing the natural cunning and deceit within himself he realized in a flash of insight that the other dragons were certainly capable of the same; as well as much, much more. He paced back and forth across the huge stone floor.

"What would you have me do, Shalintess?" he growled, but Shalintess did not answer, could no longer answer.

Shalintess had loved, inspired, and shared his idealistic dreams of a peaceful monarchy. She had also shared in his dreams of doing away with the harsh image of the Dragon King, but now he understood that he could not change that image any more than he could change the nature of his people. Rhendak was now aware of the magnitude of the treachery before him. That was why the first dragon kings had instituted the laws. They, too, had shared in his idealism, dreaming of peace between dragons and all other races, but they understood better than he the inherent difficulty in achieving that coveted peace. Stories about his people were not wrong, the stories that depicted them as ravenous beasts who laid waste to the countryside and made off with whole flocks of sheep and the occasional beautiful maiden. His people were strong in magic and will, and they could rule by terror and cunning, but they were also small in numbers and had been overwhelmed by the other races. Fear of the dragons had been their undoing. And so, the first King, and the first Elder Council of the dragons had instituted laws that were strict, that were harsh, that would be more fearsome than their own nature, in order to save themselves. It was an eye-opening realization, and Rhendak found his mind reeling as he accepted the truth he had never seen before: that his idealism and the Law were one and the same.

The traitors had known him to be merciful, they had known his ideals, and they had used his own personality to their advantage. They had played upon his sympathies, played upon his mercy, and played him for a fool. Rhendak was no longer in a rage; he was cool, calm, and clear-headed. He saw how easily he had been tricked and how dangerous these traitors really were, but he could be dangerous too. He finally understood what the Council had tried to explain to him over and over again: as King of the dragons, it was his duty to be more dangerous than his subjects, to channel their strength and their capabilities in such a way that their entire race was strengthened. And now Rhendak smiled; once the traitors were dealt with, he knew exactly where he would channel the strength of his people. Perhaps he would be able to lead the myth-folk above-realm sooner than anyone had believed possible. Perhaps, with a little dragon cunning and strength, he just might save them all.

Brant and Oraeyn were traveling silently, speaking little. They went swiftly, breaking pace only to eat or to sleep and then only for very short periods of time. Brant was impressed with the youth's stamina, for he never lagged behind or asked to rest for longer than Brant allowed.

Oraeyn found that he had plenty of time to think, as they traveled. He wondered often about the tall man with whom he was traveling. Brant was quiet and calm most of the time, and yet there were moments when Oraeyn was almost afraid of him. Something like fire lurked in the depths of Brant's dark eyes, something old and wild, something that Oraeyn could not quite identify. Oraeyn spent a long while trying to piece together the things that he knew of Brant and succeeded only in becoming more confused. He remembered when they had met him in the middle of the Mountains of Dusk, a peasant or a farmer was all Brant had seemed to be; and yet he had amazed them all by proving that he could move through the land without making a sound and leave a campsite without even a trace of evidence that could be discovered, no matter how hard a tracker looked. Oraeyn had been impressed with Brant's familiarity with weapons and battle skills. The man could handle a sword and sit a horse like no other. They had assumed that he lived his entire life in small towns and among peasants, yet Brant was acquainted with Calyssia, could read Old Kraïc, and knew his bearings throughout Aom-igh. He always knew where he was and how long it would be till their destination. He was familiar with wizardry and shape-shifters, had known Yole to be a dragon, and was constantly surprising even Dylanna with his vast knowledge. On top of all this, perhaps the most alarming of the small store of facts about Brant was that a Dark Warrior had actually fled from him.

It was this last thing that Oraeyn could not understand. It was the single thing that did not fit into the puzzle that was Brant. He could understand a farmer who had traveled the country as a young man, perhaps even spent some time training as a knight, and maybe meeting Calyssia and learning about magic and Old Kraïc from her. However, Oraeyn could find no spot which explained why a Dark Warrior would fear Brant. Oraeyn's recent experience confirmed the stories he had heard about Dark Warriors. They were fierce, relentless, and skilled fighters. They did not wear helmets or armor, and yet they entered battle fearlessly. Oraeyn had defeated one, but knew that luck had played a major part while Brant had killed two outright and the third fled when facing Brant alone. The only conclusion that made any sense was also the thought that must be impossible... was it possible that the Dark Warriors knew who Brant was? Surely that could not be true... could it?

When he was not wondering about who, or what, Brant really was, Oraeyn was puzzling over the words of the wood nymph. What was the meaning of her baffling riddles? He possessed no magical abilities, and for that matter he had never wanted to. He pondered the sword at his side. Perhaps the blade was, after all, the Lost Sword of King Llian, gift of the dragons. The two dragons had certainly recognized it, calling it by name: the Fang Blade. He remembered King Rhendak giving him a strange look, a look that he had dismissed at the time, but now he understood that look to be both recognition and surprise. No, not surprise, more like a suppressed delight. Oraeyn touched the sword hanging at his side, thinking hard. He allowed himself to believe for a moment that what he had found actually was the sword that the King of the dragons had fashioned for Llian, that he really was a direct descendant of the great King who had ruled over six hundred years ago. Maybe the sword had not only been fashioned by dragons but somehow embedded with dragon magic during its forging as well. That would explain much of his unusual experiences these past several weeks since the sword had claimed him.

"We stop here for the night." Brant's voice cut into Oraeyn's thoughts, startling him.

Oraeyn looked around and found, to his surprise, that the Dragon's Eye had already set and that it was growing dark. He had lost track of all time, wrapped as he had been in his thoughts.

"That Dark Warrior fled from you," Oraeyn said, giving words to the first thing that popped into his head.

Mentally he kicked himself, wondering why he had blurted that out, but Brant did not look angry with him. The man gazed at Oraeyn with a weighing look in his eyes. Oraeyn winced a little, wishing he had not spoken aloud.

Brant finally nodded. "And you want to know why."

Oraeyn froze. So the warrior really had fled from Brant; the man was not denying that. Whether he had fled in terror or in wisdom it did not matter, he had fled, and that meant that he did not dare to face Brant alone in combat. Oraeyn nodded.

"Yes, I want to know why."

Brant sighed, the sigh of a man who has carried too much on his shoulders for far too long, and stared off into the darkness of the coming night. He was silent for a few moments, as though he wanted to be sure of his words before they escaped his mouth. Oraeyn waited.

"A man cannot choose his own birth."

Oraeyn raised his eyebrows and leaned forward in expectation.

Brant's face seemed to lose all expression as he paused, then started again. "In my youth, training and study was all I knew. It was, in fact, all that I loved. My training included travels throughout the Stained Sea, and in these travels I lost my teacher and friend and became prey for evil men. In desperation and good fortune, I found myself in the Harshlands, where I soon lost all sense of direction and time. For the first time in my life, I was lost and without hope... and that is when Arnaud found me. He brought me to his aunt and uncle, where I regained my strength and my life. I shared their home with my new brother, and I trusted Arnaud with my soul. But then, Arnaud was given the throne, and I needed the open road over the comforts of the palace. For many years, I traveled throughout Aom-igh as the King's Protector and Servant. Arnaud preferred me to stay with him as adviser, but I had no desire to settle down. A restlessness borne in my spirit made me keep to the road, and I learned this country well.

"Eventually, I discovered my way into Pearl Cove, only to learn later that it was the Keeper who found and called me there. I spent three years learning under Calyssia. She replaced the teacher and friend I had lost, and I was reminded of my love for training and study. She taught me the Dragon Tongue and the way of wizards and much of history. She taught me to love the land, and to love people, to set aside fear and contempt for trust and compassion. I found something of myself, something that I could understand, and something I had never known: the yearning to rest and spend the rest of my days in the peaceful Cove. Yet I was not ready to stay in one place. I thought I was, but Calyssia knew better. You may well believe that three years in that place would have been sufficient temptation for any man to stay there forever. I thought so too, at first, but it was not enough for me. She knew my stay would be brief; she told me as much when I first entered her Cove. I did not believe her then. I heard her words, but it was not until many years later that I understood the truth of her vision or the depth of her wisdom.

"After three years, I grew restless again, and I left, just as Calyssia said I would. I came back and learned that Aom-igh was overrun with murderers and thieves, so I returned to the palace where I was received with open arms. I told Arnaud that I was there to help him; I wanted no pay except horses and the approval of the King to track down any and all lawbreakers and bring them to justice. Arnaud accepted my offer and sent me out as the 'King's Warrior' and that title became respected and feared. I knew the country and had both the King's justice and Calyssia's wisdom behind my sword.

"My fame spread before me and even out to the islands in the great chain that separates the Soothing Sea from the Stained Sea. It is likely that my name even reached the Dark Country; perhaps the Warrior we faced was young and overawed by a name that has long laid at rest. After many years of hard and dangerous work, justice and wisdom prevailed and the people were safe once again. It was then that I left my role as the King's Warrior. It was also then that I met Imojean. She quieted my restless spirit and woke a contentment inside me I had never known. If we were to have children, I wanted to raise them apart from my old life, to know me for who I had become, and not for who I once had been. King Arnaud gladly released me from my oath to a freedom I had never sought, but was very glad to claim." Brant stopped suddenly and said no more.

Oraeyn mulled over Brant's words. He felt, somehow, that there was more to Brant's story that he was not telling. Oraeyn was positive that the man had spoken no untrue word; however, he got the feeling that Brant had not said everything either.

However, he knew that Brant had said all he meant to, and so he did not press for anything further.

They set up camp together but neither slept for a long while. Sitting by the small campfire next to Oraeyn, Brant stared into the orange flames. He was aware of Oraeyn's eyes, watching him, and he knew that the young man had not been satisfied with his story. He frowned and rubbed the palm of his hand, flexing his fingers as if in pain.

"That's an odd place for a scar," Oraeyn said quietly, gesturing at the palm of Brant's right hand, the palm he had been rubbing. "There must be a story there."

Brant looked up, startled. How long had it been since he had even noticed the blemish? He stared at the scar and frowned.

"Yes, there is a story behind that," he said slowly. "When I was very young, I took an oath to protect and serve my country for the rest of my life, no matter how long that might be. It was a blood oath."

Oraeyn nodded, curiosity in his green eyes. "I've never heard of that... I mean, I've heard of blood oaths, but not that particular one. How does it go?"

Brant's dark eyes seemed to glaze a bit as they filled with old memories. "Courage, purity, truth, and honor. These things will I walk with and give my life to uphold, I swear this by my blood and by my sword." He intoned the words softly and slowly, and Oraeyn got the feeling that the words were as much a part of Brant as the scar on his palm was.

"That is beautiful. I have never heard one like it."

"No, you would not have."

Oraeyn frowned. The certainty in Brant's voice was unsettling. He thought back through his training, but it was true; he had never heard of that particular oath. Something, the barest shadow of a thought, whispered to Oraeyn that this was important, but he could not catch hold of the idea and shrugged it away. They lapsed once more into silence, gazing into the dancing flames of the fire. At last, Oraeyn went to sleep, leaving Brant to take the first watch. He wanted to think more about what he had learned from the tall man, but his eyelids grew heavy and he fell into a deep sleep.

The next morning, Brant woke Oraeyn with a gruff, "Let's move."

Oraeyn groaned and grumbled about getting up at such an early hour, but Brant would have none of it. So Oraeyn got up, complaining about the inhuman and cruel pace that Brant was setting and muttering that he would give his sword arm for one good night's rest in a real bed. When he discovered that Brant had cooked eggs and rabbit stew for breakfast his whining subsided, and he remarked that it really was a very beautiful morning. Brant laughed at that, and Oraeyn wondered what was so funny. He also wondered if he had ever heard Brant laugh before, but he did not have long to ponder this thought, for the man was impatient to continue their journey.

Within a few hours of swift noiseless travel, they reached a tiny village that had been built within a large clearing of the forest. Spotting a nearby secluded cottage, Brant commented that information could be useful and suggested they knock at the door of this home. Oraeyn, quick to agree to any form of rest, consented readily. The two walked up and knocked on the door; an elderly couple promptly greeted them.

The woman stared at them. "Me goodness!" she exclaimed. "So many new faces around these parts of a sudden!"

Brant was instantly on his guard. If Oraeyn had not been watching for it, he would not have seen the change that came over him. There was a slight shift in his stance, a clenched muscle in his jaw, and wariness in his eyes. He wondered if Brant suspected that Dark Warriors had been through this small village, but he kept quiet, allowing Brant to do the talking and questioning.

"What do you mean?" Brant asked carefully.

"Just what I be sayin', we've been having many visitors of late," the woman smiled amiably, then gasped, "but I do be forgettin' me manners in all this excitement! My name is Marghita, and this be my husband Enreigh." The man nodded, and the woman continued, "But come in, come in, we can be giving ye a warm meal before you must be traveling on. And perhaps ye can be tellin' us a bit o' news from outside, because certain sure you're not from these parts."

Oraeyn and Brant followed the two into the charming cottage. Marghita stirred a pot over the fire from which emanated a heavenly aroma. The brew turned out to be a heavy chicken stew that warmed their stomachs and tasted as good as anything Oraeyn had ever come across. They both praised the stew with enthusiasm, causing Marghita to blush.

"That's me mother's secret recipe, rest her soul."

Marghita turned out to be a shameless gossip. As they sat around a small, sturdy table, the woman chattered on endlessly, answering any and all questions that Brant asked.

"You mentioned other visitors to your village," Brant inquired, his tone one of easy conversation.

"Oh my! That is a story!" Marghita exclaimed. "It was stormin' out the other night, and shortly after the Dragon's Eye had set and the rain was pourin' down in sheets, I heard a knock on the door. Lo and behold, there were two chiluns standing upon me doorstep while the tempest was likening to drown the poor dears. I offered them a place to stay, being a right proper housewife, and they came right on inside, shivering with wet and cold. They told me where they was headed, asked me directions too. I thought that they was a-lyin' to me, for I took them to be the runaway laborers of our neighbor Iosten. It gets lonesome like out here on the outskirts, we sometimes have a bit o' a problem with contract-breakers. I suppose they heard me say that to me husband here when he came home later that night, for when I woke in the morning, the two had fled away and were long gone."

"Were they the two runaway laborers?" Brant asked mildly, not really interested.

"Oh me goodness, no! And more's the pity of it that they run off before they could find out they was in no trouble. The two laborers were found, not really runaway, just lost and scared and cold because they hadn't been able to find no place to get in oot of the rain."

Oraeyn suddenly leaned forward, interest written across his face. "These two who stayed at your house, what did they look like?"

"Well let me be a-thinking, the boy had dark skin, looked as though he had been outside most of this Warm-Term, working out in the fields. That's how I took them to be the runaways, don't you know. One of them was a small boy with dark brown hair, and the other was a girl, pale, rather tall, maybe a wee bit shorter than ye, lad. I never did see her hair, she kept a hood on, and I figured that it was cut short or something and did nae ask aboot it, not wanting to shame the poor lass. Why do you ask? Do you be a-knowing them?"

Oraeyn looked disappointed. "No, I thought for a moment... but no, thank you ma'am."

Then Brant spoke again, "These two, where did you say they were heading?"

Marghita looked up from her soup. "Did I nae mention that? It was the most interesting part of the whole story. Said they was heading to a village near the Harshlands to visit their brother, bless their souls. The boy is gettin' married, see, and they wanted to be there fer the happy day."

"Did they mention any names?" Brant asked.

Oraeyn stared at him. Marghita's description of the two travelers who had stayed in her house sounded nothing like Kamarie or Yole or Dylanna. He could not figure out why Brant was so interested. Yes, the visitors in Marghita and Enreigh's home *had* been a young boy and a girl who could have been Yole and either Dylanna or Kamarie, but there were probably hundreds of places where they could find a young boy traveling with his older sister or young aunt or some other such relation. Also, Oraeyn could not picture Kamarie afraid of being mistaken for a runaway laborer and fleeing in the night from that misinterpretation of her identity.

"Aye, they did tell me at that. I remember because they were odd names. They said they called themselves by the names Ian and Leota," the woman said, bobbing her head. "Do you be knowing them then?"

Brant shook his head, "No."

But there was something about the way he said it that made Oraeyn look at him sharply. Brant just looked back at him mildly and said nothing, as he continued to eat his soup and listen to Marghita. Oraeyn could not puzzle out the man's strange behavior, so he did the only thing he could and turned back to his stew.

"The strangest part of the whole thing," Enreigh said, speaking for the first time, "they left a gold ryal on the table 'fore they left. That more 'n anything made us believe they was more than just runaways."

Oraeyn frowned. That kind of money could only have come from someone noble, but how could Kamarie and Yole have changed their appearances so drastically? They finished their soup, Marghita prattling on the entire time about this or that crop and this or that neighbor who had done something or other. Oraeyn really did not pay that much attention to her words. He was relieved when Brant stood up.

"Thank you ma'am," Brant said, "for the bit of rest and the warm food." He pushed his chair back under the table and placed something unnoticed by his glass.

"And welcome ye be." Marghita smiled brilliantly.

"Come again," Enreigh said, finally getting a word in edgewise.

Oraeyn smiled and followed Brant out the door. He was very relieved to get away from the odd woman and her endless talk of things that did not concern or interest him.

As they walked through the village, Oraeyn asked, "Why were you so interested in the two people who stayed at that house?"

Brant glanced at him and continued walking, "Because it was Kamarie and Yole, and I wanted to find out if they were still traveling to the Harshlands. I also wanted to make sure that they were safe and unharmed."

"Kamarie and Yole!" Oraeyn exclaimed, "The descriptions that Marghita gave were nothing like Kamarie and Yole!"

Brant allowed a small smile to pass across his face. "Skorch root and dragon-berries can be mixed in hot water to make a brown dye. That explains the tanned skin color and the young boy's brown hair. The dye would not have worked in Kamarie's hair though, it is too dark, and that is why she hid her hair under a hood. She said it was raining, so Kamarie's dye must have gotten washed off. Besides, who else could afford to pay a gold ryal for a stew dinner and two blankets on the floor? You should learn to pay closer attention to details, lad. I am surprised you didn't pick up on the biggest clue."

Oraeyn looked at him quizzically, "What clue?"

"Their names," Brant said simply. "Ian is a root form of the word 'dragon' in some country dialects, and Leota means…"

"Woman of the people," Oraeyn finished irritably, trying to prove that he did, at least, know *some* things; then he let out a low whistle and looked up at Brant in admiration. "How did you figure all that out, and why would they flee in the night when they heard that they had been mistaken for runaways?"

"First of all, they were not fleeing from fear. Kamarie is not the type of girl who would want to spend precious time explaining that she is not a runaway when she could be traveling further towards her destination. And as to how I figured all of this out, well… when you have been solving riddles for as long as I have, you will understand how to search for clues in every word you hear."

A small, knowing smile tugged at the corners of Brant's mouth, but he kept silent, causing Oraeyn to pause mid-step and wonder.

"How old *are* you?" Oraeyn asked.

"Old enough," was all that Brant would say.

CHAPTER THIRTEEN

Oraeyn woke in a cold sweat, his heart racing and his breath coming in short, ragged gasps. He had dreamed that there were dark shadows creeping up all around him, silhouetted by the dying embers of the small campfire. He took a deep breath to calm himself and sat up, the dream still clinging to him. He looked around warily, and then he went very still, motionless with horror. The dark shadows had been no dream. They were there, slinking towards him from behind the tall trees. Like smoke, the figures seemed to rise out of the ground. The pale glow of the dying campfire made them appear as ghosts.

Terror gripped his heart. His ability to cry out a warning was choked from his throat by fear. Oraeyn looked wildly towards the spot where Brant had been sleeping and an icy finger of dread snaked through him. Brant was gone. He was alone, surrounded and outnumbered by the fell force of menacing figures that approached him with silent, slow footsteps, drawing closer with every breath he took. He groped frantically for his sword, but whether in his terror or his haste, he could not find it. With almost impossible speed and agility, one of the dark figures leaped at him and wrapped strong, supple fingers around his throat choking the breath out of him. Oraeyn screamed, his voice hoarse and rasping. He thrashed about, but the enemy's grip was like a band of iron about his neck. Then the shadow spoke; words came from the faceless terror that seized him by the throat.

"Oraeyn, Oraeyn!"

"No!" He tried to scream, tried to lash out, but his efforts were futile.

"Oraeyn! Wake up!" The voice was Brant's.

Oraeyn felt himself being shaken by the shoulders, and he opened his eyes with a gasp, squinting in the sudden brightness of the rising Dragon's Eye. Brant was kneeling next to him with a concerned look on his face.

"Are you all right?"

Oraeyn stared at the man in confusion. The light was so bright compared to the darkness that he had been engulfed in, and for a moment he could not comprehend what was real. Then he began to shake, a great shudder coursed through him.

"A dream, it was nothing but a dream."

Brant looked at him in concern. "Dreams can be powerful."

Oraeyn nodded silently.

"We need to get going," Brant said, "would you like to tell me about your dream?"

Oraeyn stood up and shook his head, and then he changed his mind and nodded. "There - there were dark shadows all around me, tall and strong like the Dark Warriors. And you weren't there. I tried to call out to you, but you were gone, and I couldn't find my sword. Then one of the shadows jumped at me and wrapped its fingers around my neck, choking me. I could not breathe or cry out for help…" Oraeyn trailed off.

He began rolling up his blanket and organizing his pack. He kept his head bent, ashamed of his fear. He was suddenly embarrassed that the dream had terrified him so badly, and he was even more ashamed that Brant had seen his terror. Oraeyn knew that the man would think him a coward now, unfit to ever be a knight of the realm. His shoulders slumped as he stuffed his blanket into his pack.

"Oraeyn." There was none of the reproach or disappointment that Oraeyn feared to hear in Brant's voice.

Oraeyn dared to lift his eyes and look at Brant.

"There is no shame in being afraid, the shame is found in not being willing to face that fear."

"But I thought that courage was the absence of fear," Oraeyn protested. "Brave men are described as such because they are not afraid of anything. You are the most courageous person I know. You're courageous *because* you're not afraid. Dark Warriors fear *you*, not the other way around!"

Brant shook his head. "I do not lack fear. Don't you understand? Courage is not found in lacking fear, courage is found in not allowing your fear to rule you. Think, young knight, would there be any courage required to face that which you do not fear?"

"Well... I suppose not...no...I guess you're right." Oraeyn bit his lip as Brant's words sank in. "Huh, I never thought about it that way before. I... I guess then that courage is really... just facing fear."

Brant slapped him on the back. "He can be taught!" A grin spread across his face. Oraeyn was startled, he wasn't sure he'd ever seen Brant really smile before. "Now we really must get moving, or it will be night again before we have even taken a step from our campsite."

Oraeyn laughed in spite of himself, for the Dragon's Eye had only just risen fully above the horizon, and it was what most people would consider very early in the morning. It felt good to laugh, the sound of it dispersed the rest of the shadows of his dream.

Kamarie did not allow herself or Yole to rest again until they were many miles from the small village. Although they were both tired, much time would be lost if they were not careful. Finally, much to Yole's relief, she stopped.

"We are safe now," she said.

"What were we running from anyway?"

"The people we were staying with thought that we were runaway laborers," Kamarie explained.

"So?" Yole was outraged, "We weren't! We could have stayed there and proven that we weren't! We could have done it easily. We ran all night because of *that?*"

"You're right, we could have proven that we were not who they thought we were, but it would have taken up precious time, and we need to get to the Harshlands as quickly as possible. We must travel with the swiftness that Brant expected of us or we will miss the others and never get home."

Yole calmed down a bit at her words and tone, but it was clear that he was still upset.

"We can rest now, I promise there will be no more running tonight."

Yole sighed. "Now that tonight is almost over."

"Well, we can rest for a few hours at least."

Yole sighed again, sounding like one who has long suffered many injustices. His sigh caused Kamarie to grin, though she was careful not to let the boy see it. Although quite mature for his age, Yole sometimes acted very young.

"Get some sleep now," Kamarie said. "You will need it. And from here on out there will be no more villages for us. Not even if it *snows!*"

Yole groaned but said nothing as he stretched out on the ground and fell asleep. Kamarie smiled down at the sleeping form, feeling a fondness for the boy. For the first time in her life, she wondered what it might have been like to have a younger brother or sister. Then she curled up in her own bedroll and slept peacefully.

"Kamarie."

Kamarie woke to an insistent whisper and someone tapping on her shoulder. Yole was kneeling next to her, and the look in his eyes told her that something was wrong. She stood up and drew her sword with the practiced grace that had impressed even Brant.

"What is it?" she asked in a hushed voice, crouching down next to the boy, her eyes darting from shadow to shadow straining to see what the threat was.

"Someone is watching us."

Kamarie glanced around, but she could see no one. She could, however, feel the watching eyes on them, and it was enough to convince her that they were in danger. With skillful, swift movements, Kamarie set about striking their camp. She rolled up her blankets and shouldered her pack within seconds. She saw that Yole had already done so, and she nodded in approval. She turned and set out in the direction that they had been traveling; she did not run or hurry, but there was stealthy speed in every step she took. There was nothing else that she could do but wait for the enemy to make the first move. She could not attack what she could not see, and yet, the hidden eyes watching her made the skin on the back of her neck prickle with nervous anticipation.

Yole tried to match every step that Kamarie took, keeping his movements through the trees silent. He was glad that they were not out in the open; at least here in the forest there were places to hide. He tried to ignore the presence of the unseen eyes on his back, but he could not. He wondered if he was just being paranoid and glanced over his shoulder. He could see nothing; if something was watching or following them, it was keeping itself well hidden.

They continued traveling in this manner throughout the day. Neither of them spoke, hoping that they had lost their pursuer and fearing that any extra noise would attract more attention if they had not. They neither stopped nor slowed their pace; the feeling of being hunted would not allow them to rest. However, as the day drew to a close, despair began to well up within Kamarie. She did not know how much longer she and Yole could keep up this pace, for they had not stopped to rest or eat all day and they would be at a disadvantage when night fell. She was weak with hunger, despite managing to eat a few trail rations that she kept in her pockets. Instinct told her that the attack would come when darkness enclosed them. She felt helpless: knowing when the enemy would make his move, yet powerless to do anything to prevent it.

Kamarie glanced around, her sharp eyes taking note of their surroundings. The underbrush had become very thick immediately to their left; she could see no end to the bushes and small plants. There was a narrow space under the bushes where it was conceivable that a small child could crawl through them. It would be fairly easy for someone to vanish into that thicket if that someone was small enough. To their right the trees had thinned, and through the trees Kamarie could see more wide-open plains. Directly in front of them was more of the thick, dark forest that would grow even darker in the quickly approaching twilight. Kamarie took a deep breath, a plan forming in her mind.

She drew closer to Yole. "Listen carefully," she whispered.

He nodded wordlessly.

"Do you think that you could fit through that small opening under those bushes and crawl unseen through the thicket deeper into the forest?"

Yole stiffened a little, knowing that she was suggesting that he go that way on his own, but he nodded again.

"Do you think that you could find a good place to hide where no one would be able to find you?" Kamarie asked, hoping that her plan would work.

"Yes," Yole whispered, so quietly that Kamarie almost missed it.

"Good," she said. "When I give the word, you crawl under there and go as quickly and as quietly as you can. Find a good place to hide and then wait. If morning comes and you have not heard the shrill whistle of a shadow-lark, then you must travel on to the Harshlands without me. But, if you hear the whistle of a shadow-lark, then you will know that it is safe to come out."

Yole twisted his neck so that he was looking up at her, he had a puzzled frown on his face. "How will the shadow-lark know if he should whistle or not?" the boy asked seriously.

Kamarie almost laughed at Yole's naïve question, but the danger of the situation held her to a small smile. She whispered quietly, "I'll be the one making the signal. Do you know what it sounds like?"

Yole's eyes widened as he understood. He nodded. "I do."

Twilight fell, and the forest grew dark even as the presence of the unseen eyes weighed upon them more heavily. At length, Kamarie realized that they had reached a spot that felt defensible. She reached out and touched Yole's shoulder.

"Go, now!" She pushed him towards the dense thicket.

He broke away and ran towards the bushes. He dropped onto his stomach and rolled quickly into the underbrush that lined the path. Kamarie heard him wriggle through the branches, and she heard the rustle of dead leaves, and then the forest went silent again. She inwardly congratulated the boy on his stealth, and then she whirled to face the silent watchers, sword drawn.

For a moment, she wondered if she had been wrong or if the watching eyes had been nothing more than her imagination. There was no one behind her, no movement in the trees, no sound of footsteps through the forest, no sound at all except the slight, chill breeze that softly whispered around her. She crouched, anticipating an attack. Her instincts told her that she was not wrong, that the enemy was coming. She waited, her sword drawn, her heart beating fast and her fear mounting. She backed up to the large oak tree she had seen as a defensible position. It would offer at least a little bit of suitable protection for her back. Her eyes darted everywhere, and she backed into the tree until she could feel its rough bark pressing against her. Kamarie relaxed a little in the minute amount of protection that the tree offered, but her muscles stayed tense.

She was beginning to think that she was going crazy and had only imagined that there was someone following them when she saw movement off to her left, following the exact way that she and Yole had come. Her heart sank when they came more fully into view. It was another band of Dark Warriors, three of them this time.

Kamarie was suddenly assuaged by doubt and fear. She had learned well how to use her sword, she could hold her own among the other squires and had even beaten Garen once or twice. She still believed that he had let her win, no matter what he said otherwise. But she had never fought against anything real; none of her opponents had ever been trying to hurt or kill her. The Dark Warriors were altogether different. These were soldiers who were trained to hunt, fight, and kill, and she knew for certain this was no game.

In that singular instant, she was frozen with self-doubt and fear, but in the next moment she had gotten a hold of herself. This stand she was taking was hopeless; she acknowledged that. She knew very well that there was no hope of rescue or survival; this first real battle would also be her last. But she had to give Yole time to get away. He was under her royal protection, and there was nobody else standing between him and the enemy. Kamarie held up her sword to face the enemy and readied herself to die.

Brant and Oraeyn had found the spot where Kamarie and Yole had spent the night, and now they were following their trail at a near run. It was obvious that they were gaining on their friends with great speed, for the trail was warm.

Darkness was gathering, but Brant said not a word about stopping and Oraeyn did not ask. Urgency drove them, and they hurried on through the woods even as the Dragon's Eye sank below the horizon. Oraeyn sensed that they were very close to rejoining Kamarie and Yole, as if they would turn a corner any minute now and see their friends, and he did not want to stop until he knew they were safe.

Brant continued to push on well after dark. There was something menacing in the woods, and danger and anger fueled his pursuit while caution and concern guided his thoughts.

One of the Dark Warriors approached, the other two hanging back to see what would happen. Kamarie marveled at the grace of her foe. His fluid movement reminded her of a cat or a predator bird.

"Jaret," one of the two spoke, his voice uncertain.

"Quiet, Kyan," the warrior who was approaching Kamarie snapped.

"But... it's just a girl," Kyan persisted.

"And she's seen us," Jaret replied.

"Who is she going to tell? There isn't a house for miles, by the time she reached anyone worth telling, we would already be long gone," Kyan argued.

"She has seen us. Surely I don't have to remind you of the Council's orders, of the King's orders?"

"We were ordered to find a criminal with no description and no name and to leave no trace of our passing. Surely this does not include the sacrifice of our honor?" Kyan asked.

Jaret seemed to falter slightly, pausing in his advance. His face, which had been stony a moment ago softened just a little. As Kamarie watched him wavering, she was struck by the feeling that she knew this man from somewhere, his face seemed familiar.

"Here, little one," Kyan spoke to Kamarie now. "You're not going to tell anyone you've seen us, are you? We mean no harm to you or your companion."

It would have been better for Kamarie to agree with him. Kyan had already put a seed of doubt into his comrades' minds about their orders and their honor, and if she had simply agreed with him, they probably would have faded away into the night. However, Kamarie was already struggling to keep her identity a secret from everyone they met, a task which was taxing her harder than she had imagined. She was tired and she was scared and she was alone, and these men had stepped out of her worst nightmare. She truly believed that she could not trust a word they said, and so she very rashly spoke her mind.

"No harm? Tell that to the slain families in Peak's Shadow. I have seen the handiwork of Dark Warriors. Keep your 'mercy' and your 'honor,' for I have seen that you have none. I will make no pact with you."

"Well said," Jaret grinned. "Well, Kyan, you heard the girl."

Kyan's face dropped in disbelief as Kamarie brandished her sword. He shook his head sadly; he had hoped to convince his comrades not to kill this one, to leave her in peace, but her little speech had ruined any hope of that. He nodded at Jaret.

"Go ahead then, but make it quick."

Jaret advanced towards Kamarie's position. He moved in absolute silence and astonishing speed; one moment he was moving stealthily along, and the next instant he pounced, his sword coming down at Kamarie's head with shocking force.

Kamarie met his sword and held off the blow, barely. She pushed Jaret's sword away. Her own sword seemed to spring to life on its own as her arm remembered the patterns that she had practiced over and over again. Kamarie blinked and saw the warrior staring down at her with an expression of shock on his face. She had somehow flipped the sword out of his hand and was now holding her blade stretched out, the point resting near Jaret's throat. He did not look as though he was accustomed to being held at sword point, and he held up his hands in surrender.

Kamarie was not sure what to do. She could not just lower her sword and let him go pick up his own, for she assumed that her skill had simply caught him by surprise. She did not want to face him when he was on his guard. But she found that neither could she kill him, especially now that he had no weapon.

An instant later the question was answered for her. Kamarie had forgotten about the other two Dark Warriors. She heard a tiny movement to her left and glanced that way; in that moment

Kyan, who had come up on her right side, grabbed her sword arm and wrested the blade from her hand. Too late, she realized her mistake. She let out a single, piercing scream, but it was cut off as the silent, third warrior, who had crept up on her left to distract her, brought the hilt of his sword crashing down on her head in a blow that knocked Kamarie out. She was aware of shooting pain that raced through her skull and, then, blackness.

From somewhere ahead, there came noises that did not belong in the forest. There was the brief sound of metal striking metal as though sword blades were crashing together. Then there was a short period of silence. Brant and Oraeyn slowed, straining their ears. Out of nowhere they heard a piercing scream that was cut off immediately after it started.

"That could be Kamarie!"

Oraeyn looked at Brant, a question in his eyes. Brant nodded his head in answer, and both of them broke into a run. They raced towards the sound, and then proceeded with caution as they approached a clearing ahead.

Brant laid a hand on Oraeyn's shoulder, stopping him and pushing him down, closer to the ground. Oraeyn jumped, startled, but he followed Brant's example without question as he crouched low to the ground.

"Dark Warriors," Brant whispered, "three of them."

Oraeyn peered cautiously into the darkness as they crept closer. There indeed were Dark Warriors ahead of them on the path. They were dragging a limp body away from one of the great tall oak trees.

"Now what do you suggest we do, Kyan?" one of the figures asked.

"Don't take that tone with me, Raelf, I'm your commander here. You should have killed her instead of knocking her out. If it was dishonorable to kill a woman in combat, it would stain all of us to kill one who is unconscious."

"Be quiet, both of you," a third voice said in an exasperated tone. "We'll just have to tie her up and take her with us."

"That will slow us down, Jaret," the one called Kyan argued.

"Then we'll tie her up and leave her here."

Oraeyn saw the face of the prisoner and his eyes widened. He made to stand up, but Brant's hand on his arm kept him down.

"Brant, it's Kamarie."

"And charging in there and getting killed is not going to help her. They're still arguing about what to do with her, which means she's alive. We have to be smart about this, there's three of them. On my signal," Brant said to Oraeyn in a hushed whisper, "you stay here, I am going to circle around and catch them off guard."

Oraeyn nodded wordlessly, and Brant slid off into the darkness. Not for the first time, Oraeyn was amazed at how quietly Brant could move. The man was a shadow, for all the noise he made. It was not just when he was trying to be quiet either, Oraeyn suddenly noted; Brant moved with the same quiet stealth even when they had been running, even when they were traveling along in broad daylight. Oraeyn did not have much time to marvel, however, for Brant was already in position.

Brant made a twig crack beneath his foot, and all three of the Dark Warriors looked up from their argument in his direction. Oraeyn, recognizing Brant's action as the signal, raced as quietly as he could towards the warriors. Brant came rushing out towards them as well. When the warriors saw their two attackers, they put up a good fight, but they had been taken by surprise. Brant ran his sword through the one who had argued for tying Kamarie up and leaving her, and Oraeyn managed to stab the other one in the leg. The one called Kyan turned to face Brant and stared directly into his face. His own visage drained of all color and he did the one thing that Oraeyn never would have expected him to do; he grabbed his wounded comrade by the arm, and together they turned and fled into the night. Oraeyn stood watching them run, his sword lowered and his mouth hanging open in surprise. Brant also watched the warriors as they fled, but there was no look of surprise on his face. When they had checked the area to make sure that there were no more Dark Warriors hiding in the shadows to jump out at them, they turned their attention to the princess.

Oraeyn lifted her shoulders off the ground and laid her head in his lap. "Kamarie!"

Her eyes were closed, and for a moment Oraeyn was afraid that she was not breathing. He put his ear to her lips and was relieved to note that she was, in fact, breathing, though shallowly. She was very still and did not move or wake when he called her name a second time.

"She received a blow to the head," Brant said, "she will recover."

"Why were they tying her up?" Oraeyn asked, glad to hear that Kamarie was going to be all right. "Why didn't the Dark Warriors kill her?"

Brant shook his head. "I have no idea. Perhaps Kamarie will tell us when she awakes."

Oraeyn was not going to let Brant get away with any flimsy explanations this time, and he burst out in an accusing tone, "You know why the Dark Warriors won't face you in combat, you know what questions they wanted to ask Kamarie, why won't you tell me? Are the Dark Warriors after you? You told the King you thought this whole invasion is because of you. Why would you say something like that unless you were absolutely convinced that you were right? Who are you, really?"

Brant's face became dark as Oraeyn spoke. When the young man stopped yelling long enough to take a breath, Brant spoke in a voice of control and quiet anger, "I have my reasons for not telling you the whole truth. Suffice to say that you are right, about some things. I don't know if those three wanted to question Kamarie, or if they simply couldn't face the dishonor of killing a woman. Honor is very important to the Dark Warriors, despite their actions against your country, they do have honor... most of them, anyway."

"What do you mean, 'your country'? Isn't it your country too? How do you know so much about them? Everything you say sounds like a half-truth. It's our lives you're risking, and you don't even have the decency to tell us the truth. I don't know what the truth is, but I know it's not the bits and pieces you've told us."

"You speak of things you do not understand, could never understand," Brant's voice was sharp.

"Of course I don't understand! You won't explain it to me!"

Brant merely looked at him, but the look silenced Oraeyn. The young man stared down at the ground, not sure what to say, but refusing to apologize for his questions. He was ashamed of his outburst though, and set about busying himself with setting up camp. When he dared to look up again, Brant seemed to have forgotten the whole incident.

"Help me move her over onto these blankets," Brant said in a friendly tone. "Gently now, be careful!"

They spread out their bedrolls and extra blankets, arranging them into a soft bed, and then laid Kamarie onto it. Brant broke his own rule about not having a fire, and then he went hunting. He came back with a pheasant and two rabbits, which he cooked over the small fire. The two men ate quietly, but the silence was not an angry one. Brant glanced in concern over at Kamarie, who still lay unmoving.

Oraeyn caught the worried expression. "She is going to be all right, isn't she?"

"She has been asleep for longer than I expected."

"But she will be all right," Oraeyn said again, needing reassurance.

"I don't know."

Oraeyn's shoulders slumped. Then Kamarie moaned and began muttering feverishly. Oraeyn and Brant hurried to her.

"The shadow-lark," Kamarie muttered. "Yole, I'm sorry."

"How could we have forgotten about Yole?" Oraeyn closed his eyes, mortified. "Do you think he's still nearby?"

Brant stood up and walked around the area, scanning the signs quickly, then he pointed. "He went through there."

Oraeyn looked to where Brant was pointing. "Into the thicket? Why?"

"They must have known that something or someone was following them. Kamarie probably told Yole to go through there and find a safe place to hide. She knew that she would have a better chance if she only had to protect herself, and she couldn't have fit through there. They probably had a signal set up so that Yole would know if he should come back or continue on alone," Brant said.

"But we don't know the signal," Oraeyn spoke quietly.

"Maybe the call of a shadow-lark?"

Oraeyn tried it a few times, but there was no answer. He kept it up until his lips were too tired to whistle any longer, and then he gave up. There was no sign of Yole.

"I am afraid that Yole will have to go on alone. We cannot continue until Kamarie is back on her feet, and we cannot go searching for the boy because neither of us is small enough to follow him in the direction he went," Brant said.

Oraeyn opened his mouth to argue that they could not just let the young boy wander towards the Harshlands alone but found that he could not come up with a single better idea. He tried calling Yole's name a few times, but if the boy could hear him, he was not coming out until he heard Kamarie's signal. Oraeyn fell silent again. He stared off in the direction that Yole had gone, hoping that the boy would be all right and that Kamarie would be all right.

Kamarie woke the next day and surprised even Brant with the speed at which she recovered. In spite of the serious blow to her head, Kamarie was able to rise and walk. Although dizzy and disoriented at first, after a good meal and some additional rest, she was soon back to her old self.

Brant allowed Kamarie to rest for two days, knowing that she was not up to traveling until she regained some of her strength and confidence. Brant and Oraeyn needed rest as well, since they had been setting a fast pace and were more worn out than either would care to admit. On the morning of the third day since the attack, they were all restless. Oraeyn and Kamarie got into a pointless argument at breakfast, and Brant commented to himself that it was good to see Kamarie had regained her fire.

After they had finished eating, Kamarie said, "Brant, I can continue traveling now. I have cost us two days already, and I don't want to delay us further."

"Are you sure? I had planned to allow one more day for rest."

"If we remain here for another day I will either go crazy or Oraeyn and I will kill each other."

"All right," Brant said, smiling faintly. "If you are well enough to argue with Oraeyn again, then you are well enough to travel. Let's get moving."

At that, Oraeyn felt like dancing and cheering. He threw himself into cleaning up the camp with an energy he had not known he possessed. The atmosphere improved now that they could finally look forward to continuing their journey. When their campsite was concealed they made their way through the great southern forest towards the Harshlands. Their concern now turned to Yole, but there was nothing they could do except hope he made it to the Harshlands safely.

The remaining band of Cove People huddled together under the shelter of a massive rock overhang carved in the ravine pass of the Mountains of Dusk, waiting for the violent storm to pass so that they could once again continue towards Ayollan. They had decided to offer their help to the King. They had faced the Dark Warriors and were determined to help Aom-igh in the coming battle. They also had vital information that the coming attack would not be a simple frontal assault, but that there was at least one party creeping up on the castle from behind. They traveled with swiftness borne of desperation, knowing the urgency of their information while fearful of being overtaken by the enemy behind. Traveling through the ravine pass when the storm hit, the air turned bitter cold and the wind sliced through them like an icy blade as the driving rain chilled them to the bone. The punishing gale was unknown to people who had so long lived in the beautiful warmth of Pearl Cove.

They had been traveling for days, bearing their wounded on drags: beds that were held together with light poles and covered in leaves and soft blankets.

Rena sat curled up in a back corner, her shawl pulled tight around her shoulders. She held her daughter, Kaitryn, on her lap and rocked the little girl back and forth, singing quiet lullabies between her tears. Kaitryn had neither spoken nor eaten since leaving their home.

After sending their families ahead, with promises of seeing them again, the defenders of Pearl Cove awaited the onslaught from the Dark Country. These men were not warriors by training, but neither did they lack courage, and they fought well while buying their families time to escape. Some of these men were able to keep their promise, but most were not. As they returned, Rena had run to greet them, anxious to find her husband, but her eyes found only sadness. One of the men brought her news that Wessel was gone. He was pierced with several arrows after bringing down many Dark Warriors in his fight. She kept reliving the exact moment when she had been told of her husband's death. She could still hear the words ringing in her head, could still see the expression of sympathy and compassion on the face of the one who had brought her the hard news. The grief that welled up within her and threatened to overwhelm her still throbbed as though she had been pierced with those same arrows. Her mind and soul revolted at the reality that Wessel was gone. That had been a terrible day; only a few of the men had survived what was already being called the "Defense of the Cove." The following days were filled with grief and sadness as the families who, like Rena, ran with hopeful greeting in their hearts and found only emptiness. A fog descended on them, and they trudged forward only because they could not go back.

Rena found the task of telling Kaitryn that her father was not coming back to be the hardest thing she had ever done. She returned to the spot where Kaitryn was playing and told her, very gently, that Wessel had not come back with the others. Kaitryn looked up, a big smile on her face.

"Daddy's still fighting the bad men who attacked us from the sea," the little girl said, a note of childish pride in her voice. "He'll join us when the enemies are all gone and can't come bother us anymore, and then we can go home!"

The child's words broke Rena's heart all over again. "No, Kitry," she said in a choked voice, "Daddy's not coming to join us, not ever again. And we'll never go home, we'll have to find a new home, I'm sorry, darling, I..." Rena knew she was babbling, that her words made no sense, but she could not seem to gather them in, and she could not stop the flow of words. It was the look on her daughter's face that stopped her.

Kaitryn stared up at her, confusion and hurt on her face. "But he promised," she cried out in distress, her lip starting to tremble, "he promised he'd come! He always keeps his promises!"

Rena nodded, feeling her throat close up tightly with emotion as she tried to find the right words that would somehow explain the situation and make everything all better. "I'm sure he tried harder than anything to keep his promise, Kitry." Her voice broke in the middle of the sentence, and the tears she had valiantly kept at bay poured down her face.

It was the sight of her mother's tears that made Kitry understand the truth. Rena saw the weight of reality suddenly hit six-year-old Kaitryn all in a single moment. The little girl stared at her mother with her large eyes filling up with sorrow: wise, sad eyes that were too old for the youth of her face. Kaitryn had not cried; she had huddled up inside of herself and refused to speak to anyone or eat anything. She withdrew from the rest of the world and retreated with her pain to a place that Rena could not reach.

Rena's friends watched in sympathy, but there was little they could do for they were all struggling with their own pain and hardships. So many were drowning in their own grief and heartache, and had little to offer in the way of comfort to anyone else. Even as the urgency of their mission weighed upon them, even as they left behind all they had known, they traveled wrapped in private pain, isolated from all the rest and unable to share their shattered hearts.

However, Rena, almost sick with heartache over the loss of her husband and her hurting daughter, had done what no other had been able to find the strength to do. Despite her own pain that pricked her heart afresh whenever she saw something Wessel would have loved or whenever she looked into Kitry's hollow eyes, she began to reach out to the other people in her own unique way. She sang. Her songs were sometimes bright and joyful, and sometimes they were sad and mournful, but whatever she sang, the music raised the spirits of the people. Often they would stop what they were doing, enchanted by the sound of singing that seemed so out of place in the atmosphere of grief that clung around them. As they journeyed through the mountains, Rena's beautiful, haunting voice echoed off the rocks above them and served to ease a bit of the pain, a fraction of the weariness. Slowly, ever so slowly, Rena's songs began to mend the broken hearts and penetrate the misty shadows of sorrow, allowing a breath of joy to once again enter their lives. At night, preparing for rest, the children would gather around Rena and she would sing silly nursery rhymes to them, making them giggle and laugh and forget where they were and why they had been sad. Then she would sing a lullaby, and the children would drift to sleep to the sound of her voice.

It was Rena's songs that bound up the broken spirits of the Cove People and reminded them how strong they really were. It was Rena's beautiful voice as she sang nonsense rhymes to the children that reminded them how to laugh again. It was Rena's selfless heart that taught them how to reach out to one another and comfort each other even through their pain. And, eventually, it was Rena's songs that drew her own daughter Kaitryn out of her protective shell.

On this morning, Rena was again entertaining the children with her song. It was very silly with words of utter nonsense - the kind that led its listeners to mentally fill in the next word with one that rhymed, but then she would surprise them by inserting a word that didn't rhyme. It was a fun song to sing and Rena had begun taking any opportunity to laugh or make the children smile. They were too young to bear such heavy burdens on their shoulders, and so she tried with all her might to ease the load they all carried.

Kaitryn, as usual, was sitting a short distance away, hugging her knees to herself and staring back the way they had come. The song was making the other children giggle, and some of them were laughing too hard to sing. Rena even began to laugh at the sight of some of the little children, flopped on the floor and trying to sing between giggles. Their laughter rose up into the fresh new morning air as the Cove People gathered up their things and prepared to leave the shelter of the overhang and continue on their way.

Suddenly, as Rena was singing and the children were laughing, she heard a small noise that began as a whimper and then turned into a full-fledged sob. She spun around and saw Kaitryn. The little girl stared at her mother with large eyes filling up with sorrow, wisdom, and sadness too old for the youth of her face.

"Mommy!" the little girl cried, standing up and holding out her arms.

Rena ran to her daughter and picked her up, cradling her, sheltering her, and murmuring all the while, "It's all right, it's okay, shhh, dear one, darling, I love you so much."

"I miss Daddy," the child sobbed.

"I miss him too," Rena managed to choke out before the tears that she had held back for so long began to slide down her face.

"Why? Why couldn't he keep his promise?"

Rena had no answer; she simply rocked her child, allowing her to cry. She kissed Kaitryn's forehead and held her tight, not speaking, not doing anything, just holding her and crying with her. Their broken hearts bled openly for the world to see, drawing the others to them, and even as the tears spread, so did the healing. The pain did not diminish, it would not heal in an evening of tears, but the healing had begun. Rena knew that one day, in the distant future, the wounds would close, replaced by scars that would only ache every now and then at the unbidden memory of what they had lost. But for now, those wounds were sharp and fresh, and would never fully heal.

CHAPTER
FOURTEEN

Tobias walked slowly to the doors of the audience chamber. Through the crack between the great doors, he could see King Seamas sitting easily on Prince Elroy's throne. The ruler of Roalthae stood nearby, a glimmer of a frown on his young face. Slightly behind the throne stood Seamas' uncle, Captain Ramius. Tobias clenched his jaw. On the Council, Ramius was the worst of the three, the most bloodthirsty, the most impulsive, and the greediest. Tobias knew that the man had begun whispering in Seamas' ear a long time ago, even before King Stiorne died. As such, Ramius held much of the blame for Seamas' most recent actions, at least in Tobias' opinion. Taking a deep breath, as though getting ready to swim a long way under water, Tobias pushed the door open and entered the chamber.

"Tobias!" Seamas' voice resounded through the room. "Approach the throne."

It was impossible to tell what the King was thinking from his tone. Tobias hesitated for the briefest part of a second, and then he held his head high and approached his king. If he was to die, then so be it. When he reached the edge of the slightly raised

dais upon which the throne sat, he knelt and saluted, fist to heart.
A moment later, he felt hands pulling him up, and then the King
himself was embracing him.

"Have they found him?" Seamas whispered in his ear.

Tobias shook his head. "Not yet, Sire."

Seamas stepped back and raised his voice, "You have done a
great work for us, Tobias. The weapons we ordered are complete.
The ships are stocked and stand waiting for us to board them.
The warriors we sent ahead are in position. All that is left now is
to wait."

"It may still be a week before we set sail," Tobias replied
cautiously.

"Details," Seamas waved a hand. "What is one more week
when I have waited this long? What I seek will not escape me
again. Now, let me see the maps that our scouts have brought
back, and let us review our strategy once more. Come, let us
retire to the council room and give our good host back his chair."
Seamas smiled at Elroy, and the prince jumped slightly.

They adjourned to a large room near the center of the castle
with a huge table and great tapestries on the walls depicting
historical battles. Several high ranking aethalons joined them, and
they immediately began hammering out the final details of their
battle plans. Tobias tried to stay focused on the plans, but his
thoughts were still reeling from the reception he had been given.
Had he been forgiven? Or, an even more startling thought: did
the king not even realize Tobias had once given him false
information? Or was Seamas biding his time, waiting for the right
moment to punish him? Perhaps Seamas was waiting to see if the
reports he had received were accurate, for the King was the only
one who would be able to verify them. Or perhaps Seamas would
simply place Tobias in a spot where he would be sure to perish
during the battle. Tobias felt uneasy, and his skin prickled as if
trying to warn him of his danger. A hand clapped him on the
shoulder, and he turned to look up into the bearded face of
Captain Ramius.

"Sir," Tobias said.

"You've done a good job here," Ramius replied, steering him towards a corner away from the others. "His Majesty is well-pleased with you."

"I live to serve him."

"But you do not approve of this bid for conquest." It was not a question.

"It is not my place to question the will of my King," Tobias replied.

"Then it is the Council you do not approve of, and you believe this invasion was our doing?"

Uncomfortable with the accuracy of the captain's inquiry, Tobias shrugged and allowed his lips to twitch in a slight smile. "The Council was appointed by the King, and is therefore safe from my judgment. As I said, I stand for my King."

"And what of the King's other agenda, the one he has kept secret from all but his oldest friend?"

"And who might that be?"

"You, of course. You served with him when he was part of the King's Helm, he appointed you to the leadership position of the Helm when he took the throne. You are the one he turns to most often for advice, in spite of the Council being raised."

"If the King told me of any secret agenda and I am the only one who knows about it, then why would I betray his confidence and discuss it with you?"

"Because the quest he has set for us all could stain his honor. I may be a member of the Council, but the king is still my nephew. I would not see him brought low simply to further my own political ends. To tell you the truth, I would rather be sailing my ship, but Seamas asked me to join his Council, so..." Ramius shrugged and took a sip of wine, "here I am."

"How could the King's agenda hurt him, precisely?" Tobias asked.

Ramius raised an eyebrow. "Shrewd, Captain, very shrewd. But you and I both know that Seamas is keeping something to himself. I thought you might know what it was. I can only guess, and my guesses leave me cold. The others on the Council are not as honorable as I, and I fear they do not have my nephew's best interests at heart. Ah well, if he has not confided in you..."

Tobias kept his face blank as Ramius glanced at him questioningly. The old ship's captain, reading nothing in the younger man's face, shrugged again and continued. "I only hope that when it comes to light it does not mean the ruin of us all."

As Ramius walked away, Tobias breathed deeply. *That was interesting,* he thought. *I never would have expected him to worry about honor. Or maybe it is only his own skin he is worried about. I wonder how much he knows? If he suspects the truth... would he help Seamas, or would he try to seize power himself? He certainly would not try to talk the king out of this madness.* Tobias let his shoulders droop. None of his options were looking good.

It was raining again. Yole sat shivering under a bush and pulled his soaking blanket tighter around his shoulders. The blanket was too wet to offer any comfort, and he whimpered, his teeth clacking together as another wave of cold hit him. He thought back to the horrible events of several nights ago. No shadow-lark had called to let him know that it was safe to return to Kamarie; Yole knew that this meant Kamarie had been captured or killed, and he was miserable at the thought of either.

He had pressed on, trying to head east as Kamarie had instructed, but the going had been difficult. He was still traveling through the thicket, and sharp thorns and razor-thin grasses had slashed through his light clothing, covering his arms and legs in numerous tiny cuts that stung. He was sore and his muscles ached. Each morning it was harder to get moving. He had to push his way through the thick brambles, and at times he had been forced to crawl when he could not stand in the thorny thicket. His hands and knees were blood-stained, leaving a trail that anyone could follow.

Yole stood as the rain began to let up and left his meager shelter. Squaring his shoulders, he wiped his nose on his torn and filthy sleeve, and set off once more towards the Harshlands.

Kamarie had told him to keep going if the shadow-lark did not call. She had entrusted him with the duty of continuing on alone so that he could tell the others what had happened to her, and this mission he was determined to complete, even if it killed him. He *would* reach the Harshlands, and he would find Brant and Oraeyn and Dylanna, somehow.

Yole trudged on, weary footstep after weary footstep, until he came to a break in the forest. He found himself standing on a road that wound on in an easterly direction. He stood for a few moments, debating with himself as to what he should do. The open road was dangerous; it meant that he had a better chance of coming in contact with people. But, somehow, that threat did not sound all bad to the boy who had been traveling on his own through the dark, shadow-filled forest for three days. He knew that he should probably stick to the forest, but he was tired of fighting his way through brambles and weeds. As he looked at the quiet path before him, the dark, tangled forest seemed a dreadful and fearsome place to travel alone. He stared at the trees, wondering how he had come through it as far as he had. Then, with a confident nod to himself, Yole followed the dirt road, trusting that it would, by some miracle, lead him to the Harshlands.

A few hours later found him traveling with a much lighter step and whistling a merry tune. The rain had stopped, and the Dragon's Eye was shining down brightly, warming and drying the youth. He knew that his food supply was running low, and he missed Kamarie's lessons and her cheerful outlook on their plight, but these were minor trials. Yole was beginning to remember that he had spent most of his life traveling alone. He liked the feel of the dirt road beneath his feet and the wind in his hair once more, and he was even starting to forget all the terror of the past few days.

Quite unexpectedly, Yole heard a familiar sound up ahead of him on the road. It was the unmistakable noise of wooden cart wheels and the jingle of a harness. Yole walked quickly, but still with the caution that his days of journeying with the others had taught him. Shortly, he caught up with the cart and found its owner sitting by the side of the road munching on something that smelled of roasted meat and recently baked bread. The delicious aromas made Yole's mouth water. Then he caught sight of the cart and almost forgot his hunger. The cart was so brightly colored that it assailed the eyes. It was covered in a hodgepodge of all the colors that Yole had ever seen, and it had windows on each side with little wooden shutters that looked absolutely ridiculous on a traveling cart. And yet, there was a definite appeal, a cheerfulness about it that made Yole smile just to look at it, though he could not have said what it was he was smiling about.

Convinced of his own stealth, Yole was surprised when he heard a cheerful, "Hello there. I'm not as blind as all that." Yole hesitantly stepped forward, wondering how he had been spotted.

The man jumped up in a flurry of too-long limbs and came over to shake the boy's hand. "Hello again!" he said with enthusiasm. "I haven't seen another creature's face in two day's time! Come and share my lunch?"

Yole was more than willing to share lunch and said so. The man laughed and clapped him on the back good-naturedly. Then the two sat together on the side of the well-worn path, munching on roast turkey sandwiches and drinking bowls of foaming goat's milk. As they ate, Yole studied the man sitting across from him.

The owner of the cart was tall and lean. He had a shock of blond hair that stood up in all directions as though it had never been brushed and bright blue eyes that twinkled with laughter when he spoke. Yole could just imagine the man telling tall tales and making people believe them just by the look in his eyes. His face was young and unremarkable and, yet, Yole got the impression that there was a depth and age behind that face. He also got the odd feeling that the man was familiar, but he abandoned that idea as soon as it made its presence known; such a notion was ridiculous. The owner of the cart had long hands with slender fingers, which had calluses on the tips as though he played some sort of stringed instrument. He was dressed in practical clothes for traveling, but the cloth was a patchwork of as many different colors as could be found on his cart, some bright and some dark. In all, the man looked rather gawky and ungainly. He was even somewhat funny looking, Yole thought, though he never would have said something so rude out loud.

"And who are you?" the funny looking man asked. "Perhaps I could write a song about it: the youngling who wandered alone the open roads of the southern realm. Ah! But that would make a magnificent tale!"

As he spoke, his hands moved quickly, bringing out four brightly colored round objects. Throwing them up in the air, he tossed them back and forth in intricate patterns that took Yole's breath away. Yole laughed delightedly and clapped his hands.

The young man smiled and stood up to take a bow. "You like my juggling?"

Yole nodded enthusiastically. "Yes, I do!"

The strange man smiled again at the delight of his young audience, but then his shoulders drooped and his smile faltered. "It is truly a pity that no one else seems to," he sighed dramatically.

Yole looked at him quizzically. "What do you mean?"

"I am completely unappreciated by many of my audiences," the man sighed again and put a hand to his forehead, his voice was plaintive but uncomplaining. "I tried to get an audience at the castle, but they have too many minstrels already, or so they told me. Then I tried to juggle and sing for the rich merchants, but they are all more interested in the newer stories and the fancier tricks, bah! Fancier tricks! Why, when I juggle I make their heads spin, but that's the way of the rich, they're alright until you want to be paid, then they get stingy on you and hem and haw about how little talent you really have. Hah! They wouldn't know talent if it reached out and pinched their noses, now there would be a sight! Ha ha!" The man's voice changed with each turn of his story, as if he were weaving the words into an intricate pattern on some unseen loom.

Yole laughed at the antics of the minstrel. The minstrel did not notice, but continued talking, almost as though to himself.

"No siree, there is no greater talent beneath the Dragon's Eye than that of the Great Kiernan Kane! No, the Magnificent... oh, hello there," the Great Kiernan Kane abruptly halted his flow of words as he suddenly seemed to remember that he had an audience, small though it was. "What is your name? I completely forgot to ask you."

Yole suppressed a smile. "My name is Y... Ian," he said, catching himself just an instant before he slipped and gave away his real name.

"Y...ian? Marvelous!" The minstrel said, "And my name is K... iernan K... ane. Kiernan Kane the Magnificent Minstrel, they call me in the large cities, (they also throw rotten fruits and vegetables at me, just goes to show how unappreciated I am) but you can call me Kiernan."

Yole laughed, but did not correct the man about his name, finding it all too funny for words and, yet, he wasn't too sure that the man needed correcting.

"Now, where are you headed my boy?"

Yole pointed. "Towards the Harshlands."

"Splendid! Wonderful! I am headed there myself. There is a witch-queen living in the Harshlands, and I thought that since nobody else likes my singing or my juggling, that I would travel to see her and perhaps she will like one or two of my jokes and hire me as her jester or something... I really am getting tired of not being able to find a steady job. Or at the very least, she will give me something to eat. Hopefully she won't turn me into anything nasty."

Yole brightened at Kiernan's words. "Could I travel with you to the Harshlands?"

Kiernan grinned at him, looking very much like a youth just out of school. "I was just about to suggest that myself," he said, "in fact, I insist upon it! Perhaps I will even teach you how to juggle and do front flips! Then we could really have a show for the dreaded witch-queen of the Harshlands."

"She's not a witch," Yole said, "she's a wizardess."

Kiernan stood up, curiosity in his eyes, looking for all the world like a long-legged frog. When he had finished unfolding himself and managed to stand up straight, Yole wondered how the man had managed the feat with such speed. Kiernan looked so ungainly that it seemed that he would fall over at any moment

"Whatever you say my boy, witch, queen, or wizardess perhaps she won't turn us into toads before giving us a bit of bread and perhaps a sip of tea. Maybe she will even ask to see our show! I don't mind being turned into a toad so long as I can have a last meal and a last chance to strum a few notes on my mandolin!" Kiernan began to climb up into his cart.

"What's a mand... mandolin?" Yole asked in curiosity as he clambered up into the cart next to Kiernan.

"What is a ...!" Kiernan trailed off as he stared at the boy in horror. "Why, Y... ian! The mandolin is the trade instrument of all minstrels and jesters and even the high court bards! I myself am quite good at playing the thing, although I may not good be enough to be a court bard, not yet anyway. Well, hop on up here into the cart, and we shall be off and away into the fair light of the failing Dragon's Eye yonder. Gee-yup, Silver!" he shouted loudly at the old mule that was pulling the cart.

The donkey, whose coat could be called gray but was nothing like silver, glanced over his shoulder with a look that closely resembled that of patient exasperation and bemusement. Then the faithful animal began pulling with gentle and steady steps, going at a slow and easy pace.

Ships had continued to arrive in Roalthae transporting hoards of Dark Warriors, or at least that was what King Arnaud was told. His intelligence network informed him of the frantic efforts being expended to prepare the ships of war in the Port of Roalthae.

Apparently the Dark Country was readying their final assault against Aom-igh. Attacks against their villages had ceased, and although a relief, it was also a concern. Where were the marauders? What was their purpose? Surely they had not simply disappeared.

King Arnaud walked along the high wall that allowed him to look beyond his castle keep, and his gaze was drawn to where the Dragon's Eye was rising over the sea. He studied his soldiers as they kept their vigil, and he smiled with pride.

"Majesty?" a voice pulled Arnaud out of his thoughts.

"What is it Garen?" he asked, turning towards the older knight.

"I need to tell you something."

Arnaud looked sharply into his face as he heard the quiet and serious tone. "What?"

"I know I shouldn't have, but I've spent the past few years training young Kamarie to be a squire. She begged me so to teach her to ride and use a sword and to keep it all a secret, well; I couldn't bear to let her down. I thought some of the skills might be useful to a princess, and I always meant to put an end to the lessons when she got older, but somehow, I never could turn her away. I know I should have told you right from the start, but I just couldn't seem to work up the courage, and I couldn't break my promise. But I did want to tell you about it before the Dark Warriors get here because I might not get another chance to do so."

Arnaud did laugh now, and clapped a hand down on Garen's shoulder. "I noticed you'd been quiet lately. That is what has been worrying you? You've been feeling guilty about this?"

The knight nodded.

Arnaud sobered, seeing that his oldest and most trusted advisor was about to take offense at his laughter. "Garen, I am not laughing at you. I've known about your secret training of my daughter since her first lesson. I watched when Kamarie would climb down the trellis from her room to the stable yard. I watched you teaching her how to wield a sword and shoot a bow and I've also seen her clout *you* a few times on the head with a staff in the more recent days. Kamarie needed this training, and more importantly she needed the secret. The life of a princess, much like that of a king, is on public display at all times, and her time with you has helped her endure the trials of that responsibility. Your confession just now has simply given me the opportunity to thank you. I always knew she was in good hands. The one you really need to be worried about is what Zara or Dy... Darby will say."

"You are thanking me?"

Arnaud nodded. "You were right, the things you've taught her are useful skills for a princess. She ought to know how to track an animal or enemy through the forest, she ought to know how to ride a horse and defend herself. She wanted to be a squire so badly, and she thought that I would refuse if she asked me outright. I can't say whether I would have refused or not, but to tell you the truth, the only reason I felt comfortable sending her off the way I did was because I was confident that she could take care of herself. I couldn't very well come out and say that I knew what Kamarie was doing, though; Zara would have my ears if she found out I knew about all this and did not put a stop to it. Zara is very protective, as you well know, and she wouldn't want Kamarie doing anything she thinks is dangerous. So perhaps we had better continue to keep this particular secret."

Garen let a smile appear on his stern face, but then sobered again. "There's one other thing, Majesty."

Arnaud sighed. "More skeletons, Garen? And call me Arnaud: it's my name, and there are too many years in our friendship for all that bowing and scraping between us."

Garen chuckled; he had been a knight of the realm since a few years before Arnaud had been given the throne. He still remembered the day the youth had been all but dragged to the castle to take the throne. The lad had not wanted anyone calling him "Majesty" or "Highness" then either.

"Kamarie doesn't intend to become a knight."

"I see. But you think I should encourage her to take the test anyway?"

"It could be a very valuable asset if she ever has to rule the kingdom alone."

"Well, we shall see what happens. If there is still a kingdom to rule when all this is over, we will discuss it further."

"You don't think we stand a chance, do you, Sire?"

"I have to believe we stand a chance. I'm the king. I don't have the luxury of doing otherwise."

"We are all standing behind you, Arnaud. We'll fight and live for you and Aom-igh. We will not easily be defeated."

Arnaud smiled. "Thank you, Garen. I know."

CHAPTER

FIFTEEN

"Leila! Open this door at once!"

At the loud pounding and the shouts demanding entry, the great wooden doors to the stone mansion swung slowly inwards, and Leila stood in the doorway. Leila took one wide-eyed look at her visitor, and then pulled her inside, shutting the door quickly.

"What is it Dylanna? What brings you all the way out here?" she asked, motioning for her sister to sit down while she went for tea. "And why have you suspended your illusion?"

Dylanna began to sit down but the angry yowl of a cat startled her. She jumped and stared down at the long furred, gray body curled up on the chair. The cat glared at her with a look that could have frozen fire, anger and wounded pride glowed in the green eyes that bored haughtily into her own.

"Leila!" Dylanna exclaimed in frustration.

Leila looked up, then grinned. "Oh, that's Shandy's chair, sorry. Try the green one. I think Switch is out hunting, so you should be able to sit there in peace."

Dylanna shook her head as she sank down gratefully in the unoccupied chair. "I do believe you think more of animals than you do of humans sometimes."

Leila busied herself with pouring the tea and then breezed over towards her sister with steaming refreshment. Dylanna watched her younger sister with a small smile; she looked so out of place, pouring tea without spilling it all over the place. Leila had always been the wild one. Her magic rarely worked indoors. She hated doing things like sitting around sipping tea when there were wondrous trees to climb outside, just calling her to play. Leila had always been the child of the family, though Zara was truly the youngest. Leila was the innocent, the easily delighted, the whimsical one, especially when it came to animals.

She had always surrounded herself with animals both wild and domestic, although Scelwhyn had made a strict rule that no animal was allowed inside the house. Leila, of course, had broken that rule often, smuggling little creatures up to her room and opening her windows to allow birds to fly in and out freely. However, if Scelwhyn had known about any of it, and Dylanna doubted that there was any way he could *not* have known, he never said anything.

Leila had striven to learn the language of the wild things. It had been her special dream. Scelwhyn had told the girl that it was a hopeless task, but Leila had a stubborn streak that would not allow her to give up. Even now, Dylanna was amazed at how completely Leila seemed to understand animals, and they seemed to understand her as well. The animals had always flocked to her, and even now creatures of all shapes and sizes always found their way to Leila's home.

Finally, Leila sat down across from Dylanna, shooing Shandy out of her chair. The big gray cat tried to assert his right to the chair, but Leila fixed him with a violet-eyed glare equal to his own. Finally, Shandy stepped off of the chair. He moved regretfully with a kingly air of wounded pride at being thrown out so cruelly, but he left. Leila smiled after him fondly, shaking her head, and then she sat forward and rested her chin on her hands. Once again, Dylanna was amazed at how young Leila looked.

"Now, what has brought you out of your disguise, and particularly, what has brought you here to the Harshlands?"

Dylanna smothered a laugh; her younger sister never had been able to comprehend the notion of small talk. Direct and to the point, Leila was and probably always would be. Dylanna forced herself to return to the present. Her face and voice turned serious.

"Calyssia has left the Pearl Cove."

Leila gasped in shock. "But she took an oath! She took an oath never to leave that place. She has to stay in the Cove lest the power that holds the shield together be broken completely. It was her final promise to Graldon, though it took her long enough to get around to keeping it. She vowed never to leave until…" Leila trailed off as the meaning of Dylanna's words sank in. "You mean she has gone back to the sea?"

Dylanna nodded quietly. "She must have been losing strength. She seemed different when we saw her, she must have known then that she was dying."

"You spoke with her? You saw her? When?"

"A few days before she returned to the sea. She led us into Krayghentaliss, and while we were down there the Dark Warriors invaded the Cove, and she took the last chance that she had to leave. I can't imagine she would have left her people in danger if she hadn't been near death."

"What? Dark Warriors? Why would they invade Pearl Cove? Dylanna… you aren't telling me something."

"Forgive me." Dylanna closed her eyes and took a sip of her tea. "I'm tired, and I'm not doing a good job explaining. Let me start at the beginning."

Dylanna told her younger sister of all that had happened since the first hints of the invasion had reached King Arnaud's ears. Leila hung on every word, asking questions throughout. The night grew late, until Dylanna finally finished speaking. They sat together in silence for a few moments, and then Leila shook herself.

"How incredibly rude of me!" she exclaimed in dismay. "You must be weary, dear sister."

Dylanna sighed as her long travels mixed with concern for her companions, reminding her again of the exhaustion she had been fighting off for so long.

Leila directed her sister to a guest chamber that was "animal free."

"Go get some rest, and in the morning we can set guiding-wards for the princess and her companions so that they will have no trouble finding my house."

Dylanna walked up the stairs to the bedroom that her sister had mentioned. She was relieved to see that the room was, in fact, free of cats, and all other wildlife for that matter. She flopped down on the big bed and fell into a deeper sleep than she had for days, finally feeling safe enough to let her guard down.

The next morning, Dylanna came downstairs. The night of sleep had done wonders for her, and she had awoken feeling refreshed. She found herself noticing the interesting decorating job that her sister had done. The house was a strange dichotomous maze of nooks and corners alongside great open rooms. Dylanna was sure that there was a secret passageway or two in the meandering floor plan. The house was decorated with flowers and vines and the walls were all painted in soothing, earthy tones. The entire place had a very outdoorsy feel about it. Dylanna found that the good night's sleep had also restored her ability to worry about her companions and had brought to memory another question she had for her sister. Leila smiled at her as she came down the long, winding staircase. When Dylanna explained her request, Leila looked at her oddly.

"Show it to me," she commanded.

Dylanna produced the silver pipes that Rhendak had given to them. Leila took them and turned them over in her hands, examining the instrument from all angles. She marveled at the craftsmanship of the pipes, but then handed them back to Dylanna with a regretful sigh.

"I cannot play them," she said, shaking her head. "The dragon magic cancels out my own, or perhaps it is the other way around, but either way, the instrument is useless in my hands. Pity too, for they are beautiful and just looking at them inspires an odd longing to hear them."

Dylanna nodded, looking upset. "That is what I had found. I believe the pipes were not meant for wizards. But then who can play them? Surely the dragons would not have given us a useless gift."

Leila smiled. "Perhaps you already know who can play them."

"What do you mean?"

"The dragons would not have given you a tool that they knew you were incapable of using, so they must have believed someone in your group had the ability to play the instrument," Leila said.

Dylanna shook her head in confusion. "But who?"

Leila shrugged. "From what you have told me, any one of the people you have been traveling with could be qualified to play the thing. Oraeyn already holds the sword of the Great King Llian, so we know that he can use the gifts of the dragons. Yole himself is a dragon, so he would most likely be able to play them. Brant is the only person you have told me nothing about, but from what you have said, it seems as though he would probably be able to play them as well. But if Kamarie is, as you and Zara think, the first dragon ward born in a century, then it may be she is the one that the pipes were intended for, but..."

Dylanna interrupted, "But we do not know for sure that she is a dragon-ward or not. She seems to have inherited your way with animals, but that could mean anything or nothing. As she grows older, I begin to think that our hopes for that will not come to pass through Kamarie. She exhibits none of the signs, and she has now met with several dragons and shows none of the restlessness that comes to a dragon-ward after meeting dragons for the first time. I am not ruling it out completely, but I no longer believe Kamarie is a dragon-ward. No, I don't believe the pipes are meant for her, although if you think it wise, I will indeed give them to Kamarie. I just don't want to give them to the wrong person."

Leila shrugged. "I was not suggesting that you do anything quite so reckless or hasty as *that*. You did not let me finish. I was about to mention that the dragons are more patient and thus more far-sighted than we, it has something to do with their sense of time. They know someone is destined for these pipes and for now, they have been entrusted to your care. I do not think you will be able to give them away in error. Perhaps they have seen someone in the future who will be able to play them. It may be a survivor from Pearl Cove. If anyone alive in Aom-igh is close enough to the dragons to be touched by their magic, it would be the inhabitants of Calyssia's realm."

Dylanna was intrigued. "That's true. You could very well be right. I suppose I must carry them a while longer."

"I wouldn't worry, sister, the gifts of the dragons tend to make their own choices about whom they will call."

Dylanna nodded slowly. "This is also true. For once you actually have a point that is grounded in common sense."

Leila pretended to pout. "I have plenty of common sense."

"Oh, sure!" Dylanna retorted sarcastically. "As I recall, locking ourselves in the basement of the palace was full of common sense! I do believe it was your idea to play 'prisoners' that day. I also recall a large stone door that blocked the sound of our voices from getting through when we called for help. I seem to remember two days of hating you for that while we waited to be missed and found. That idea was definitely brimming with common sense."

Leila grinned. "But it makes a great story, doesn't it?"

Dylanna groaned. "You will never grow up, will you?"

Leila's grin grew even wider. "I'm working on it."

As the three travelers continued to journey east, the forest grew thicker and the going became much more difficult. Often they had to chop their way through the tangled branches. Oraeyn tried to do as little damage as possible with his sword as he cleared the path in front of them. He tried to cut only the dead branches, of which there were plenty, for he could not help but remember the childlike wood nymph, and he did not wish to destroy anyone's home with a careless stroke of his sword. Oraeyn casually mentioned this to Brant and Kamarie as they journeyed along. Brant gave a thoughtful nod, and both he and Kamarie grew more careful with their swords as well.

"We are drawing near to the Harshlands," Brant said when they stopped to catch their breath after a particularly difficult stretch.

"How do you know?" Kamarie asked between gasps for air as she drew out her canteen and drank, forcing herself to sip slowly.

"The forest grows thickest right before you get to the Harshlands. This thick, tangled wood borders most of the desert; but in the Harshlands themselves there are scarcely any growing things to be found. It is nothing but a great, flat, windblown desert of barren rock that puts a strangle-hold on all life and fights against it with a malice."

"It can't possibly be as bad as it has been portrayed in the stories and tales of the knights," Oraeyn spoke up. Since visiting the Pearl Cove, he had lost all faith in the tall tales that he had grown up hearing in the squires' rooms back at the palace.

Brant nodded slowly. "You are right," he said, "it is worse."

Oraeyn stared at him, disbelief written plainly across his face. But there was something in Brant's eyes that told him the man was serious; Kamarie's eyes widened at Brant's words. She had only heard some of the stories about the Harshlands, but they had been bad enough. Not so bad that she was in any way deterred from wanting to journey there someday but terrifying enough to give her a healthy respect for the place. Brant nodded and then stood to continue their battle through the thick forest.

He began chopping through the dead branches, but Kamarie's concerned voice made him halt.

Kamarie surprised herself, saying something that she never thought she would say, but she was loath to continue on without reassurance. "But is it safe to go there then? Even if we could find Aunt Leila's house without Dylanna's help, can we hope to make it there alive? I mean, if the place is truly as bad as you say it is."

Brant turned towards her, his patience running thin. "No, it isn't safe. But with the threat of Llycaelon's attack on Aom-igh growing greater every day, is anything truly safe?"

Kamarie shook her head and stood up, feeling a little more like her old self. "You're right," she said.

Oraeyn also stood. "Llycaelon?" he asked. "What is that?"

Kamarie's brow wrinkled. "It sounds familiar... where have I heard of it before?"

Brant stared at them, and Oraeyn thought he caught a glimpse of surprise deep in Brant's dark eyes, but when he looked closer, it was gone. Brant's voice was calm.

"Llycaelon is the name of the Dark Country. The people of Llycaelon do not call themselves 'Dark Warriors' either, they are known as aethalons. The name is two-fold: it means one who was born in Llycaelon, and it is also the term for 'warrior.' All aethalons train to some extent in the art of combat, and so the term is appropriate."

The information was delivered without expression or change in tone. Both Kamarie and Oraeyn wanted to ask Brant how he knew this; however, there was something about the look in his eyes, or perhaps his too careful tone of voice, that warned them to keep their questions silent.

Although the pace of Silver, the old gray donkey, was quite a bit slower than traveling with Brant, Yole was glad of the sturdy little animal that pulled Kiernan's cart. The little donkey and the ridiculously painted cart seemed like a king's chariot and a brace of prancing chargers to the young boy who had been traveling by foot through the tangled forests for what seemed like forever. The wooden wheels of the cart bumped along as they traveled ever closer to the Harshlands. Kiernan insisted that the path was a short-cut to the Harshlands, and so their slower pace did not bother Yole as much as it might have.

When he was not asking Yole about his own story, Kiernan talked incessantly about his adventures. Yole told Kiernan as much as he thought was safe, but soon found that it was quite simple to distract the young minstrel and evade the questions altogether. The best way to divert Kiernan's questions about Yole's story was for Yole to ask questions of his own. The only problem with this ploy, however, was that once Kiernan began talking about himself, it was next to impossible to get him to stop. Yole found the size of the minstrel's ego to be both highly amusing as well as quite irritating. As they rolled along, Yole sighed. Kiernan was right in the middle of a long-winded tale about how he had once performed for the King and Queen of Quenmoire. The tale seemed to be a mixture of a ballad lauding Kiernan's skill at minstrelsy and a story about his own prowess at defeating a dragon in fair combat for the hand of some princess. Whatever the story was about, Yole believed that the whole thing was just a lot of hot air and rot. He was growing tired of these endless stories that probably had next to no basis in reality. Besides, the minstrel kept using big words that Yole did not understand, and talking about places and people that Yole had never heard of.

"How soon will we get to the Harshlands, Kiernan?" Yole asked, breaking into Kiernan's monologue and hoping to cause the minstrel to forget about his story.

Kiernan stopped his flow of words abruptly. "Ah, that is a good question Y... ian," he said, "we should reach the castle of the witch-queen tomorrow. Silver may not be the fastest mule in Aom-igh, but this is the most expedient road to take if one wishes to peregrinate to the Harshlands."

Yole nodded, glad to know that they only had one more day of travel left. He did not even bother to ask what "expedient" or "peregrinate" meant. Whenever he asked the minstrel those kinds of questions, Kiernan would launch into a lengthy definition of the word and usually ended up using a variation of the word itself in his definition. On the whole, Yole had found that it was better, and less confusing, not to ask. He still found it difficult to hold back a smile when Kiernan called him "Y... ian" but he managed to keep a straight face this time.

"Now, where was I in my story?" Kiernan asked.

"I think you had just finished," Yole lied, yawning.

"I did?" Kiernan looked amazed. "Well of course; I must have. Did I ever tell you of the time that I sang the *Ballad of the Dragon King* to the King of the dragons, Graldon himself?"

Hoping to spare himself from having to listen to any more stories, Yole nodded.

"Yes, you did. Great story, Kiernan; shouldn't we stop and set up camp? The Dragon's Eye has long since set."

"Why I even…" Kiernan was launching himself into yet another tale, but he stopped when Yole spoke. He glanced up at the sky and smiled. "I do believe that you are right. Jolly good observation old chap, jolly good. We will set up camp now and approach the ice palace in the morning!"

The next morning was chilly and wet. It had rained in the night and a great mist hung over the ground like a wet shawl. Yole and Kiernan found that there was no way to get dry, for the wetness of the fog clung heavily to them. The air itself was dense with water and the clouds hung low, threatening more rain. Yole helped Kiernan pack up the cart again, and then they climbed aboard. Yole was miserable. He did not like being wet or cold, but Kiernan seemed to relish it.

The minstrel grabbed the reins and began talking to his mule in a soothing voice, "Steady Silver, there's a good mule." He glanced over at Yole and then reached under the cart seat and produced a thick blanket. He handed it to the boy. "Don't be frightened of this mist, Yian, it's only eerie and spooky and bound to be full of ghosts and creepy, clammy things slithering out from the sides of the road with the intent of catching us and pulling us off the cart and eating us for dinner, right, my boy?"

Kiernan's tone was quite cheery, and Yole found it to be comforting and heartening. He pulled the blanket around his shoulders, basking in its softness and the faint smell of alfalfa that clung to it. He nodded enthusiastically in response to Kiernan's words, until he realized what the minstrel had actually said. Yole furrowed his brow in confusion and looked at Kiernan with an expression of alarm. The problem was that in the fog it was impossible to make out Kiernan's face. The mist hung so thick that Kiernan appeared only to be a ghostly shadow, even though he was no more than a foot away from Yole.

Kiernan let out a great laugh. "I'm only kidding, don't worry, lad! I've traveled this road a thousand times and no harm has come to me yet."

Yole would never have admitted it, but he breathed a sigh of relief to hear that the minstrel had not been serious. The mist gave everything a hollow, spooky feeling, and it deadened all of Yole's senses. Believing that there were dangerous creatures with sharp teeth and long claws hiding in the mist was not difficult at all. Yole was allowing his imagination to take over, and he thought he saw two large hands reaching out of the fog to grab a hold of him and drag him back into the forest where he would never be found. He jumped and turned back towards where Kiernan was sitting. The mist seemed to be letting up a little bit, or perhaps it was just that the day was growing lighter; Yole could now at least see Kiernan's face.

"Will we still get to the Harshlands today?" Yole asked, to take his mind off the possibility of ghosts.

"Yes, we will. I told you we would reach the palace of the witch-queen, and we will, if I have anything to say about it."

Yole spoke up defensively, "I don't know why you keep calling her names if you haven't even met her yet. She doesn't sound all that bad to me. In fact, I even know two of her sis…

uh, stories, and they are wondrous tales about her saving people from death."

Kiernan laughed out loud, not seeming to notice Yole's slip. "Ah, I must hear those stories sometime, perhaps it would improve upon my impression of the Wizardess of the Harshlands."

"If you think she is so bad, why are you traveling to her house?" Yole asked. "And if you have never met her, then how can you say that you have traveled this road a thousand times? I thought you said that this was the most ex… uh… expi… that big word that you said."

Kiernan let out a great laugh. "My stories are not matching up, are they? Ah well, that is perhaps why I get rotten fruits and vegetables thrown at me more often than not." He sighed, "The truth, my lad, is that I actually have met the wizardess before, several times. We know each other quite well; as a matter of fact, I sort of stretched the truth a little when I told you that I had only heard of her. And I call her names because I feel that it is my right. Name-calling is my only way to get back at her."

Yole was surprised. "Get back at her for what?"

Kiernan sighed again dramatically and pressed his right hand to his chest. "For breaking my heart."

There was a moment of silence, and Yole was brimming with new questions, but he remained quiet, hoping that Kiernan would explain things. He sensed a story that he might actually be interested in, and Kiernan did not disappoint him.

He spoke slowly and drew the story out as though he were spinning cloth on a loom, "You see, Y… ian, I have known Leila the wizardess for quite some time, at least ten years or so. We have become very good friends over the years. If you must know, I think she is the most beautiful woman who ever lived and I love her dearly. However, she has refused all of my requests to marry her. Do you know what she claims? She claims that she is too young to get married. Too young! As if the girl weren't a hundred and seventy already! I don't know how long she expects me to wait, she's not going to live forever you know." Kiernan's tone, normally so light, darkened a bit as he said those words.

Yole shook his head wordlessly. Kiernan continued on as though he had once again forgotten that Yole was traveling with him. He gave a piteous sigh and spoke in a tone of quiet fondness, as if to himself. "But that's just it, the lass knows I *would* wait forever if she asked it of me. And I would too."

"Why?" Yole asked.

"Why?" Kiernan nearly shouted, sounding aghast.

He leapt up and stood on the bench of the cart and flung his arms wide. Then he dropped them back to his sides and moaned, pressing his hands to his chest just above his heart. He staggered around upon the bench and Yole feared that the man would topple over at any moment, but he could not help laughing at the minstrel's antics. Then Kiernan flipped into a handstand and smiled. The mule flicked an ear but continued his steady plodding with a bored air that seemed to say he had seen it all before.

Kiernan continued to speak, a look of anguish on his face, but in a confidently cheerful voice, "Because she has not only broken my heart, but she has *stolen* it too! And she won't give it back, how very rude of her. So you see my boy, all the tales about the wicked witch are true, except the ones that you heard about her saving lives, those were obviously shameless lies. The wizardess of the Harshlands is no human, she is carved from ice, and her heart is stone. But now you know, she has stolen something from me and that is why I must keep going back... ahhh," the minstrel sighed and flipped off his hands to sit next to Yole once more, "but such is the nature of love."

Yole would have been aghast at Kiernan's words, if it had not been for his merry tone and the look of absolute adoration for the wizardess that shone in his bright blue eyes. It was obvious that the minstrel thought quite highly of his "dastardly witch-queen." Yole also suspected that if anyone else tried calling her names, Kiernan would be swift to become her most ardent defender.

Kamarie and Oraeyn stood in shock, staring out across the rocky desert. They had come upon the Harshlands all of a sudden, with a swiftness that had been breath-taking. One moment they had been fighting their way through the thick, tangled forest, chopping away dead branches and wondering if the trees would ever end, and the next instant they emerged from the trees and stood standing with the great forest at their backs, gazing out across a vast sea of wind-swept rock with loose sand whirling around in miniature tornadoes. The Harshlands were all that Brant had promised: forbidding, filled with a relentless wind and devoid of any and all growing things. A barren, lifeless wasteland of rough and rocky terrain stretched out before them. Sharp, jagged peaks jutted up harshly into the air. Perilous crags and fissures lined the landscape with valleys and rifts. Rough, red rock expanded to fill the horizon as far as the eye could see. A dark and overcast sky and a gray, sand-blasted air were the predominant features of the Harshlands. And yet, despite the sharp contrast between the lush, green, living forest that they had just exited, and the lifeless reds, browns, and oranges of the terrain that now faced them, there was something innately beautiful about the Harshlands. Perhaps it was the way the air was filled with the smell of spices. Perhaps it was the intense dry heat after days in the damp forest. Perhaps it was the way that the rocky desert floor seemed to sparkle whenever the clouds parted, albeit briefly, and allowed the Dragon's Eye to peek through. Or perhaps it was something about the way that the shadows fell across the rocks. Something about the way that the wind whipped through the loose grains of sand and made them dance glittering through the air. Or maybe it was a combination of all these things, creating a view that was magical and awe-inspiring in a dangerous sort of way.

"It's ... beautiful," Kamarie breathed in tones of wonder.

"Until it kills you, yes." Brant pulled some long cloths out of his pack and handed them to Kamarie and Oraeyn. "Bind these around your faces, make sure you cover up your neck, mouth and nose. Pull your hoods down as well, you want to cover up as much of your face as possible."

"Why?" Kamarie asked, as she obeyed Brant's instructions.

"Once we get out onto the open plains of the Harshlands, the wind whips at you like a hurricane. As you can see from here, there is a loose layer of sand covering the ground, and when the wind picks up it drives the sand before it with ruthless force. If you do not cover up your skin as much as possible, the blowing sand will sting any exposed flesh like a thousand tiny needles. Anything that gets hit will burn like fire the next morning. The sand can strip your skin completely off if you don't take the necessary precautions."

Kamarie grimaced and double-checked her knots, making sure that her face was completely covered. When they had pulled the hoods of their cloaks up and were ready to face the Harshlands, Brant nodded and began striding forward. Within moments of leaving the protection of the forest the three travelers were plunged into a windstorm. They struggled on, pressing through the wind and holding their hands up to shield their eyes. The wind tore at them, tugging their cloaks. Oraeyn could feel the tiny grains of sand whipping at him and penetrating his layers of clothing through minuscule openings in the fabric.

Oraeyn had pulled his sleeves down over his wrists and was holding the ends of them bunched up over his hands in an attempt to protect them from the biting sand. He wondered if the others had done the same thing, but he did not have any spare energy to waste wondering about that. It was taking every last bit of willpower he had just to keep putting one foot in front of the other. He trudged along, his head down, looking up every so often just to make sure that Brant and Kamarie were still within sight. Together, the three of them trudged, heads down, fighting the wind at every step.

The swirling windstorm continued, driving the sand around them. Even with their scarves and hoods pulled securely around their faces, the sand still managed to get into their mouths.

Kamarie was not sure how much longer she could continue. Her strength was giving out. They had been fighting their way through the storm for hours, and the going was painfully slow. Her whole body ached with the effort of walking through the gale, and the sand was beginning to sting, even through her thick cloak. Just as she thought that she could go no farther, Kamarie tripped over an unseen outcropping of rock and fell forward. She flailed her arms, trying to keep her balance, letting go of her cloak as she fell; she held out her hands and broke her fall a little when she hit the rough, uneven, rocky ground. A dull sting of pain shot through her as her exposed palms scraped against the sharp rocks, but she was too tired to notice. Her cloak and hood were blowing almost straight upward in the wind only attached to her by the ties around her neck and arms. Her scarf had also come loose in the fall.

Kamarie pushed herself up from the ground slowly and painfully. She had scratches all along her arms and deep gashes on her palms from her fall. Blood dripped from the wounds, and she felt the throb of pain at her bruised left knee. As she stood up she yelped, having forgotten the wind and the driving sand, which had not affected her as she lay on the ground. The sand stung her cheeks, forehead, and arms. She wrestled for a few minutes with her cloak, trying to draw it back around her for protection, but the wind was too strong and she was too drained of energy to fight it. She had the brief thought that it was amazing how much something as tiny as sand could hurt; sand seemed too small and harmless a thing to be able to inflict such agony. Her scraped up arms were burning as though they were on fire as the sand hit them and caused the already smarting wounds to sting with a vengeance.

Kamarie gave up on the cloak and dropped back down to the ground, huddling with her head buried in the rock. She pulled her arms in around her, trying to find some sort of protection from the wind and sand. She tried to pull her cloak down around her, but when she reached up the sand drove into her wound and made her cry out in pain. *I am going to die,* she thought, *I am going to die here in the middle of this wasteland. The wind will simply continue to blow, and in less than a week I will be nothing but a pile of sand-polished bones.*

Then, for a moment, the wind seemed to stop. She could still hear it whistling around her, but it was no longer pounding sand at her. She looked up and saw that Brant, who had seen her fall, had come back to rescue her. He was now kneeling in front of her, blocking the wind. His cloak was spread out around them both. He helped her stand up and pulled her cloak back into place. Then he helped her tie her scarf around her face once more and pull her hood down tighter. She gazed up at him gratefully, wanting to thank him but not being able to find the right words.

"Are you all right?" Brant practically had to shout to be heard.

Kamarie nodded. "You saved my life," she said, hearing the words fall flat in the wind. She tried to think of something that she could say that would express how much she owed him, but could find nothing.

Brant looked down at her in concern, noticing the blood oozing from her arms through the cloak. "Can you keep going? It's just a little farther. I can't tend to your wounds until we get out of this wind."

Kamarie nodded wordlessly, then looked around. "Where's Oraeyn?" she yelled, trying to make herself heard above the noise of the howling, hostile wind.

Brant pointed in the direction that they had been going. "There's a small shelter over there, not much of anything really, just a hole in the ground, but it will serve as some protection while we wait out the storm. Oraeyn found it, almost broke his neck falling into it, but the small protection it offers will be very welcome. We all need rest and some food before we go any farther. I can clean and bandage your wounds there."

Kamarie gave a weary nod and followed as Brant led her to the cave. She kept her eyes on the ground now, not wishing to risk stumbling again. They fought through the wind and finally reached the shelter. As Brant had said, it was little more than a hole in the ground. Although the blur of blowing sand made it difficult to see anything clearly, Kamarie could still discern the outcropping of rock that Oraeyn had stumbled across. It looked as though the rocks had split in some kind of land-quake with one side risen up above the other, creating an overhanging entrance. Crawling inside, they found that the cave was deeper than they had first thought. Kamarie rushed in, thinking that the ground would be only a foot or two down. She fell further than she had expected, and for a brief moment she envisioned herself falling and falling and never reaching the bottom. She let out a frightened scream, and then two arms reached out and caught her as her feet hit the ground. Without Oraeyn's help, her knees would have buckled under the greater than expected impact and she may well have broken her legs. However, he caught her and helped soften her landing. Brant leapt lightly down after her. Kamarie looked around, trying to get her bearings. It was dim in the cave, and her eyes had not adjusted yet, which meant she could barely see her companions. She found that she was a little afraid to be down in the hole, but she was relieved to be out of the wind.

Brant's voice sounded tired, "I want to look at your arms when I can see a bit better and tend to your wounds. We will stay here for the night, and hopefully the windstorm will have broken by morning so we can travel on again. I don't want to go out in that storm again, but our water won't last long."

"I'm sorry." Kamarie's voice was small.

"It's not your fault. The ground is uneven, and the storm is far worse than I expected for this time of year. Let me see your arms, and then we should all try to get some sleep."

Brant was as sparing with the water as possible, and though he was surprisingly gentle, Kamarie could not help but let out a few whimpers as he cleaned the cuts and scrapes and then bound her arms with some strips of cloth taken from his pack. When he was finished, they hurried down a quick meal of dried jerky and then huddled on their blankets trying to sleep in spite of the howling wind above. Kamarie thought that the pain in her arms and the noise of the storm would keep her from sleeping at all; however, within moments of lying down, exhaustion overtook her, and she fell into a deep sleep. Oraeyn dozed off too, and even Brant slept a little. The wind howled above them, but they were safe beneath the shelter of the rock above and the sand did not find them.

Kamarie awoke feeling refreshed; the long sleep had been good for her. She sat up and shook the remnants of clinging sleep from her head. She sat for a moment, staring blankly at the stone wall in front of her, trying to get up the motivation to move. Her arms ached, but they were not as painful as they had been the night before. As the fog of sleep lifted and she began to remember the events of the day before and where she was and how she had gotten there, she realized what had woken her up. All night long the wind had howled and screamed, sounding like some sort of wild animal. The sand had whipped above with a steady noise not unlike that of rain, with the occasional drum beat of larger rocks rolling across the stone roof above. Now, though, the noise had stopped, and their cave was deafening in its silence. Kamarie scrambled to the entrance, and in the faint light of dawn, she saw that the drop was not so severe as she had thought the night before. Poking her head into the new day above, she saw that the storm indeed had stopped. It amazed her that, even in this vast desert of rock, the storm had left no trace of its passing.

Kamarie rushed back down into the cave and woke Brant and Oraeyn. Brant went outside to take stock of their surroundings, and Oraeyn and Kamarie began packing up and getting ready to leave. A few moments later, Brant returned.

"The storm has truly passed, and only a little while ago too. The sky is clear, and I do not believe that we will come across another windstorm any time soon."

Kamarie and Oraeyn looked relieved at these words.

Brant smiled, and then continued, "We need to take advantage of this time that we have. We are going to have to travel more quickly than before if we want to use well this blessing we have been given."

Kamarie groaned, but said nothing in protest; instead she asked a question that had been bothering her for some time, "Do you have any idea of how to find Leila's home?"

"Dylanna gave me some idea of its location, and I noticed a few of the landmarks yesterday that she mentioned. I believe we are going in the right direction."

"How could you notice anything in all of that wind?" Oraeyn asked.

"It was difficult," Brant admitted, "but I had no desire to wander around lost in the desert, and I have been in the Harshlands before."

Yole was speechless at the sight of the Harshlands. He had expected a land blackened by the Dragon's Eye, peeled by the driving wind and altogether dead. As he and Kiernan entered the desert, however, Yole realized just how wrong he had been. The Harshlands were indeed barren of any growing things or greenery, but there were so many other colors of reds, browns, and golds that made up more than a thousand-fold for the lack of green. The patches of light from the Dragon's Eye, penetrating through the gray vapor, accentuated the rich colors of the rock formations in a dazzling display of artistic brilliance. Enhancing this canvas were the deep silver shadows that filled every crevice and the flashing gold swirling through the backdrop. The biggest surprise, however, was that the moment he stepped into the desert Yole discovered that the whole land was alive; it was a fierce life, a harsh and unrefined life, but it was most definitely life.

Kiernan almost toppled off of the cart in his laughter at Yole's wide-eyed amazement. He was so amused that it took him several moments to answer Yole's glare and demand of, "What's so funny?"

"I'm sorry my boy, it's just that your amazement at the Harshlands reminds me of myself the first time I came here. You expected the place to be dead, didn't you?"

Yole nodded.

"Yes, most people do. Something about the name, I think; for some reason the term 'Harshlands' puts that notion of death and darkness into people's minds. But the place wouldn't be nearly so fearsome if it were dead, now would it?"

Yole furrowed his brow, trying to figure out what Kiernan meant. He was certainly afraid of things that were dead, and he definitely thought that the Harshlands would be more frightening if they were the grim, dark plains that he had been picturing. Now that he had seen it, he could not understand why people were so afraid of coming to this beautiful, sparkling place that was so filled with life. After a few moments of thought, he still was not sure what Kiernan was trying to say. He shook his head in what he hoped was agreement with whatever it was that the minstrel was trying to explain, and Kiernan seemed satisfied with his answer.

"The Harshlands have not always been feared, you know," Kiernan went on. "Long ago, dragons lived in the Harshlands. Yes, my lad, there really were dragons living in Aom-igh. They also resided in the Mountains of Dusk, but all of them preferred the Harshlands. To dragons, this land is indeed alive. While we might think of this land as harsh and barren and colorless, the dragons could see a myriad of colors and dazzling shades of silver and gold and a most startling color of black that would astound you, er, us. It's a pity that only dragons and creatures of magic can see it, for it is truly a sight to see... or so I have been told," he added with a twinkle in his eye. "The dragons are the oldest of creatures, and thus their magic is the strongest. It permeates and surrounds the Harshlands, and it is that magic that even you are sensing. The very land itself moves and shifts with a life of its own because the dragon magic is so deeply embedded in this place and in such quantities that it will never depart these lands. The land before you is alive with dragon magic! What do you think of that, Yo... ian?"

Yole was not sure what he thought of that. He was beginning to believe that nothing would ever surprise him again. He was also wondering what Kiernan would think if he knew that he, Yole, was a dragon himself. And then he frowned, although Kiernan appeared every inch the foolish, lovesick minstrel that he seemed, Yole got the strangest feeling that Kiernan Kane knew exactly what Yole was. In the face of such a frightening possibility, Yole found that he was oddly comforted by the idea that Kiernan knew the truth. He did not have time to puzzle over this strange notion, though, for the minstrel was chattering at him again, breaking into his concentration.

"Well, my boy, we should be arriving at the wizardess' house just in time for lunch! Does that sound as good to you as it does to me?" Kiernan asked cheerfully, changing the subject abruptly as was his wont. "As long as *we* aren't lunch," the minstrel added dolefully.

Yole laughed, having learned to take comments like that as a joke. Kiernan's sense of humor was foreign to the boy, but after a few days traveling with the man, Yole was beginning to understand the twists of irony hidden within the minstrel's words. Yole may have felt uncomfortable with the Minstrel's odd ways, but he had never felt safer in his life.

Kiernan looked at him and frowned, as though puzzled by Yole's laughter. "Does the thought of feeding the evil wizardess' cats amuse you? Because it certainly does not sound like *my* idea of a good time."

Yole only laughed harder, shaking his head and holding his sides because they were starting to hurt from laughing so hard. The sight was so comical that Kiernan could not keep a straight face any longer. He burst into a great roar of laughter as well, laughing as long and as hard and as loudly as Yole. They both laughed until they ran out of breath and were left gasping for air.

Kiernan slapped Yole on the back. "My friend Y... ian, you have certainly made this trip quite enjoyable. The road can become very boring when there is no one to talk to. I must say I am very lucky you happened to be traveling the same road at the same time that I was."

The youth smiled back at Kiernan. "Well, I am sure that I would have gotten lost if I had not found you, and at least now, if I am lost, I didn't have to walk all this way."

Kiernan laughed and patted Yole on the head. "Quite so, youngling, quite so."

CHAPTER SIXTEEN

Hours had passed when Oraeyn grabbed Kamarie's arm and pointed. "Look!"

Kamarie peered towards the horizon and then rubbed her eyes in disbelief. There, in the distance, stood a solitary stone cottage, which jutted from the ground in generous proportions. Despite its lonely vigil, it did not seem at all out of place, for it had been built of the same red and brown stone and seemed more a part of the landscape than a home. With a cry of relief, Kamarie began sprinting towards the house as though it would disappear if she did not reach it in time. She ignored Brant's shouts to slow down and approach the house with more caution and continued to run towards the apparition. The distance was greater than she bargained for, and when she reached the stone steps leading to the entry, she found herself overcome with both exhaustion and awe. There were four strong columns supporting the roof above and two sturdy oak doors boasting large metal rings indicating the entry to this forbidding yet charming structure. Kamarie stared up at the large doors, breathing hard. She had felt such a great urgency to get to the house, but now all she felt was fear and doubt. She suddenly realized that perhaps this was not her Aunt Leila's home after all. She had met her Aunt Leila once before, and surely this lonely existence could not be hers.

Brant and Oraeyn finally caught up with her, and they all leaned against the columns, panting for breath. Brant looked at Kamarie and shook his head, but he did not say anything out loud. Oraeyn asked what was on all of their minds.

"Is someone else going to knock, or should I?"

Kamarie shook her head as she caught her breath. "No, it ought to be me."

Oraeyn and Brant both opened their mouths to protest, but before either of them could say anything, Kamarie knocked boldly on the door. For one terrifying second there was no sound at all except the echo of the loud knocking. Then the door swung open with aching slowness.

Kamarie felt her heart race and her body tense to run if whatever was on the other side of the door looked threatening. She held her breath and waited, her muscles coiled and ready to burst into action. Then the door swung all the way open, and Kamarie felt herself engulfed in an enthusiastic embrace.

"Kamarie, dear! How wonderful to see you again!"

Kamarie recognized the voice and hugged her aunt back, her fear sliding away like a discarded cloak. Oraeyn and Brant also stepped forward, seeing that it was indeed Kamarie's Aunt Leila. Seeing them approach, Leila stopped hugging Kamarie, though she did keep one arm slung protectively around her niece's shoulders, and with the other arm she beckoned to the others, inviting them to follow her inside.

"You must be Brant and Oraeyn. Come in, please."

As they entered the house, Leila continued talking, saying something about a long journey and how they must be tired, but Oraeyn did not listen to her words; instead he focused on her voice. Leila's voice sounded as though she was accustomed to laughter. It was not the beautiful voice that Queen Zara was famed for, nor was it the deep echoing tones of Calyssia's voice.

Leila's voice was natural and real. Oraeyn thought that she sounded very much like Kamarie: kind and cheerful, with a tone that was natural and comforting.

Oraeyn jerked himself out of his thoughts, realizing that Leila was still speaking. "Dylanna has told me much about your journey, I recognized you at once. She will want to see you all right away, we've been trying to locate you with our magic for days and she is beside herself with worry. It's not an exact science, you know, trying to find someone when you don't know where they are. Much easier to see them when you know their location. My goodness, you all look exhausted. Please, follow me this way, you will want food and drink and rest before you return to your quest."

"Dylanna is here?" Kamarie asked, managing at last to get a word in.

"Yes, I am here." Dylanna suddenly appeared from a room up ahead of them and, embracing Kamarie warmly, she smiled in obvious relief. Oraeyn noticed that she was dressed in a long, flowing blue dress, and her hair cascaded down over her shoulders in waves of deep brown. As he looked at her, all traces of Darby were finally erased from his mind. He could never think of her as a simple lady's maid again; from that moment on she would forever appear to him as Dylanna, a beautiful, powerful wizardess.

"Kamarie, Oraeyn, Brant, you do not know how good it is to see you all alive and well," she stopped and looked around, then spoke again. "But where is Yole?"

Nobody answered her question, and Leila cut in before Dylanna could say anything else, "Come in, sit down, rest, and I will bring you food and drink, then you can tell us the whole story without interruption."

The weary travelers followed Dylanna and Leila into the house and sank into the comfortable chairs and couches of Leila's main room. As Kamarie sat down, her tiredness threatened to overwhelm her and she was grateful for the cozy chair beneath her. She thought that it would be nice to never rise from her place again. Leila brought them tea, fruit, and bakery goods fresh from the oven that invited them to eat. They accepted with grateful murmurs and dug into it with enthusiasm. The tea, which Kamarie normally did not care for, was delicious and tasted of cinnamon and some other spice that was rich and tangy and not at all tea-like. The rolls were lightly buttered, and there was a bowl of raspberry jam that they added liberally to their bread. The croissants were hot and laced with warm, melted chocolate and the flaky bread literally melted in their mouths. Both Leila and Dylanna were brimming with questions about their travels, but they kept silent as the three travelers devoured the food and drink before them. When they had finished, Leila spoke.

"I know you all must be tired, perhaps the story should wait until you have had a chance to get a few hours of sleep in comfortable beds. Then you will be refreshed and clear-headed, and answering questions will not seem so much a chore."

"Perhaps that would be best," Brant agreed after studying Kamarie and Oraeyn for a moment.

Leila led them upstairs to her guest rooms. All of them were amazed at the size of Leila's house, though none of them said anything. Kamarie chose the first room that Leila showed them. Nodding at the others, she yawned and smiled.

"Good night," she said.

Kamarie closed the door behind her and crawled into the big, soft, pillowy bed. She did not have time even to admire the beautiful decorations of the room or feel grateful for the clean, cotton sheets. Exhaustion swept over her as she lay down and breathed out, relaxing her aching muscles. The last thing she remembered before she fell asleep was pulling the thick, fluffy blanket up to her chin and thinking that she had never felt so comfortable.

Morning came much too quickly for Kamarie's liking. She sighed as she opened her eyes, and then she stretched luxuriously. Sitting up, she blinked. For a moment she thought that she was back in her own room in the palace and that everything had just been a dream. As she woke up more fully, however, she realized that the room she was in was not her own, though there were many similarities. Swinging her legs over the edge of the bed, Kamarie got up and wandered around the room. Someone had attended to her injuries and set out a fresh change of clothes, and there was a bowl of hot water for washing on the table beside the bed. After enjoying this luxury, she changed into clean clothes, and headed downstairs feeling much brighter and more cheerful.

She found the others at the table, eating a breakfast of eggs and bacon and thin hotcakes topped with berries and sugar. They welcomed her with big smiles. She greeted them cheerfully and sat down. As the smells of breakfast reached her nose, she discovered that she was very hungry. She loaded up a plate of food and began eating with a will borne of hunger. It appeared that Brant and Oraeyn had washed and been given clean clothes as she had, for the layer of traveling dust had been cleared away from them, and they looked refreshed.

Leila entered the room with a smile. "Kamarie! You're awake, good! When you're done with breakfast, there is someone outside who wants to see you. He is very impatient."

Kamarie looked at her aunt, mystified. "Who?"

Leila's eyes twinkled with mischief. "I can't tell you who, that would ruin the surprise, but don't rush your breakfast."

Dylanna had a wide grin on her face, and Kamarie was annoyed by the fact that everyone seemed to know what this was all about except for her. Despite Leila's instructions not to rush, Kamarie hurried through her meal, wondering who the mysterious visitor was. She also wanted to know how whoever it was knew that she was here. When she finished eating, Leila smiled and then told them all to follow her. She led them to the back door and then flung it open. Kamarie blinked at the sudden light; then her eyes opened wide as a smile spread across her face.

"Tor!" she cried, running towards the silver horse and flinging her arms around his long neck.

The horse nickered and nudged her shoulder with his nose.

Kamarie laughed. "I'm glad to see you again too! I was so worried when you weren't at the Pearl Cove."

Tor shook his head vigorously and then lowered his eyes and gave her a reproachful look.

Kamarie sobered. "I'm sorry for leaving you behind, but you really would not have liked Krayghentaliss. It's all underground and it was dark and there were dragons."

Tor nibbled at her pockets, a gesture of forgiveness as plain as if he had said so.

Kamarie giggled. "I'm sorry Tor, I didn't know you were here or I would have grabbed an apple. I'll bring you one later, I promise. And some sugar, too." She turned to Leila. "How did he get here?"

Leila and Dylanna had both watched the whole exchange with understanding smiles on their faces. Oraeyn, however, could not have been more shocked than if Tor had actually opened his mouth and spoken audibly. Oraeyn's mouth dropped, and his eyes were wide with shock. Brant, if surprised, showed no visible signs of his astonishment. Looking at him, no one would ever have been able to guess that anything out of the ordinary had occurred.

"Tor should have taken the other horses home when Calyssia set them free to return to the palace. But your ornery horse insisted that he just absolutely *had* to visit me first. They all arrived here shortly after Dylanna did because the other horses apparently wanted to do some sight seeing." Leila smiled. "Tor also came here because he believed you would come here before you went home. That is a smart horse you have."

Oraeyn shook his head, rubbed his eyes, scratched his head, and then gave up, deciding that whatever he was hearing probably had no easy explanation. Brant was watching Kamarie and Leila carefully, and after a few moments a small, knowing smile crept up to the corners of his mouth as though he suddenly understood. Dylanna turned around to look at Brant, but by the time she was facing him, Brant's face was as unreadable as ever. Her eyes closed to slits as she stared hard at him. Brant looked back at her easily, his face clear and open but expressionless. Dylanna watched him for a moment, then shook her head and walked back into the house muttering something unintelligible under her breath.

Kamarie patted Tor one more time, then turned to follow the others back inside, "I'll come back out to visit you later," she promised the horse.

Once they had all gathered back in Leila's main room, Dylanna and Leila begged Kamarie, Brant, and Oraeyn to tell them all about their journey to the Harshlands. So Brant began telling what had transpired along the trail since the Dark Warriors had sprung upon them and caused them to separate. He told of coming to Marghita and Enreigh's house, and Oraeyn chimed in explaining about how Marghita would not stop talking or let any of them get more than a single word in edgewise, not even her husband. Leila laughed at that and said that she knew someone who reminded her of his description of Marghita.

Then Kamarie explained about how she and Yole had fled in the night to save time and how they had felt that someone or something was watching and following them. Then she recounted her instructions to Yole and told of the three Dark Warriors who had attacked her. Dylanna shuddered at that part. Oraeyn finished the story with an explanation of their decision to make for the Harshlands in the hopes that Yole had indeed found his way to Leila's home. He added that Brant had expressed confidence that Dylanna would come to no harm in her travels; at this, Dylanna glanced at Brant, who simply nodded in recognition of their shared confidence.

"We must find Yole," Kamarie said worriedly.

Dylanna put a hand on Kamarie's shoulder. "The confidence that Brant placed in me is the same I place in our young dragon friend."

Kamarie smiled. "Yes, he's fairly resourceful, and quick too. I was teaching him a bit of forestry along the way, and he caught on very fast."

Just then a loud knocking on the front door caused them all to jump slightly. They all followed Leila to the door to find out who the unexpected visitor was. As they approached the door, they heard a voice from outside, shouting loudly, but none could understand the words.

"Oh, my!" Dylanna said in shock as the words became audible.

Whoever was outside seemed to be bellowing at the top of his lungs, "I know you are in there, so don't pretend you aren't home! Is this how you would treat visitors? I know that your heart is as cold as an iceberg and as black as your cats' fur, but I did not know that you left your guests standing in the cold on your doorstep to freeze! Come out if you dare, Witch Queen of the Harshlands!"

Kamarie and Oraeyn were shocked to hear these accusations. Brant calmly reached for his sword while Dylanna looked at Leila in shocked curiosity. Leila herself looked rattled for a moment, and then she burst out laughing. She approached the door, but Dylanna grabbed her shoulder.

"Sister, do you think it is safe?" she asked.

Leila smiled at Dylanna's concern, then chuckled and said, "As safe as a wandering bard ever is."

Yole had tried to stop Kiernan from yelling through the door. He tried to say that the knocking would bring someone to open the door eventually, but Kiernan insisted that he must shout or they would be left standing outside for eons and ages. Yole personally thought that the minstrel just wanted an excuse to speak more loudly than normal, but he kept his thoughts to himself and buried his face in his hands while Kiernan shouted to the wizardess through the door.

Just as Yole was beginning to think that perhaps nobody was at home or that the wizardess could not hear Kiernan's ranting, the door swung open.

"Kiernan!"

A pretty young woman flung herself at the minstrel and hugged him.

"Beautiful ice princess!" Kiernan said cheerfully. "Ah, so you don't leave your guests to rot on the doorstep. That is good to know."

Leila's face turned red and her violet eyes flashed as she tossed her head, "I do not own any black cats either, and for your information my heart is *not* carved out of ice!" She sounded angry, but there was a twinkle deep in her eyes. "And only you would claim to be freezing in the desert during the end of Warm-Term."

Kiernan smiled agreeably and nodded. "Well then, so the rumors aren't true."

Leila laughed. "As though you don't start half the rumors concerning me."

Kiernan opened his light blue eyes wide, the picture of innocence. "Me? Why, how *could* you accuse me of such a thing?"

"Easily."

"My dear woman, you do me a great injustice," Kiernan said in injured tones, as he did his best to look as though her comments had wounded him deeply. "I have never had anything but respect for you, and only speak of you with words of highest regard."

Yole rolled his eyes.

Leila snorted in exasperation. "You are as impossible as ever."

Kiernan smiled irritatingly. "Admit it, you would be disappointed if I was ever less impossible than ever."

"Your word games never cease to amaze me, dear minstrel."

"She called me 'dear,'" Kiernan whispered loudly to Yole, "that's always a bad sign."

Leila fixed the minstrel with a bemused stare, then directed her attention to Yole and asked, "And who is this?"

Kiernan flung his arms wide. "My darling wizardess, allow me to introduce to you my apprentice, Yo... ian! Well, actually, he is not exactly my apprentice; I just offered to teach him some bits of the trade as we traveled along. We met up quite by chance as we journeyed along the road. Poor young... ster had lost his way, but he insisted on traveling to these dangerous parts and what could I do? Let him wander alone? He's picked up the juggling quite well but the poor boy is as tone deaf as Silver."

Yole glared at the minstrel.

Leila smiled. "Welcome to my home, Yo... ian."

"Milady," Yole said, blushing, "I must confess, I have not been completely honest with this good minstrel. You see: my name is not actually Y... ian."

Just then Kamarie caught a glimpse of the boy and ran towards him. "Yole!"

She and the others rushed outside and surrounded Yole, peppering him with questions about how he had gotten there, and taking turns hugging him. Yole was overjoyed to see them, and even happier that he had not missed them by arriving too late. He smiled and tried to answer several of the questions, but soon gave up, deciding that he would tell them all about it when everyone calmed down a bit. Kiernan watched all of this with a bemused expression on his face.

"Now what is all this about? You know these people?"

Yole spoke up, "I am sorry Kiernan, but as I said, I have not been exactly honest with you about myself. I hope you will understand that anything I said that was untrue was only to protect you and anyone you might come in contact with. My name is actually Yole, not Y... ian. These good people are my companions and friends. We lost each other as we were traveling to Leila's house."

The minstrel scratched his head and seemed to be doing his best to look puzzled, but then he brightened. "So that means you all must have quite a story to tell. Come, let us go inside and you can tell me your tale and then I can turn it into a ballad that will be sung for as long as the Dragon's Eye rises each morning."

They all agreed that Kiernan's idea was a good one, and they went into the house. They spent the rest of the day exchanging tales and recapping what had happened since the attack of the

Dark Warriors had first separated them. Kiernan was fascinated by their tale, especially the part about their wanderings through Krayghentaliss. He asked many questions about the dragons and their tunnels, seemingly awed by the fact that there was a whole world within Aom-igh that he had never visited, and yet the questions he asked revealed an insight that put Brant on his guard. When they were all caught up, Kiernan leaned back and stretched out his long legs.

"I say, that is quite the story!" he exclaimed. "Well then, it's settled."

"What is settled?" Oraeyn asked.

"Why, the fact that I am going to travel with you," Kiernan said, as though it were the most obvious thing in the world.

"No, I do not think so," Brant said quietly, but firmly.

"But I must!" Kiernan cried. "I am a minstrel and all of you are in the middle of a greater adventure than any I have ever heard sung! I must continue on with you so I can find out how the story ends!"

Brant shook his head. "We cannot have anyone else traveling with us, especially not a minstrel. We must make all haste back to the palace. It is normally a three day's journey, I intend to be there two days hence."

"If you do not allow me to travel with you, then I will follow you, and you cannot stop me from doing that," Kiernan said sulkily. "Besides, you are going to let Leila travel with you, and I am much less trouble than she is."

"We may as well take him with us," Leila said with a sigh, "he is as stubborn as that old mule of his when he sets his mind on something."

Brant sighed as well, realizing this was one battle he didn't need to fight. "All right, I suppose you can come with us. But leave your cart and mule here and ride a real horse like the rest of us, otherwise there is no way that you will be able to keep up with our pace."

Kiernan turned his head to one side. "I am not sure if Silver would like it very much if he heard you implying that he is not what you call a 'real horse," he said mock seriously, but then he seemed to decide to stop being difficult and he nodded enthusiastically. "Of course, of course, Silver will not mind staying behind, he needs some rest anyway, I promised him a vacation a long time ago. May I stable him here Leila?"

Leila nodded. "Of course you may."

Brant blew a short breath out through his mouth and let his shoulders drop. "We are leaving at first light. Anyone not ready to go when I say 'move out' is staying behind."

The aethalon stood trembling before Tobias. It was not the Captain of the King's Helm who was causing the trembling, however; it was the nearness of King Seamas. The king had insisted upon hearing the reports as they came in, and his presence made the men a touch nervous.

"Why have you returned? You were not in any of the scouting parties," Tobias kept his voice calm.

"No, sir, but..." the man glanced towards the king, "I think I might have found the one His Majesty is looking for."

If Seamas heard, he did an excellent job feigning disinterest. Tobias breathed an inner sigh of relief. At least his king was still sane enough to act his part.

"Tell me what happened."

"Well, sir, our food supply was low, so me, Jaret, and Raelf split off from the party to do some hunting. We hadn't much luck, when we came upon the trail of two travelers. We followed them because we didn't know if they were a threat to our purposes or not. It was dark when we approached, and we were surprised to discover that our prey was alone, and a girl. Uncertain as to what we should do, I assured the girl that we meant her no harm, but she had either seen or heard about what had happened at Peak's Shadow, and she knew that we were Dark Warriors, as they call us. She was proud and defiant, and we knew that we could not simply threaten her to silence. She carried a sword and Jaret tried to disarm her, but she could wield her blade and she surprised Jaret with her skill. We eventually subdued the girl with a blow to her head, and then we didn't know exactly what we should do with her. We couldn't just leave her, as she would eventually waken and warn her countrymen. We couldn't kill her, unconscious as she was, and we certainly didn't want to drag her along with us. It was then that two men attacked us. They came out of nowhere, sir, they just materialized out of the trees and they fought well. The big one killed Raelf, and the younger one wounded Jaret. I turned to face the taller one, but..." the man trailed off. Silence hung in the room like a tangible thing. "I opted to try to get Jaret to safety. I got him back to camp and left him to mend. Then using one of the long-boats I made my way back to Roalthae to report my findings."

"Why did you run, Kyan?" Seamas' voice cut like a blast of frigid air through the room.

"I - I had to, Sire... the man we faced... it could have been *you*."

"What?" Seamas and Tobias both stared at the man.

"What do you mean?" Tobias asked after another long moment of silence.

"He... he looked just like the king," Kyan replied. "I thought it *was* the king, I didn't understand... I was surprised to see you here, Your Majesty, I thought you were... but now I see it couldn't have been. I was mistaken, a trick of the light, the Toreth, the forest, the shadows... forgive me, I became confused." The man knelt, awaiting punishment.

"You have done well, Kyan," Seamas said. "Get some rest and then make ready to invade Aom-igh."

"Sire?"

"Do not question me," Seamas' voice thundered down the hall. Kyan rose, bowed at the waist, and hastily exited the room.

When he was gone, Seamas turned to his trusted adviser, a strange gleam in his eye. "Tobias, my friend, they have found him."

CHAPTER
SEVENTEEN

A scout had returned to Ayollan to report to King Arnaud that the enemy warriors were making ready to board their ships. Weapons and other supplies and horses were being loaded onto the Roalthaen vessels.

"They plan to set sail in two days, Sire," the scout reported.

Arnaud took this news stoically and issued orders to his men to get some rest but to remain ready; the period of waiting was nearly over. He was walking the eastern wall when Zara came out to speak with him. She looked lovely, but troubled. Her forehead was creased with a worried frown, and her eyes had a stormy look in them.

"What is wrong?" Arnaud asked.

"There are people in the Throne Room who seek audience with you," Zara said in clipped tones.

"What do they want?"

Zara turned her eyes up towards him; there was a flame of absolute fury written across her face now. "They want... no, I will let them explain it to you."

Arnaud hurried after her as she walked with long, purposeful strides towards the Throne Room. As he followed her, he wondered what could have happened to make Zara so angry; he was certain he had never seen her so furious in all the years that he had known her. At the door, Zara halted.

"You attempt to put sense into their heads, I have already tried," she said.

Arnaud nodded, and then, trying to hide how mystified he felt, he entered. As he came through the doors onto the dais, he found five very fashionably and expensively dressed courtiers. He silently placed their names with their faces: Baron Sauterly of Drayedon, the Duke and Duchess Frantell of Coeyallin, Baron Yatensea of Urith, and Duchess Selynda of Zrheden. They were well-known to Arnaud. They were young, idealistic, and keenly interested in affairs of state.

Arnaud nodded at them with cautious cordiality. "Ladies, gentlemen."

He waited silently, letting them take the floor. They shifted and exchanged glances, as though unsure how to begin.

Finally, after a long pause, Baron Yatensea spoke, "Your Majesty, we come representing many of our fellow citizens, and ask that you bear this in mind when you hear our suggestion. For starters, we, all of us here, are of the opinion that you have placed the people of Aom-igh at risk of war, without pursuing every avenue of peace available to you."

Arnaud's face tightened, but he remained silent. Yatensea winced visibly, but continued to press on, hurrying to make his point before anyone interrupted him.

"No one we know has ever journeyed as far as the Dark Country, and as far as we know, no one from the Dark Country has ever journeyed to our fair Aom-igh. We do not know if the Dark Country or the Dark Warriors truly mean us harm. We could be needlessly launching ourselves into a bloody battle that we will regret later.

"Our plan is simple and involves no risk to anyone but ourselves. We propose that we be granted a small ship. We wish to sail to Roalthae and seek an audience with the leader of the Dark Country to sue for peace. If we succeed, we may be able to avoid much suffering."

Arnaud's eyes filled with sorrow and he spoke quietly, "The time for speaking of peace has passed. Perhaps you are right, perhaps I have not looked hard enough for a peaceful solution. Perhaps I simply focused on the threat too much and missed the opportunity for peace. However, these have been my decisions, and now that moment, if it ever existed, is gone."

"We do not believe that is true. It is never too late to speak of peace," Baron Yatensea pressed.

"I have always seen you as an honorable man, Ryen," Arnaud said. "It seems I misjudged you. I never would have expected you to stir up a rebellion against me."

"No, Your Majesty!" The Duchess Selynda exclaimed in horror, her pretty blue eyes widening. "You do us all a grave injustice, Sire. Our first loyalty is, as ever, to you and our country. Our mission is not a bid for power. We truly wish only for peace. We do not wish to see anyone die needlessly, and we believe very strongly that the coming violence can be avoided if we can just find out what it is that the Dark Warriors want."

Duchess Frantell spoke up, "If we succeed it will say nothing against you at all, it will instead laud your wisdom at being able to listen to the advice of others who perhaps see things differently than you. Our view is that you may have been perhaps a little too hasty in your decision to prepare for war when we do not know the true intent of the Dark Country, but that is nothing against you as a ruler, rather it shows your desire to protect the people of our fair land, that could only ever be construed as a credit to you, Sire."

Arnaud's spoke quietly, "What about the events at Peak's Shadow do you not understand? What possible intent could justify the murder of those peace-loving families? Is that not enough to persuade you of your own folly? Do you truly not understand? You charge me with placing the people of Aom-igh at risk of war while the enemy is already here and has struck! War is upon us, and not by my choice. Weeks of agonizing study and the intelligence from our scouts has confirmed this. I do not seek battle, but only a careless fool would allow his people to remain unprepared. Whomever you claim to represent, know this for certain: their King is no fool. For this reason alone I cannot allow you this foolhardy attempt. You will be murdered as certainly as the families of Peak's Shadow."

The courtiers looked down. None of them spoke for a long moment. But then Duke Frantell spoke up.

"Yes, Your Majesty, we have considered that possibility. We know this mission could go awry. We know we could end up in a very dangerous situation; we know we may even be killed. But we have considered that with care, we have all set our affairs in order, and we have decided it is worth the risk. The benefits of our possible success far outweigh the cost of our possible failure."

Arnaud shook his head in disbelief. "You are willing to foolishly trade your own lives for the mere *possibility* of peace, even though everything in the world is telling you that it is a hopeless endeavor? And what if your sacrifice does not save anyone?"

"You would not even let us try? You would not even consider the possibility of our success?" Duchess Selynda's voice conveyed her shock.

Arnaud looked at her solemnly. "No, foolish lady, I would not. I thought your intent was to undermine your King, but I have misjudged you, and I beg your pardon. But that aside, however genuine your purpose, I cannot allow you to attempt this needless and useless waste of lives that I indeed value."

"You think there is no chance of it working." Selynda said flatly. "What do you know? You have spent too much time reading dusty journals about the past. There is the possibility that much has changed in the Dark Country since those words were penned, it has been over five hundred years since anyone made contact with the people of the Dark Country."

"What I know or don't know regarding the Dark Warriors will soon be revealed, but this much is certain: such a plan as yours is doomed for disaster, and I would spare you that," Arnaud replied.

"Well," Baron Sauterly said, "we have asked for your permission and we have listened to your arguments against our plans. You do not believe that our mission will work; you do not believe that there is any way to prevent this war from happening. That is your prerogative as king and commander of our military forces. However, we know what we are up against and we are willing to take the risk."

Arnaud shook his head. "I will not keep you here against your will, but you have my command to desist from this madness. Heed the wisdom that has been offered."

The five courtiers bowed.

"We understand, Your Majesty," Baron Sauterly said.

They departed without presenting any further arguments. Arnaud watched them go, suspicion in his thoughts. They were taking his decision far better than he had expected. He thought they would at least try to talk him into giving them a ship; instead, they almost seemed relieved at his words. That could only mean one thing: they already had a ship at their disposal. He sent a message to the Port Command with instructions that no vessels could leave or enter without written permission from the King under threat of death.

Arnaud watched the messenger go, but a premonition of disaster pricked at the back of his mind. He tried to distract himself with his duties, but found himself staring out the window towards the harbor. At length, Arnaud gave up and called for Garen.

"I cannot set myself at ease about the courtiers who petitioned a ship earlier this morning," he explained. "I sent a message to the Port Commander, but I cannot focus. Something feel amiss."

Garen did not wait to hear more, but raced to the stables. Together, they made for Port Aolla. When they were in sight of the Harbor, his urgency accelerated and Arnaud out-paced his Guard. The Captain of the Port Command met Arnaud at the quay and handed him his sword. Arnaud was startled as the man kneeled before him.

"What is all this?" Arnaud demanded. "What is the meaning of all this? I don't have time for this ceremony. There are five nobles headed this way bent on their own destruction and under no circumstances are you to let them set sail. Is that understood?"

The captain nodded. "Only too well, your Lordship. They set sail thirty minutes ago, and just moments ago, I received your message."

Now, the king understood the actions of his captain. Arnaud pulled the man to his feet and returned his sword. Looking the man in the eyes, he said, "Your devotion to duty is unmatched and my harbor could be in no better hands than yours. The 'threat of death' in my message was meant for the fools who set sail, not for the worthy soldier before me."

Arnaud then turned, fighting back tears, not only for the five fools, but for his brave commander whose life had been mistakenly placed in his hands. The thought scared Arnaud, and he learned a hard lesson as his thoughts rebuked him: *if you had acted with the same authority when the five were in your chamber, they would still be alive, and your captain would never have been in a position to believe his life was unjustly forfeit.* Arnaud's grief slowly turned to anger, and if his resolve before was uncertain, it was now steel.

He knew with terrible certainty in his heart that he would never see those five people alive again. Although no one would ever blame him for the deaths of the nobles, he knew that he would always blame himself. Arnaud closed his eyes tightly, trying to shut out the sight of the little boat disappearing over the horizon. A long, deep sigh escaped his lips. Then he opened his eyes and set his jaw. Those five had known their mission was doomed before they even set off. They knew of the merciless raid at Peak's Shadow. They knew that the Dark Warriors had not hesitated to kill women and children, and yet they had insisted upon trying to talk of peace with the enemy. He had warned them of the vicious nature of the Dark Warriors, and yet they had stubbornly insisted upon sailing off on their fool's errand anyway.

In a way, Arnaud found that he was forced to admire their courage and their deep love for peace. He even admired their willingness to throw away everything for what they considered to be a higher goal. But he could not condone the actions that had placed a good man in harm's way, and may well endanger many other innocents before all was said and done.

"Sir Garen," Arnaud barked, "send out runners to evacuate this town. I want everyone relocated by tomorrow morning, we're running out of time. Our enemy is coming in ships, and this port is surely their destination."

"Will we be setting up a defense in the town?" Garen asked, he knew as well as the king that they did not have the ships or the sailors to be able to make any kind of attack at sea.

Arnaud shook his head. "No, we will stick to the plan and set up our defense with our backs to Fortress Hill. We will make them come to us."

Oraeyn shifted with impatience as he watched Brant move forward with painstaking care. They were following the Farrendell River through the Mountains of Dusk, and Brant had warned them to follow his movements and proceed with extreme caution. The Farrendell wound its way through the mountain pass with rapids and falls and the path was slippery and treacherous. A misstep could prove fatal.

They were forced to dismount and lead their horses as they traveled this part of their journey. Brant went first, testing the ground and cautioning the others. He alerted them to loose rocks and soft sections of the trail. Several times he almost fell himself, but he was always able to jerk himself back upright and continue on. The rest were grateful for their guide, and they attended to his directions closely. They traveled in silence for the most part, each of them focusing their full concentration on the path before them. The result was a solemn and somber group as they trekked through the pass. The foremost thought in each of their minds was the wish to get through the mountains and past this dangerous part of the journey.

The river was on their right, rushing and swirling mere inches below them. Immediately to their left was a sheer rock cliff that wanted to crowd them off the trail and into the roaring river. The trail was only about four feet wide, and that left little room for mistakes, especially with the horses.

Brant had not wanted to travel along this path; he had warned them that the trail was treacherous and difficult, but Leila and Dylanna had declared that it was the fastest and most direct route back to Ayollan. Brant had given in, having no desire to waste any more time arguing about it, but it was clear he was not happy with their decision. Oraeyn was starting to believe Brant had been correct about the trail; it was too dangerous to be attempted. Whatever time they could have gained because this path was the quickest road to Ayollan they lost because of their travel speed, or lack thereof. Oraeyn was also worried about any attack they might face as they traveled along the riverbank. If Dark Warriors, or any other villains, were to attack them here, they would have nowhere to turn.

Suddenly Brant held up a hand and the party halted, wondering what had happened. Brant took a few more steps forward, then turned around. Oraeyn could not see past the man and could not see what was wrong, but Brant's face was grim and set. The man's eyes told Oraeyn that there was something ahead that he did not like and did not want to face.

"The trail has been washed away," Brant declared in a voice loud enough for all of them to hear. "Up ahead of us, perhaps a dozen more paces or so, the water has carved away at the path and at the mountain. There is a shallow cave in the side of the cliff face, but the path is completely gone."

Dylanna spoke up in concern, "How much of the path has been washed away?"

Brant shook his head. "I don't know for sure, it looks like a width of ten to fifteen feet or so before the path reappears above water."

Dylanna pursed her lips. "That's not a very big gap. We will just have to swim across then."

Brant glared. "It's too dangerous to attempt, I say we turn back, the current is strong and it may be too much for the horses to cross, let alone us, and I can assure you that some in our party are not strong enough to make it across."

"Of course you would want to turn back, you did not want to take this path in the first place," Dylanna said, her voice turning stubborn. "I say we cross. It is not like we are trying to cross the river itself where the current could wash us downstream."

"It's too dangerous," Brant maintained. "The current could drag us into the cave beneath the cliffs, and there would be no way of swimming out again."

"We are running out of time, we must get back to Ayollan with all speed, we are more than halfway through the mountains by now, if we turn back, we lose a whole day that we cannot spare."

Brant's mouth tightened into a thin, angry line and his eyes narrowed. "All right, I will get you all across the river, but we do it my way."

Dylanna nodded shortly. Oraeyn shrank back, seeing how angry Brant was. His face was stone, giving away nothing, but fury radiated from him as if it were tangible. Brant moved in abrupt, harsh motions as he lifted a long coil of rope from the place where it was secured behind his saddle. Then he removed his cloak and put it into his saddlebag. He also removed his boots and attached them to the front of his saddle.

"Do as I do," he barked.

Oraeyn followed his example, and from the sound of the others moving behind him, he assumed that they also were taking off their cloaks and boots. The path was too narrow to waste energy in turning around to confirm what his ears told him, so he kept his eyes on Brant, waiting for instructions.

"Pass this back and have everyone hang on to it. Keep several feet between each person, we will need as much room to maneuver as possible," Brant ordered sharply, handing Oraeyn the coil of rope.

Oraeyn obeyed swiftly, uncoiling a length of the rope to hang onto and then passing it backwards over his shoulder to the next person in line, repeating Brant's orders as he did so. Brant tied his end of the rope to his belt and then he turned and walked forward, leading his horse cautiously along the path. As they continued to walk, Oraeyn peered up ahead and saw where the water had caused the riverbank to deteriorate and was now rushing into a shallow cavern in the side of the mountain.

"When you enter the water, hold tight to your horse's saddle, and hang on to the rope, keep yourself between it and the cliff," Brant ordered, demonstrating.

They all obeyed, and Brant waded into the water. The current tugged at Brant's legs, surging around him in miniature whirlpools. His great black horse shied away from the water, but Brant calmed him, speaking soothingly and softly until the horse relaxed. The black horse finally lowered his head and followed Brant obediently into the rushing water.

The water was deep, above Brant's shoulders after only a few paces. Brant had left a lot of room between him and Oraeyn on the rope, and he told Oraeyn to wait until he was on the other side to enter the water. Brant continued through the water, holding onto his horse's saddle. In this way half swimming, half walking with great effort he reached the other side. He clambered up the bank, secured his end of the rope to his saddle, and turned to wave Oraeyn across.

Oraeyn waded into the water and soon found that he could not touch the bottom. He clung to his saddle with one hand and gripped the rope pulling himself along it with his other arm. As he got near the middle, the current became much swifter and too strong. His fingers grew numb and stiff. He tried in desperation to paddle against it, but found himself being dragged by the current towards the actual river. The current suddenly pulled him under the surface of the water, and he let go of his horse in his panicked attempts to paddle his way back up to air. Oraeyn surfaced and gasped for air, clinging desperately to the rope, and then was pulled under again. The current swept him under the side of the cliffs, and his head struck against a jagged rock. The pain almost sent him spinning into unconsciousness. His arms felt leaden, and he wondered how much longer he could hold his breath. He could still feel the rope clenched in his fist, but he did not know how much longer he could hold on. He tried to kick but the river was too strong. He strained with his arms, hoping he could use the rope to pull himself to shore, but his strength was giving out, and so was his air. Although his eyes were closed and he was underwater, he felt as though he could almost see the world slipping away, fading into blackness as he prepared to open his mouth and take that deadly gasp for air that would ultimately drown him. However, before he could open his mouth, Oraeyn felt himself being jerked back above the surface of the water. He gasped for air and opened his eyes, blinking through the water drops that clung to his eyelids. He heard shouting and wondered where it was coming from. Something large bumped against him and he wrapped his arms around it, clinging to the solidness of it for dear life. He felt himself being pulled along, but he did not care as long as he was no longer under water. He took great, gulping breaths of air and dazedly wondered why he had never noticed what a wonderful thing breathing was. A few moments later, large hands pulled him up out of the water and he let go of the great solid thing that had saved his life, finally feeling safe. Something pulled at his fingers and he clenched his fists reflexively, then relaxed, someone was simply trying to get him to let go of the rope. He relaxed his grip and tried to open his eyes, but it was too difficult and he eventually gave up, letting darkness and the pain in his head overwhelm him.

Oraeyn woke several hours later to the sound of voices raised in anger. He was wrapped in blankets, and there was a fire roaring next to him. A bandage had been wrapped around his head, but the pain was gone. The palms of his hands ached, and when he looked down at them he saw angry red welts. He dully realized that they were no longer on the riverbank and he wished he knew where he was, but he could not dwell on it because he was still very tired and the angry voices were too distracting.

"I don't care if that path *was* the fastest way to get through the mountains, your stubbornness almost got Oraeyn killed!" It was Brant's voice.

"But it did not get him killed, he kept hold of that rope, and we were able to pull him above the surface of the water. You yourself said that he will be just fine. We got him dry and warm quickly enough that we do not have to worry about him freezing or catching cold, and Leila's healing magic seems to have worked to close the wound. He won't even have a scar." Dylanna's voice was icy, but there was some kind of undertone in her voice, something that told Oraeyn she had been very frightened.

"But the water *could* have been colder, the rope *could* have broken, he *could* have let go of the rope, we *could* have been stuck on that trail for hours, even days longer, and even with the rope, we almost lost a good horse and a good man," Brant was almost shouting now.

"*Could* have, but did not," Dylanna shouted back, as if trying to prove some point.

Oraeyn wanted to speak up and tell them to stop arguing so loudly so that he could go back to sleep. He wanted to say that he was fine and the ordeal was over and ask where they were now, but his throat was dry and hoarse. He could not speak above a whisper. He tried to lift himself up, but he was wrapped too tightly in blankets to move.

"He's awake." Kamarie's voice cut through the tension.

Brant and Dylanna both suddenly came into view. Their faces were both concerned, and although they had just been shouting, they both looked weary and worried. Brant knelt next to Oraeyn.

"How do you feel?" he asked.

Oraeyn opened his mouth and whispered hoarsely, "Water."

Dylanna swiftly brought him a canteen of cold water and propped up his head so he could drink. He drank deeply and then sighed and nodded for Dylanna to take the canteen away. Then he looked back and forth between them.

"What happened ... where are we?" he asked, his voice returning.

"The current turned into a very strong whirlpool as you reached the middle of the river. Both you and your horse were immediately dragged under. Luckily for both of you, you had stayed to the right of your horse, and he was not dragged past the rope. You went under several times and struck your head on a rock. We pulled you to the surface, and fortunately your horse is a strong swimmer. He got you to shore and we hauled you up the bank. The whirlpool abated and everyone else made it across without incident. Now we are resting and concerned for you."

Oraeyn nodded and sighed; closing his eyes. "I am slowing everyone down."

Dylanna spoke up quickly, "No, you are not. We are ahead of schedule because we took the river pass."

"Yes, but we could continue on even faster if I had not gotten pulled under. I should have kept a hold of my horse," Oraeyn argued.

"You would not have gotten pulled under or even ended up in the river at all if we had not taken the river pass," Brant said, "so don't blame yourself for anything, you'll be ready to travel in the morning if you get a few hours of sleep. We will continue our journey tomorrow."

Oraeyn shook his head. "You should leave me here and keep traveling. I know you want to get there quickly."

Brant looked shocked at Oraeyn's words, and he shook his head. "No! No one is leaving anyone behind."

"But isn't that what the argument was about?" Oraeyn asked.

"No," Dylanna said softly, "we were finishing our argument from before about whether or not we should have taken the river pass. Perhaps I was too stubborn - forgive me Oraeyn - the fault was mine."

Brant looked up, startled at Dylanna's words, then he lowered his head. There was a grudging look of respect in his eyes, but he did not say anything. Oraeyn caught the look and wondered why Brant kept silent, but he did not ask about it, sensing that the time was not right to bring it up.

Dylanna looked at Oraeyn. "You just get some rest, that is the most important thing, there's nothing wrong with you that a few hours of sleep won't mend."

Later that night, as Dylanna lay on her blankets, she found that she could not sleep. She resisted the urge to toss and turn with the restlessness she felt. The others were all sleeping the deep, sound sleep of exhaustion, worn out by their arduous journey through the river pass, all of them except Brant.

Brant was sitting on the other side of the fire, taking the first watch. The firelight flickered back and forth. He had not spoken to her since Oraeyn had regained consciousness, but he had gone about securing the camp with a stony expression on his face. Brant had become silent and brooding and had hardly said a word to anyone else all evening. Dylanna had tried to approach him a few times, but an unaccustomed timidity had stolen over her and kept her from speaking. She frowned, wondering what was wrong with her. She never cared what other people thought of her, and she was used to being in charge, the one others looked to for answers. It was rare for her to find herself tongue-tied and awkward, yet that was how this strange, silent man made her feel.

Finally giving up on trying to fall asleep, Dylanna sighed and got up from her blanket. She walked around the fire and sat down on a log next to Brant. She sat there for a few long moments, staring into the fire, watching it eat the wood and dance along the branches in a ghostly semblance of life. She glanced sideways at Brant, feeling altogether too much like a little girl who has been reprimanded. Brant sat with his arms folded and his legs stretched out in front of him. He, too, stared into the fire, as though mesmerized by its movement, yet she knew he could be standing with his sword drawn in an instant if he heard anything out of place. She tried to read his expression, but his face could have been carved from stone. She waited, quiet and calm on the outside but far more nervous on the inside than she ever would admit.

Without looking at her, Brant spoke, "Yes?"

She sighed again and then spoke in a very small, very quiet voice, "This is not easy for me."

Brant did not move as she spoke. He stared unblinkingly into the fire without so much as twitching a muscle. Dylanna felt very cold, but she continued to speak, her voice slow and hesitating. The words came, but they were hard to form; they felt awkward and ungainly, but she said them anyway, cursing herself for being unable to keep the tremor out of her voice.

"I was not trying to get anyone killed, Brant. I honestly believed the danger was minimal, I... Brant...." She could have kicked herself for sounding so weak, for pleading, but the words were already out.

Brant did not turn towards her but continued to stare into the fire. After an agonizingly long moment he spoke, his voice cool, "I don't mind that you thought the river pass would get us through the mountains quickly, I don't even mind that you were stubborn enough to get your way. What I do mind is that you were reckless with someone else's life. I am upset that you were so confident in your own plan that you could not see past it to the true danger that was present, perhaps not to me or you, or even your sister, or the minstrel, but the danger was very real and very great for Oraeyn and Kamarie and Yole."

His words pierced the air like icicles falling off a roof and shattering in the cold, making Dylanna wince. In the face of this stone man, she felt younger than she had in years. She wanted to cringe backwards and return to her bedroll and cry, but she did not. Instead she stayed still and tried to say the words that were weighing heavily upon her.

Finally she opened her mouth again, daring to break the stormy silence, "Brant, I... m-my confidence was not in my own stubborn belief that the river pass was the quickest way. My confidence was in you, in your ability to get us safely through the mountains no matter which path we took. You have gotten us through everything else...." She trailed off for a moment but then spoke again, "It is hard for me to admit that, I haven't had to rely on anyone else since my father died and my sister went to the Cove. It has been my job to look after my younger sisters and Kamarie...." Dylanna stopped, feeling as though there was something more that she ought to say, but not being able to think of what words would convey what was troubling her heart.

Brant had turned towards her as she spoke and was now looking at her with a deep, searching gaze. Dylanna looked down, unable to meet his dark eyes. She felt a lump forming in her throat.

"I know my behavior today seems inexcusable. I know I acted horribly... but I wanted you to know that I only continued to argue because I was worried about Oraeyn; only I- I did not know how to show it. I am not accustomed to making such an error of judgment."

Brant sighed and grimaced. Dylanna waited for a moment in the silence, hoping that he would say something, but the silence stretched on. To her horror, Dylanna suddenly found herself fighting back tears. Shocked and embarrassed at such a childlike response, she hurriedly stood up to leave. She murmured a quick "good-night" to Brant and started to walk away.

With astonishing speed and surprising gentleness, Brant reached out and grabbed her wrist. She stopped, a little uncertain, and looked at him. His sudden grip startled her, but it did not hurt. The firelight made the shadows move like living creatures crawling across the contours of his face. Dylanna could feel her eyes filling with tears, and she was very glad Brant could not see her face in the darkness.

He did not look away from the fire but continued to gaze into the wildly dancing flames with a deep intensity that almost scared her. For a long moment he did not say anything, and she wondered if he had forgotten that she was still standing there, held there by his own hand. Then he turned his eyes to her face and spoke, his voice so quiet that she almost did not catch the words.

"Do not let your resolve waiver, we will need your strength in the battle to come."

He stared into her face for a moment more, his gaze both stern and kind; then he loosened his hold on her wrist and she turned away again. She heaved a great sigh and realized that she no longer felt like crying into her pillow like a little girl. She returned to her bedroll where she fell asleep immediately.

The courtiers landed on the shores of Roalthae as night fell. They decided to approach the palace in the morning, so they set up camp and spent an uncomfortable night. None of them were used to sleeping on the ground surrounded by the cool night air and strange noises. And, although they each firmly believed that their mission would meet with success, they were each a little nervous about what the morning would bring. They were going to see Dark Warriors by the light of day, perhaps speak with their king, something no one from Aom-igh had ever done before to their knowledge. It was a long, cold, sleepless night.

Morning dawned, and the five nobles set off on the short walk to the palace of Roalthae. It was not so grand a palace as that of Aom-igh, but it was a beautiful and delicate structure, built out of white marble that reflected the rays of the Dragon's Eye, dazzling the eyes of all who beheld it by the light of day. They did not walk far before they were halted by armed guards. After they had been questioned and thoroughly searched for weapons, a messenger was sent to the king.

"Sire," the young gyrfalcon addressed his king, "we discovered spies in our camp this morning."

Seamas frowned and glanced at Tobias. "Spies?"

The boy stopped, a perplexed look crossing his face. "Well... we assumed they were spies. But they claim to be from the court at Aom-igh, here to sue for peace."

Seamas' expression turned from disbelief to bewilderment. "Show them in, Jemson, but keep them well guarded," he commanded. He turned to Tobias and whispered, "What can this mean?"

"I don't know, Your Majesty."

The five people who were ushered into the room did not, at first glance, look like courtiers. Their clothes were rumpled, their faces were covered in dust, and their expressions were a mixture of confusion, nervousness, and pleading. However, upon closer inspection, Seamas noticed that their garments were made of elegant fabrics, material that did not stand up well to sleeping on the rough ground. He noticed the way they carried themselves, with pride and confidence. And they looked him in the eye, as if they believed themselves his equals.

"My warrior tells me you hail from Aom-igh and have come to sue for peace," Seamas began.

The tallest of the three men took a tiny step forward. "I am Duke Kal of the province of Coeyallin, and my comrades and I have indeed come to discuss terms for peace. We do not want this war to go any further. Simply tell us what you seek, and we will lobby King Arnaud to resolve the matter peacefully. He does not seek war, but he is prepared to defend Aom-igh."

Seamas glanced at Tobias, who gave a slight shrug. The room was long and lined with pillars. In the shadows between each set of pillars, guards stood motionless as statues. Behind the throne were four or five chairs for the king's most trusted advisors, men who were allowed to sit in the king's presence and would come forward if he felt the need to confer with them on a particular decision. After a moment of thoughtful silence, Seamas spoke, his voice full of tightly controlled rage.

"I want the traitor your people have been harboring for thirty-five years."

Kal's eyes widened, and he took a step back. "Who?"

"I don't know what he calls himself now, but he is one of us, a 'Dark Warrior' as you call us. He has betrayed the Crown, his people, and our honor. He will be brought to justice by willing consent or brutal force. If your king will return this fugitive to me, there will be no war."

"Majesty!" one of the men who had been sitting behind the throne gasped, standing and coming forward. He was tall, like all the men of his race, but his face was lined with age and his hair had begun turning gray at the temples. His dark eyes glowered at the five messengers, and they each took an involuntary step back.

"What are you saying?" the man asked. "What of the promises you have made to the Council?"

"How dare you approach me without being summoned, Alarek?" Seamas rose from his throne and glowered down at his councilor. "I care not for the ambitions of the Council. My one desire is to see the traitor found and brought before me to face justice."

The five courtiers had been conferring together in confused whispers, but now Selynda stepped forward, raising her chin. "Sire, we will find this traitor and bring him before you, if it means preventing this war." She reached into her cloak and drew out a silver metal object that glinted in the light pouring through the high windows above the throne. "If you can just..."

"A weapon!" Alarek snarled. "Guards!"

Arrows hissed across the room, and the five courtiers fell to the floor, looks of bewildered surprise painted on their faces. Seamas, still standing, whirled on his councilor, his face dark with rage.

"Alarek! What is the meaning of this?"

"The woman was reaching for a weapon, Sire. They obviously came with the intent to murder you. Do you think five nobles would really come to sue for peace? The only peace they could be sure of was the assassination of their enemy."

Tobias had rushed down the steps the moment the arrows stopped flying. He knelt beside Selynda.

"Why?" she whispered, staring up at him with the life already fading from her eyes. "All we wanted.... was peace..." Her hand slipped out from beneath her cloak, clutching a silver container.

Tobias took the container and opened it. Inside was a rolled up parchment and a quill pen. He rose, holding them up for Seamas to see.

"A pen and paper, Alarek," Seamas snarled, "these are the weapons you so cleverly protected me from." With a mighty sweep of his arm he backhanded the older man across the jaw. Alarek stumbled backwards, shock creeping into his eyes. "You are useful to me for now, so you will not be thrown into the dungeons of this place," Seamas growled. "But the next time you see fit to give an order in my presence without my consent, I will see you executed for treason. Now get out of my sight."

Alarek left the room with as much speed as dignity would allow. When he was gone, Seamas sank back onto the throne. He waved a hand and warriors moved out from behind pillars and took the bodies away.

"The Council has an eye on your throne," Tobias said bluntly. "They want this war, for very different reasons than your own."

"I know," Seamas sighed. "Perhaps I have always known. Sometimes I think..." his face darkened. "I will see this through, and I will deal with the Council when the time comes. Alarek, Reichard, even my uncle, Ramius, I will deal with them all once the traitor has been found. Ready the men, we leave at dawn."

Tobias grimaced. "Yes, Sire."

"At least I have one man near me whom I can trust."

CHAPTER
EIGHTEEN

Queen Zara stood alone in the yard behind the palace. She was lost in deep concentration, focused, calm. She heard someone come up to her, but she did not allow the new presence to distract her. The person had the good sense not to speak, and she loosed her arrow. It flew straight and true and buried itself in the center of the target. Zara smiled, a bull's eye from fifty paces was not bad at all, especially since she had not practiced for quite some time.

"Brilliant shot, milady," the voice drew her back to the present and she glanced down at the errand boy.

Zara smiled and wiped her forehead, then asked, "Now, what brings you out here? Are you on a break? Would you like to learn how to shoot?"

The boy looked hopeful at her offer, but then his eyes widened. "I almost forgot! I was looking for King Arnaud, but I can't find him. There's a group of people who have arrived outside the castle; they say they've come to help, but they look half-starved. They asked to see the King."

The boy tugged at her sleeve. Zara started to protest that she could not come until she had freshened up and was wearing something more suitable. She was dressed in leather breeches and a loose brown tunic with a leather jerkin over it. She had her quiver of arrows still slung over her shoulder and her hair was flying all over the place, although she had tried to tame it by pulling it up out of her face with clips and pins. As she followed the boy, however, she stopped protesting. If these people just needed food and a place to rest and a listening ear, then perhaps it would be better if she appeared to them as she was.

Upon reaching the visitors, Zara was glad that she had not taken the time to change into a fancy dress. Men, women, and children all stood in the room, looking uncomfortable and out of place. They were dressed in clothes much like hers. There was pride in their eyes as well as weariness and hunger, and Zara perceived that they had not come to beg for aid, but to offer it. She whispered to her young guide, who then departed for the kitchens, under orders to bring back refreshment for these strangers; then she turned her attention fully upon them.

"I am Queen Zara," she said, "how can I help you?"

A man stepped forward. "My name is Clyet."

Zara nodded for him to continue and he bowed slightly. "My queen, we are the people of the Pearl Cove."

Zara's eyes widened, and she looked around, as if searching for a particular face.

"Where is Calyssia?" she asked.

Clyet stepped back, seeming a little bit shocked that Zara knew of Calyssia, then he spoke softly, "She has left, milady."

Zara lowered her head a little, whispering a soft farewell. Tears glimmered in her eyes, but she blinked them away rapidly. A few of the women noticed and exchanged puzzled glances. Then Zara looked up again.

"What is it that you want?"

"Only to help fight back the darkness that threatens," Clyet said. "The Dark Warriors invaded our home, the Pearl Cove, shortly after the Keeper left. We fought them, and struck a fair blow, but they were too many for us. Many of our men, good men, died at the hands of the warriors.

"We seek safety for our families and offer our weapons and fighting skills, to defend our country and serve our King, and in a way, to serve our Lady."

Fighting tears, Zara replied, "We accept. Consider it done."

At that moment servants arrived with food-laden carts, and Zara invited her countrymen, and these friends who loved her sister, to partake. "Please eat, and I will bring my husband to you. He will want to learn all you can tell of these Dark Warriors."

On her way out, one young woman caught Zara's attention. The woman was no more than thirty years of age. She was holding a young girl on her lap and crooning to her softly. Zara was not sure what it was about the woman that held her attention for so long. The woman was small and lithe, and she had a fairy-like quality to her looks. She had shoulder-length brown hair that curled at the ends and bright blue eyes. The girl on her lap could have been no more than six. Her hair was longer, darker, and very curly. Her eyes were large and brown, framed by long, dark lashes. There was sadness in both the woman and the child, and it seemed to weigh heavily upon their shoulders. And yet, Zara sensed a strength about both of them as well, a strength that shone through them with such force that it caused her to pause and marvel.

Arnaud plied the men of the Cove with questions about their recent battle with the Dark Warriors. He was satisfied that these men, who served his sister-in-law and now served him, were as true-hearted and brave as he could hope for. He warmly accepted their offer to fight and thanked them for their service already given. As he made ready to leave, one of the men spoke.

"There is one more thing, milord. You may have heard that the enemy is loading ships of war and will soon attack when these reach your shores. Do not be deceived. The enemy is only a day or two behind us, and through long conversations with

Calyssia before she departed, we have reason to believe they will attack from the Harshlands as well."

Leaving his new recruits, Arnaud hurried to the War Room and sent for Garen, requesting his immediate presence there.

"What is it, Majesty?" the old knight asked in concern.

Arnaud smiled. "We have just received information from unexpected friends that confirms my suspicions. When we spot the sails of our enemies, you will send a third of our force to greet them. But you must make it look as though I have sent my entire army, can you manage that?"

Garen nodded, mystified. "Yes, Sire, I can manage that. But to what purpose, if you don't mind my asking?"

Arnaud shook his head. "We won't be facing their entire army on the beach. Our new friends have already confirmed that one enemy army is coming from the direction of Pearl Cove, and they have passed along the wise caution that an attack from the Harshlands is also likely."

The older knight nodded slowly. "I thought a frontal assault seemed a bit too straight forward, especially after the past few months of covert attacks and raids for information."

Arnaud's face was grim. "They want us to underestimate them."

"Well, we won't."

Garen left quickly, eager to carry out his king's instructions. Arnaud made his way for Zara and found her immersed in conversation with her new friends from Pearl Cove. She was drawn to them for obvious reasons and could not resist asking questions and listening to their answers and stories about her beloved sister.

"Zara," Arnaud said quietly as he entered the room.

She turned to him. "Yes?"

"I need you to lead the women and children up to Fortress Hill. You will be safe there so long as we can hold back the Dark Warriors. They will not come from that direction, the way is too steep. Make sure of your weapons and put bows and quivers of arrows in the hands of all that can use them. We will need your archers to cover us from behind; it could mean the difference for us."

"You believe that the castle will fall," Zara said quietly. The words were concerned, but her voice held no emotion.

Arnaud nodded. "This palace is not well-suited to a siege. It was never intended to be a fortress. The castle will be the aim of their first attack, then they will fight us in the open ground below Fortress Hill. If they get to the Hill, all is lost. But I do not intend to let them come that far."

Zara nodded, and then repeated his words to the people in the room. They gathered their children and their few belongings and followed their new Lady. Soon thereafter, an army of women and children followed their queen to the top of Fortress Hill.

Fortress Hill was so named because it looked like a tall tower. The hill was not dome-shaped like most normal hills, but it rose up in a shape that was decidedly square. It had four definite sides and was very tall, almost as tall as the tallest tower of the palace it sat behind. The two sides nearest the palace sloped considerably, but not so steep that a person could not hike up them. The two sides of the hill that faced away from the palace were sheer, rocky cliffs. The top of the hill was large and flat, making a good place for those who were defenseless to flee to in times of attack. In the past, it had also served as a good place to hold certain important ceremonies, such as the coronation of a new king or the christening of a new prince or princess.

There were many stories surrounding the hill, and few knew quite what was myth and what was real. Some had said that King Llian had driven back the Dark Country from the top of Fortress Hill. Others said that King Artair had climbed to the top of this hill to pull the legendary sword from the stone. Still others claimed that the hill once had secret passageways running through it and that wizards had lived within its caves. The caves and passages were still there, but wizards have a way of hiding their workmanship. Most believed that the stories were just fables, but Zara knew that they were all quite true.

Fortress Hill was very steep. The climb was difficult without help, which made for slow progress. It took hours, but Zara saw them all to the top. The hill was west and south of the castle, with dense forest on three sides. The eastern face sloped down to a great, open plain that reached the sea.

The ships were traveling swiftly and steadily towards the shores of Aom-igh. It was dark, for Seamas planned to arrive and bring battle at dawn. A wild light had begun to glow deep in Seamas' dark eyes. He stood more and more often near the prow of the ship, his head thrown back as the wind and the waves whipped at him. His men trod warily around him. No one dared to question any of his orders. Seamas looked like a madman on the verge of going over the edge, and no one wished to be near if that happened. Seamas knew his men were afraid of him, could feel their fear of him rising, but it did not matter. It was right that they be afraid, for he was in a mood to kill.

He smiled, the expression stretching across his face; it was not a kind or cheerful smile, it was cruel and fierce. He was invincible this day, he could feel his own power and he knew what power there was in the great army he commanded. He commanded the warriors of Llycaelon and today he would bring the traitor, the one who had eluded him for so long, to justice. Today Seamas would even the score. No one would challenge or question his right to the throne ever again. Today, Seamas vowed, he would wipe away the look of regret that had lingered in his father's eyes when he named his eldest son as heir. No longer would that look haunt him in his dreams, no longer would he have to remember and know that his father believed the wrong man had been chosen. Today he would prove to his people that the right man had been on the throne all along.

He heard footsteps coming up the deck behind him but he did not bother to turn around. He knew those steps well by now. It was his Uncle Ramius, the captain of this ship. Only he could approach Seamas this day without fear, for he was family, and he had been the only one who ever truly understood Seamas' plight. For some strange reason, Seamas' thoughts drifted back and into the past, to a memory he had buried long ago, a memory of himself as a young boy without worries or cares or any idea that his birthright had already been given to another. Seamas remembered that day as clearly as though it had happened an hour ago. It had been a day of revelations and lessons. It had been a day that had shaped his entire future as a man.

He had never seen such a huge animal as the proud golden horse that his uncle had brought to the palace one day in the early Warm-Term. Seamas had been amazed and a little afraid when his uncle told him the horse was just for him.

"For me?" young Seamas asked.

The grizzled sea captain, nodded. "For you my boy. The eldest prince ought to have a horse all his own. He needs a good horse. A horse on which to ride into battle."

Seamas did not want to admit that he had never been on a horse. He was embarrassed to say he could not ride, and he could not be rude and say he did not want the horse. His father, the king, had spared him from having to explain by mentioning it lightly. The man had been outraged.

"The prince does not know how to ride?" he had asked incredulously.

The king had shaken his head. "He is young yet."

"But he is your eldest son! Is he not the heir?"

At his uncle's words, Seamas looked up, a quizzical expression on his face. He wondered at his uncle's assumption that he was something special. He had never been treated as anything special. He did well at everything he turned his hand at, but he had never been treated like... like this, as though he would one day be something so much more... Seamas shook his head, unwilling to allow dark thoughts to enter his mind on this day, his day of glory.

Ramius took Seamas outside and threw him up onto the great, prancing beast of a horse. Seamas gripped the reins tightly, terrified. His uncle slapped the horse, and it took off without any warning.

Seamas immediately half-toppled, half-threw himself from his precarious perch and landed on the hard-packed ground. The impact shoved the air from his lungs and left him gasping in pain. That had been more than enough to convince him that, eldest prince or no, he had no desire to learn how to ride a horse, ever. As he was about to race back into the palace his uncle clutched his shoulder with a hand that was formed from iron, stopping him mid-step.

"Get back on the horse." If Ramius' hand was made of iron, his voice was edged with steel.

Seamas turned a frightened look at his suddenly fearsome uncle. "I don't want to."

"Get back on the horse."

There was no arguing with that voice. Seamas obediently got back on the beast. The horse sensed his fear and bucked him off. Seamas flew over the horse's head and landed in a heap on the ground. As he landed, he began to snivel and tears escaped his eyes. His uncle jerked him off the ground and placed him back on the horse.

After four more falls and a horse trough full of tears, Ramius threw his hands up and stormed out of the paddock in exasperation muttering something that sounded like, "completely worthless." Seamas stayed crumpled on the ground for a few moments, crying into the dusty earth. Then something hardened within him. He became angry at his uncle for giving up on him, at his father for allowing his uncle to try teaching him to ride, at his mother just because he was angry at everybody right then, and especially at the good for nothing horse that he could not conquer.

Seamas picked himself up off the ground and approached the horse once more. The horse paid little attention to him, flicking an ear as if to say, "Oh, it's you again."

Determined to make the beast bend to his will, he jumped into the saddle, grabbed a handful of mane, and dug his heels into the horse's sides. The horse reared and bucked, but Seamas hung on, clutching at the horse's mane and bridle. With a scream of anger, the horse took off, but Seamas stayed on, determined to show his uncle that he was not worthless. After a few minutes, the horse, who really was a well-trained animal, decided that Seamas was not going to fall off again and began to behave and listen to his signals. Seamas rode up in front of the palace at a stately and controlled trot.

His father and uncle had looked up; they were alongside the path talking when Seamas rode into sight. The boy kicked the horse into a canter and headed straight for his uncle with the half-formed intent of trampling him. The captain, however, merely stepped to the side and grabbed the reins, halting the horse mid-stride. Then he pulled the boy from the saddle. The king wore an expression of astonishment and fury at what Seamas had tried to do, but his uncle looked at him with gruff pride. From then on, the stern old sea captain had taken a special interest in Seamas and had taught him many skills that he would need to have as king.

Seamas shook himself out of his memories and turned to speak to his uncle, "It is a good day for battle."

His voice was eager, yet there was a dark, hard undertone to it that betrayed his true mood. He was filling with anger and a cold, hard emotion that he could not name. It felt as though there was a layer of ice covering his words. He felt as though all he had to do was reach out and touch Aom-igh and it would be his.

"Aye, a good day for battle it is, Sire, 'twould be better were the sky dark and the rain hanging heavy in the air," his uncle said, and Seamas noticed that being at sea brought out the accent that Ramius had learned to hide as one of the Council. "Barring an unfavorable wind, we will reach the shore of Aom-igh by dawn, Your Majesty. How would you have me instruct the men?"

Seamas smiled slowly, hearing that he would be standing on the soil of Aom-igh within a few short hours. Soon he would be close, so close, to his final goal.

"Make sure that every man is ready to fight the moment we leave the ship." Seamas paused, then continued, "Remind the men that the soldiers of Aom-igh are expecting us. They will not be caught by surprise. They will attack as soon as we are within range of their arrows."

The captain nodded sharply to show that he understood. Seamas did not watch him leave, but turned back to the front of the ship, gazing once more towards the approaching shore. Soon his hand would reach clear across the sea, and no one would be able to stand against him; no one would dare try.

As soon as the lookouts had spotted the sails through their spy-scopes, Arnaud signaled to Zara atop Fortress Hill. She immediately reached for her magic. It rushed to her easily, and she smiled with pleasure; it had been too long since she had used it, especially for something so demanding. She quickly wove a protective shield around the hill so that no one seeking to do her, or those with her, harm would be able to climb more than five paces up the hill before they would be forced to turn back. The shield shimmered a little from the inside, and a few of the women turned to look at her, questions in their eyes.

"It reminds me of the Pearl Cove," one older woman murmured.

Zara smiled, but offered no response. Her heart went out to these people. They were so strong, so noble, and so peaceful. They had lost so much already. It made no sense. What purpose could...

"Look!" shouted one young woman as she pointed towards the harbor. "The ships!"

Zara could not fully fathom what she was seeing. The heavy ships of war had sailed much nearer to shore than was possible. She furrowed her brow in bewilderment. Ships of this size could not maneuver in such shallow depths, they should have struck bottom before now.

Slowly, a thought took shape, and she understood how the enemy had tried to fool them. These ships were far lighter than they appeared, and that revelation brought a knowing smile to Zara's face. The report from the Cove People was now confirmed, and Arnaud was indeed prepared.

Garen and his men were ready and waiting, hidden from view. The ships glided into port easily, even though the docks were meant for much smaller and much lighter boats.

Garen cautioned his men to save their arrows and wait until their targets were in range. Even the best archers cannot hit what their arrows cannot reach. Earlier, his men had set campfires ablaze deep in the woods and placed empty helmets on tall stakes all along the forest that stood between the harbor town and the palace. The deception would not add to their strength, but it might add caution to their enemies; it might cause them to hesitate a moment before their charge, and that moment was something Garen was counting on.

"Hold steady men," he shouted. "They'll be coming over the side in a moment and we must be ready to hold them back. Steady, let them come to us, do not rush them, let them make the mistakes, you just be ready to take advantage of those mistakes."

Garen noticed the fear on the faces of his men. Many were young, but for almost all of these defenders, today would be their first, genuine experience of battle.

Garen turned and faced his men: "My soldiers... my friends... remember why we fight." Pointing to Fortress Hill he continued, "We can fight for King, we can fight for country, we can even fight for honor... but what we really fight for is our loved ones. Remember your wives, your sons, your sisters, your nieces, your nephews: their future and their freedom is at stake. Will we stand by and let that future fade?"

A resounding NOOOO! filled the pending battlefield.

"Will we stand by and allow some enemy of men to rob that freedom and future from our families?"

NOOOOO! came the thundering reply.

"On this day, I fight for you and your families! Will you fight for me and mine?"

YESSSS! Came the roar from his men, and it was echoed from atop Fortress Hill with a harmony of YESSSS! At Garen's signal, the arrows were released, and the battle was struck!

The Dark Warriors swarmed from their great ships amidst the rain of arrows and hesitated for a moment.

"NOW!" cried Garen. The men of Aom-igh did not hesitate at his command and raced to face their enemy with shouts of "For Aom-igh! For the King! And for Garen!"

Garen led the charge, but even his great heart paused when he saw the first wave of warriors flow from the ships. He quickly understood that they were outnumbered, and when the second wave of attackers emptied from their ships he and his men would be crushed. Garen did not expect the Dark Warriors to show them any mercy. However, long moments of fighting passed, and no more men came out of the boats. Suddenly, Garen understood; this onslaught was just a decoy, meant to pull their attention away from the true attack. Spirits rising as he finally understood Arnaud's plan, he parried a vicious thrust and backhanded his opponent over the head with the hilt of his sword, then he pulled out his horn and gave two short signal blasts. The fighting grew more intense, but the warriors of Aomigh began to give ground as ordered.

The travelers were in the forest not far from Ayollan when they heard the sounds of battle erupting ahead.

Brant stopped his horse, holding a hand out to hush the others. Then he stood up in his stirrups and leaned forward, listening. The rest of them sat forward and strained their ears as well. All of them, that is, except Kiernan.

Kiernan had not seen Brant stop, and he continued to ride forward, chattering on about how exciting this adventure was and what a great tale it would make. He passed the others, talking to no one in particular. He seemed completely oblivious to the fact that everyone had stopped until Brant reached out and grabbed the reins of the minstrel's horse, jerking the beast to a halt. The horse the minstrel was riding stopped so suddenly that it forced Kiernan to stop his monologue in the middle of a word. He uttered a short cry of alarm as he nearly tumbled out of his saddle and over his horse's head. He pulled himself back into the saddle, got his feet back in the stirrups, sat up straight, and looked around, curiosity filling his bright blue eyes. Brant fixed the minstrel with a dark, serious glare. Kiernan stared back at Brant, his expression unconcerned.

"What did you do that for?"

Brant spoke in a fierce whisper, "If you will not pay attention to my signals and keep quiet, I will be forced to tie you up and leave you behind before you get the rest of us killed." He emphasized each word as he spoke.

Kiernan let out a hearty laugh, but then cut it short when he noticed that Brant's expression had not altered. The minstrel's face fell, and his normally boisterous, confident voice faltered a bit.

"Y-you... *are* joking?" he asked, a little more quietly than Oraeyn had ever heard him speak.

Brant did not reply. He merely looked at Kiernan; his dark gaze pierced through the minstrel. Kiernan fell very silent as he tried to hold Brant's gaze, the whole forest heldits breath as Brant glared into Kiernan's bright blue eyes. The blood drained out of Kiernan's face, and he grew very pale. Finally, after a few long seconds, the minstrel dropped his eyes and nodded. His demeanor slumped, and he directed his horse once more to the end of the line.

Oraeyn had watched the whole exchange with a feeling of shock that grew within him as Brant spoke. He stared at Brant in horrified disbelief as Kiernan slunk back to his spot in quiet defeat. Oraeyn wanted to speak up, to say that the minstrel had not meant any harm but just did not think; but the words refused to come. He waited for Brant to break the horrible silence and say something reassuring, but the silence stretched on as Brant sat very still, listening intently to the sounds of battle. More than anything, Oraeyn wanted to ask Brant if he had meant what he had said. Surely he could not have truly meant that he would tie the minstrel up and leave him behind; such a fate might be better than what waited for them at the palace, but it could also be a death sentence if he were found by the wrong people. But the words were stuck somewhere inside of him, and they could not seem to find their way out. His throat felt dry and parched, and it seemed difficult for him to even force air out of his windpipe. His whole world had gone dark and cold and dangerous. In a few, sharp words, Brant had become someone he did not know, someone cruel and heartless, and Oraeyn felt that he could not live if that were true of the man.

At length, Brant turned to face the rest of the group. His face held no hint of expression as he spoke quietly, "The Dark Warriors have beaten us to the castle. By the sound of it, they are already attacking Ayollan and laying siege to the palace." Kamarie's face fell, and Brant held up a hand, speaking quickly, "But all is not lost. We must travel even more swiftly and silently now. Perhaps we can sneak in from behind and take the Dark Warriors by surprise. Even though we are few, it has not been uncommon in the past for one man to be the deciding factor in battles between armies of thousands of men."

They nodded quietly in understanding. Oraeyn opened his mouth, but no sound came out. He felt a great agony welling up within him, but he could not find a way to express what was on his heart. Brant glanced at Oraeyn and saw the anguish written across his face. He seemed puzzled for a moment, then he looked back towards Kiernan and a light of understanding broke across his face. Something twinkled deep in Brant's dark eyes, and the corners of his mouth twitched in something very like a smile. Then he winked at Oraeyn and swung around, urging his horse forwards.

Oraeyn sat completely still for one stunned moment, then a light seemed to dawn in his eyes. He heaved a deep sigh and smiled. His smile grew into a full-fledged grin, and he almost laughed, but he held back, remembering the danger. He looked at Brant with a new respect in his green eyes and shook his head. He urged his own horse on, much relieved of his worry, a little bit rueful, and a little bit wiser.

CHAPTER
NINETEEN

Proceeding cautiously with her companions, Kamarie began to recognize the landmarks around them. They were very close to Fortress Hill and not far from the palace. As they neared the castle the sounds of battle grew steadily louder and their stealth increased accordingly. They emerged from the forest just south of Fortress Hill. The battle was before them on the shore and through the Port of Aolla. Kamarie's face reflected her concern.

"I thought my father would have committed more men to defending the town," she commented.

Oraeyn nodded in agreement, then looked to Brant for an answer. Brant was watching the battle intently, as though he were searching for something.

"Arnaud is no fool," he commented to no one in particular.

Dylanna looked at him quizzically, but Brant did not seem to notice as he was deep in thought. His eyes moved across the battlefield again.

"He must have anticipated the tactics of this enemy," he continued. "He must have known this naval attack was simply a decoy."

"What do you mean?" Kiernan asked, speaking for the first time since Brant had reprimanded him.

Brant turned towards the minstrel and explained, "I am guessing that the Dark Warriors sent a large number of ships with a small number of men on board. They are experienced in warfare, so they would know that their armada would be spotted long before they approached the harbor. They also must have known that Aom-igh has no navy, but they would be uncertain of our shoreline defenses, so they would not want to commit their entire force to the ships. They took the information they were certain of and used it to their advantage and made it look as though their entire army was coming from one direction, which is why I called it a decoy attack.

"However, in light of the number of men who are actually fighting, I have to assume that Arnaud must have seen through the decoy. Perhaps he noticed that the ships were riding too high in the water, or maybe he watched them enough to see how many men were on each ship, maybe he even received advance warning from his intelligence forces, I don't know. The point is not how he saw through the decoy, but that he did see through it. That is why only a part of the army is down there fighting. The safest bet is that the rest of the knights are elsewhere, waiting to receive the main attack."

"How can you know all this?" Leila asked in an awed voice, her eyes wide.

Brant shrugged a little. "Just speculating really," he said, his voice indifferent.

Dylanna, made no comment. She was busy glancing around as though she were trying to find something. She closed her eyes for a moment, then opened them and looked around again. Nobody paid much attention to her. Nobody paid any attention to Kiernan, either, or they would have seen the sharp look of understanding and approval in his eyes.

"What should we do?" Oraeyn asked.

Before Brant could answer, Dylanna pointed up to the top of Fortress Hill. "Zara is up there."

Leila looked at her curiously and then waved a hand at the hill. The air shimmered between them and the slope, reminding Oraeyn of the Pearl Cove. Leila smiled.

"She has grown strong indeed to be able to hide a protective spell of that magnitude from me so well."

"She will need help," Dylanna said. "Strong though she is, she cannot hold that up for long. She gave up her training when she married Arnaud. Leila and I must join Zara."

Brant nodded. "Better take Yole and Kamarie with you."

"What?" Kamarie cried. "You can't send me away from all the excitement. I won't go!"

Oraeyn turned to her and spoke soberly, "It isn't exciting Kamarie."

Kamarie glared at him. "I am just as much of a squire as you! Give me one good reason why I cannot fight alongside the other knights."

"Because I won't let you," Brant and Dylanna spoke in unison before Oraeyn could come up with a good response.

"A battlefield is no place for a young lady," Brant said quietly. "Especially when that young lady is the Princess of the Realm."

"But I…" Kamarie started to protest, but Dylanna cut her off before she could start.

"And you *are* a young lady, whether you act like one or not," she said. Her voice was stern but there was a soft fondness in her eyes.

Oraeyn struggled to hold back the laugh that bubbled up within him at Dylanna's words. One look at Kamarie's face, however, was enough to quell any desire he had to laugh. Her eyes were a stormy dark blue, and her face was set in a glower.

Suddenly Leila broke the tension by asking, "How are you with a bow, niece?"

Kamarie considered for a moment. "I'm a fair shot," she said, forgetting for a moment that she was upset.

Leila spoke again, choosing her words cautiously, "The barrier that your mother set up is a rather tricky one: it only affects those who would do harm from getting inside. It does not affect friends from passing, and it does not prevent anyone or anything from getting out.

"I am certain that an extra archer placed up top would be a great asset to our cause. If you are good enough?" Leila asked.

Kiernan Kane spoke up immediately, "And such a great song it would make! The lone princess upon the hill, fending off the enemy with her glowing bow and her deadly arrows, her dark hair streaming behind her in the breeze..." he stopped, looking a little crestfallen. "Um... well, I mean, it *would* make a great ballad, but it wants an ending."

Kamarie tilted her head to one side, the minstrel's words carrying her imagination up the hill. His words made sense and spoke to her of glory and renown, urging her to accept this noble duty. She did not see the sly look that flitted briefly across Kiernan Kane's face as he spoke. She thought about Leila's idea for a moment more. Then she nodded.

"I suppose I really have no choice," she said. "Very well, I will take my place at the top of Fortress Hill."

She never would have admitted it, but she felt something like relief. She was almost glad that she had been forced to stay out of the battle. After her fight with the Dark Warriors, she had discovered that she really did not relish the idea of real battle with real danger and real death.

Yole would have liked to argue as well. He felt as though he were being treated like a child, and he did not like the feeling. He did not say anything, however, because he did not think there was much of a chance that he would succeed where Kamarie had failed.

Kiernan spoke up hesitantly, jerking Yole out of his thoughts, "Um, I, ah, really am not much of a hand at fighting or, ah, handling weapons. I knocked someone out with my mandolin once, but I do not think that would be much help here. I will come along with you if you want, Sir Brant, but I fear that I will be much more harm than help to you."

Brant looked at the minstrel for a moment. Kiernan met his gaze this time, his blue eyes open and honest. Then Brant nodded, as though reaching a decision.

"You will go up to the top of the hill as well then," he said shortly.

Kiernan nodded, and then turned to follow the others up the hill. Brant watched them go and then swung his horse around nodding to Oraeyn.

"Follow me," he said.

Oraeyn obeyed and urged his own horse to follow Brant and his black charger. He suddenly found that he was scared, more scared than he had ever been. This was nothing like facing the two treacherous dragons or the Dark Warriors who had attacked them on the road. That had been nothing but reflexes and reaction without having time to think. This was much harder and more terrifying. He was heading into battle against thousands of skilled warriors, and he was not even a full knight yet. Oraeyn had complete confidence in Brant though, and he found that his confidence in Brant seemed to cancel out most of the fear in himself. Suddenly he realized that Brant had taken it for granted that he was coming. There had been no question about whether or not he was going to follow Brant into battle. He realized what a great compliment he had just been paid, and he found himself smiling broadly. Pride welled up within him, banishing the remnants of his fear.

"It… is a good thing," Kamarie said between gasps for air, "that this hill… is not any taller. Because it is certainly… steep enough."

"I… quite… agree," Kiernan said.

The hill was too steep to ride up on horseback, so they had been forced to dismount and lead their horses behind them as they climbed. The going was difficult, and they were exhausted after their two-hour climb to the top. Kamarie was surprised by the sight that met her eyes. Fortress Hill was covered with women and children, most of them unknown to her and she unknown to them. Kamarie focused her gaze until she found who she sought. Her mother was standing at the bluff's edge, overlooking the battle.

Zara's long, blond hair was bound back in a great golden braid. Wisps of hair had come loose and were blowing around her face in the gentle breeze. She held a bow in her hand and was staring intently down at the battle. In that instant, she looked so like a warrior that Kamarie caught her breath in a sharp gasp, amazed. As Kamarie watched, Zara notched an arrow and drew the bow up to her cheek. She gazed down the long shaft of the arrow, her brow furrowed in deep concentration. Beads of sweat glistened on her forehead and she looked exhausted. She pulled the arrow back and then loosed it in one fluid motion. The arrow flew from her bow and found its target.

As soon as she had shot the arrow, Zara dropped the bow back down to her side. Her arm hung limp and she grasped the bow loosely, as though she would drop it at any moment. Kamarie could see the weariness in the way that her mother stood and she knew that she did not have the strength to draw another arrow.

"Mother!" she yelled across the crowd.

Zara turned towards the sound of Kamarie's voice and looked around, her eyes searching. Kamarie pushed her way through the crowd of people and ran towards her mother, feeling as though she were moving in slow motion. Zara caught sight of her daughter through the crowd and broke into a run herself. Near the center of the hill, mother and daughter met and embraced.

They held each other in a hug. They both knew that there was no time for questions and even less for answers, so neither of them spoke. Then Zara saw Dylanna and Leila making their way through the crowd, Kiernan and Yole trailing along behind them. Zara let go of Kamarie and greeted her sisters with a warm smile and moist eyes that read, "I'm so glad you are here."

"You are worn out," Dylanna said, "Kamarie will take over your bow, and Leila and I will help maintain your rather ingenious magic shield."

Zara sighed gratefully and handed her bow to Kamarie. "Dear sister, ever the organizer."

Kamarie took the bow and slung the quiver over her shoulder. She walked back over to where Zara had been standing and took up her position. Dylanna and Leila both helped Zara to sit down, and then they both took some of the strain of the magical shield from her. Zara sighed again.

"I will never know how Calyssia did it, maintaining that shield for so long all by herself," Zara said quietly.

"So you know that she left," Dylanna said without looking at Zara.

Zara nodded. "Yes, the Cove People told me that she went back to the sea. Half of the people up here are from Calyssia's Cove. Was there truly nothing that she could have done?"

Dylanna shook her head. "Her time had come, and she was completely drained. She was dying even when she spoke to us, though I did not realize it at the time. As you have found on a slightly smaller scale, the energy required to keep up such a shield is beyond measure. That is why she had to stay so close to the Cove, why she never left its boundaries. She wove a part of her own life into the place, and she knew that when she left, the boundaries would fail and the magic would fade, as it did shortly after she returned to the sea."

Zara managed a small smile. "I meant to go visit her... I wanted to see her again before she left, but I thought I had so much time. I suppose I should have known, but I never guessed how much it had taken out of her. I just didn't understand what she was doing, and now it is too late."

"But she loved it Zara," Leila broke in, "Calyssia would not have done anything differently if she had the chance to do it over. She had no regrets."

Zara nodded, her eyes weary. "I suppose you are right. I know I wouldn't make any different choices, given the chance."

She glanced over at Kamarie and love for her daughter shone in her eyes.

Oraeyn followed Brant quietly, weaving through the forest. Their horses were left behind. They were headed for the opposite side of Fortress Hill. Brant had told Oraeyn that the real attack would come from either side of the battlefield. The Dark Warriors would lie in wait until they were convinced they had captured their prey's full attention in one direction, and then they would swoop down from either side with the killing blow.

Oraeyn did not bother to ask Brant how he knew this. He had come to realize that every time he asked the man a question, he just ended up feeling more confused than before. Brant had a way of answering all of his questions with riddles that seemed to serve no other purpose than to weave an even thicker layer of mystery around the man.

Suddenly Brant stopped and dropped to the ground. Oraeyn dropped to his stomach, lying flat and wondering what Brant had seen. Brant began to inch backwards and Oraeyn slipped back as well. When they had retreated a distance, Brant crept behind a tree, motioning for Oraeyn to follow him. Oraeyn obeyed without a sound and crouched, his heart beating rapidly.

"A skirmish line of Dark Warriors," Brant whispered, "posted to screen the movements of their larger force. We now know where one attack will come from. The problem for us is how to get around them and how long will that take. If only there was some way..."

Brant trailed off and Oraeyn waited patiently to find out what their next move would be. He hoped Brant would not suggest that they take on all of the Dark Warriors who were hiding in the grove of trees up ahead. Then Brant got an odd look on his face; if Oraeyn had not known any better, he would have called it mischievous.

Brant began to move away from the tree to the left. "Follow me," he whispered.

Oraeyn felt relieved. He knew Brant would never do something so foolish as taking on a whole army of Dark Warriors single handedly, but he still felt better knowing they were going to go around, rather than through, the army. After they had retreated deeper into the forest away from Fortress Hill, Brant stopped again but did not crouch down. He glanced around and muttered something to himself.

Suddenly he whispered, "Ah, that just might work."

Oraeyn followed Brant's gaze and saw that the man was gazing intently at two trees. "What?" he asked quietly. Brant shook his head and put a finger to his lips.

Working swiftly, Brant pulled a length of rope from his pack. Then he went over to the two trees; they were standing quite close to each other. One of them was a young sapling, and the other was not much more than an old hollow log that was standing on one end. Brant knocked lightly on the hollow tree and smiled in satisfaction when it echoed back a little bit louder than he had knocked, it also seemed to move a bit, which Brant noted with a nod. Then he handed the rope to Oraeyn.

"When I give the word, I need you to loop one end of the rope around this sapling, and then pull the rope as taut as you can and tie it off at the base of the nearest tree. You'll understand shortly."

Oraeyn was starting to wonder if Brant had lost his mind. Mystified, he watched as Brant carefully bent the sapling towards the ground, away from the hollow tree. He pulled until the top of the sapling was almost touching the ground. Finally, his muscles straining at the exertion, he nodded to Oraeyn.

"Now!" he gasped.

Understanding taking shape, Oraeyn quickly tied one end around the sapling, pulled the rope tight, and then secured the other end. When Brant was satisfied that the knots were tight, he let go of the sapling. He stood back and surveyed their work critically, then nodded.

"It'll do," was all he said.

Then, using his knife with painstaking care, he cut through the rope until there were only two remaining strands securing the sapling in place. Oraeyn watched in growing fascination, but he remained mystified about what Brant was trying to accomplish. Brant glanced up at him.

"Now, give me your rope," he said, still talking in a hushed whisper.

Oraeyn pulled out his coil of rope and handed it to Brant. His question was written all over his face, but Brant did not speak.

He tied Oraeyn's rope tightly around the area that he had frayed and then he motioned for Oraeyn to follow him. Uncoiling the rope as they crept through the underbrush, Oraeyn was bursting from curiosity, but knew his questions would have to wait. Brant stopped when they reached the full-length of the rope.

"I am going to need help with this," he said. "Stand in front of me and hold the rope with both hands like I am."

Oraeyn did so, and Brant continued, "Good, now, when I count three, tug on the rope sharply with all your strength, ready?"

Oraeyn nodded, reaching forward with his arms while leaning backward with the rest of his body. "Ready," he said.

"All right then, one, two, THREE!"

Together they tugged the rope with all their strength. The rope tightened and then went slack, causing them both to tumble backwards. Before Oraeyn could get up, he heard a loud cracking noise like thunder, followed by a mighty crash. A flock of birds flew up into the air, frightened by the noise.

"Good, it knocked the hollow one over," Brant said as he stood up. "I didn't even hope for that."

Brant hurriedly coiled up the rope and tucked it back into Oraeyn's pack. Oraeyn turned to him, not quite understanding what had just happened. Before he could ask any questions though, Brant put a finger to his lips and pointed back the way they had come.

"Listen."

Oraeyn grew very still and listened as hard as he could. For a moment he heard nothing but the beating of his own heart, then he heard voices and shouting and the underbrush being trampled. Oraeyn's eyes widened and he made a small noise that sounded like, "oh!" Then he looked at Brant and grinned.

Brant smiled back then turned sober again. "That will not distract them for long, but it may buy us a little space and a little time. Hopefully it is enough."

Continuing now through the recently vacated terrain, they hurried their way to the far side of Fortress Hill. Suddenly there was a sound like the roar of the sea followed by the war cry of their enemy.

"The Dark Warriors have sprung their trap, Arnaud had better move soon," Brant said. "Come, now is the time!"

Abandoning stealth they raced to the battlefield where the fighting raged the hottest. The new forces of Dark Warriors were fresh and rested, and now they outnumbered the knights ten to one. Then there was another mighty shout from either side of Fortress Hill. The Dark Warriors slowed their attack and stared around in confusion as the rest of Arnaud's army raced down onto the battlefield.

"Caught in their own trap," Brant muttered, then pointed. "See that man? The one wearing the crown?"

Oraeyn's eyes darted to the person that Brant was talking about. He squinted, even at a distance the man's features were familiar. "Yes," he replied. "What about him?"

"That is their leader," Brant said, and then he drew his sword.

Oraeyn did not ask how Brant knew this; there was no time for questions. Instead, he drew the Fang Blade, and it hummed as it left its sheath. The sword seemed to glow in his hand, and it throbbed with energy. Oraeyn looked at the sword for a moment in awe. He knew he would never get over how the sword could seem like a living thing and yet become a part of him at the same time. He did not have much time to wonder over the phenomenon, however, because Brant began to race towards his opponent, and Oraeyn followed close behind.

Fighting their way through, they carved a path for themselves, ever moving towards the center, where the leader of the Dark Warriors stood. Brant's blade flashed again and again, and Dark Warriors fell away from his sword as he cut his way through. He strode forward with a purpose, towards the center of the battle. The few men who tried to stop his advance soon discovered their error, but by the time they realized it, they were already dead.

Oraeyn struck out with his own sword and found himself fighting with confidence and skill borne of necessity and the reflexes of his training. His sword was light and easy to handle in his grasp, and it swung through the air in patterns almost as though it were moving on its own. He did not follow Brant through the fighting; he just cut his way through whatever enemy he found before him. His blade twirled and danced as he moved through the Dark Warriors.

The men of Aom-igh fought hard. Oraeyn saw that many were not even knights, they were just patriots who had joined the battle. But even though they had taken the Dark Warriors by surprise for a few precious moments, they were still outnumbered three to one, and the Dark Warriors began to force them back.

Oraeyn was bleeding, but he could not recall being wounded. He fought furiously, with more skill than he had ever believed he possessed, and still the Dark Warriors pressed forward. Oraeyn swung his sword fearlessly and with every last bit of his strength, but he knew it was not enough. They were losing ground, and the Dark Warriors kept coming.

Yole paced back and forth along the top of Fortress Hill restlessly. He kept his eyes on the battle, never taking them from the scene below. He had shouted in triumph when the knights of Aom-igh had swarmed in and taken the enemy by surprise. But he could see that, though the Dark Warriors had lost a little precious ground in their surprise, they were now pressing back with renewed efforts, and he could see from a distance what Oraeyn sensed in the midst of the fray: the Dark Warriors would prevail.

As he watched, Yole spotted Brant, he was striding through the enemy as though towards a specific goal. He was making slow progress, for the enemy continued to attack him from all sides. He cut many of them down and continued cutting through the enemy, but the Dark Warriors seemed to be growing stronger as the battle wore on. Yole's eyes swept the battlefield, and he found Oraeyn. The young man's golden blade was flashing brightly as he fought. He fought tirelessly, but the enemy continued to come on, and Yole knew that it was only a matter of time.

He paced the top of the hill, feeling both restless and powerless. He wished there was something he could do. He thought about what Rhendak had said, that he was a dragon. He wished he knew how to turn himself into a dragon. He continued to pace, his thoughts a turmoil of fire and sharp claws and flight. Suddenly, a woman near him screamed. Yole stared at her in confusion. The woman was looking at him in horror, her eyes were huge and her face pale. He looked towards Kamarie to ask her what the trouble was.

Kamarie had turned to see what the commotion was, when she saw what the woman had screamed about, she almost screamed herself.

"Kamarie?" Yole asked in concern, his voice sounding too loud in his own ears.

Kamarie seemed to gather her wits back to her as she stared. "Yole? Is that you?"

"Of course it's me. Why is everyone acting so strangely?"

"Well," Kamarie spoke slowly, "you're a dragon!"

Yole blinked at her, and then he lifted his hand and looked at it. The great, curved claws gleamed up at him, and he smiled, baring long golden teeth in a terrifying grin. He glanced over his shoulder and saw that two huge, leathery wings were protruding from either side of his back. He pumped them experimentally, and he rose off the ground. Delighted, he swooped up into the air and flew over the magical barrier that Zara had created. He was amazed to find that he could see the barrier clearly now, could see how it had been made, and he instinctively knew how much strength Zara had poured into it. He could see how Dylanna and Leila were maintaining it. The barrier was weakening, as were the wizardesses. In an instant he saw how the wall could be made to stand on its own. Without knowing exactly how he did it, Yole reached out and pulled a blanket of wind around the barrier, and then he reinforced the wall with a deep, living flame. Satisfied that the barrier would hold itself together now, he flew down towards the battle.

Dylanna stared up at the great dragon. She knew that it was Yole, but somehow she could not believe it. Then she felt the barrier slipping from her grasp. With a cry, she reached after it, as it was wrenched out of her control, but she could not find the end of it. She stared at Leila, who looked back at her with wide-eyed wonder.

"He figured out how to make it stand on its own," Leila whispered.

"That's all very well and good, but will he know how to clean it up when the barrier is no longer needed?" Dylanna grumbled in irritation, still reeling a little. She rubbed a hand across her eyes; the shock of so much magical weight being lifted from her shoulders in so little time had left her with a pounding headache.

"He does need some pointers on his technique," Leila agreed, wincing a bit. "But it does free us to use our magic more actively."

"I suppose we'll have to thank him when this is all over," Dylanna sighed. "Bother."

Yole flew down at the enemy with a great roar. He opened his great jaws and threw a burst of flame at a group of Dark Warriors. They fell backwards with cries of disbelief and shock, and then their cries became frantic shouts as they tried to put out the fire.

Yole laughed a great dragon laugh. He felt strong, stronger than he ever had. He delighted in the feeling of freedom that came from being stronger and larger than his enemies, but even as he relished in his newfound body, he realized he could not turn the tide of the battle alone. Already the enemy warriors were beginning to point their bows his way, and although an arrow or two would not hurt him, enough of them could bring him down. He would need help. Instinct drove him, as it had when he strengthened the barrier around Fortress Hill; he stretched out with his thoughts and *called*. For a moment he thought nothing had happened. Then he felt a voice in his head saying, "Friend? You called?"

He looked and saw in the distance the dragons silhouetted against the horizon.

"We are being defeated, will you help?" he asked.

"We were already on our way, youngling," the voice replied.

Several dragons, gryphons, and pegasi joined in the fight. Yole was disappointed at how few had come, but then he thought, *how many dragons do you really need?*

The warriors of Aom-igh flinched a bit at the sight of the great beasts who suddenly covered the sky, but as it soon became apparent that the creatures were fighting against the Dark Warriors, the knights redoubled their efforts with renewed ardor. Yole was flying low over the enemy, the wind from his wings wreaking havoc on the enemy arrows, when he spotted Rhendak. The great silver-green dragon was flying just a little to his left. The King of the dragons was soaring and diving and blasting fire down at the battle as though he had no care for himself or his own safety. Yole stopped and stared in awe. Rhendak fought with ferocity and precision. His eyes were solid silver and seemed to shoot sparks of molten steel down towards the enemy. His claws gleamed like deadly silver sabers in the light of the Dragon's Eye, and his rows of teeth shone like golden daggers when he roared his challenge to the Dark Warriors. Death gleamed in his silver eyes as Rhendak raged over the battlefield.

The creatures of Krayghentaliss rallied behind the fearsome wonder that was the Dragon King. But despite the fearsome beasts and the renewed energy of the men of Aom-igh, the Dark Warriors still held the advantage of numbers. A gryphon fell to an arrow, and then a dragon fell, seven flaming arrows tearing holes in its wings; as the huge beast crashed to the ground, the Dark Warriors surged forward, their confidence and courage restored.

As the enemies discovered that the creatures they now faced were not invincible, they regrouped and began turning their bows upwards, shooting arrows at the dragons and other creatures. Yole's concern grew as this counter-attack took effect. He saw that when the myth-folk got within range, the well-aimed arrows managed to severely wound and kill many of their number. The enemy warriors now gave a great cry of triumph and surged forward again. Yole felt his heart drop; even with the help of Krayghentaliss, the people of Aom-igh were still losing.

The top of Fortress Hill had suddenly become a chaotic panic of women and children as they watched the battle rage below. Zara, Dylanna, Leila, and Kamarie tried to calm the others, but their efforts were in vain. The feeling of defeat hung heavy in the air, and helplessness reigned at this last line of defense for Aom-igh.

Working tirelessly to turn their despair into resolve, Dylanna remembered. She stopped, reached into her pocket, and drew out a small object. She removed its wrappings with care, and stared at it as it lay atop the blue handkerchief in her hand, glistening in the dying light of day: the Dragon Pipes. The instrument whispered of hope, but Dylanna also knew that they were not hers to wield. She glanced around and caught sight of a flash of dark hair. Certain that it was Kamarie, she made her way through the throng of people and pressed the instrument into the girl's hand. Turning her attention to Leila's call for help, Dylanna simply said, "Play this!" and turned to run to her sisters. Glancing back and catching a glimpse of the woman's face, Dylanna realized her mistake.

Rena was searching for her daughter. Kaitryn had gotten separated from her in the confusion, and Rena was growing both frantic and desperate. She had visions of her daughter getting trampled or wandering down the hill into the battle, and she was quickly becoming terrified. *Where is everyone going?* The angry thought flitted through her mind. *There is nowhere to hide.* The top of the hill was approaching pandemonium, and nobody seemed to know what to do. Someone pressed something into her hand and ordered her to play. She turned to argue that she had to find her daughter, but when she turned around whoever it had been was no longer there.

Rena stared down at the object she was holding. It was a set of shepherd's pipes, but they were much more beautiful than any she had ever seen before. Silver in color with just a hint of green, they seemed to be formed from some kind of metal. They shimmered and glittered in her hands and seemed to beg her to play. Just holding them gave her a sense of peace amidst the commotion, and she wondered what it would be like to hear the music from such an instrument. Without any conscious effort on her part, Rena raised the pipes to her lips. She blew into the delicate instrument, and a single, lovely note came out of the pipes. Suddenly, all other noise ceased. The women and children on the hill turned towards her as if frozen in time. The sound of battle slowed as the note hung in the air.

Rena took the pipes from her lips stared down at them with awe and just a little fear. Then, as if against her will, she raised the pipes to her lips again and she began to play. She had never played such an instrument before and was shocked to hear the unfolding melody that sprang from the instrument. The pipes chose their own song. The sweet, fragile notes strengthened into chords and danced across the breeze.

As she played, she began to lose herself in the music. It carried her far away as if she had wings. She flew along the chords, her soul aching with the beauty of the music and the land and the people. As she played, she poured herself into the song: she played for the men who had given their lives, she played for the women and children who had lost their husbands and fathers and sons in the war, she played for the people of Pearl Cove who had lost their homes, she played for the time before the war, mourning its loss, she played for peace, and she played for victory. The song seemed to spread out all across Aom-igh, and the hearts of the people rose.

At the first note, Oraeyn's sword jumped in his hand as if in recognition. He turned to the music, drawn by some irresistible impulse, listening. The song floated down across the battlefield, and as he looked around, he saw the men around him begin to smile. The music played on, freezing time. It tugged at something in Oraeyn's heart, making him remember what he was fighting for. He felt as though he was being carried away on the wind, staring down at Aom-igh from high above, his heart leapt at its beauty. He saw the people of the realm, working for their living in peace; he saw families drawing together and laughing together as they worked and played. He saw their enemies, and they were no longer the stuff of legends and scary bedtime stories; they were simply men, men who were attacking his people for unknown reasons, but still just men. And, in that instant, Oraeyn knew that they were capable of winning the battle, because they were not fighting nightmares, after all.

The melody swelled and then softened and then ended. As the song faded away, the knights of the realm, the farmers, the workers, the shopkeepers, even members of noble families, all who had donned armor, taken weapons and entered the fight joined together once more and began to slowly beat back the enemy. They had all seen similar visions as Oraeyn, and they were all filled with a new determination and confidence. The music had strengthened something within each one of them, reminding them that they were stronger than they believed. The tide turned, and the Dark Warriors now fell back, unable to stand against the swords of their foes. The battle raged, but now it was the Dark Warriors who were losing ground.

Arnaud also heard the music and felt renewed as he looked up towards the hilltop. Dressed in simple armor and fighting alongside his countrymen, he was where he had always wanted to be. He, too, cut down the enemy and fought with a grace and a ferocity that would have astonished his daughter had she been able to see him. Arnaud caught sight of Brant through the battle, and he fought his way closer to his old friend, determined to fight at his side one last time. Brant had a cold, fierce expression on his face, and he did not see Arnaud; he was moving through the enemy with single-minded purpose.

At almost the same moment, Oraeyn also saw Brant. He found he was much closer to the man than he had thought and fought his way towards him as well. As he fought his way through enemy warriors, he noticed Brant's determined visage and realized where the man was heading. As Oraeyn looked towards Brant's goal, he felt a chill go through him. Brant was directing himself straight towards the leader of the Dark Country. The leader of the Dark Country watched as he came, a fierce smile on his face. His black eyes glittered cruelly. And it was in that instant that Oraeyn realized why the man had looked familiar: he could be Brant's brother.

Seamas stood and watched Brant come. He had seen and recognized Brant the moment he had stepped out of the forest. But Seamas had been waiting for many years, and he could afford to wait a few minutes longer. He had not gone to meet Brant but had waited, knowing that Brant would come to him. He smiled now as Brant came closer, and he bit back the urge to laugh. Finally, after so long, Brant stood before him. The battle around them raged, but the two men glared at each other swords drawn, as if in the very eye of the storm. With wary looks, they circled each other, and then paused.

As he stood facing Brant, Seamas' smile turned harsh. He had dreamed of this meeting. He had planned for years what he would say. Now, after all of his dreaming and all of his planning, the dream had finally become reality. His carefully planned words poured out of his mouth in a torrent, almost without his bidding.

"So, we finally meet again, brother. I have waited for this day for many years. They all thought you had traveled beyond the pathways of men, and they all mourned your death deeply. But I did not mourn. I would have known if you had died; after all, you are my brother. No, I knew you were still among the living, and I was glad, because it meant that I still had the chance to kill you myself."

Seamas took a step closer to Brant; the two were of equal height. The battle nearest to them had slowed to a half-hearted buzz, and those who could see and hear them had stopped fighting in order to watch and listen, each man holding his breath, irresistibly drawn to the strange conversation that was taking place in their midst. The silence moved out from around the two men like ripples in a pond, until the battle came to a complete halt. It was obvious to all who were watching that the two were related. Their faces could have been carved from the same slab of stone. They both had the same dark hair and dark eyes, and their build was very similar, although Brant was perhaps a hair shorter than the man he faced.

Seamas continued talking, his voice growing louder and more agitated, "I was the firstborn son, the crown should have been mine by birth! I should have been the heir! But no, the prophecy ruined all that, changed all that, and I was overlooked. You were the one who was chosen as heir."

Seamas' voice deepened into a snarl of rage, "Well, the throne ought to have been mine, and I vowed that it would be mine someday. I have known for some time now that I would have to kill you. At first I did not like the idea of killing my own brother, but it is the only way to secure my position as king. I thought this would be hard, but it is not, now that you are standing before me I find that it will be easy. You are no longer my brother, you are just a shadow that I must sweep away. I have hated you for so long, and now I have finally found you." He paused, a sneer written on his face. "Now," he continued, "I am going to kill you."

The last words were uttered in a flat, expressionless tone, but Seamas' eyes were gleaming. His whole face was contorted into a snarling mask of vengeance. Oraeyn, standing just a few feet to the left in the circle that had formed around the two, was terrified.

Brant did not flinch or show any signs of emotion at all as Seamas spoke. As the King of Llycaelon uttered his final words, the corners of Brant's mouth twitched in what Oraeyn recognized as a smile, but the light in Brant's eyes was hard and cool. He raised his drawn sword and stepped back into a fighter's crouch.

Then he spoke, and his voice was so soft that Oraeyn had to strain to catch the words, "You can try."

A noise very much like a growl rose up in Seamas' throat. He bared his teeth, his face contorted into a hideous mask of anger and hatred. Brant met the furious gaze calmly. A muscle twitching in his jaw was the only visible sign of how hard he was working to maintain his exterior calm.

"I will make you pay dearly for those words, *brother*," Seamas' mouth twisted around the word "brother" as though he did not like its taste. He swung his sword at Brant's legs. Brant stepped back and parried calmly. Another blow, and another parry. Brant's parry threw Seamas off balance, but instead of pressing his advantage, Brant stepped back to allow the other man to regain his footing.

Brant stared unflinchingly into Seamas' eyes, and Oraeyn thought he saw sorrow in the man's dark eyes. "Then you will have to strike the first blow, for I will not raise my hand against you except in defense. You say you have hated me for years, but know this, brother, I have never hated you. I have never desired anything that was yours. I never wanted to be king, and I still don't. But if you must kill me to feel secure on the throne that is rightfully yours, then you must try. I warn you, though," Brant's voice became edged with ice, "do not begin something you don't intend to finish. I am not a child anymore Seamas. I am acquainted with death and battle, and I am not easily defeated."

"You will run, and I will hunt you down. You will be the one who cannot finish what you start. You have always run, and you always will. You never had the strength to complete anything, you never had the steel, you never had what it takes to be king."

Without warning, Seamas attacked with an overhand swing of his sword at Brant's head. Brant met him with a parry and kicked at Seamas' knees, forcing the other man back. He held his sword up in a defensive position.

"I am not running anymore, Seamas. I have learned how to stand my ground, and I will never run again, not from you, not from anyone. I suppose I should thank you for that lesson, the lesson of brutality that you taught me when you had my home attacked and my family killed!"

A glimmer of surprise flitted across Seamas' expression, and he half-lowered his sword as a whisper of shock rustled through the ranks of the Dark Warriors. "If you had not run away in the first place, they never would have been in danger. You endangered them with your presence; you should have known I would never rest until I saw your actual body. I never believed you were dead, not even when my wife told me that you were, not even when the captain of the King's Helm, my oldest and most trusted friend told me you had died."

"Who threatens you, Seamas?" Brant half shouted, half growled the words. "Are you so insane that you could not see I was never coming back? I did not know the aethalons would suffer themselves to be led by a madman. The only threat I see here is you! You are the one who has caused this bloodshed and this grief, and it has all been unnecessary."

"Their deaths are on your head, and on the heads of the aethalons who disobeyed the code of honor, not mine," Seamas said almost flippantly. It was the wrong thing to say, and Brant's expression grew even harder.

"You gave the orders, *brother*. Do you know that your orders were carried out flawlessly? Did you think that there was even a chance they wouldn't be? You know better than that! Who carried your orders to your men? Were they trustworthy messengers? Or were they men with their own agenda? Aom-igh is a great prize to promise, a prize that would corrupt most men. Do you know that you ordered innocent women and children killed? Do you know that the noble aethalons performed these brutal deeds because of their undying loyalty to you? What does that say of their king? You have manipulated your warriors to bear a tarnished stain on their ribbons; do you want your name to be recorded as such? As the king who ruined the reputation of his people over a petty childhood jealousy? In your quest to find me, who is actually ruling Llycaelon?"

Seamas' glare deepened, and the tension in the air between the two warriors thickened almost visibly. Oraeyn was almost surprised that there were no sparks flashing in the air where their gazes met and clashed. A knight bumped into Oraeyn, and he turned to see who it was. As he turned, he realized that the raging battle had stopped. The men from both armies had gathered around Brant and Seamas in a large ring and now they stood watching, transfixed.

The whole world seemed to be holding its breath, waiting to see what would happen. Then, with a loud yell, Seamas attacked again. Holding his sword in both hands, he swung the blade in a great arc over his right shoulder, aiming it at Brant's head. Brant brought his own sword up and met the blow, blocking it with ease.

"I would have thought, brother," Brant said quietly, "that you would have changed your tactics a little over the years. That attack has never worked, in all the years we sparred as children."

Seamas gritted his teeth angrily and sliced down towards Brant's leg. Brant brought his sword down, blocking the blow again. He had not yet made an offensive move.

"Seamas, Seamas," Brant shook his head, "will you never learn to take the unexpected strike?"

Seamas glared. "I took the unexpected move when I attacked Aom-igh."

Brant sighed. "Yes, but your plan had a hole in it, and your prey saw through your decoy and you still ended up being the one who was taken by surprise."

"That doesn't matter," Seamas said, thrusting his sword at Brant's throat, "I have you here in front of me at last."

Brant pushed Seamas' blade to the right with his own. "No, I suppose it did not matter, your army outnumbered your enemy's by at least three to one."

Seamas brought his blade in a chopping motion towards Brant's waist. Brant moved to block it but at the last moment Seamas switched directions and swung his sword down in a slice at Brant's right leg. The maneuver should have worked, but Brant simply jumped backwards, causing Seamas' blow to swing wildly through the air, hitting nothing.

"I suppose I should be flattered: all this effort, the subterfuge, the strategy, the resources, all just to find me. Did your men know what you were really after? Or did you fill their heads with the glory of expanding Llycaelon across the seas?"

Seamas stepped back, keeping his sword up. "Will you not attack?"

"Do you really want to die?"

"It is you who will die."

"I beat you once, brother. I can do it again."

Seamas' face turned red, and his eyes seemed to glow in his rage. "Prepare yourself, brother! After I kill you I will hang you in the palace garden and let my wolves devour you!"

Brant's face lost all expression and became hard and implacable. His jaw tightened, and his eyes became burning embers. He stood on guard and nodded at Seamas.

"As you wish."

All who were watching took a step back, realizing that the duel had just become much more serious.

Seamas let out a yell, but this time as he rushed in he crouched low and made a thrust up at Brant's stomach. Brant spun away and then brought his sword around towards Seamas' shoulder. Seamas ducked and then chopped up at Brant's arm. Brant switched directions with his sword and blocked the blow. The blades screamed as they came together and sparks flew as the edges clashed.

Oraeyn watched the dance of death in fascination. The two fighters whirled and chopped and blocked and ducked at dizzying speeds. Oraeyn found that it was hard to tell which was the better swordsman; they were matched so well. However, after a while it became apparent that Brant was the stronger and quicker of the two. His sword moved in a blur that seemed to be no more than an extension of his arm. He seemed to be just a touch more comfortable with his sword than Seamas, and that tiny difference was beginning to take its toll. Seamas was breathing hard and bleeding in several places where he had not been quick enough. Seamas made one last, desperate attempt to defeat his opponent. His blade sang a deadly song as he swung it through the air at Brant's head. Brant ducked at the last moment and brought his own sword up in a final blow.

Seamas gasped as the sword went through him. For one, agonizing second, he stood staring at Brant in disbelief. Then he sank to his knees as though stunned.

"No... no..." Seamas mumbled the words. He looked pleadingly up at Brant, dropping his sword and reaching out towards Brant. Slowly, he pulled the sword from his body and dropped it on the ground, clasping both hands over the wound. "Brother..." He toppled over.

Brant crouched down next to his brother, wary of any tricks that Seamas might play; but Seamas was beyond tricks. His eyes were quickly becoming glassy, his breaths coming in short, painful gasps. Gently, Brant placed one hand beneath Seamas' head.

"Rhoyan?" Seamas blinked, and then squinted at Brant's face. "Rhoyan? Is that you?"

"I'm here, Ky, I'm here," Brant's voice was soothing. "It's me."

Seamas' lips quirked up in a pleasant smile, and the harshness of his face softened. His dark eyes had a faraway look in them, and he suddenly seemed much younger, just a boy. "I looked for you, Mother wanted you home for dinner. Hasn't been the same... with you gone."

"I know."

The expression the dying man's face twisted into one of anguish, he lifted his head, reaching up to clasp Brant's shoulder with bloody fingers. "Rhoyan... I did... something horrible. I..." Seamas' voice came in whispered gasps. "I was... wrong. Done so many... so many... terrible things. Please... forgive...me."

"I already have, brother. A long time ago."

Seamas' expression relaxed into a whisper of a smile. "You... would," he gasped in pain, his body arching, Brant held him tightly. "Please... watch over... my son. He is not... not... like me. Please... he's a... good boy. Lot of... his mother... in him. Might make... a... good... king. You de... decide." His breath left his body in a final, ragged gasp, and he was gone.

Brant bowed his head and knelt over the body of the slain king for a long moment. Then he laid Seamas on the ground and folded the king's hands over his heart. Brant stood up slowly and gazed at the people who had gathered around him. He looked weary but alert. His muscles were tensed as though he was ready for any attack. Oraeyn held his breath as the tension of the silent battlefield mounted, wondering what would happen now that the King of the Dark Country had been defeated. He tensed, ready to fight off a new attack if need be. Then one of the Dark Warriors moved towards Brant. Oraeyn tried to shout a warning but the words died on his lips as he watched in astonishment.

Brant tensed visibly as the man strode to stand before him, but the Dark Warrior made no move to attack. Instead he knelt and turned his sword to hand the hilt to Brant, holding the blade in the crook of his left arm.

"My name is Tobias," he said, in a strong yet submissive voice, "rank: Aetoli. We met once, long ago, perhaps you will not remember me. I have kept your secret these long years, though apparently it did not do as much good as I had hoped. You have defeated my king, and by the law of Llycaelon I will serve no other. You spoke many true things to King Seamas. I cannot excuse the things that I have done, I take responsibility for the orders I followed and for the men who followed me. I take responsibility for standing by and doing and saying nothing to stop the evil that has occurred by the hands of our warriors in this peaceful land. I was afraid, but I know that is a poor excuse. I will accept the consequences that you deem just, even death."

Oraeyn was confused, but Brant seemed to understand the man perfectly. He took the Warrior's sword and raised it high, then he turned it around and handed it back hilt first saying, "I remember you well, Tobias, you did me a great service once. You saved my life. Consider my debt repaid. There has been too much bloodshed done today already, your life is yours."

Tobias stood up, nodded gravely, and took his sword, sheathing it once more. "Thank you, my King." He gave Brant a meaningful look, then gestured at the warriors around them. "Will you tell them your name, my liege?"

Brant straightened. "My name is Brant of the House of Arne, though when I was younger I was known as Rhoyan," he spoke quietly, but his voice carried across the battlefield as though he had shouted.

The Dark Warriors heard in shame the words of their king, and had seen him defeated in fair battle. Thus, offering the hilts of their swords, they knelt in surrender before Brant on the battlefield of Aom-igh.

Then someone nearby started up a shout of, "Hail Brant, hail the new king!"

The battlefield was filled with a great roar of men shouting for their new king. And there was Brant, in the middle of it all, deaf to the shouts. He had fallen to his knees beside his brother, and he was weeping.

CHAPTER
TWENTY

With the death of their leader, the rest of the Dark Warriors surrendered. Many had witnessed Seamas' duel and the word spread swiftly through the ranks until all acknowledged Brant as the victor. They had seen how their leader had given challenge, and since Brant had conquered, the Dark Warriors had knelt in surrender.

There was much to be done after the battle, and Oraeyn found himself almost wishing for the "good old days" of traveling through the wilderness and running from Dark Warriors. The first thing on the list was dealing with the traitors of Roalthae. Guards were sent to Roalthae and Prince Elroy was brought back to Aom-igh in chains to face charges of treason and espionage. King Arnaud had him and several of his highest ranking aides locked up in the empty wine cellar so that they could be dealt with in due time. At present, there were more pressing matters to take care of before the traitors could be tried.

The dead had to be buried, and Brant insisted upon giving his brother, Seamas, a king's funeral. Arnaud had been loath to give his enemy such an honor, but Brant had been adamant.

They had argued about it for an entire day, and finally Arnaud had relented.

Only a few attended the ceremony. Seamas was laid in a black coffin. He was dressed in combat attire, and his crown was laid on his chest along with his sword. Brant stepped forward to say a few words.

"In life, the King of Llycaelon was ambitious, proud, and determined. These qualities were to his tribute, and he led his people well for many years. However, in the end, it was these same attributes that pulled him down."

Brant stopped and stepped back with a sigh, shaking his head. "I cannot say what needs to be said, for though he was my brother, he became my greatest enemy. He challenged me as such because he had convinced himself that his throne was in danger so long as I lived. Seamas never knew that he was the only one who ever questioned his right to the throne.

"His body will be borne to Llycaelon and buried with our father and the other kings of Llycaelon. Truly, Seamas was a good king for many years, and had he not allowed his pride and his fears to rule him, I believe he could have continued to be such."

Brant fell silent once more and motioned towards several of the Dark Warriors. Tobias and several others strode forward and picked up the casket. They carried it onto one of the ships that would sail back to Llycaelon. The rest of the people shifted uncomfortably and then dispersed in silence, returning to the undesirable task of burying the rest of the fallen.

Dylanna walked over to Brant. "I think you were too kind, but I find myself in awe of your strength. I could not have done that."

Brant gave her a weary smile. "'Speak no ill of the dead,'" he quoted. "I did not think I could do it either. But it was different when we were younger, before either of us realized there was anything special about being princes of the House of Arne, before Seamas discovered that the eldest son is usually the heir.

For a long time, we were best friends; for a long time, he was a very good man."

Dylanna wanted to ask Brant why Seamas had not been chosen in the first place, and what the prophecy was that Seamas had spoken of; she wanted to ask so many questions, but she kept them unspoken. Months of travel had taught her that Brant answered questions with cryptic words that hardly explained anything. She also knew that he was always saying more than he seemed to say, so she left him alone, puzzling over his words.

Brant stood alone for a long while after everyone else had left. A tear rolled down his face as he gazed across the sea in the direction of Llycaelon.

"You weep for him?" Kiernan's voice startled Brant, and he dashed a hand across his face as though to hide the tears.

"He was my brother, once," Brant replied.

Kiernan smiled, but it was a smile filled with sorrow. "I am sorry." Then he slipped away as quietly as he had come. Brant watched him go, wondering why the minstrel's words had sounded like a heartfelt apology rather than a statement of sympathy.

Everyone worked together to clean up the battlefield, even the dragons and the other people of Krayghentaliss helped dig graves and plant new grass. Oraeyn worked alongside Brant as much as possible during the next few days. Most of their work was done in silence, for it was not the lighthearted sort of work that leads to conversation. It was as though the silence of the fallen men they were burying had penetrated each one of them and held them captive until the task was finished. Once the grisly task was complete, Arnaud asked Brant to seek for any strays that may have been injured and escaped into the woods or surrounding countryside. Brant readily consented to this task and asked Oraeyn to join him. Both men were eager to exchange the battlefield of death for the life that blossomed in the woodlands. But it didn't really matter where Brant was headed, Oraeyn was always glad to be at his side.

"Brant?" Oraeyn said as they walked into the forest.

Brant looked back at him, but said nothing, waiting for Oraeyn to finish his thought. Oraeyn smiled a little, then continued.

"Will you be sailing back with the Dark Warriors?"

"They are called aethelons," Brant said kindly, then he sighed. "Yes, I will be sailing back with them. I am their new King."

Oraeyn's face fell a little, but he did not press the point any further. Instead he changed the subject.

"Why did the dragons come to our aid?"

Brant looked at him. "You do not know?"

Oraeyn shook his head. "No."

Brant raised his eyebrows, and then answered, "Apparently King Rhendak was trying to make a statement. You remember the two dragons who tried to stop us from leaving Krayghentaliss with the pipes?"

Oraeyn nodded, and Brant continued, "They tricked Rhendak and managed to put on a convincing show that they had lost their sanity. As a result, Rhendak spared their lives. They were placed in a locked room, but since they were only lightly guarded, they escaped with ease. Rhendak hunted them down and killed them himself. But justice came a little too late; his people, as well as the other creatures of the under-realm, were beginning to doubt Rhendak's strength as a leader.

"The Elders continued to uphold him, but even their support was not enough to curb the mutinous grumblings that arose. The only way Rhendak could see to save his position as king and rebind the loosening loyalties of his people was to lead them into action. I suppose it was lucky for him that there was a war going on. He led all of the creatures of Krayghentaliss above-realm and towards the palace. As they headed this way, they felt the presence of another dragon and then Yole called them, directing them to the battlefield."

"All of the creatures followed Rhendak into battle except for the unicorns," Oraeyn commented. "Why?"

Brant snorted. "Typical of unicorns."

Oraeyn would have pressed the question further, but a noise ahead of them made both men stop and listen.

"What is it?" Oraeyn whispered.

"Listen."

They moved forward with caution, aware that whoever it was might not know the battle was over. As they drew closer to the source of the noise, the sound became clearer. Oraeyn stared up at Brant in confusion.

"Someone is creeping through the bushes."

Brant's brow furrowed, and he moved silently ahead on the path. He pulled back some branches, and suddenly there was a flash of steel. Brant leapt back hurriedly, barely missing being cut by the sword.

"Go away!" a voice shouted angrily. "Leave me alone! I wish to die, let me die in peace!"

Brant and Oraeyn shared a confused glance. Then Brant darted back to the bushes and reached towards the branches. The sword flashed again, but this time Brant was ready. He ducked away from the blade and then reached with his left hand and grabbed the arm that held the sword. He pulled the owner of both the sword and the arm from behind the bushes. Oraeyn stared in surprise at the figure. It was a young man, about the same age as himself. The boy had dark hair and eyes, and he resembled Brant a little. Seeing that he was held captive, he dropped his sword and stared at the ground in defeat. Blood encrusted the side of his head, and his hair was matted with it.

Brant kicked the sword away. "What is your name?"

"Jemson."

"What are you doing out here alone, Jemson?" Brant asked, his voice kind.

"I don't..." he stopped. "I don't know. I remember the battle, but I think I got hit in the head. When I woke up, everything was quiet." He pressed a hand to the wound on his head and winced.

"You were fighting in the battle?" Oraeyn asked.

"Yes," the boy grew defensive, "I am young, but I am strong, and as good a swordsman as any aethalon."

Brant did not look surprised. Squinting a little, he asked, "What is your father's name?"

Oraeyn looked at Brant questioningly. There was a note in the man's voice that said he knew more than he was letting on.

"My father is Seamas, King of Llycaelon," Jemson said. "And now you know. You have the prisoner you need most, but you should know my father will not ransom me, this war..." the boy stopped and stared up at the sky, "it has consumed him. Some say he is mad, others say he is searching for something or someone...." The boy paused again, looking at Brant as if seeing him for the first time. "Wait... I took you for being from Aomigh... you're dressed as one of them... but surely, surely you are from Llycaelon?"

Brant nodded. "I am from Llycaelon. You have missed much, the war is over, has been for five days."

"You say the war is over?" His eyes grew haunted. "My father?"

Brant shook his head. "I'm sorry."

"Was it you? Were you the one... the one he was looking for?"

Brant hesitated, then he nodded. "It was I."

Jemson seemed to understand the double meaning and he stiffened slightly. "Why?"

"It is a long story, but you should know, your father was my older brother."

Jemson's eyes widened. "The prophecy?"

Brant sighed and his shoulders fell as though a heavy weight had been laid upon them. "Yes."

"Then I think I understand. Am I right in assuming that you were not the threat he thought you were?"

"You seem to know more about this than most would, at your age."

"I was his son," Jemson replied simply.

Brant placed his hand on the youth's shoulder. "I'm sorry, but you have a responsibility to more than just yourself now. You answer to the people in your father's place."

At these words, Jemson raised his chin and nodded. Though he straightened his shoulders and followed them with strong, sure steps, Oraeyn noticed the brightness in his eyes and knew that the young man was very near tears. Oraeyn watched him with furtive glances, feeling akin to this sad boy. Though he could not remember it, he knew that when his parents had died and left him orphaned he, too, had been lost and scared. The knight who had brought him back to the palace and trained him in the ways of the Knights of the Realm had been like a father to him, and Oraeyn never forgot what his life might have been had his mentor-knight not taken pity on him. Oraeyn wondered what would become of this boy, when he returned to his own country. He did know this for certain: this boy had the best uncle in the world and was confident he would soon learn that on his own. A twinge of jealousy gnawed at Oraeyn's heart for a span of a few heartbeats, but then he shrugged it aside. Who better to be friends with than Brant's nephew? And what could be more pointless than wishing to be in the place of someone who had just lost his father?

When they returned to the castle, Jemson was given a room in the palace in the wing where the aethalons were staying. He washed and dressed in clean clothes, and when he reappeared, he looked every inch a prince. Brant took the boy aside and sat down to talk with him in private.

"You have gleaned much about me, and you have inferred a great deal correctly. I was meant for the throne, though it was never my desire. I had no wish to rule Llycaelon, and I had no feelings of enmity towards your father. I am sorry for what has happened, but I did all I could to prevent it. You may hate me, but your father did ask me to look after you... is your mother...?"

Jemson shook his head, and Brant looked at the boy with sympathy in his dark eyes and continued, "I am sorry, I met her, once. She saved my life." There was silence for a moment, then

Brant continued, "Then allow me to fulfill my promise to my brother and my nephew, when we return to Llycaelon."

The young man gazed at him steadily while he was told all of this. He nodded gravely to show that he understood but could not yet give an answer. There was a sadness in the strength of this young boy, and Brant recognized this as the blessing and curse of the House of Arne. Jemson truly was a son of kings. He wanted desperately to restore this boy to the joy of youth, but wondered if that would ever be possible.

As the days passed, more unpleasant duties demanded their attention. There were prisoners and traitors to deal with, wounded to tend, and missives of sorrow to be sent to many families whose loved ones would not be returning home. Everyone noted how King Arnuad walked slowly, as though he were carrying a great burden upon his shoulders.

Arnaud entered his chambers one evening after a long day. Zara looked up as he came in and immediately grew concerned.

"What's wrong?"

Arnaud shook his head. "I am not the right man for this job." He sighed and sat down, weariness etched in every line on his face.

Zara smiled at him, a quiet smile. "Then who is?"

He looked at her and shrugged. "Not me."

"Someone like Seamas, who believes that he is the right man?" Zara asked. "Or like Elroy, who cared for little else than gaining a throne?"

Arnaud shook his head. "No, of course I don't think that. The throne needs to be held by a good man, someone who cares about his people but not about power. The throne needs to be held by a strong man, but also by a kind man."

"And how does any of that disqualify you?"

"I never wanted this! I never wanted all of this responsibility. I am a simple man, I hate living in the palace, I hate the laws of the court, and I hate the power I hold. It is not right that I hold so much!" Arnaud burst out, then he calmed, seeing Zara's gentle smile. "You are laughing at me," he accused, but there was a smile tugging at the corners of his own mouth.

Zara shook her head. "No," she managed to get out before she collapsed into giggles.

Arnaud tried to stare at her sternly, but he could not keep the solemn expression on his face, and he began to laugh himself. Arnaud finally stood up, getting his laughter under control.

"We need a banquet," he declared.

Zara stopped laughing and gazed up at him with a puzzled expression on her face. "What?"

"We need a banquet, a great gathering of peace. The people need something to rejoice over, and the country needs healing. We need to find a way to put this bloody war behind us, and focusing on the future is the only way that I know of to do so."

"When?" Zara asked.

"How long do the cooks need?"

Zara thought for a moment. "Two weeks," she said quietly, "preparing food for so many is no easy task."

"Splendid!" Arnaud declared. "The Banquet of Peace will take place in two weeks' time. I will send out the declaration. Brant will understand the time that needs to be taken, and his people will stay as long as he does. We must put things back to rights around the castle; the banquet hall must be ready for this great event! There will be dancing and food and music and stories. Did not a minstrel come with your sisters when they arrived?"

Zara smiled, catching his enthusiasm. "Yes."

"I am sure he would be willing to sing a few tales for us, minstrels always like to be asked to play at occasions like this," Arnaud continued, planning out loud.

"I will go and alert the chefs."

"Yes, certainly," Arnaud replied. "I will ask Brant to delay his departure and then send out the proclamations."

The Great Banquet of Peace was declared throughout the countryside. All were invited. This, Arnaud proclaimed, was to be the largest and finest banquet ever held. Craftsmen, seamstresses, shopkeepers, and cooks were kept busy long into the evenings in preparation for this great festivity. Excitement and genuine delight filled anew the streets of Ayollan as the people turned from grief to celebration. As the day approached, the entire countryside was abuzz with anticipation, and King Arnaud glowed with delight at the smiles and laughter he saw among his people.

Brant sent the aethalons ahead to Llycaelon, as they would need to make preparations for his return. However, he stayed behind with his nephew, as well as a score of aethalons who insisted on staying as his honor guard, for the celebration of peace.

At last the day of the banquet arrived. Thousands of people gathered inside the castle walls while tens of thousands more gathered in the courtyard and the surrounding palace grounds. Even the myth-folk were invited as honored guests, and they attended in human form. They too were ready for a celebration and a renewed association of peace above ground.

It was very odd, Kamarie thought to herself, to be standing in her own room again. It was as though she had never left, and yet she felt she was no longer quite the person she had been. There was something stronger, something braver, and something wiser about the girl who now stood in Princess Kamarie's chambers.

She gazed at herself critically in the mirror. Whoever this new person was, she had been completely hidden within yards of satin, strings of pearls and other assorted jewelry. She was dressed like the princess that she was, but for some reason, for the first time in her life, she did not feel like one. The green satin dress was brand new, and the circlet on her head had been polished until it shone as brightly as though lit by a fire that glowed from within. Her maids had spent hours doing her hair, complaining all the while that no princess' hair should have so many tangles in it, and didn't she even *comb* her hair while she was off gallivanting across the countryside? Though she loved her maids dearly, Kamarie was glad when they finally left. She lifted a fold of satin and sighed, the person in the mirror was hardly even recognizable.

Kamarie looked longingly at the outfit that was lying on her bed. The comfortable, light brown tunic with the dark green belt; the soft leather breeches; and the high, soft-soled brown boots. Her maids had been about to throw the clothes away, but Kamarie had threatened to knock them into the moat if they touched her traveling wardrobe. Her tailor had sighed the deep sigh of one who has suffered much and been asked to do the impossible, and then he had taken the clothes away to be washed and mended. They were returned in perfect condition, although there was a very stubborn stain on the left sleeve that refused to come out. Kamarie smiled; she liked that the clothes were a little worn and unable to be mended.

Kamarie considered, looking at her reflection once more. She wrinkled her nose and stuck out her tongue at the mirror. Then she sighed again and walked out into the hall, making her way towards the rooms where the banquet was being held. She really was looking forward to the banquet; she just wished she could go in something more comfortable.

TWENTY-ONE

The great banquet hall was filling up quickly. Servants carried platters of food into the hall and set it on the great long tables. Many of the squires had been given the duty of serving the tables, but Oraeyn had been exempted from that task as he was one of the honored guests.

He found it very strange to be sitting in the huge banquet hall, at a table full of hundreds of people, especially when some of those people were Dark Warriors. *Aethelons*, he reminded himself sternly. King Arnaud was using this gathering of all who were present as a great send-off before the Aethelons returned to their own country. He called it the Banquet of Peace, but Oraeyn sensed there was more to it than that. King Arnaud had been too quiet lately, and Oraeyn wondered what the King was planning for this Banquet of Peace.

Oraeyn was sitting near the head of the table, to the left of Queen Zara. Kamarie was sitting between her parents, and Brant was sitting on Arnaud's right. Dylanna and Leila sat to Brant's right. Yole was on Oraeyn's left, and the boy was trying very hard not to squirm. Jemson was sitting next to Yole. Oraeyn liked Yole well enough, but he was intrigued by the young aethalon and had hoped to be seated next to him at the banquet. Yole had shifted back into his human form after the battle, but Oraeyn saw the look of longing in Yole's eyes whenever the boy looked up towards the sky.

The table was laden with a feast of every kind of food that Oraeyn could think of. He stared, sure that he had never seen so much food in one spot at one time. Actually, most of the people in the room were thinking the very same thing. Everyone attending was dressed in their best finery. The knights did not wear their full armor for it was too heavy, but they were dressed in light vests of mail that gleamed from much polishing. The farmers and tradesmen were all wearing brightly colored scarves or sashes. But most bedazzling of all were the outfits of the courtiers. Oraeyn had not known that such colors could be woven into fabric or that any one outfit could contain such brightness. But none were quite so grand looking as Kiernan Kane. The minstrel sat near the great fireplace, strumming his mandolin with seeming indifference, but the music was achingly pure and every note perfect. The minstrel himself wore a maroon tunic and black trousers with a silver sash tied around his waist. He looked reserved and formal, and the courtiers had been eyeing his stylish, yet regal, outfit with envy all evening.

Arnaud stood, and a hush fell across the banquet. He surveyed the great assembly in silence for a moment. He raised a hand, and the room fell silent.

"Let the Banquet of Peace begin!" King Arnaud's voice thundered through the marble room, but it was a cheerful sound, not a menacing one.

With that, the silence was broken, and the people who were sitting at the tables began eating heartily. There was much laughter and chatter as the feast wore on. Several great stone fireplaces lighted the rooms that had been opened for the banquet, and they cast a romantic red and gold glow throughout the halls. There was a sense of friendly companionship and safety that filled the air. Comfortable, that was how Kamarie would have described it.

She gazed around the room at her people in wonder. Everyone was at ease, the tensions of the past few months flowing away upon the wind, distanced from memory for a time. The cheerfulness of the people struck her deeply, and she realized that this peace was all that many of them had to look forward to. Tomorrow most of them would return home and return to the mourning of their dead, but today they could relax and enjoy life and feast upon a banquet that offered them so much more than food. It was not only for the banquet that these people had come; it was for the opportunity to lay down their burdens, great and small, and leave them at the door for a short time.

The Dragon's Eye began to set, and the feasting slowed. The people sat back in their chairs, full and satisfied, with smiles on their faces as they continued to talk and joke and laugh with their neighbors. It was then that Kiernan began a dancing reel, his fingers moving swiftly across the strings, the music swelling out into the hall.

King Arnaud stood up and offered his hand to his wife. "May I have this dance?" he asked her with an air of debonair gravity.

Zara covered her mouth politely with her napkin to keep from laughing. "You may," she said smiling as she took his hand and allowed him to lead her onto the dance floor.

The music grew and intensified, so light and cheerful that soon others joined the King and Queen as they danced. Soon the great ballroom floor was crowded. The people smiled and laughed as they danced across the floor, keeping time to the fast pace of the music. Oraeyn looked around to find Kamarie, but saw that she was already dancing with Yole. He smiled to himself and turned to Dylanna.

"May I have the honor?" Oraeyn asked, offering his arm.

Dylanna grinned at him, having seen his glance towards Kamarie. "Of course," she said laughing. Together they glided out into the crowd.

Not all joined in the dancing, however. Brant had moved back to stand in the shadows of the fireplace. He had not danced, seemingly satisfied to stand back and watch the others on the ballroom floor. The look on his face was both calm and content. His arms were crossed and he leaned against the marble wall, looking more relaxed than he had in all of the past few months combined.

"Why do you not join in the dancing?" a young, sweet voice asked from the shadows near him.

"Why do not you?" Brant countered the question with a question of his own.

He heard a low laugh that was devoid of all cheer, and then the voice replied, "I am in mourning."

"Are not we all?" Brant asked.

"You did not answer my question."

"I rarely do."

The voice fell silent, but Brant did not turn to look at the young woman who was standing next to him. The silence stretched on for a long while, but it was not an uncomfortable silence. Finally Brant spoke again.

"You played the Dragon Pipes during the battle, didn't you?"

Rena started back a little, surprised, then she nodded. "Yes, I did."

They stood in silence for a moment more, then Rena spoke again, more quietly this time and there was a hint of apology in her tone. "I have to go find my daughter and put her to bed, it is getting late. If you would excuse me...?"

Brant nodded. "Certainly, Rena. But do not fear to come back to the banquet, you are one of the heroes in whose honor this occasion is being held."

Rena's heart was filled with many things that she could not speak, so she hurried away from the strange man. She had sensed an odd closeness to the figure that she could not see, a bond of some kind, and it frightened her. The voice had been strong and sure, and yet sadness had lingered in his words: a sadness that she identified with. Rena did come back to the banquet hall after seeing to Kaitryn, but she did not dance.

As the Toreth rose up high into the night sky, the dancing gave way to sitting around the fireplace. Kiernan put his mandolin aside and began to entertain his audience with feats of juggling, tumbling, and antics that drew steady laughter and delight. However, what the crowd wanted most were stories, and finally Kiernan relented.

The minstrel took a few requests and first sang the *Ballad of the Dragon King*, which was Yole's request, never guessing that the actual King of the dragons sat not more than ten paces from him. Yole had to admit that, for all of Kiernan's boasting, the minstrel was a wonderful storyteller, and he was excellent at playing his eight-stringed instrument. After that, Kiernan played the *Song of Llian's Sword*, and then he told several tales of the legendary King Artair. He spun the tales with words that cast magic throughout the room, and those who listened were spellbound as though they were actually seeing the things that Kiernan sang. The strings of the minstrel's mandolin jangled long into the night. As his finale, Kiernan sang a song that he had composed about the recent events leading up to this banquet. His words and his music brought many to tears as he captured the heroism of the men who had given their lives in the great battle. Brant found himself moved beyond words at the way the minstrel told of the two brothers who had lost each other and, in losing each other, had lost pieces of themselves. The minstrel sang of how sorrow and anger and bitterness had turned one man's mind to madness and how he had become consumed by it until he at last faced the monster of his own making: his own brother, who had never wished him harm, but had been content to live in exile rather than fight with his blood-kin. The tale expanded to a crescendo as Kiernan sang of the tragedy that had forced the exiled man to kill his brother in order to save two nations. The words were poignant and painted the story in such a sad and beautiful light that many found themselves weeping for both of the men in the tale. Brant wondered at the minstrel's accuracy: how had he learned the details of the story? He wondered if Kiernan had spoken to Jemson. He glanced at the young man and saw tears on his nephew's face. Jemson caught Brant's look and smiled slightly, nodding his head in a gesture of forgiveness.

After a few more songs, each more cheerful and less compelling than the story about Brant and Seamas, King Arnaud motioned for Kiernan to step down from the hearth. The lanky minstrel unfolded himself from his sitting position and stood up. He took a bow and his audience clapped and cheered, applauding him loudly. Kiernan blushed a deep shade of red and stammered a little.

"I must say, this is a rather new experience for me," he admitted, "usually people throw things at me when I finish. It sometimes seems as though they cannot get rid of me quickly enough."

Everyone laughed at his words, and Kiernan stepped down from the hearth, bowing and smiling to his audience as he went. King Arnaud strode forward to take his place in front of the people, and the room fell silent once more. There was a smile on the king's face and a spring in his stride as he stepped up to the hearth to address the audience.

"My people, my friends," King Arnaud began, "we gather tonight to celebrate the end of the great strife that has overshadowed our land for many long months. We come here to celebrate our new allies and our new-found peace with the country across the sea, the land called Llycaelon."

The people gave a great cheer at his words, and Arnaud paused, waiting. When the boisterous and excited applause had died down, he spoke again.

"But that is not all that we come together for: we come together in order to celebrate the future of Aom-igh, a future that has been preserved by its people. We come to honor the memory of those brave souls who gave their lives to save their kingdom so that we might have that future."

The room fell into a respectful silence as the memories of the many brave men who had given their lives in the battle were honored. A few tears were shed in that silent moment as images of lost friends and family came to mind.

King Arnaud spoke once more, breaking the silence and continuing his speech, "And we also come to honor those who are among us today. We come to honor those brave men and women who are still living, we come to honor those who joined the struggle and helped to bring about the end of the war with their acts of unmeasured courage and valor. Today I mean to grant them the honor that they deserve."

The room lapsed into silent anticipation. King Arnaud paused for a moment with a smile, allowing the expectancy to build. When he finally spoke again, the people hung on his every word.

"First," Arnaud said, "I would ask the new King of Llycaelon to step forward."

Brant moved forward and stepped up onto the hearth. He was not surprised at King Arnaud's words, for this part of the evening had been planned in advance. The treaties of peace between their countries had already been signed the morning before the Banquet of Peace, but Arnaud and Brant had both decided that a public acknowledgement of that peace would serve both of their lands far better than obscure documents that most people would never see.

"I would have our two countries bonded by ties of peace and friendship henceforth and always," Arnaud intoned as Brant moved to stand in front of him.

Brant nodded once in agreement. "I would have it so as well," he replied in the traditional words.

The two men, the two kings, clasped hands, sealing the agreement for peace. The people in the room, from Aom-igh and Llycaelon both, let out a heartfelt and unrestrained cheer, and the two kings smiled at each other in friendship and brotherhood.

Brant turned to leave, but Arnaud stopped him. Brant looked at Arnaud, a question in his eyes. King Arnaud raised a hand and the people quieted down once more to hear his words.

He smiled again and said, "Before this man who stands before you became a king, he was my friend. We were as brothers when we were younger, and I have always thought of him as such even though we lost touch through the years. Brant did much to save our country and the lives of our people in the past few months, and he is, as many of you know, first and foremost, among those whom we gather to honor tonight.

"I have struggled long and hard trying to think of some worthy gift of honor to bestow upon this hero of Aom-igh. Were he not already a knight of the realm, I would grant him knighthood. Were he not the king of another country, I would gladly give him half of my kingdom and name him as my heir." Arnaud stopped and turned to Brant. "It seems that I have nothing to give you that you do not already possess, so after much thought, I have decided to grant you this: ask for whatever you wish, and on my honor as the King of Aom-igh, I will do my best to grant your request."

Brant considered for a moment, then he smiled his quiet smile and spoke, "Then I can think of only one thing that I would ask of you, my friend. I would claim you as my brother, forever bound in friendship and trust."

Arnaud gave him a puzzled smile. "Granted, and gladly! But surely you know that you already have what you ask for, and no great boon is it, for I have always regarded you as such. Are you certain that you have no other request?"

Brant shook his head and replied, "To claim the friendship and trust of my brother is all I could want." His thoughts echoed, *All I ever wanted from him.*

Understanding shone in Arnaud's eyes and he embraced Brant. Turning to his countrymen he said, "No better brother could I ask for, and no greater friend to Aom-igh could we hope for. I give you Brant!"

With tears forming in his heart, Brant stepped down from the stage.

Arnaud then turned to address the crowd once more, "This is a night of recognizing many. Tonight I wish to honor the dragons for their part in the great battle as well. There is one dragon in particular whom I would like to honor. He is among us tonight, though in human form. King Rhendak, if you would?"

A tall man with red hair and green eyes strode forward. He was tall and thin, but every line of his visage bespoke him of an inner strength that could not be disguised. Though he did indeed appear in human form, King Rhendak hid his true form and nature very poorly. The crowd parted for him with a respect that was tinted with admiration and fear.

"I would have peace between our peoples as well," King Arnaud said quietly when Rhendak stood before him.

Anyone else standing next to the King of the dragons would have appeared small and insignificant; however, King Arnaud appeared in every way Rhendak's equal. Kamarie noted this with a sense of wonder and a little bit of puzzlement. The two clasped hands as Arnaud and Brant had done.

"And how do you propose that we have peace between our peoples?"

"I would have your people return to live above-realm," Arnaud said carefully, having learned from Kamarie the word that the dragons used to refer to the surface of Aom-igh.

"Long my people have hoped for such a time when we could return above-realm," the Dragon said, "but such is not possible, for among your people we are feared and hated and hunted. I will not bring my people to live in a place where they will be in danger."

King Arnaud nodded. "This I know, I offer you a chance to live above-realm but my offer is not without conditions."

Rhendak eyed Arnaud for a long moment in silence; then he said, "Speak your terms."

"I would put the condition that your people promise not to hunt or kill the livestock of the farmers and ranchers. If you consent to this I will pass a law of protection upon your people," King Arnaud said.

Rhendak looked at him. "How can you assure me that this law of protection will be abided by?"

"The penalty for breaking the law will be death," King Arnaud replied without hesitation.

He had spoken at length with Kamarie and Oraeyn and Darby and Brant about the dragons and their laws. He had discovered that the more severe a ruler came across, the more he was revered and admired by his people. He had long pondered these same questions that Rhendak now asked, and at length he had come up with answers that were acceptable to his advisors.

Rhendak thought for a few moments, his eyes never leaving the king's face. Finally he nodded quietly. "Your terms are acceptable King Arnaud, and I consent to them. Our people will return to live above-realm in our old homes in the Mountains of Dusk and the Harshlands. Perhaps we will not be seen for many years, for our people are wary and shy of humans, but we will accept your offer and return to the lands of the Dragon's Eye."

There was no cheering as the two kings clasped hands, for this was something too deep for cheers and catcalls. Every person in the room felt the weight of responsibility fall upon them as the agreement was reached, all of them except for Kiernan who told everyone around him how shocked he was to find that he had actually been in the presence of the King of the dragons when he had sung the *Ballad of the Dragon King*. His shock, Yole noted wryly, had not affected his voice in any way, nor did it seem sincere. Yole wondered at this; it seemed that the minstrel made too much of his awe and shock, as though he had not truly been either awed or shocked, almost as though he had known all along. But that could not be, Kiernan Kane was just an overconfident and arrogant minstrel, wasn't he?

Rhendak then spoke again, "I would ask your permission to speak, King Arnaud."

Arnaud looked startled. Dragons were an independent people, and they rarely asked permission to do anything, let alone speak. It dawned upon him that Rhendak was struggling to abide by the niceties of the humans that he was among. He nodded, emotions of respect making him unable to speak for a moment. Rhendak turned and faced the crowd. "Yole," he called out the name.

Yole walked up to stand in front of the King. He looked very small and very scared as he stood there under the burning green gaze of the Dragon. He stared up at the dragon and gulped loudly.

"Yes, Your Majesty?"

The dragon laughed. "Do not look so terrified my boy!" he exclaimed. "I did not call you up here to suffer some horrible fate. I asked you to come forward so that I could offer you a gift."

"What gift, Majesty?"

"I want to offer you a choice, young Yole."

"What kind of choice?"

"You have proven yourself as a mighty fighter, you have proven to be a lost one who is worthy of being given a second chance to choose. I asked you once if you wished to live with the dragons and learn our ways; you refused me because you were young and inexperienced. I see before me now one who is not so young and one who is, perhaps, a little wiser. I have seen you in battle and as the King of the dragons, it is my right to offer you this choice again: do you wish to live among the people of your birth and heritage or among the people who have adopted you and befriended you and cared for you? Consider carefully, and do not answer quickly," Rhendak cautioned as Yole opened his mouth. "You do not have to answer tonight, the choice is not quite so plain as it might seem. Not many people get to make this choice."

Yole shut his mouth quickly, then he spoke tentatively, "May I have a few days to decide?"

Rhendak smiled kindly and nodded at the boy. "Yes, you may."

"I will give you my answer as soon as I know it, Your Majesty."

They both left the hearth and now King Arnaud asked Garen to step forward. The old, grizzled knight strode up to the hearth and stood before his king as an equal, as he ever had. King Arnaud decorated him with the King's Sword, the highest medal of honor that could be given.

"You have served this country faithfully for many long years, and your acts of courage in the battle were only a continuation of your everyday service to the crown," King Arnaud declared. "However, it is not your acts of courage or valor that I honor highest, but rather, it is your continued friendship that I cherish the most."

The old knight smiled and ducked his head, embarrassed yet pleased. He said nothing, for he had always been a man of few words and he now did not know what to say. King Arnaud allowed him to return to his spot in the crowd, and then he called up several other men and warriors who had distinguished themselves in battle and service. To these he awarded the Silver Flame, which accorded them a permanent honor among the heroes of Aom-igh.

Then King Arnaud asked the knight Justan to come forward. The young man strode up to the hearth with long, confident strides. Arnaud greeted him with a smile.

"I would make you King's Warrior were it a position you would accept," King Arnaud said after decorating him with the Gold Sword.

"I would accept your offer, Majesty," Justan said gravely, but there was a hint of shock in his brown eyes at the great honor that he had just been given.

King Arnaud saw the shock and smiled slightly. "Do not discredit yourself, I do not give you this honor lightly, Justan. Your advice has been unmatched, and your love for king and country is more than laudable. You have served as spy, informant, warrior, and advisor. You have gone far above and beyond the oaths you took when you became a knight. There is no higher honor, and I would bestow it upon you."

Justan bowed deeply and then clasped hands with King Arnaud. He returned to stand next to Garen, a little dazed. Garen beamed with a father's pride and clapped Justan on the back heartily.

King Arnaud smiled after him and then spoke again. "Now I would like to ask someone whom you all know and love to come forward, the Princess Kamarie, my daughter."

Kamarie's mouth would have dropped open in shock had she not been deeply conscious of all the eyes that were turned towards her. The crowd parted as she rose and she walked calmly to stand before her father. He smiled at her, and she gave him a puzzled smile back. A light dawned across her face as she stood there, and she took a deep breath.

Before King Arnaud could say anything, Kamarie spoke. "Father," she began, "if you have called me up here to grant me knighthood, I would ask you not to. I once thought that I wanted to be a knight because I like to ride horses and I am skilled in weaponry, Garen claims that I am among the best that he has taught..."

"You say that you once desired to be a knight," Arnaud said slowly, cutting her off, "is that no longer true?"

Kamarie nodded quietly. "It is no longer true, Father. A knight is not only called to be skilled in these talents, but a knight is called upon to use these talents as well. A knight must go into battle and a knight must kill, and I have discovered that I have no desire to do so. I thought that battle would be exciting, and I was upset when Brant and Dylanna forbade me to join in the fighting. However, in my travels and while I was atop Fortress Hill, I saw enough to convince me that it is neither exciting nor is it fun. War is perhaps a necessary evil, but it is not my desire to be a part of such."

King Arnaud smiled. "Good," he said, startling Kamarie slightly, "I am glad, for it means that you will not be disappointed when I do not grant you knighthood.

"You are right, my daughter. Battle is no place for women. However, you have set a wise example in your rigorous training, and I would like to encourage this among all the daughters of Aom-igh. You will be the first of a new order, one that you may have the honor of naming. You will take the same tests required for knighthood, and you will lead and develop your sister countrymen in building and sustaining this great honor among the women of Aom-igh. Though your duties are different, your training and honor will be the same as that of your brotherhood of knights."

As Arnaud finished speaking, Kamarie beamed and threw her arms about his neck. Arnaud smiled and hugged her back; he felt a lump of emotion lodge itself in his throat and well up behind his eyes. Then Kamarie let go and returned to her place in the crowd next to her mother amid shouts of, "Hail Princess Kamarie! Hail the Lady Warrior!"

Arnaud continued, "My pride is full this evening, not because of this celebration, but because of you, my countrymen, and the courage, sacrifice, and selflessness that has been on display these past months. I truly wish I could honor each one of you individually, but time does not permit. This celebration is because of you, and nothing could please your king, your brother, more. Among those who remain unmentioned are four sisters, and I honor their request for anonymity for the sake of my own health."

The people laughed, and Arnaud smiled as well. Then he continued speaking, "There is one more whom I would like to especially recognize this evening. A young man whose loyalty to king and country took him far from the battle and excitement that he so wanted to be part of.

"He followed his orders and completed his mission, a mission that proved to be far more perilous and of far more benefit to his countrymen than ever expected. His journey led him directly into the battle he thought he would miss, where he proved his skill and courage beyond measure."

The room was suddenly abuzz with curious whispers as everyone wondered who fit the king's description. All eyes were on Arnaud in anticipation of the answer to that question.

King Arnaud paused, and then he said, "Oraeyn, would you come forward please."

Oraeyn had never been so shocked in his entire life. He had hardly even expected to be recognized and certainly not with an introduction such as that. He felt frozen in place as though rooted to the floor, and he could not move to obey his King nor could he speak to say that he could not move.

Suddenly Brant was there, the man nudged him forward, causing him to stumble a bit reminding him of his ability to walk. Oraeyn flashed him a grateful look and then made his way up to where his King stood. Within a few moments, he was standing on the hearthstone before Arnaud. Oraeyn's face was full of confusion and questions, but he found he still could not speak to utter them; his tongue felt as though it were weighed down with lead.

Arnaud smiled. "This man who stands before you is Oraeyn. He has traveled with my daughter, Kamarie, as well as with King Brant, the dragon Yole and the wizardess Dylanna. He went on that journey because I entrusted to him the safety of my daughter. Little did I know the true value of that trust.

"Oraeyn was chosen to go on that journey because he was the only squire who could be spared. However, had I to make the choice over again, I would entrust my family, my life, our kingdom with none other."

Arnaud looked at Oraeyn kindly. "This man was orphaned as a child, and he never knew his parents. However, he carries at his side the Fang Blade, the Shining Sword of King Llian. That sword was lost to us when Llian died, over six hundred years ago. Llian's advisor, wizard, and oldest friend, Scelwhyn, put a spell of protection around the blade, making it so that no one but Llian himself or one of his descendants could remove the sword from its hiding place. Oraeyn was found by that hidden place, and the sword has claimed its owner. He does not, as yet, realize the full greatness of the thing that he carries, nor does he recognize the true value of its holder. However, I do. That is why he stands before you now."

Arnaud paused again and the crowd of people held their breaths, waiting. He turned to Oraeyn now and bade him to kneel down. Oraeyn obeyed without a word. King Arnaud removed his own sword from its sheath and touched Oraeyn lightly on either shoulder with the flat of its blade.

"By my power and authority as King, I name you a knight of the realm and I bind you to their code to serve and protect the king and the people of Aom-igh, and to raise others above yourself as you choose to do what is good and right and just. I bid you rise, Sir Oraeyn."

Oraeyn stood in a daze and the people raised a great cheer for him. But Arnaud was not finished and he held up a hand.

"A man of royal blood, a knight of the realm, the holder of the Fang Blade, a man of character, courage, loyalty, and honor; to this man, I give my kingdom. It is this man whom I would proclaim as my heir." Arnaud finished speaking, and the crowd fell silent as he removed his own crown and placed it upon Oraeyn's head.

At last Oraeyn found his tongue. "No, sire!" he exclaimed. "I am not worthy of such words, I am not the man that you believe me to be! I cannot rule Aom-igh, I am not King Llian returned; I am not even of noble blood. I cannot follow in the footsteps of the great kings, of Artair and Llian and Sharlmayen and yourself!"

Arnaud smiled quietly. "They all said that they could not do it either, but they did; *that* is what made them so great. They did not believe in their own worth either, not one of those men thought that he was the right man for the throne, but that was their greatness: that they did not believe themselves to be so high.

"That belief, that conviction is your greatness as well. Stay true to this understanding, and stay true to your fellow countrymen, and you will serve well. More than courage in battle, or loyalty to country, or even royal lineage, it is the love and care that you bring to your people that defines the greatness of your effort."

Oraeyn sighed as understanding weighed on his heart. "So have I no choice?"

Arnaud looked at him kindly. "The greatest kings never do, but out of gratitude for your singular service to me and my family, I am granting you this choice."

Oraeyn opened his mouth hastily to say that he chose to be anything but the King of Aom-igh, but then he closed it again. "Kings don't get to choose, do they? They are chosen."

Arnaud nodded solemnly. Oraeyn looked at him and said, "So be it."

Arnaud's face broke into a smile of pride. "Then I proclaim you King Oraeyn of Aom-igh, a new king for a new beginning."

The stunned crowd finally found their voice again and shouted out, "Hail King Oraeyn!" over and over again. Arnaud signaled and music, refreshment, and entertainment resumed late into the evening.

"So what does this mean?" Oraeyn asked, following Arnaud back to their table.

"It means that I am no longer the King of Aom-igh," Arnaud said.

"But I thought that you were just naming me as your heir," Oraeyn protested, "how can you not be king while you are still alive? I am too young to take the throne now!"

"It has always been my wish to step down from the throne while I was still living," Arnaud replied. "I would like to return to my farm, and set aside the burdens of royalty and take on the concerns of crops and livestock once again. The challenges of kingship are great, young Oraeyn, but so are the rewards. I have enjoyed both, but Zara and I are ready to move on. As for being too young, I was your age when I was handed the throne. Young means many things, but one thing it definitely means is energy and enthusiasm, which our country will need in the aftermath of recent events. Plus, you carry the Fang Blade, and that means quite a bit to our brothers from Krayghentaliss."

Oraeyn's shoulders slumped in defeat. "Will you at least stay to be my advisor for a little while?" he asked quietly. "I know nothing of ruling a country."

Arnaud grinned, looking younger than he had looked in years. "Of course, you did not think I would leave you to figure out the intricacies of ruling a kingdom all by yourself? That would hardly be a reward, now would it?"

Oraeyn soon found himself tired, and overwhelmed. So many things he wanted to ask and needed to know, but these would have to wait. He found his way back to his room where sleep overtook him, leaving his questions unspoken.

EPILOGUE

Yole roused Dylanna and Kamarie and Oraeyn early the next morning with an urgency in his voice and gestures. They stared at him, groggy with sleep. It took him a while to make them comprehend what he was saying, but when they finally did understand it jerked them into complete wakefulness. They each got up hurriedly and dressed and then followed Yole down to the harbor.

The day was dark and drizzly, and there was thunder in the air. It was cold and gray out, as though the sky itself were weeping for something lost. The rain poured down, drenching the four lone people who stood upon the shore staring out to sea.

The final ship of Llycaelon had set sail several hours earlier and was now just a tiny speck on the horizon of dark gray sky meeting the white-capped blue waves. It rose and sank and got ever smaller as the great swells carried it away. Kamarie turned to look at Oraeyn, her brow furrowed with questions and a great sadness in her eyes.

"Why would he leave without saying good bye?"

Oraeyn could only shake his head, for there was pain welling up within his heart and he could not speak for fear that the pain would overcome him. He stared out after the ships; the sails were barely visible now. He thought about the man he had met with suspicion and reservations, he thought about how the man had gradually become a role model, a hero, and even perhaps a friend, and he thought about how he was returning to his own homeland. Oraeyn felt that he ought to have been happy for Brant, but he could not help feeling abandoned as he stood there on the shore, staring out into the angry, rolling waves that broke upon the rocks. Kamarie's question echoed in his own thoughts, but he could not summon the energy to respond.

Dylanna spoke softly, as if in answer to Kamarie's question, but there was much emotion in her voice. "His work here was done, and he is going home."

Kamarie was crying quietly, tears streaming down her face and mingling with the light mist that hung in the air, threatening true rain.

Dylanna's words hung in the air and seemed to swirl around them as the rain and the wind that drenched and chilled them. They stood there silently for a moment, watching the ship as it sailed beyond their sight.

"But why would he slip away in the early morning without saying good bye?" Yole repeated Kamarie's question plaintively, breaking the silence and asking again the question that was weighing upon each of them.

"Perhaps he doesn't like good byes."

The deep, familiar voice that answered Yole's question made the four of them whirl around with a start. For a moment the mist and fog blocked their vision of the speaker. Then they found themselves face to face with a smiling, rain-soaked Brant.

"Brant!" Oraeyn cried, wiping the rainwater out of his eyes; and now the tears did come as he threw his arms around the man and hugged him as a little child hugs the father who has returned from many months of being gone.

The rest of them joined Oraeyn, hugging Brant as though he had just come back from a long and perilous journey that had taken him away for many years. Brant laughed and hugged them all back.

"Now, what's all this? One would think that you had not seen me since last night!" Brant exclaimed cheerfully, his tone light and playful.

Then Dylanna drew back suddenly and frowned in confusion. "But your ship has left without you," she said, glancing in the direction of the vanished vessel.

Brant nodded soberly. "Yes, I know. But Llycaelon has managed without me for a long time, and a while longer will not matter to them. I have never desired the throne. Last night I relinquished the crown of Llycaelon to Jemson. He is known by our people, and his ascension to the throne will be far easier and more seamless than mine would have been. I named Tobias as his First Advisor and disbanded the Council of Three that used my brother and his tenuous grasp on sanity to try to grab power and wealth for themselves; they are being taken back to Llycaelon in chains and will face justice in our own land. The dragons have been kind enough to offer their services in flying me back and forth between the two countries when my nephew needs my aid or advice. I do not intend to abandon him to learn ruling a country, but I cannot be too visible, or it might seem as though I do not have confidence in him. The last thing he needs is for the people to believe he is a puppet king. Besides, Aom-igh still has need of me for now," he paused, and then added with a twinkle in his eye, "I thought perhaps King Oraeyn might need a better advisor than a retired king and a couple of wizardesses."

Dylanna opened her mouth and closed it several times in mock outrage. But she could not continue to pretend being angry while she was holding back a smile. Together, the five of them walked back towards the castle, arms around each other, laughing and reminiscing over their journeys that already seemed to have taken place lifetimes ago.

GLOSSARY

Aethalons (ā-ETH-ə-lohns): The people of Llycaelon.

Aetoli (ā-eh-TOLL-ee): Highest ranking warrior in Llycaelon.

Aom-igh (Ā-ōm-Ī): Home of Kamarie

Ayollan (AY-ōl-ăn): Capital city of Aom-igh

Arnaud (AR-nawd): King of Aom-igh.

Brant (brănt): Formerly the King's Warrior.

Calyssia (cuh-LEE-see-ah): Keeper of Pearl Cove.

Coeyallin (kō-ĕ-yăl-in): A province of Aom-igh.

Darby (DAR-bee): Kamarie's maidservant.

Drayedon (DRAY-ĕ-don): A province of Aom-igh.

Dylanna (dĭ-LAHN-ah): Wizardess, second daughter of Scelwhyn.

Elroy (ELLE-roy): Leader of Roalthae.

Enreigh (ON-ree): A peasant of Aom-igh, Marghita's husband.

Farrendell (FAR-ehn-dell): Main river that runs through Aom-igh.

Frantell (fran-TELL): A duchess of Aom-igh.

Garen (GAIR-en): A Knight of the Realm

Graldon (GRAIL-dən): King of the Dragons before Rhendak.

Iarrdek (ee-yar-DEK): A gryphon.

Imojean (ĬM-ō-jeen): Brant's wife.

Iolanver (ee-ō-lan-vair): Island-country southeast of Aom-igh.

Justan (JUST-in): A Knight of the Realm; raised by Garen.

Kaitryn (KAY-trin): Rena's daughter.

Kali (KĂ-lee): Brant's daughter.

Kamarie (kah-MAR-ee): Princess of Aom-igh.

Kane, Kiernan (KANE, KEE-YAIR-nen): A wandering minstrel.

Krayghentaliss (kray-ghen-TĄL-ĭss): The realm of the myth-folk

Leila (lee-Ī-luh): Wizardess who lives in the Harshlands

Llian (LEE-ĕn): King of Aom-igh during the first Great War.

Llycaelon (lie-KAY-ĕ-lahn): The true name of the "Dark Country."

Marghita (mar-GHEE-tuh): A peasant woman of Aom-igh.

Mystak (mis-TAK): A dragon.

Nnyendell (nYEN-dell): A dragon.

Oraeyn (ŏr-AY-in): Squire in training to be a Knight of the Realm.

Quenmoire (kwen-moyr): Island-country to the south of Roalthae.

Rena (RĒ-nuh): One of the People of Pearl Cove.

Rhendak (ren-DACK): King of the Dragons.

Rhynellewhyn (rin-ELL-ĕ-whin): A Pegasus.

Roalthae (rō-awl-THAY): Island-country northeast of Aom-igh.

Sauterly (SAW-ter-lee): A baron of Aom-igh.

Scelwhyn (sell-win): Wizard and advisor to Aom-igh's kings.

Schea (shay): Brant's son.

Seamas (SHAW-mŭs): King of the Dark Country.

Selynda (sell-IHN-dah): A duchess of Aom-igh.

Shalintess (shall-IN-tess): Mate of King Rhendak

Tobias (toe-BY-ess): King Seamas' most trusted friend

Toreth (TOR-eth): The moon.

Urith (OOR-ith): A province of Aom-igh.

Wessel (wess-əl): Leader of the Cove People, Rena's husband.

Yatensea (YĄcht-in-see): A baron of Aom-igh.

Yole (yōle): A young orphan boy

Zara (ZAR-ah): Queen of Aom-igh.

Zhreden (ZREE-den): A province of Aom-igh.

Read on for a sneak preview of the next book in The Minstrel's Song

SECOND SON

Available Spring 2013

The young apprentice peered up at the sky, a puzzled look in his bright eyes. "But what does it *mean*, Master? I don't understand."

"Two sons."

"*Two* sons? But there have never been two sons in the house of Arne, never!"

"Never, my boy? Never? Have you lived since the Dragon's Eye was formed then? Have you watched the line of Arne from the ancient days before their family acquired the throne? No? Then be silent with your idle words and keep your thoughts to yourself!" the old man's voice became a thundering roar and his apprentice hunched his shoulders against the storm. "You are right in one sense of the word, my boy."

"How?" the boy asked carefully.

"There has not been a second-son in that line for a very, very long time."

"The stars shoot sparks at his birth, Master, why?"

"Do not put too much stock in the stars my boy, they are fickle and distant and do not affect the lives of men by very great a margin. I see that I shall have to un-teach you much of what you have learned from your previous superstitious masters. The stars merely appear to spark more brightly now because it is a clear night and we are far away from other lights."

"Then there is nothing special or extraordinary about this child, this second-son? There's nothing to the old legends at all?"

"Nothing to the old legends…?" The old man looked surprised. "I cast aspersion on one superstition and you are ready to throw out all the old writings as well; is that it boy?"

The youth looked properly chagrined and made no further comment, waiting upon his master's words.

The old man smiled. "You learn quickly, boy."

"Thank you, Master Scelwhyn," the youth said humbly.

"I know it is tiresome for you to listen to me prattle on about events that are not taking place here in Aom-igh, but the lives of those in far-away lands do affect our own. This royal birth in Llycaelon tonight is just as important as the coronation of our own young King Jairem tomorrow."

"No, the lessons are not tiresome, master, just confusing. And there is so much I have to learn!"

"And much you have to unlearn. Both can be cured by listening and thinking, so rest easy knowing that there is nothing severely wrong with you." Scelwhyn laughed at the young man's expression. "Ah, Garen, you long more for the horse and the sword than for all this book-learning and magery, I understand that, but here, I will give you a gift."

"A gift, Master?"

"Yes, a free answer to your endless questions about the child who is being born far away in the Dark Country. A prophecy, if you will."

"A prophecy about this second-son?"

The old wizard looked down at the boy in something halfway between exasperation and amusement. "Do you listen to a word I say boy? Or do you not trust your own ears?"

The boy looked down at his feet, "I'm sorry, Master."

"Very good. Listen closely, for I will not suffer myself to repeat the dark words of the Llycaelon prophecy." The look in the wizard's eyes became faraway and distant, his voice evened out, becoming strong and soft.

> *In waning days of autumn gold*
> *A shadow shall spread across the sky*
> *A banner of darkness here foretold;*
> *Yet a second-son that darkness defies.*

> *Born 'neath the sign of Yorien's stars*
> *He comes to turn the battle's tide*
> *Wanderer he, to shores afar*
> *Warrior he, the Eagle's pride.*

ABOUT THE AUTHOR

Born and raised in the midwest, Jenelle Leanne Schmidt received her bachelor's of science degree in English Education at Taylor University in Upland, Indiana. In the tradition of J.R.R. Tolkien's writings, she aspires to produce a series of epic adventures to delight readers of all ages. Herself a reader from a very early age, the author desires to craft stories that will be loved and enjoyed by generations to come. Jenelle currently lives in North Carolina with her husband and their three children.

Made in the USA
Monee, IL
18 October 2022

16083765R00246